SYDNEY HOS... LUCA'S BAD GIRL

BY
AMY ANDREWS

THE FIREBRAND WHO UNLOCKED HIS HEART

BY
ANNE FRASER

MILLS & BOON

SYDNEY HARBOUR HOSPITAL: HOSPITAL: LUCA'S BAD GIRL

BY
AMY ANDREWS

First published in Great Britain 2012
by Mills & Boon, an imprint of Harlequin (UK) Limited.
Harlequin (UK) Limited, Eton House, 18-24 Paradise Road,
Richmond, Surrey TW9 1SR

© Harlequin Books S.A. 2012

Special thanks and acknowledgement are given to Alison Ahearn
for her contribution to the *Sydney Harbour Hospital* series

ISBN: 978 0 263 89786 9

Harlequin (UK) policy is to use papers that are natural, renewable
and recyclable products and made from wood grown in sustainable
forests. The logging and manufacturing process conform to the
legal environmental regulations of the country of origin.

Printed and bound in Spain
by Blackprint CPI, Barcelona

**Welcome to the world
of Sydney Harbour Hospital
(or *SHH*… for short—
because secrets never stay hidden for long!)**

Looking out over cosmopolitan Sydney Harbour, Australia's premier teaching hospital is a hive of round-the-clock activity—with a *very* active hospital grapevine.

With the most renowned (and gorgeous!) doctors in Sydney working side by side, professional and sensual tensions run sky-high—there's *always* plenty of romantic rumours to gossip about…

Who's been kissing who in the on-call room? What's going on between legendary heart surgeon Finn Kennedy and tough-talking A&E doctor Evie Lockheart? And what's wrong with Finn?

Find out in this enthralling new eight-book continuity from Mills & Boon® Medical™ Romance—indulge yourself with eight helpings of romance, emotion and gripping medical drama!

Sydney Harbour Hospital
*From saving lives to sizzling seduction,
these doctors are the very best!*

Sydney Harbour Hospital

*Sexy surgeons, dedicated doctors,
scandalous secrets, on-call dramas...*

**Welcome to the world of Sydney Harbour Hospital
(or *SHH*... for short—because secrets never stay hidden for long!)**

Last month new nurse Lily got caught up
in the hotbed of hospital gossip in
**SYDNEY HARBOUR HOSPITAL: LILY'S SCANDAL
by Marion Lennox**

And gorgeous paediatrician Teo came to single mum Zoe's rescue in
**SYDNEY HARBOUR HOSPITAL: ZOE'S BABY
by Alison Roberts**

This month sexy Sicilian playboy Luca finally meets his match in
**SYDNEY HARBOUR HOSPITAL: LUCA'S BAD GIRL
by Amy Andrews**

Then in April Hayley opens Tom's eyes to love in
**SYDNEY HARBOUR HOSPITAL: TOM'S REDEMPTION
by Fiona Lowe**

Join heiress Lexi as she learns to put the past behind her in May...
**SYDNEY HARBOUR HOSPITAL: LEXI'S SECRET
by Melanie Milburne**

In June adventurer Charlie helps shy Bella fulfil her dreams—
and find love on the way!—in
**SYDNEY HARBOUR HOSPITAL: BELLA'S WISHLIST
by Emily Forbes**

Single mum Emily gives no-strings-attached surgeon Marco
a reason to stay in July:
**SYDNEY HARBOUR HOSPITAL: MARCO'S TEMPTATION
by Fiona McArthur**

And finally join us in August as Ava and James
realise their marriage really is worth saving in
**SYDNEY HARBOUR HOSPITAL: AVA'S RE-AWAKENING
by Carol Marinelli**

And not forgetting Sydney Harbour Hospital's legendary heart surgeon
Finn Kennedy. This brooding maverick keeps his women on hospital
rotation... But can new doc Evie Lockheart unlock the secrets to his
guarded heart? Find out in this enthralling new eight-book continuity
from Mills & Boon® Medical™ Romance.

A collection impossible to resist!

**These books are also available in ebook format
from www.millsandboon.co.uk**

CHAPTER ONE

DR MIA MCKENZIE didn't know it yet but her night was about to go from bad to worse.

And that was no mean feat.

A full moon didn't usually bode well for emergency departments and this clear, cold Saturday night was no different. Moonbeams sprinkled like fairy dust on the world-renowned surface of Sydney Harbour, lending a deceptive calm to the view from the windows of Sydney Harbour Hospital.

But inside the walls of the emergency department it was crazy town!

At two in the morning there had been no let up from the insanity. SHH, or The Harbour to those who worked there, was living up to its reputation as the busiest emergency department in the city.

'I could have been a dermatologist,' Mia grumbled to Dr Evie Lockheart, her best friend and flatmate, as she strode out of the resus cubical, turning her back on the torrent of abuse from a drug addict she'd just brought back from the brink of death.

'They don't get abused by patients at half past stupid o'clock. You know why? Because they're sleeping. No on-call, no such thing as a dermatological emergency in the middle of the night, no urgent consults required.'

Evie, clutching a portable ultrasound unit, grinned. 'You'd be bored to tears.'

Mia's long blonde ponytail swished against her shoulder blades as she made her way to the central nurses' station with the patient's chart in hand. 'I could do bored.'

Evie snorted. 'Yep, whatever you say.'

Mia ignored her friend's sarcasm. 'How much longer are you and George Clooney going to be with the MVA?'

Evie laughed. 'The name is Luca. Dr Luca di Angelo.'

As far as Mia was concerned, the hospital's new director of trauma looked more like the devil than an angel.

He certainly seemed to be having a devil of a time with every available female walking the halls of SHH in the very short time he'd been here.

Which was fine by her. It was his life. And in a way she admired him for it. She too liked to keep her liaisons short and sweet.

But maybe that's what caused an itch up her spine whenever he was around—besides his disturbing good looks apparently honed beneath a Sicilian sun. She recognised a kindred spirit.

And didn't like what she saw.

'And he really is quite dishy.'

'Yes,' Mia mused. 'That he is.'

Evie grinned. Now, why couldn't she be interested in a tall, dark, handsome Italian who was living up to the reputation of sex god that had preceded his arrival at The Harbour a few weeks ago? Why was it the infuriating, dictatorial Dr Finn Kennedy that her brain insisted on conjuring up with monotonous regularity?

'Anyway,' she said shaking the thought away. 'We're stabilising the patient at the moment. He needs to go to Theatre for a laparotomy.'

Mia nodded. 'Okay, but when he's gone, go home. You were supposed to have finished three hours ago.'

'Yeah, yeah.' Evie grinned as she departed.

Mia had ten minutes' respite to catch up on some charts before a stocky man with swarthy features and wild eyes burst through the ambulance bay doors. 'My wife…she's in labour. The baby's coming now!' And then turned around and raced out the door again.

Mia sprang to her feet as a shot of adrenaline surged into her system. She hurried after the man, followed by Caroline, the triage nurse. She didn't notice the chill in the air, just the beaten-up old car parked at a crazy angle near the doors and a woman's urgent cries.

'Hurry,' the man yelled, wringing his hands.

Mia was there in seconds. The woman was lying on the back seat yelling, 'It's coming, it's coming.'

'Hi, I'm Dr McKenzie,' Mia said over the din. 'What's your name?'

'Rh-Rhiannon,' the woman panted.

Mia smiled at her encouragingly. 'How far along are you?'

'Thirty weeks, she's thirty weeks, all right?' the husband barked.

The man seemed hostile and had his wife's needs not been so urgent she'd have told him to back off. The last thing she needed right now while having to deliver a ten-week premature baby was a man with some kind of chip on his shoulder.

'Caroline, page the neonatology team, please,' Mia said quietly as she reached for the endless supply of gloves she had stashed in her pockets. 'And get Arthur to bring out a gurney.

'Okay, let's have a look here,' Mia said calmly.

The woman groaned again and it took Mia two seconds to identify a crowning head, despite the poor light. 'Right, well, you're absolutely correct, Rhiannon, this baby is coming.'

'I have to push,' Rhiannon yelled.

'That's fine.' Mia nodded, her heart bonging in her chest like the bells of a clock tower. 'I'm here to catch.'

Thirty seconds later the scrawny bawling infant slipped into Mia's waiting hands. 'You have a boy.' Mia grinned, laying the baby on the cloth seat and hoping that Caroline thought to bring back something warm to protect the newborn from the brisk air.

'Let me see it,' the father demanded.

But Caroline arrived, blocking his view as she handed Mia a pre-packaged emergency birth pack and some blankets fresh out of the blanket warmer. 'Neonates are doing an emergency intubation in Labour ward,' she said quietly. 'They'll get here as soon as they can.'

Mia nodded as she quickly laid the babe on a warm soft blanket, unwrapped the birth pack and efficiently clamped and cut the cord. She bundled the still crying baby up and handed him to Caroline.

'Get him into Resus so we can give him a proper check over, although his lungs seem pretty fine to me.'

Caroline laughed as she turned to go.

'Where are you taking it?' the father demanded.

'Inside,' Caroline said calmly. 'You can come too if you like.'

The father stalked after Caroline while Mia and Arthur helped Rhiannon onto the gurney. They covered her in warm blankets and pushed her inside to the resus cube next to her baby. The little boy was quiet now as he basked beneath the warm rays of a cot's overhead heater.

The father was pacing the cubicle when they arrived and seemed agitated. 'Red hair. It's got red hair,' the father growled at Rhiannon as he approached her with a sneer on his face.

'Oh, for crying out loud, Stan. Your grandfather had red hair.'

'Whose is it?' he demanded, rattling the rail of the gurney. 'Who's the father?'

Mia felt the hairs rise on the back of her neck as the father's puzzling behaviour gained some context. But context or not, he didn't get to act like a bully in her ER.

Thoughts of her own father wormed their way into her head and she quashed them ruthlessly.

'Sir!' Mia stood between him and the exhausted Rhiannon. 'You will not raise your voice in here. Whatever the issue is, this is not the time or place for it. Now, why don't you go and shift your car from the ambulance bay? When you come back, you'd better have calmed down or I *will* call Security.'

Mia was used to dealing with emotionally charged situations. Also drunks, drug addicts and a whole bunch of other people who didn't respect the sanctity of a hospital.

But she was a doctor. And Rhiannon and the baby were her patients. It was her duty to protect them.

The man scowled at her and left, muttering to himself.

'I'm sorry,' Rhiannon apologised. 'He gets so paranoid sometimes but he's harmless.'

Mia smiled. 'It's fine.'

A midwife from the maternity ward chose that moment to arrive. 'The team's going to be another twenty minutes or so,' she apologised.

'That's all right,' Mia dismissed. 'I think this little tyke's going to be fine.'

The ugly incident with Stan was forgotten as the midwife tended to Rhiannon, delivering the placenta while Mia gave the baby a check over. 'They'll probably want to keep him for the night in Special Care, given his early arrival, just to be on the safe side,' Mia pronounced, 'but everything checks out so far.'

She stood aside for the midwife to wrap the little boy up in that special way they did with babies so they looked just like glowworms, with only their little faces showing. Then Mia picked up the precious little package and asked, 'Would you like to hold your son?'

Rhiannon nodded and Mia was walking the baby over to her when the curtain flicked back a little and Stan stood there, looking slightly mollified. The time away seemed to have helped. Mia changed tack. 'Would you like to hold him?' she asked.

In Mia's experience, babies melted even the hardest of hearts. What man could resist such a gorgeous package? Hopefully this little impatient cherub would help Stan focus on what was important in life.

He looked uncertain for a moment then looked at Rhiannon. 'Can I?'

She smiled at him and Mia could see the love shining in the other woman's eyes. 'Of course.'

Mia eased the little bundle into Stan's arms. He seemed more dazed than elated but Mia knew that for some new fathers it was a big adjustment. He walked up and down the length of the cubicle with the baby, rocking him as he went, his gaze fixed on his face.

'What are you going to call him?' Caroline asked.

'I like Michael,' Rhiannon murmured.

The tight swaddling had loosened a little from the rocking and the baby stirred, displacing the wrap covering his head. Stan stopped as he stared down at a shock of red hair. He whipped around to face his wife. 'Is that his name?' he demanded. The baby started to cry. 'Michael? The man you've been sleeping with?'

Rhiannon groaned. 'Stop it, Stan. I'm sick of these accusations. You know there's only ever been you.'

'I want a paternity test,' he yelled.

Mia looked at Caroline then at a near-to-tears Rhiannon. 'Stan—'

Stan swung wildly around to face her and the baby cried louder. 'I want you...' he jabbed the air with an index finger '...to do a paternity test.'

'Stan this is ridiculous,' Rhiannon wailed, a tear trekking down her face.

Stan swung back. 'Are you refusing?'

'Okay, Stan, enough,' Mia said firmly. Stan turned abruptly and faced her. 'That is no way to be talking and certainly no way to be flinging a baby around. Listen to him, you're making him cry.'

She walked briskly towards Stan, her arms extended. 'Give him to me.'

Stan leapt back, his eyes wild again as he pulled a pocket knife out of his back pocket, flicking the blade open with one hand while he clutched his son in the other.

'Stay back,' he screamed. Caroline gasped, Rhiannon wailed and Mia stopped in her tracks. 'Don't come near me.'

Stan swung wildly from side to side, brandishing the knife as he backed slowly away from Mia.

Oh, good Lord! Mia felt a spurt of annoyance. *She did not have time for this.*

'Okay, Stan.' Mia summoned her most placatory voice as she put her hands out to calm the situation. She didn't think that Stan would harm anyone but that wasn't the way to play it when he was holding a brand-new thirty weeker in one arm and a knife in the other.

'Okay, I can do that for you,' she soothed, deftly placing her own body between Stan and Caroline.

Caroline, bless her cotton socks, picked up on her cue and quietly crept out of the cubicle. Mia knew one push of the panic button located under the desk in the nurses' station and every security guard rostered for the shift would be here in under two minutes.

'But you're going to need to give me the baby first.' She took another step towards Stan, tuning out the lusty newborn's cries and Rhiannon's pleading.

Stan slashed the blade through the air. 'No! Get back,' he yelled.

Luca di Angelo, who was passing the resus bay, frowned at the raised voice, louder even than the squalling baby. He strode in through the partially open curtain, surveying the scene rapidly.

A man with a knife. A bawling baby being held to ransom. A crying woman. A terrified nurse. And gutsy Dr Mia McKenzie—aloof, frosty little Mia—standing in the thick of it.

'What the devil is going on here?' he demanded.

Stan swung around again, slashing the air in Luca's general direction. 'Stay back,' he yelled.

Luca stopped. 'Dr McKenzie?'

'It's fine, Dr di Angelo,' she said, a placid smile plastered to her face as she inched closer to Stan. Very soon there'd be maximum force at her disposal—she could do without the Lone Ranger potentially ramping the situation up in the mean time.

Even if he did look good enough to spread on toast.

Mia's stomach rumbled.

'Stan here just wants a paternity test so he's going to give me the baby and I'll draw some blood. Right, Stan?'

'No.' Stan looked wildly between the two of them. 'The baby stays,' he insisted.

Luca watched Mia in his peripheral vision as she crept forward at a snail's pace. 'But how can we take blood when you're holding a baby, Stan?' Luca reasoned, distracting the man.

Mia, grateful if a little surprised that Luca had caught on really fast, took another step closer.

'Stay back,' Stan bellowed. The baby's cries rose another octave.

'I can't take your blood from here, Stan,' Mia soothed.

The adrenaline flowing through her system brought

everything into sharp focus. The sweat on Stan's brow. The harsh suck of his breath as he heaved air in and out of his lungs. The white spittle forming at the corner of his mouth. The way he turned the knife over and over in his palm and constantly shifted his weight from one foot to the other as his gaze darted between the two doctors.

But she was probably even more aware of Luca. Somehow it was he who dominated the room, not Stan. He towered over the knife-wielding man, all lean and broad shouldered, in sharp contrast to Stan's stocky stature. And despite the deceptive casualness of his hands-in-pocket stance, Mia could see the hard clench of his jaw and sense the coiled rigidity in those muscles barely contained behind the snug-fitting polo shirt.

She reminded him of a taipan, ready to strike. Swift and deadly.

Just then there was a commotion behind them as several security staff arrived at once.

Stan looked over Mia's shoulder. 'What are they doing here?' he roared, his hold on the baby tightening and causing further lusty protest.

Luca held out his hand as Stan's agitation increased. 'It's standard hospital procedure,' Luca soothed, moving a little closer. 'It'll be all right, though. I'm going to ask them to stand back, okay?'

'I don't think that's a good idea, Doc,' the chief security officer said.

'Back! You heard him, get back!' Stan shouted, brandishing the knife a little too close to the baby's head.

The midwife gasped.

Luca turned to the security contingent. 'It's okay,'

he assured them. Then he turned back to Stan. 'They're going, see?' Luca said as he heard the guards shuffling away.

Mia kept her gaze focused on Stan and the baby. 'Okay, Stan, now we've done something for you, you've got to do something for us.' She covered up her next step closer by holding out her arms. 'Give me the baby. He's scared and hungry. Listen to him. I'm sure a nice feed will settle him down and we can talk about this without upsetting him any more.'

And, frankly, the infant's cries were getting on her last nerve. The situation was fraught enough without the distinct urgency of an escalating newborn baby's cries.

'She's right, Stan,' Luca agreed as he edged nearer too. 'This isn't something a baby should be part of.'

'It's not my fault.' Stan's voice cracked as his face beseeched them. 'I work hard all day and she repays me by sleeping with half the neighbourhood.'

Mia felt a chill as if a ghostly hand from the past had stroked down her spine. She ignored it.

Luca nodded. 'I know. Believe me, I know.' And he did. He understood the desperation that Stan was feeling, the sense of betrayal. *Intimately.*

Mia glanced sharply at Luca. There was empathy, real empathy, in his tone.

'We can talk about all that, Stan,' Luca continued. 'Just give the baby to Dr McKenzie.'

Stan looked from one to the other and Mia saw the uncertainty on his face, saw that even Stan in his crazed state had registered Luca's compassion. She took advantage and moved forward slowly, unsurprised to sense Luca doing the same.

'It's okay, Stan, you're doing the right thing,' Mia reassured him.

Stan shook his head from side to side. 'I just need to know.'

'Of course,' Luca murmured. 'Of course you do, Stan.'

They were close now and Mia could sense Stan weakening. His grip on the knife had slackened. But so had his hold on the baby. Everything inside her urged her to leap forward and snatch the bawling infant from him but she knew any sudden movements would be a bad idea.

'Give your little boy to me, Stan,' she implored quietly.

Stan looked down at the crying bundle, the red hair even more vivid against the white of the wrap. He shook his head, his grip tightening again.

'He's not my baby!' he roared, lunging the knife at her.

Everything slowed as Mia watched it come towards her chest. She wasn't conscious of anything else, just the hypnotic arc of the blade as its point drew closer to her heart.

'Mia!'

Luca reached out and grabbed her, pulling her towards him. The sweeping slash of the knife missed her torso completely but sliced into the flesh of her upper arm. Mia gasped as bright, piercing pain stole her breath.

Luca swore in his native tongue as his hand shot out and crushed Stan's wrist in a vice-like grip. Stan yelped and dropped the knife.

'Security!'

His voice cracked like a whip into the charged atmosphere and in an instant five burly guards had entered the fray. The fight instantly went out of Stan at the sight of overwhelming force.

'The baby,' Luca demanded, and the midwife leapt forward, snatching the squalling infant.

'Go easy,' Luca ordered as the guards hauled a now passive Stan away. 'Are you okay?' he asked switching his attention to Mia.

She nodded automatically as the baby, now safe in his mother's embrace, began to settle. 'I'm fine.' Even though the hand that had instinctively covered the wound to apply pressure was sticky with her own blood. It had quickly oozed through the material of her cotton shirt.

Luca looked at the dark red blood running down her arm and shook his head. Most women he knew would have been hysterical by now. But not Mia. She'd kept her head in the face of an emotionally overwrought father with a knife and had dismissed what looked like a substantial wound as if it were a paper cut.

'Go to the minor ops room, I'll take a look at it.'

'It's fine, just superficial,' she said dismissively.

Luca pointed. 'Blood is running down your arm.'

Mia looked down at the thick trickle, surprised to see it. 'I'll get Evie to look at it.'

'I sent her home.'

'Dr di Angelo?' Caroline interrupted them. 'The psych reg is on the phone. He wants to speak with you.'

Luca quirked an eyebrow at her. 'I can't have one of my staff expiring from blood loss. It wouldn't look very good. Minor ops. Now. I'll be along after the call.'

Mia watched him go, a well of resentment rising in

her. She'd been looking after herself for a lot of years, she didn't need Mr Tall Dark and Handsome pulling the boss card and she certainly didn't need him fussing over her.

No one had ever fussed over her. *And that was just the way she liked it.*

A couple of steri-strips and she'd be fine.

A few minutes later, Mia pushed into the on-call room and plonked herself down at the table in the kitchen area, spilling her supplies on the cluttered top. Her arm hurt like hell and all she wanted to do was crawl into one of the private rooms off to her left and collapse on one of the pull-out beds.

The adrenaline had worn off and her earlier tiredness had taken hold and intensified.

And if she was asleep, the memories that Stan's actions had unleashed tonight couldn't bother her.

It was quiet in the room as she fumbled one-handed with the buttons of her blouse. The sleeves had a firm cuff that sat snugly around her biceps and couldn't be rolled up enough to gain a good visual of the damage. She winced as she slipped the blouse off, every movement jarring though her lacerated deltoid.

She tossed it on the floor—that was going straight in the bin.

She inspected her spaghetti-strapped top, pleased to see that no blood had seeped into it. This kind of undergarment was a permanent fixture beneath whatever shirt she was wore on a night shift. The hospital air-conditioning seemed to reach freezing point at around four in the morning and, even in summer, the extra layer helped.

Mia was especially grateful for it tonight.

She looked down at the wound on her upper arm. The blood had dried and crusted, making it difficult to tell the extent of the laceration. It looked ugly, though, as she gently probed it with her index finger. It was quite long and for a moment she let herself think about what could have happened had Luca not pulled her out of the way.

She noticed her hand was trembling and she dropped it from the wound, clamping down on her thoughts.

She hadn't been stabbed in the chest. She hadn't died. *Luca had pulled her out of the way.*

But it didn't stop the trembling from spreading to all her limbs and then to her insides. She took a couple of deep breaths, desperately trying to quell the outbreak.

It was a reaction, that was all. It would settle.

But the longer she sat, trying to get control of her breathing and the shaking, the more vulnerable she was to her emotions and thoughts. And she hated that—she'd learned long ago they didn't get you anywhere.

But tonight she didn't seem to be able to stop them.

Was that how her own father had felt when he'd found out about the paternity of her stillborn sister? Like Stan? Desperate and enraged? If there'd been a knife or a gun handy, would he have used it on her mother?

He'd walked away from them that day but she hadn't known why until years later. Years of blaming him for abandoning them, years of hating him, only to find out that it had been her mother's infidelities that had driven her father away.

Mia shook her head. *Stop it. Stop it!*

This situation tonight had come too close to home but there was no need to fall apart. She wasn't ten years old any more. She was an adult.

Clean yourself up and get back out there again!

Mia forced herself to action. To tend to the wound. Open the dressing pack, pour in some antiseptic lotion, pick up the gauze, work away at the dried blood.

It was awkward and hurt like the blazes but she welcomed the distraction from her thoughts and her shaking hands settled with a familiar routine.

Two minutes later Luca strode through the door. Mia glanced up at him, feeling strangely naked with her blouse discarded. Which was ridiculous—she was more than adequately covered. She ignored him, returning to the task at hand.

Luca lounged against the table and smiled to himself as Mia barely acknowledged his arrival. 'You're making a mess of that,' he mused.

Mia glared at him. 'It's a little difficult.'

'I do believe I told you I would attend to your wound.' He folded his arms across his chest. 'But you don't like asking for help, do you, little Mia?'

His slight accent gave his deep baritone a very sexy edge as it rolled over her. 'It's Mia, or Dr McKenzie. Please refrain from addressing me any other way.'

Luca chuckled as he pushed off the bench. 'Okay, *Mia.*' He sat on the chair next to her. 'Allow me,' he said as he picked up some gauze and dabbed at the wound.

Mia didn't protest—she was making a hash of it anyway. His touch was gentle as he coaxed the dried blood from the cut and she shivered. His fingers were dark against her paler skin and long.

Her father had long fingers. A pianist's hands. He was tall too, like Luca. He'd told her he was her prince and she was his princess and they'd be together for ever.

And then he'd left.

She squeezed her eyes shut. *Stop it. Stop it.*

Luca watched her. It was the first time he'd spent any length of time in her company and he was curious. He'd already noticed on their brief acquaintance she was a good-looking woman with a cute mouth and a sassy swagger.

But up close she was really quite exquisite.

Her face was long, as were her eyelashes. A frown appeared between her brows and her lips parted. She looked in pain.

'Am I hurting you?' he murmured.

Mia's eyes fluttered open. *How had he got that close?* She could see the individual whiskers making up the smooth blue-black of his jaw and just make out the black pupil in the middle of his bottomless brown eyes. His hair, as dark as his eyes, was thick with a slight wave that brushed his forehead and the tops of his ears.

And his mouth. The full curve to that bottom lip was wicked.

His fingers stroked gently over her skin as he cleaned the wound and it reminded her it had been a while since a man had touched her.

She lowered her gaze to the column of his throat. 'No.'

Luca was captivated by the slide show of emotions in her large blue eyes as magnificent and as transparent as a stained-glass window. The husky timbre of her voice wove between the bands of steel around his heart. 'Are you okay?'

Mia nodded, keeping her gaze firmly fixed on his throat. The long tanned column of his neck was also shaded in blue-black smoothness. She remembered how she'd loved the sandpaper roughness of her father's neck as he'd cuddled her close to read to her at night.

Damn it! She gripped the back of the chair hard. 'I'm fine.'

'You've been through an ordeal tonight. That knife came very close to—'

'I said I'm fine,' Mia interrupted, raising her face to scowl at him. 'Just clean the damn wound.'

CHAPTER TWO

LUCA paused in his ministrations for a moment, the blue of her eyes frosty now. He'd only known her for a few short weeks and while he'd been impressed with her empathy for patients and her good rapport with her colleagues he'd also sensed she was a woman who preferred to keep herself pretty much to herself.

But she'd always been polite about it.

Something was definitely eating at Mia McKenzie tonight.

He shifted his attention back to the wound.

'It's borderline,' he mused, looking at the clean ten-centimetre laceration. 'It's deeper laterally, could probably do with a couple of sutures there.'

Mia nodded to the pile of medical supplies on the table. 'Steri-strips there somewhere.'

'Sutures would be better.'

'Steri-strips will be fine.'

'The scarring will be worse if we use steri-strips.'

Mia shrugged. 'I don't care about a scar.'

Luca looked at her for a moment then fished around for the strips. 'Most women would,' he murmured when he located them. He doubted he'd ever been with a single woman who didn't obsess over the slightest blemish.

'I'm not most women.'

Luca chuckled. 'Yes. I think you are right.'

Mia sat still as he opened the packet and secured the wound edges together, applying firm tension through each sticky strip. Then he applied an adhesive dressing over the top. She watched as he absently brushed the pad of his thumb back and forth over the dressing as if he were a parent, rubbing a boo-boo better.

Just like her father had done.

'You look like you've got a lot on your mind,' he murmured.

Unfortunately, he was right. She hadn't been able to stop thinking about her father since Stan's episode. It had probably been the first time ever she'd been confronted with how emotionally untenable it had been for him to stay.

'It's busy,' she said brusquely, rising from the chair and clearing away the detritus from her dressing and tossing it in the bin. 'We can't just skulk in here all night.'

'The team have got it covered. And you're not going back out there until you've had a break. Try and get some sleep.' She opened her mouth to protest and he stood. 'That's an order.'

Great! What in the hell was she going to do alone in here with a bunch of unwanted memories that wouldn't quit? *Things she just wanted to forget.*

'What if a bus crash comes in?'

Luca grinned. 'I'll come and wake you.'

Mia felt the grin right down to her toes. It twinkled

in his eyes and gave the devil a whole new degree of wicked.

The fact that she noticed his twinkling eyes rankled. 'Are you flirting with me?' she demanded, crossing her arms.

Luca chuckled. She didn't beat around the bush. 'Would it be a bad thing if I was?'

'Yes,' she said. Something told her he wouldn't be an easy man to walk away from. Not disposable, like the others. 'Stop it. I have no desire to become a notch on what I understand is your very crowded bedpost.'

Luca regarded her for a moment. In her top and jeans, arms crossed, a frown knitting her brows, she looked quite fierce. But Luca knew women. He knew them well.

And Mia McKenzie was definitely protesting too much.

His gaze slipped to her mouth. 'Are you sure?'

Mia felt her lips tingle beneath his heated stare and felt her resistance ebb. *Now, he was something that could make her forget for a little while.*

Luca grinned, pleased to have discomforted her. 'Goodnight, Mia. Don't let the bed bugs bite.'

By four a.m. Luca was ready to head home. The craziness had settled and things were quiet—for now anyway.

He'd checked on the MVA from earlier—the laparotomy had found a perforated bowel. Stan had been admitted to the psych unit on a ninety-six-hour hold. The baby was settled into the special care nursery for overnight monitoring.

And his paperwork was up to date.

Just one last thing to do—check on Mia.

He hesitated, his hand on the doorknob of the on-call room. Prickly little Mia probably wouldn't appreciate being checked up on.

Her prim *I have no desire to become a notch on what I understand is your very crowded bedpost,* had played on his mind ever since she'd uttered it.

She obviously disapproved.

What the hell was wrong with indulging in a little flirtation here and there? Spending an enjoyable few hours with a woman who was fully aware that one night was all he was interested in?

He was always open and honest about his intentions. And he never made the mistake of giving false hope by going back for seconds. He knew his limitations where relationships were concerned—had learned them at a very early age.

Best not to set expectations—that way you couldn't let anyone down.

He loved women—bronzed, natural, fun-loving Australian women in particular—and they loved him. And he was a healthy adult male.

Still, Mia intrigued him. Her resistance even more so. He'd be lying if he said he didn't want her.

He twisted the knob and opened the door. She wasn't around and the light had been turned out. Sleeping room one had its door shut and he padded over to it, knocking lightly when he reached his destination.

No reply was forthcoming. He hesitated again before gently twisting the knob and opening the door a crack—checking on her *was* the right thing to do.

The sight stopped him in his tracks.

She had fallen asleep in a semi-upright foetal position on the triple-seater couch. Her head was snuggled against the fat cushions of the sofa, her spine propped up against the squishy arm, her legs, tucked in close to her bottom, had fallen sideways to rest against the back of the couch.

She'd taken her hair out of its clasp and it fanned around her shoulders and the couch cushions. Her feet were bare. A medical journal lay open on her chest.

The lamp on the table beside the couch illuminated her relaxed profile in a warm yellow glow. His gaze tracked the outline of her nose, the slope of one cheekbone, the plump fullness of her mouth.

He was satisfied to see the journal on her chest rise and fell in a regular rhythm. His eyes dropped to the white dressing covering her upper arm and he absently noted there was no fresh ooze.

She was obviously fine.

As he watched, a little frown wrinkled her forehead and a soft mew escaped her mouth. He wondered what she was dreaming about. Her near-death experience? The flash of a blade? The bawling of a baby?

His question—*are you sure*?—from earlier?

She mewed again and he realised he was staring at a sleeping woman who would most definitely not appreciate the attention. He left the door ajar and turned away.

Mia was trapped in a dream she didn't seem able to fight her way out of. It was one she hadn't had since she'd been a little girl but it was disjointed, jumping back and forth between now and then. Between Stan and her father. Each slash of the knife through the air shunting the dream to the other person, to another time.

Her mother was there too somewhere, holding a

wrapped bundle that Mia knew was her stillborn sister. Her mother was sobbing those deep, gut-wrenching sobs that had been indelibly woven through the fabric of Mia's life.

She was holding her father's hand, her little ten-year-old fingers tugging at his long ones, asking him not to go. And then Stan would yell to get back, get back as the knifepoint came ever closer.

Daddy, don't go. Don't go.

Slash. Back, get back. Slash.

Please, Daddy, don't go.

Slash. Slash. Back! Get back!

Daddy!

'Daddy, come back!'

Luca was almost at the door when he heard her cry out. Without thinking, he hurried back to her, pushed open the door and strode over to the couch as Mia cried out again, flinging her head from side to side. The journal had already fallen to the floor.

Luca took her by the shoulders and gave her a gentle shake, mindful of her injury. 'Mia! Mia.'

Mia heard a voice. A different voice. And the urge to run towards it, to run away from the feelings of hopelessness, was overwhelming.

Luca? Luca?

'Mia.' He shook her again. 'It's Luca. Wake up. Wake up.'

Mia's eyes flew open. *Luca?* Luca was here?

The mellow lamplight bathed his strong masculine features, softening them—his jaw, his cheeks, his mouth—and he finally looked like that angel. She blinked away the crazy thought as tendrils of dread clung to every heartbeat.

Mia tried to sit up but her limbs wouldn't co-operate and her arm throbbed. 'Luca?'

'Shh,' he murmured, the pads of his thumbs absently stroking her shoulders. Her large blue eyes reflected her confusion. 'It's okay, you were having a bad dream.'

Mia nodded. 'It was…there was…'

'Your father?'

Mia blinked up at him. He pronounced the *th* softly, giving the word a gentleness it hadn't had in the dream. Her head was crowded with memories. One after the other, battering her brains and beating against the locked door to her heart.

Old and long forgotten. Supposedly.

She had to make them stop.

'Are you okay?' Luca asked.

She looked at him, into eyes so deep and brown it was like falling into a well.

He could make them stop.

'Mia?'

She shook her head. 'Not yet.' *But she would be.*

Then she leaned forward and pressed her lips to his.

Luca stilled at the tentative touch. He pulled back and searched her eyes. 'Mia?'

She shook her head and, supporting herself on her good arm, leant in close, locking her gaze with his. 'Kiss me,' she murmured, her mouth a whisper from his.

In fact, she was close enough that Luca could almost feel those two little words branding his lips from the sudden heat rising between their bodies. He dropped his gaze to her mouth—so near, so luscious—and he was instantly hard.

'What happened to not wanting to be a notch on my bedpost?'

'Stan,' she muttered.

After that Luca wasn't sure who closed the hair's-breadth between them. But he did seize control.

His mouth opened over hers and demanded she follow suit. And follow him she did, opening to him eagerly. He thrust his tongue into her mouth and the little whimper at the back of her throat implored him to keep going.

He tunnelled his hands into her hair, angling her head back to accommodate more, and the kiss escalated. Got deeper, wetter, hotter. His body moved over hers, forcing her knees down, crowding her back against the cushions, imprisoning her against the couch, her head falling back over the arm.

His hand brushed the side of her breast and she moaned deep and low. He drew it lower, to her waist, her hip as his mouth broke from hers to ravage her neck, stretched out before him, the pulse at the base beating as madly as his own.

Mia felt the memories disappear into the ether as a veritable storm of sensations swept through her body.

Yes, yes, yes.

'Yes,' she cried out as Luca licked along her collar bone. 'Yes,' as he nipped at the base of her neck. 'Yes,' as his hand squeezed the exact spot where, beneath her jeans, butt met thigh.

One-handed, she pulled his polo shirt out of his jeans and ruched it up his back, his skin hot and vibrant beneath her palm. She kept pulling till it was past his shoulders and gave a triumphant cry when Luca ducked his head through the opening and she pulled it off him entirely.

His smooth chest was totally bare to her touch and she pressed a kiss to a flat brown pec, then his collarbone, then the hollow at the base of his neck.

She breathed him in, his scent intoxicating. Potent. Virile. Male. It filled up her senses. Like a drug.

And left her wanting more.

He claimed her mouth again, pressing her deep into the cushions, and she revelled in his weight, in the tangle of his legs, in the oh-so-right angle of his pelvis.

Luca felt the agitated circling of her hips and ground himself against her. He swallowed her gasp, making her moan more deeply as his hand travelled back up her body, pushing beneath her top. He needed to touch her breasts. To see them. Taste them. To feel them rubbing against his chest.

He pushed the fabric up, his hand filling with soft, delectable female. Satin, lace and heaven all in one sweet handful. He rubbed the hard point with his thumb and she gasped.

Luca broke away from her mouth, his lips instinctively following the dictates of his body as his tongue stroked down her neck, over her collarbone, the slope of her breast then finally her nipple. The lace was rough against his tongue as he sucked the tip right through the material of the bra.

Mia's breath hissed out as her back arched involuntarily. It jarred painfully through her sore arm and she cried out in pain this time, her eyes squeezing shut.

'Mia?' Luca broke away. 'Oh, sorry, did I hurt your arm?'

Mia shook her head, her eyes still shut. 'It's okay, it's settling.'

Luca groaned, dropping his forehead onto her chest. Her heart beat frantically there as her ribcage heaved in and out. His own breathing was loud and ragged in the silence.

Mia's eyes slowly fluttered open as the pain ebbed. She looked down at his head, his thick wavy hair tousled from their ministrations. It was suddenly absurdly funny and she felt a bubble of laughter rise in her chest. She bit down on her lip to stop it from spilling out.

But her ribcage shook with the effort to keep it in and it bubbled up anyway.

Luca felt the vibration against his forehead and glanced up just as she laughed. Their breathing was still erratic, they were both half-undressed and thoroughly bedraggled, he had a raging hard-on—and she was laughing.

It was absurd. So he laughed too.

'You're crazy,' he said after their laughter had died down.

Mia shook her head. 'This is crazy.'

Luca had to agree. Even if his hard-on didn't. 'You want to stop?' he murmured.

His husky voice thickened his accent and a surge of lust welled deep down low in her. Mia shook her head. She couldn't have stopped now even if a bus had crashed right through the walls of the on-call room.

She was a healthy adult woman, and it had been a couple of weeks since her last liaison. 'That would be even crazier.'

Luca grinned, dropping his mouth to her chest, run-

ning his nose lightly along the slope of a breast and upwards to nuzzle her neck. 'Pure insanity.'

She stretched her neck to give him better access.
'Certifiable,' she agreed.

Luca laved the pulse half way up her neck with his
tongue. 'Utter lunacy.'

'I think we should get the door, though,' she managed through the haze of lust descending on her.

Luca's head snapped to the doorway. He swore softly
against her neck at its partially open state and was rewarded with another throaty laugh. He kissed her hard
on the mouth.

'Take your clothes off,' he said, before pushing off
her, padding over to the door and locking it.

'You do realise this is a one-off, right?' she said as
she tried to wiggle out of her jeans essentially one-
handed.

Luca turned and watched her. He could clearly see
her nipples through the lace of her bra and it made him
harder.

He undid his zip and peeled off his jeans. 'Of course.
My bedpost is littered with one-offs. Or hadn't you
heard?'

Mia went to grin but it died on her lips as the pure
male beauty of his physique was fully exposed to her.
Long, lean legs, dusted with black hair. Flat, flat belly.
Broad in the shoulder, narrow in the hip.

And if the bulge in his snug cotton boxers was anything to go by, large, in all the right places.

She'd seen a marble statue just like him in Rome
many years before. Luca di Angelo had *Made in Italy*
stamped all over him.

Then he came to her, towering over her, snapping the

lamp off, helping her out of her jeans, kissing her everywhere, arching her back over the arm of the lounge, thrusting her breasts upwards towards his eager mouth. Making her sigh. Making her whimper. Making her come.

And, best of all, making her forget.

Three days later Dr Finn Kennedy, chief of Surgery, strode into the emergency department on what he was sure was going to be a fool's errand. He was tired. His upper arm had ached all night despite several shots of whisky, and he rubbed at it absently. His eyes felt scratchy and his damn nuisance thumb was numb and tingly.

He pulled up short as Evie approached him. Great, just what he needed. Dr Evie Lockheart. *Princess Evie.* Born with a silver spoon in her mouth, working in her granddaddy's hospital, a place still generously supported by the Lockheart family trust and her father in particular, who was treated like royalty by the boffins upstairs.

With absolutely no idea how hard ordinary people had it.

And the only woman in the entire hospital who seemed to be able to push his buttons. She didn't simper or cower. Just looked at him patiently with those damn hazel eyes.

'Dr Kennedy,' she greeted him.

'There's a consult for me?' he asked, not bothering to acknowledge her greeting. He had a feeling that she saw beyond his curt exterior and he didn't like it.

The only other woman to have done that had been

Lydia—his brother's widow—and that had been an un-mitigated disaster.

Evie refused to give Finn the satisfaction of seeing how his brusqueness grated. He wasn't in the army any more and she wasn't one of his soldiers to be ordered around. Instead, she launched straight into her spiel. Still, it didn't stop her heart from pounding like a runaway train in her chest—she'd made an amazing incidental find and despite his gruffness she was desperate for his approval.

'Twenty-two-year-old female, with a painful lump in her breast. Ultrasound identified a small benign cyst—'

'Are you kidding me?' Finn glared down at her, hands on hips. 'You do know I'm a cardiac surgeon, right? That means stuff to do with the heart.'

Evie held his gaze and her tongue and continued as if he hadn't just rudely interrupted her. 'She also complained of fatigue, shortness of breath and intermittent chest pains. Incidental finding reveals bicuspid aortic valve with associated ascending aortic aneurysm.'

Finn stared at her. Was in hell was she on about? 'Sure,' he said sarcastically as he held out his hand. 'Radiographer report?'

'There isn't one. Radiology was backlogged and the ultrasound was performed in the department.'

'I see. By who, exactly?' he demanded.

Evie's gaze didn't waver as his piercing blue eyes dared her to blink. 'By me.'

Finn snorted. 'You? You diagnosed a complex heart condition through a breast ultrasound?'

Evie crossed her arms too. 'Yes.'

'That's not even remotely possible,' he snapped.

Until right now, Evie would have agreed. 'It is if the woman in question has very small breasts.'

Finn glared at her. Princess Evie—her place at the prestigious SHH emergency department no doubt paid for by her father's huge donations—wasting his time. 'Where's the patient?'

'Cubicle fifteen,' she said calmly.

'What have you told her that I'm going to have to untell her?' he asked silkily.

'I told her I couldn't get a good enough angle and I was going to call for someone more experienced,' Evie bristled. 'I did *go* to medical school, Dr Kennedy,' she said frostily.

'Really? Daddy couldn't fast-track you, then?'

Evie ignored the dig. 'I graduated top of my year.'

'He gives to the university too, then?' Finn retorted, before turning on his heel and heading for the indicated cubicle.

Evie's heart tripped in her chest as she struggled to keep up with his long-legged stride. But even falling flat on her face would be worth it just to see the look on Finn's when her diagnosis was confirmed.

Finn snapped back the curtain and introduced himself to a petite young woman in a hospital gown who was chewing on her bottom lip. He smiled at her. 'Hello. Bethany, is it?' he asked, consulting her chart. 'I'm Dr Kennedy. Dr Lockheart's asked me to have a look at you.'

'Is something wrong?' Bethany asked, looking from one doctor to the other.

Finn patted her hand. 'Give me one minute and I'll be able to tell you.'

He turned away to the compact mobile ultrasound

machine and shot Evie an exasperated look. It was hardly the most sophisticated machine in their radiology arsenal. He found it hard to believe anyone could diagnose a potentially fatal heart problem on something so basic.

He picked up the transducer from its cradle fiddled with the pulse settings and the screen brightness and turned to back to Bethany, who'd already opened her gown and put her arm above her head.

Finn squeezed a blob of warmed gel on Bethany's chest, noting that she did indeed have practically non-existent breast tissue. 'Okay, here goes,' he murmured as he ploughed the transducer through the middle of the gel.

He ignored Evie, who was standing at his elbow, and concentrated on the small screen as the grainy grey and black image of Bethany's pumping heart came into view. It took him less than a minute to concur with Evie's very impressive diagnosis.

He flicked a glance at her and met her unwavering hazel gaze. There was no triumph or smugness there, just complete confidence in her diagnosis, and he felt a rather foreign feeling of grudging respect.

Maybe there was more to her than the Lockheart name.

'Is everything okay?' Bethany asked.

Finn shook his head. 'No. There's a problem,' he admitted. 'But it's okay,' he added quickly. 'I can fix it.'

Evie listened in awe while Finn sat with Bethany and explained how the small benign-looking cyst in her breast was nothing compared to the real problem, and what he could do about it. For such an arrogant, rude, human being he had amazing rapport with patients.

When they walked out of the curtain thirty minutes later Evie had seen an entirely different side to the infamous Dr Finn Kennedy. She'd known he must have had a heart in there somewhere but it was the first time she'd ever seen any evidence of it.

'Organise a bed for her in CCU,' Finn said briskly, handing Bethany's chart to her.

Evie nodded as she accepted it, trying not to feel discouraged. She hadn't really thought he'd congratulate her, had she?

'Good catch, Dr Lockheart,' he murmured. 'Maybe you're not Daddy's little girl after all.'

And then he turned in the opposite direction and strode away.

Evie blinked as the back-handed compliment sank in.

High praise indeed!

CHAPTER THREE

WHEN Mia came on duty later that afternoon the first person she spied was Luca. Which wasn't difficult, given that his very presence seemed to attract attention. She'd bet whoever had invented the term *chick magnet* had met Luca di Angelo.

Of course, she could also just have conjured him up—she couldn't deny she'd been thinking about him and their illicit liaison in the on-call room a little too often on her days off.

She squeezed her eyes shut tight for a few seconds then opened them again. Nope—still there.

And looking right at her.

Smiling at her, actually. Like he knew all her dirty secrets. And that he was one of them.

She graced him with an indifferent glare and a cool nod of the head as she slung her stethoscope around her neck and deliberately walked in the opposite direction.

Luca chuckled to himself as he watched the hypnotic swish of her blonde ponytail. She seemed all prim and neat, her dark grey tailored trousers classically elegant, her high-necked, capped-sleeve blouse in sapphire blue crisp and stylish.

Not a wrinkle. Or a hair out of place.

Very different from the Mia of the other night. Who had looked rumpled and disturbed and hadn't cared about either.

A hum coursed through his blood at the mere thought. It certainly hadn't been the way he had envisaged that night would turn out. In fact, if someone had asked him who'd be the woman least likely to sleep with him, he would have said Mia McKenzie.

But it had been pretty damn amazing. Once she'd made up her mind she hadn't held back. She hadn't done that irritating talking/fishing-for-compliments thing that a surprising amount of women did during sex. Or tried to twist herself into some uncomfortable position because she knew it was her best angle.

She hadn't even asked him what he liked in an effort to make it all about him.

No. She'd known exactly what she'd wanted and she'd taken it. But she'd given, too. She'd been confident and assured and had met him as an equal.

It was the most uncomplicated one-off he'd ever had.

Now, if he could just stop thinking about it…

Mia moved through the shift with her senses on high alert. Her skin prickled when he was near. The hairs on her nape stood to attention. Her nipples seemed to stay in a state of permanent erection. It seemed every cell in her body was well and truly tuned in to Luca.

And it didn't help that they kept running into each other.

The first time had been in the lift after she'd been on for half an hour. She'd just caught it before the doors had shut and squeezed in with several other people sharing the space with a transport bed. The patient had been almost lost amidst the equipment on the bed and the stuff hanging off the rails had made it an even tighter fit.

She'd smiled at the patient as the doors had shut and turned to stare at the opposite wall, only to be confronted by Luca's slow, sexy smile.

'Dr McKenzie,' he murmured.

'Dr di Angelo,' she replied, dropping her gaze to the knot of his tie rather than the knowing look in his eyes.

'How were your days off?' he asked innocently.

Mia couldn't believe how intimate it could feel between them in a lift full of onlookers. She kept her gaze firmly on the knot at his throat.

His long, tanned throat she'd licked every inch of.

'Fine, thank you.' *Apart from daydreaming about you.*

His grin broadened as if he could hear the words she hadn't said. 'I trust your arm is getting better?'

Mia had felt sure that if his voice could cure wounds hers would have miraculously healed on the spot. She kept her gaze resolute, trying not to think how erotic the smooth glide of his jaw had been against her breasts.

'Thank you, yes.'

'I can look at it later, if you like. I think there're still some dressings left in the on-call room.'

Mia's eyes flicked up before she could stop them and his smile gained a slight triumphant edge. A blast of heat arced between them and Mia was surprised that it hadn't incinerated everyone in the lift.

'Thank you Dr di Angelo. I can manage,' she murmured as the lift doors opened and she walked out on legs that felt like wobbly jelly.

The second time she'd worked with him on a fifty-two-year-old construction worker who had come in from an industrial accident, having sustained major chest and abdominal injuries. He'd placed a chest tube and done the intubation while she'd inserted a central line.

They'd worked in tandem, like a well-oiled machine, but she'd been aware of him and his every move every second. Their gazes had locked regularly. At one stage their heads had even bumped together, competing for the same line of sight. He'd apologised, but their faces had been very close. His gaze had dropped briefly to her mouth and her mind had strayed to exactly where she'd put it on his body.

The third time she'd been plastering a fifteen-year-old-boy's broken arm when he'd lounged in the doorway to the plaster room. He hadn't announced himself but something had alerted her and she'd looked up to find him propped against the doorframe.

'Haven't you got something better to be doing?' she asked testily, returning her attention to the job. How was she supposed to avoid him when he seemed to be wherever she was?

Luca shook his head. 'All quiet. I thought I'd *skulk* here for a while.'

She'd glanced up at his use of the word 'skulk' and he grinned at her. He advanced into the room and she tried not to notice how his beautifully cut trousers and khaki business shirt fitted him to perfection. He could easily have been strutting a Milan catwalk.

'You the boy who was having a light-sabre fight with your little sister?' he asked the teenager.

The boy nodded glumly. 'She's never going to let me live it down.'

'Sisters can be very unforgiving.'

'You've got sisters?'

Luca nodded. 'Three.'

'Man, that's harsh.'

Mia slid him a sly glance. His accent had thickened and his words had seemed tinged with something she hadn't been able to put her finger on. Then the two of them got into a conversation about *Star Wars* and Mia gritted her teeth and pretended Luca and his mouth were in a galaxy far, far away.

By the time he passed her in the hallway at ten o'clock she was walking a very fine line between homicidal mania and sexual frustration. The man was everywhere—in the department and in her head—and, heaven help her, she wanted to push him into the nearest available private space and tear his clothes off.

But it had been a one-off.

They'd agreed.

'Oh, Dr McKenzie, I meant to tell you earlier, I've arranged for a debrief session with John Allen from Psych for you.'

Mia slowed and turned. How could she want to kill him and kiss at the same time? 'Cos she did. *She wanted to kiss that smug Sicilian mouth so badly she could scream.*

'I don't need a damn debrief,' she snapped, tossing her head, daring him to push her. 'I'm fine.'

Luca smiled at the flash in her eyes—like sun shining on a cathedral window. He liked the way her chest rose and fell just a little bit too fast. And how it pulled at her blouse in all the right places.

He pushed back. 'I'm sure you are. But you're having one, anyway.'

That was it! Mia put her hands on her hips, barely

suppressing the juvenile urge to stamp her foot. 'Oh, no, I'm not.'

He nodded. 'Ten tomorrow morning.'

Her gaze locked on his mouth the same time his locked on hers. Something stirred deep in her belly. A primal recognition of attraction. A potent force.

She lifted her chin. 'You can't make me.'

Luca felt a subtle shift in the signals emanating from her. Had that challenge been sexual? A nurse bustled past and gave them a strange look.

Luca inclined his head to a nearby door. 'Shall we discuss this in private?'

Mia knew it was the on-call room. 'Fine,' she muttered, her heart rate suddenly trebling.

She followed him through the open doorway into the empty room. 'I'm not seeing a shrink, Luca. You can—'

Luca turned abruptly, cutting her off with a swift, hard kiss, crowding her back towards the door, shutting it with the combined weight of their two bodies.

Every cell in Mia's body leapt to life. She grabbed the knot of his tie, pulling him flush against her.

She groaned, or was it him?

Madness, it was madness.

She broke off. 'We said once,' she gasped.

Luca nodded. 'I know.' And then he went back for more.

Mia gave herself up to the urgent press of his mouth. The bold stroke of his hand against her breast. The hard thrust of his erection.

She whimpered as he ground his pelvis into hers and rubbed herself shamelessly against him. Her hands travelled to his butt, urging him closer, nearer, angling him just right.

She shut her eyes as he hit the spot, her head lolling back against the door. His mouth moved lower to the mad flutter at the side of her neck.

The flutter was everywhere. In her breasts and her belly and between her legs. It thrummed through her ears in a deafening thunder like the roar of the ocean or the call of the wild.

Luca. Luca. Luca.

Not even the peeling of an emergency beeper pierced it. It took two squealing beepers to manage that.

Mia pushed on Luca's chest as the sound finally penetrated. They were both gasping, their clothes askew as they automatically reached for their pagers.

Damn! 'Cardiac arrest two minutes out,' Mia panted.

Luca nodded as he read the same message on his beeper. 'Great timing,' he murmured.

Mia took a few seconds to straighten her clothes and clear the heavy fog of lust from her brain. Luca followed suit.

'How do I look?' she asked as she quickly retied her hair to its pristine smoothness.

Luca smiled. 'Like you've been thoroughly kissed.'

Mia glared at him.

That was exactly what she'd been afraid of!

The following night, Mia snuggled into her ancient duffle coat as she and Evie left The Harbour behind them and crossed over the road, heading for the flashing neon sign that read 'Pete's'. It was nearly ten o'clock but Wednesday was traditionally staff discount night—if you could produce an SHH badge, drinks were half-price—it was an ingrained part of The Harbour's culture.

Not that the majority of people letting their hair down at tables needed to produce ID. Pete, the owner, had been running the popular bar for the last twenty years and not only knew who was who but usually who was doing who as well.

Of course he would never have disclosed such information. Like every good barkeeper, discretion was his middle name. And it was definitely the reason why Pete's had been *the* hangout for SHH staff over the years.

Sure, proximity and comfy booths also helped but when down-time was limited, a cosy place nearby where a busy professional could talk and unwind and not be *on* for a while or worry about gossip, which was already rife enough in their work environment, was definitely appreciated.

He was also fiercely protective of the hard-working staff at Sydney's most prestigious hospital. He didn't tolerate customers who complained to him about bias or hassled his favourite clients in any way. After all, the good staff of The Harbour had been his bread and butter since he'd opened.

But it was more than that. The doctors and nurses of the SHH were special. Too many times he'd seen them walk through his door with weary, haunted expressions. They saw things on a day-to-day basis that were the stuff of most people's nightmares. And if a drink or two at his bar managed to take their minds off that then Pete considered he'd done a good day's work.

Mia welcomed the blast of heat as Evie opened the heavy wooden door to Pete's. They shrugged out of their coats and headed to the bar, greeting several people they knew along the way.

'It's freezing out there,' she said to Pete, thrusting out her hands. 'Just feel these.'

Pete smiled at them and dutifully folded Mia's chilly fingers in his big warm mitts. 'Cold hands, warm heart,' he quipped.

Mia grinned at him. 'You are a romantic.'

'Nothing wrong with that, love. Right, Evie?'

Evie, distracted by Finn chatting to a busty blonde further along the bar, answered automatically. 'Right.'

'Pete, Pete, Pete,' Mia tutted. 'Romance belongs in books.'

'Maybe you should read a couple,' he jested.

'Books? We don't have time for books, do we, Evie?' Mia asked.

'Nope,' Evie murmured, sliding a surreptitious gaze towards Finn.

'Journals are all I get a chance to read,' Mia lamented.

Pete sighed. 'No time for a man either, I suppose?'

'There are men,' she protested. Being happily married for thirty years had rendered Pete's vision permanently rose coloured.

Pete gave her a reproachful look. 'Men, sure. But one man, Mia? That's what you need.'

Mia rolled her eyes. 'If I were a man, would we be having this conversation?' She looked around and spied Finn with a vaguely familiar blonde—Suzy someone? One of the scrub nurses from the OT. 'Do you say this sort of stuff to Finn?'

Pete clutched his heart in a wounded fashion. He was

like the SHH fairy godfather, wanting happily-ever-afters for *all* his regulars.

'Of course. I say it to Finn most of all.' He deliberately looked at a distracted Evie. 'That man needs the love of a good woman more than anyone.'

Evie looked at Pete sharply and didn't say anything for a beat or two. 'I'll have a tequila shot followed by a bottle of lager, thank you, Peter.'

'Just the usual for me,' Mia added.

He grinned at them. 'Okay, okay. I can take a hint.'

Pete served Evie's shot first and she snatched it up and threw it straight down her throat, revelling in the burn. As she slammed it back on the bar she glanced Finn's way. He was looking at her with those piercing blue eyes and for a moment their gazes locked.

Was that disdain? Judgement? Disapproval?

Too bad, so sad.

'Orange juice for you,' Pete said, placing it on the bar in front of Mia. 'Beer for Evie.'

Evie picked up her drink. 'Let's go over there,' she said, moving off the bar stool in the opposite direction to Finn, before Mia even had a chance to lift her juice. She shrugged at Pete and followed.

Unfortunately, Evie was heading to a booth Mia would rather not be at but it was difficult to change direction now the occupants had spotted them and waved them over. And she didn't want to have to explain to her friend who would no doubt put two and two together and come up with five.

'Move over,' Evie announced. 'We're coming in.'

Mia tried not to look at Luca as she was forced to take the seat next to him. But she could feel his eyes on hers and the heat of him immediately enveloped her as her body responded in an almost Pavlovian fashion to his proximity.

The booth was spacious but with three bodies either side it was a cosy fit.

'Mia, long time no see.'

Mia smiled at John Allen, the psychologist she'd been forced to see that morning by Luca. Susie, his wife, was also there and greeted Mia warmly. Of course she saw them regularly enough anyway, given that they too lived at the nearby Kirribilli Views apartments where a lot of The Harbour staff resided.

'How did the debrief go?' Luca enquired.

'Mia's fine.' John winked.

She glared at him. 'I *am* fine.'

'Sure,' he soothed.

'You know, Mia, it's not a bad thing, to talk this kind of thing through.' Rupert Davidson, head of Neurology, entered the conversation.

'He's right,' Teo Tuala, SHH's head of Paediatrics, agreed.

Mia looked at all of them, exasperation bubbling inside her. She inclined her head towards Luca. 'He didn't. He was being threatened too.'

'Yes, but I wasn't lunged at with a knife. Neither did I have my arm slashed open by said knife.'

Mia took a long swig of her drink as his voice, so close to her ear, took her right back to the on-call room. 'I'm fine,' she repeated.

'Well, you know where I am if you want to talk any more,' John offered.

Mia couldn't help but think that a sweaty twenty minutes with Luca had helped more than an hour's conversation with John but it was a dangerous path for her thoughts to take given how aware she was of Luca right now.

'Absolutely.' She nodded. 'What's happening with Stan?' she asked, deftly moving the focus of the conversation off her. 'His ninety-six-hour hold must be up by now.'

John nodded. 'He's staying on voluntarily. He's had increasing paranoia episodes over the last few years apparently. We want to get his meds right and get him well supported before we discharge him.'

Mia nodded and soon the conversation drifted to other subjects.

Ten minutes later, Evie finished her beer and stood. 'Gotta go. I promised my father I'd drop by some hideous dinner party he's having. He's sending a car for me.'

Mia leapt at the opportunity to escape and stood as well. 'I'd better go too. I'm on in the morning.'

'Oh, Mia, no,' Susie objected. 'Don't leave me alone with all these men talking shop. Stay a bit longer.'

Mia looked at Susie's beseeching gaze and acquiesced. It had absolutely nothing to do with every cell suddenly crying out for Luca's heat to be squashed back up against her again. 'Okay, I guess I can stay for one more.'

'I'll get another round,' Luca said. He climbed out of the booth and watched bemused as Mia took a step back. 'Is that vodka and orange?'

Mia shook her head. 'Just orange.'

He frowned. 'You're not on call, are you?'

'Nope. Just not drinking.'

Luca slid a glance at the table, where the merits of a journal article were being debated. He looked back at

Mia. 'Are you worried you may lose your inhibitions?' he murmured, dropping his voice a little. 'I don't need alcohol to lose mine.'

Mia, aware of how close he was standing, felt the pronunciation of *inhibitions* slide right down her spine. His English was perfect but the occasional word leant towards his native Italian.

'I wasn't aware you had any,' she said, her voice steely.

Luca walked away chuckling, deep and low. Unfortunately, that was exactly where Mia felt it—deep and low.

Standing at the bar a couple of minutes later, Luca rattled off the drinks order and waited for Pete to return with them.

'Here you are, Luca,' Pete said, placing them on a round tray.

'Thanks.' Luca handed over the money.

'You're with Mia, I see,' Pete said casually. 'Great girl.'

Luca nodded, his gaze straying back to a smiling Mia. She was wearing a long skirt, a turtle-neck skivvy and black knee-high boots. He'd been fantasising about her in those boots, just the boots, all day.

'Yes,' he agreed. Except they weren't the words he'd have used. Sexy, feisty, prickly seemed to suit her so much better.

'Fantastic doctor,' Pete pressed, joining Luca in his observation of Mia.

Now, those were words Luca would use. 'Yes, she is,' he agreed.

'Hard to believe someone like that's still single,' Pete mused.

Luca looked back at the bartender. 'And why is that, do you think?'

Pete looked Luca direct in the eye. 'Men these days scare too easily. They buy into her *I'm fine* exterior.'

'And she's not?'

Pete shook his head. 'Of course she's not. She just doesn't know it yet.'

They watched her again for a moment or two. 'But don't tell her I told you that,' Pete added.

Luca laughed, picking up the tray. 'Deal.'

'So, Luca.' Susie, desperate for a topic change, watched Luca slip back in beside Mia. 'Sicily, huh?'

Luca nodded as the familiar feeling of dread and loss and yearning threatened to swamp him. He pushed them back. 'That's right.'

Mia glanced at Luca as she felt his thigh, jammed against hers, tense. This close to his delectable profile she could see the clench of his jaw.

'Where exactly?' Susie continued, unaware of Luca's reluctance to talk about his past. Especially his home.

Luca forced himself to breathe out, to loosen the suddenly tense muscles of his neck. 'Marsala.'

'Like the wine?' she asked.

Luca nodded. 'Yes. Like the wine.'

'We never got to Sicily,' Susie said. 'But we adored Italy, didn't we, John?'

John nodded. 'Europe as a whole. We're actually going skiing in France at the end of the year.'

Luca slowly relaxed each muscle group as conversation moved to travel but a pall had been cast over the evening. If it wasn't for the alluring press of Mia against his side, he'd have excused himself almost immediately.

But her nearness held him in check. He'd been aware of her since she'd first entered the bar and he could tell she was more than aware of him. There was a crackle between them that had nothing to do with the delicious rub of their thighs.

And after the way the conversation had turned tonight he couldn't think of a better way of keeping the memories of Marsala at bay than getting lost in Mia for a while.

To hell with their one-off pact.

Teo drained his cola and stood. 'I have to go back to The Harbour and check on a patient then I'd better head home. Emma's teething and keeping Zoe and me up most of the night.'

'Teething already?' Susie marvelled. 'Isn't six months a little early?'

Teo shook his head. 'Every baby is different.' And he grinned at them because even with the sleepless nights, Zoe and Emma had made him happier than he'd ever thought possible.

'Aw,' Rupert, also happily married, teased. 'Ain't love grand?'

Mia, barely able to suppress an eye roll at Teo's goofy expression, saw her second chance at escape. 'Yep, me too. Early start.'

'Same here,' Luca said, letting her out. 'I'll walk you to your car.'

Mia felt a thickening in the air between them as their gazes skittered past each other. Yep, like that's what she needed right now. *Sex-on-legs escorting her anywhere.*

But, sensing he was as desperate to get away as she was, she nodded her head graciously. They said their goodbyes and made their way through the throng to the coat stands by the front door.

'I'm not driving,' Mia said as she shrugged into her coat. 'I live just down at Kirribilli Views. I walk to work. I don't need an escort.'

Luca smiled as he adjusted the collar on his suit jacket. 'What a coincidence. So do I.'

Mia's fingers fumbled with the tie of her coat. *Of course he did.* 'Of course you do,' she said faintly. She hadn't seen him around but it was a big place populated with shift workers.

Luca chuckled as he opened the heavy wooden door and gestured for her to precede him. He looked back over his shoulder as he departed. Pete grinned and gave him a thumbs-up.

CHAPTER FOUR

Mia buried her hands in her coat pockets as her warm breath fogged into the night air. She glanced at Luca, who had only his suit jacket to fend off cold winter fingers. But he looked warm and vital—like a walking hot-water bottle. She shook the tempting image of her wrapped around him in bed from her head. It was disconcerting to say the least when the streets were dark and practically deserted and they kept passing interesting alcoves and alleyways where two people could warm up really quickly.

Mia clamped down on the direction of her thoughts and the strange undulation of her pelvic floor muscles. 'Aren't you cold in that?' she groused.

Luca shrugged. 'Two beers help.'

Mia nodded. 'I don't drink much,' she replied.

Why she felt the need to share that she had no idea, but she could feel his pull and knew she was on a slow march towards an inevitable ending. This wasn't how it was supposed to be between them and she felt suddenly nervous.

'You don't like it?' Luca enquired.

Mia shook her head. 'I went through a stage where I liked it a little too much.'

'Ah,' Luca said, intrigued by the nugget of information. Was this what Pete had alluded to? 'Care to elaborate?'

Not bloody likely! Mia couldn't believe she'd told him that much. Damn this man! But there was something about him, a recognition that they were the same, that seemed to loosen her lips around him. Still, she had absolutely no intention of reliving two years of booze and bad men with him.

The past was the past.

'No,' she said. He quirked an eyebrow at her and she said, 'It's complicated.'

They walked in silence for a few moments. 'I suppose a man from Marsala probably doesn't understand that.'

Luca tensed. He'd been enjoying the build-up between them as each footstep took them closer to their apartments. To their beds. The footpath had narrowed and their arms brushed; her body warmth mixed and flirted with his. Their footsteps matched, their breathing synchronised.

But suddenly that was forgotten.

Mia turned her head to face him. 'How long ago did you leave?'

Luca bit down on the urge to laugh at her choice of words. Leaving implied consent. He hadn't been given a whole lot of choice. 'I was sixteen.'

She whistled. 'That's a long time.'

Luca chuckled, trying to divert the conversation. 'Are you implying I'm old?'

Mia laughed too and let it peter out. 'You're a long way from home, Luca,' she mused.

Although she, more than anyone, knew that geographic proximity had nothing to do with that sense of 'home'. She'd grown up a twenty-minute drive from here and it may as well have been Italy for all the connection Mia felt to the brick and mortar house where her mother still resided. Mainly on the couch.

Luca kept his gaze firmly fixed on the illuminated arch of the Sydney Harbour Bridge he could just see through the treetops. 'Yes.'

Mia smiled. 'Care to elaborate?'

'No.'

'Word on the grapevine is you studied medicine in London. I thought Italian mamas liked to keep tabs on their sons. No decent universities in Italy?'

Luca saw his mother's broken face again on that horrible day that had changed everything. The sorrow and disappointment etched in lines that had seemed somehow instantly deeper. He schooled his expression as he looked at Mia and repeated her response.

'It's complicated.'

Mia nodded. If anyone understood that, she did. And she understood the underlying message—butt out. She got that too.

They lapsed into silence again but she was aware of him large and silent beside her. Aware of his tension and his potent, brooding masculinity.

'Here we are,' she announced unnecessarily as the doors to the ten-storey apartment complex loomed ahead.

Luca dragged himself out of the sticky web of his past. 'Yes,' he murmured. He looked down at her. 'Your place or mine?'

Mia swallowed. She should have been outraged at his assumption. But he was looking at her intently with that

devil mouth and heat was flooding through her belly
and tightening her breasts.

*She didn't do repeat performances, that was her
golden rule, but, heavens above, she wanted him.*

'Yours,' she murmured huskily. 'I share with Evie.'

He held her gaze for a moment before opening the
door for her and following her to the lift. They rode it
to the ninth floor in silence, Luca propped against one
wall, staring across at Mia propped against the opposite wall. The bold way she returned his gaze tugged at
his groin and his whole body tightened in anticipation.

Mia felt utterly dominated as Luca lounged against
the wall, arms crossed. His gaze raked her body lingering on her breasts, her thighs, her boots. Then travelled
all the way back up again to rest on her mouth.

The seconds ticked by as his eyes locked on her lips.
Her tongue darted out to moisten them, a nervous gesture.

His nostrils flared. She swallowed.

His arms dropped. Her heart skipped a beat.

He took a step towards her. She tensed.

The lift dinged. He stopped. She breathed again.

'Ladies first,' he murmured. 'Number nineteen.'

Mia walked on legs made of Plasticine to the indicated apartment, aware of his eyes on her the whole
time. She could barely breathe by the time she pulled
up in front of his door.

Absently she reached for the doorhandle the same
time he did. He sucked in a breath. 'Your hands are
freezing,' he murmured.

'Yes,' she agreed. That was because all her blood had
drained to her belly and breasts. In fact, apart from her

torso she felt cold right through to her bones. She even shivered involuntarily.

Luca grinned at her as he pushed open the door. 'I have the perfect solution.'

He tugged on her hand and she followed him into the toasty centrally heated apartment.

Luca strode into his bedroom, Mia in tow, flipping lights on as he went. He walked straight past his bed, turning right into a spacious en suite. He ushered her in, shut the door, flipped on a wall-mounted heater, opened the shower screen and turned the hot tap on full bore. Instant heat puffed into the air from the shower head.

He turned to look at Mia, shrugging out of his jacket. 'Get naked.'

Mia quirked an eyebrow at his imperious command. 'Boy, you sure know how to seduce a woman.'

Luca grabbed her by her coat lapels and hauled her up against him. He lowered his mouth and on a groan unleashed a truly devastating kiss.

Mia's response was instantaneous. His mouth was hot, hot, hot and it fanned the flames burning in her belly to the rest of her body. Raising herself on tiptoe, she tunnelled her hands into his hair, pressed her breasts hard against the solid warmth of his chest.

His hands cupped her bottom, dragging their hips into alignment. Mia rubbed herself against him, causing a delicious friction that spread more warmth to every part of her body.

Luca groped for the tie of her coat and yanked it loose, his hands invading the cocoon of heat around her belly and stroking down her sides and back. He felt for her zip and undid it, pushing the skirt off her hips.

Mia broke away from the drugging intensity of his

mouth, her rough breath almost as loud as the teeming shower that poured an endless supply of steam into the hothouse atmosphere.

She was hot now. Very, very hot.

She quickly stepped out of her skirt, removed her jacket and followed it with her skivvy.

Luca's breath caught in his throat as she stood before him in matching champagne-coloured underwear and a pair of black knee-high boots.

He breathed out reverentially. '*Mia bella*,' he murmured. Thoughts of the mess he'd left behind in Marsala were now a distant memory.

Mia blushed. She had no idea what that meant but it sounded pretty damn complimentary to her. Which spurred her on even more. Removing the clasp from her hair, she shook it free so it fell down her back and flowed over her shoulders in a golden stream.

Aware that Luca, hands on hips, was watching her every move between heavy eyelids, she lifted a booted foot and placed it on the edge of the bath. She leaned forward until her breasts were brushing her thigh and slowly—very, very slowly—undid the side zipper on her boots.

Luca heard every one of the zip teeth release as he watched Mia intently. She had her back to him and his gaze roved hungrily over the brief triangle of fabric encasing the enticing wiggle of her butt cheeks. He lifted it higher to the indentation that formed the small of her back. Higher still to the long delicate stretch of her spine partially obscured by her long blonde tresses.

Mia looked over her shoulder at him and smiled as she straightened and flicked the boot off. The steam was building in the bathroom and her face felt flushed, although the kick in her pulse told her it had more to do with Luca's smouldering look than the atmospheric conditions.

When she turned back to bend over the other boot, Luca couldn't hold back. He moved in close behind her, pushing her hair off one shoulder and leaning forward to drop a kiss. His hands gripped her hips and pulled her against him, snuggling her bottom into the heat of his groin.

Luca was consumed with the erotic image in front of him. He fully clothed, his erection straining for release, Mia scantily clad and bent provocatively in front of him. He wanted to tear her knickers off and take her right here and now.

He pulled her in tight.

Mia's hand faltered on the zip as Luca circled his hips against her. She shut her eyes as he created delicious havoc in just the right spot, her breath coming faster. The boot forgotten, one foot still propped on the bath edge, she straightened, arching her back against him, her arms snaking up behind her to clasp around his neck, gratified to feel both of his hands slide up from her hips, over her belly and higher.

'Mia,' he groaned into her ear as his hands found her satin-clad breasts.

Mia whimpered, biting her lip as he squeezed and flattened then peeled the cups aside and ran the pads of his thumbs against her tight, bare nipples.

'I want to be inside you,' he murmured, his lips finding her neck and licking all the sensitive areas.

Mia opened her mouth to answer but one of his hands moved lower and dipped beneath the band of her underwear, seeking the slick heat of her. He ploughed a finger through her aching sex and found just the right spot, causing her to lose all vocal ability.

'Mia,' he murmured as she bucked against him. 'You are hot here. Very, very hot.'

Mia couldn't speak as one hand teased a nipple and the other moved rhythmically between her thighs. Her knee buckled slightly and she was vaguely aware of Luca pulling her back against him.

Her hands, however, had a mind of their own and while she left one anchored around his neck the other one sought to touch him as intimately as he was touching her.

She reached behind her, grabbing for his belt as her brain liquefied. One-handed and on an inexorable march towards orgasm, she managed the buckle and the zip and finally she was freeing him, his hard length surging into her palm.

Luca threw his head back on a groan, squeezing his eyes shut as she gripped him firmly and ran her hand up and down the length of him. The urge to bury himself in her, ram into all that slick heat as far as he could go, roared through him as his fingers picked up their pace.

Mia could feel the edges of her world starting to fray and she gripped his neck hard as a wild heat started to boil out of control in the deepest part of her. Her hand clamped around his girth became dysfunctional and un-coordinated as the all-consuming urge to ride his finger, seek her own pleasure, became a blinding imperative.

She sagged against him as standing upright became impossible. 'Luca,' she moaned.

'Yes,' he whispered in her ear. 'Yes.'

'Luca-a-a-a!'

She bucked as the orgasm slammed into her. It picked her up, whirled her round and smashed her back down only to lift her again—higher. She gasped and jerked against him, rocking her pelvis in sync with his fingers, squeezing every last liquid drop of pleasure out of it.

'Yes, Mia, yes,' he urged, rubbing harder and faster, pushing a finger deep inside her, feeling her clamp hard around him.

Mia moaned loudly as her body automatically accepted his penetration. It was shockingly satisfying and she cried out as another finger filled her.

Luca held her tight against him as she whimpered and gyrated her pelvis, grinding herself against the hard intrusion of his fingers.

The orgasm began to fade and Mia felt as if she was walking through a rainbow. Cool mists of colour stroked her skin like sighs, caressing and cradling, bringing her down gently despite the frantic beat of her heart and the tortured sound of her breath.

Finally her feet touched the ground and she opened her eyes. Became aware that she was leaning heavily into Luca, his hands were cradling her hips and his erection still coursed hard and potent in her hand.

She moved against him. Dropped her leg to the floor, kicked off her boot and turned in his arms.

Luca brushed her hair off her shoulder. 'Warm now?' He grinned.

Mia laughed. A part of her was vaguely aware the floor tiles were warm underfoot and that he could obviously afford to fork out for one of the more luxuriously appointed apartments. And that he no doubt had Bridge and Opera house views too.

But none of that mattered as she plastered her lips

to his. It only mattered that she could make him groan just like that. And…she rubbed herself along the length of him…hard just like this.

'Shower,' she murmured, pulling back and quickly divesting herself of her underwear before stepping into the spacious cubicle.

She turned through the cloud of steam. 'Are you coming?' she asked.

Luca, captivated by the water running over her naked body and her hair turning dark gold as the spray doused it, didn't move for a moment.

'Luca,' Mia growled impatiently, taking in his partially undressed body and his very, very aroused state. 'Come here and do me against the tiles.'

Her provocative words galvanised him into action and he tore at his shirt, toeing off his shoes, grabbing for his wallet before he divested himself of his trousers, pulling out a foil packet, ripping it open and hastily donning the protection he never went without.

Two steps and he was in a cloud of steam, enveloped by hot water and her. He plastered her against the requested wall and plundered her lips and her neck and her breasts with his mouth. Then he boosted her up the tiles, positioned her slippery body at just the right height and plunged straight into her, his mouth swallowing her guttural cry.

Luca pounded into her relentlessly, satisfied to hear her gasps, to see the loll of her head as each thrust rocked her entire body. He tongued her breasts, her heat and her sweat and her essence in each drop of water sluicing over her nipples.

Pressure built strongly and relentlessly as each drive took him closer. In his veins, in his head, in his loins.

Pleasure, so intense it hurt, coiled low in his gut. She cried out and bucked in his arms and the coil whipped out, cracking like a lightning strike, zapping every erogenous zone, every cell.

She tightened around him and he came and he came and he came.

Luca was in the kitchen, percolating coffee in nothing but a low-slung towel, when Mia came out of the bathroom dressed in the clothes she'd arrived in half an hour earlier.

Minus her underwear.

And the earring she'd lost somewhere in the midst of the head-banging sex. Down the drainhole, she suspected. Her hair was hanging in wet strips down her back and her body ached all over.

In a good way.

'Coffee?' he asked.

Mia shook her head, distracted by the perfection of him. Broad shoulders, trim hips, flat belly. His damp hair curled around his nape and ears. She felt the slight ache inside her begin to throb in carnal recognition of him and the things he could do.

It'd be so easy to take four or five paces forward and whip that towel away. Drop to her knees. Show him she was a pretty dab hand at doling out pleasure too. Go again right there on the kitchen floor as her traitorous body was demanding.

But then what? Once more after that? Stay the night?

She wasn't a stay-the-night kind of girl. It was why she always went to the guy's place—easier to leave and never look back than to tell someone to go.

'No, thanks,' she murmured. 'I'm going to head home.'

Luca lounged against the bench and crossed his arms over his very impressive chest. 'You're not clingy. I like that.'

Mia nodded. 'Good. Looks like we'll get along just fine, then.'

'I think you're the first woman I've met who didn't want to be held afterwards.'

Mia shook her head. 'Not the cuddling type, I'm afraid.'

Luca regarded her silently for a few moments. He could almost buy into her act. Except he'd seen another side to her that first night. Sure, Mia McKenzie seemed feisty and tough but there was definitely a vulnerable side.

She was an intriguing woman.

'And why is that?' Luca mused.

Mia knew exactly why. She wasn't blind to the scars that growing up in an emotionally barren house had left. Sex was a quick, easy connection—she'd found that out at uni. But cuddling—staying?—was hard. Sex was physically intimate. Cuddles emotionally intimate. Certainly not something she'd had an awful lot of experience with from the main male role model in her life as she'd been growing up.

Cuddles called for a certain level of trust. And she'd been too scarred to trust anyone at any level—particularly men.

He was standing patiently, all big and solid, looking at her with expectation. She could have easily opened her mouth and told him the reasons.

But it was none of his damn business.

'It sends the wrong message,' she said.

Mia shifted slightly as Luca studied her with his big brown eyes. It was kind of unnerving.

She straightened her shoulders. 'Do you have a problem with that?'

Like she cared if he did.

Luca stayed very still. 'No. It just seems like something a—'

'What?' she interrupted, scorn lacing her voice as her blood pressure rose a couple of notches. 'A man? Like something a man would say?'

Why was it okay for men to use women for sex but not for women to use men?

'It's a new century, Luca. Gotta move with the times.'

Luca chuckled at the sudden glint of fire in her stained-glass eyes. Her whole body had become animated. His gaze drifted to the bounce of her unfettered breasts before it flicked back to her face. 'Sicilian men aren't known for their tendency to move with the times.'

Mia shoved her hands on her hips as her nipples responded to his blatant stare. 'You going to go all Neanderthal on me, Luca?'

Luca pushed off the bench and moved towards her. 'Not at all. I am a highly evolved Sicilian. I like a woman who knows what she wants.'

Mia watched him prowl closer and felt that ache intensify. How was it possible to look sexy and menacing all at the same time?

He stopped in front of her, close, nearly touching. But not. 'Especially one who appreciates the type of liaisons I also happen to favour.' He dropped his gaze to her mouth for long moments before returning it to her face. 'Where have you been all my life?' He grinned.

It took Mia a moment to reel her body in enough to respond. Kissing him seemed the best course of action but she needed to go home.

She. Must. Go. Home.

And never come back.

Mia took a step back. 'Goodnight, Luca. See you in the morning.'

Luca watched the sway of her hips as she made her way to the door and felt himself twitch beneath the towel. 'I'm having a party in a couple of weeks. Everyone from work is coming. You should too.'

Mia's hand paused on the doorknob. 'No,' she said, without looking back.

One thing she knew for sure was that Luca wasn't like any other man she'd known. In a brief time he'd got firmly under her skin and she wasn't about to lose the upper hand to him.

There wouldn't be a next time. Certainly not a party.

Luca's wicked chuckle mocked her as she turned the handle and slipped out of the apartment.

Evie bustled through the deserted outpatients department at seven o'clock the next evening. She'd begged a chart from Enid Kenny, the NUM of the department earlier, who'd relinquished it only after Evie had promised faithfully to personally return it before she left for the day.

Someone else might have sent a courier but not Evie. Sister Enid Kenny was an institution around The Harbour and not to be messed with! Hence the sweet note and box of chocolates she was also clutching in her hand.

She turned right, passing a row of examination rooms

on her way to Enid's office. She noticed a light on in the far office. Voices floated out. Male voices. She frowned. Who on earth was working this late?

Then, to her utter surprise, Finn stepped out, followed by Rupert Davidson. Evie faltered and dived into the nearest exam room. Recovering quickly, she cautiously peeked around the door. In the empty department their voices carried easily and she eavesdropped unashamedly.

She watched as they shook hands and Rupert said, 'You're entitled to a second opinion, Finn. But you know as well as I do that the conservative approach is only a sticky plaster and you can't keep going on like this. Surgery will have to happen at some stage.'

Then Finn nodded but even from a few metres away she could see that familiar set to his unshaven jaw. 'Thanks, Rupert. I'll think about it.'

And then he turned and walked away in the opposite direction.

Evie fell back against the wall of the examination room, her heart pounding. What the hell had that been about? She grappled with what she'd heard and seen, trying to make sense of it.

Finn was seeing Rupert? A neurologist? *You can't keep going on like this.* Was there something wrong?

She recalled the uneasy feelings she'd had for a while now that something was up with Finn, and the rumours that he'd been wounded on a tour in Afghanistan when he'd been in the army. Had he sustained injuries during his time there? Injuries that could affect his job?

Eric Frobisher, SHH's officious medical director, would be furious if that was the case. He and Finn already butted heads on a regular basis.

Evie drummed her fingers against the chart as curiosity and concern for Finn warred within her. She told herself it was pure collegial interest. One doctor looking out for another. Even if said doctor was the most surly and unappreciative man she'd ever met.

Making a decision, Evie waited for a couple of minutes before pushing herself off the wall and heading towards her original destination. She stopped in midstride as she passed the last office and blinked at Rupert with what she hoped was her very best round-eyed surprise.

'Rupert?' she asked. 'What are you still doing here? Burning the candle at both ends?'

Rupert, who was writing in a chart, laughed as he put down his pen. 'No such luck. Just a late appointment.'

Evie nodded, glancing at the chart trying to see a name. 'Gosh, that's dedication.' She smiled.

Rupert shrugged. 'It was a favour.' He nodded at the package in her hand. 'What about you? Those chocolates for me?'

She laughed. 'Oh, no, these are major sucking-up chocolates for Enid.'

Rupert laughed back. 'You're coming to Luca's party in a couple of weeks?' she asked.

Rupert nodded. 'Wouldn't miss it for the world.'

'Great,' she said as she backed out the door, her head still swimming with what she'd just witnessed.

What in the hell was wrong with Finn Kennedy?

CHAPTER FIVE

Two weeks later Mia was watching the clock, thinking that for once in her working life she might actually get off on time. Her shift, one of those rare short shifts, was due to finish at two and things were looking good. With Evie going off to Luca's party tonight—the one she was *not* going to attend, no matter how much Evie begged— she had a quiet night of reading planned.

The latest blockbuster novel had been sitting on her bedside table, gathering dust, for too long.

She glanced nervously over at the man in question as he spoke on the phone at the other end of the central monitoring station. She'd managed to keep her attraction at bay this past fortnight—until last night. A cluttered, semi-dark storeroom had seriously tried her resolve to keep away when they'd both ended up inside. His body had been big and close, his lips had kicked up into a frank smile, his gaze firmly fixed on her mouth.

How she hadn't pushed him against the wall and ravaged him she still wasn't sure.

But she hadn't. She'd caught herself at the last second. Remembered that she'd already broken her golden rule once and she wasn't going to do it again. Even if he was the most skilled, most exciting lover she'd ever known.

Unfortunately, the buzz from last night's near kiss was still vibrating through her system and they'd been trading furtive glances all morning. He'd looked at her with undiluted lust half an hour ago and she still could barely see straight.

His gaze met hers again, his brown eyes knowing, and her pulse picked up a notch.

'Ambulance two minutes out.'

The urgent note in Nola's voice dragged her attention back to reality and Mia looked down to where the efficient triage nurse sat, the red emergency phone to her ear, speaking out loud as she wrote the details down from the ambulance coms centre.

'Thirty-year-old male. Jumper. Two storeys. Bilateral comminuted fractured tib and fibs, right compound fractured femur, query fractured pelvis, query spinal injuries, fractured right ribs, GCS twelve, major internal injuries, query ruptured spleen, hypotensive and tachycardic.'

Luca joined them, all business now as he read the details again over Nola's shoulder.

'I'll page Ortho and General Surgery,' Mia said, grabbing the phone nearest her as the distant wail of a siren permeated the thick walls of the hospital.

Luca also picked up a phone. 'I'll alert blood bank that we might need to initiate the massive transfusion protocol.'

By the time the ambulance pulled up a minute later, everything was prepped and Luca and Mia were standing outside, ready to receive the patient.

Luca grabbed the ambulance doorhandle and pulled

it open as the paramedic driving the vehicle joined them, launching into a rapid-fire handover of injuries, actual and suspected.

He and the treating paramedic pulled the gurney out of the back of the ambulance. The patient was moaning, his face covered by an oxygen mask.

'Pupils equal and reacting,' the paramedica continued as they pushed the gurney towards the entrance, Mia and Luca keeping pace. 'BP ninety over sixty, pulse one hundred and forty, resps fifty and shallow. Right chest tube inserted on scene, two IV cannulae wide open.'

'Do we know what happened?' Mia asked, clinging to the gurney rail as they practically flew inside to the prepared trauma cubicle.

'Paternity test showed he wasn't the baby's daddy,' the paramedic stated dispassionately.

Mia felt a prickle up her spine as she and Luca shared a look. 'Is his name Stan?' she asked.

The paramedic nodded. 'Stanley James.'

Repeat customers—especially suicides attempts— were reasonably common in the department. As were frequent-flyer drug addicts and patients with chronic conditions. Mia treated them all with courtesy and professionalism, careful not to get emotionally invested in them.

But this man had held her at knifepoint. Had yanked her back into the convoluted emotions of her childhood. Had been the catalyst for what had happened later that night with Luca.

Mia felt sick as two nurses descended and between the four of them they quickly transferred Stan to the hospital gurney on the count of three. Whether she liked it or not, she and Stanley were connected.

And she really didn't want to have to deal with that.

Stan pulled his mask off and grabbed her hand. 'I told you,' he said. 'I told you she was cheating on me.'

Mia looked into his anguished face, trying not to see her father, trying only to see the man who had menaced her with a knife. But he looked…broken.

Just like her father.

'It's going to be okay, Stan,' she murmured, replacing his mask as people bustled around her. 'We're going to get you patched up.'

He pulled it off again. 'No. Just leave me. Just leave me to die.'

Mia and Luca's gazes met for a moment. She felt rage build inside as she looked back down at Stan. He'd taken the coward's way out, just like her father. Her father had walked, Stan had jumped—both ways showed very little regard for the people left behind.

For a tiny baby. For a bewildered ten-year-old girl.

'Please, just let me die,' Stan begged.

Mia bit down on the urge to tell Stan that if he'd really wanted to die he should have jumped from a higher building. The fact that he hadn't spoke volumes about the incident. She doubted it was a true attempt—more like a cry for help.

And she was damned if she was going to let him die on her watch.

She put the mask back. 'Can't do that, I'm afraid, Stan.'

'We need X-Ray,' Luca said. 'And get Psych down here. I want to consult with John Allen.'

Luca and Mia, their personal situation forgotten,

worked methodically over the next hour to stabilise Stan for Theatre. They intubated, placed lines and another chest tube, gave blood and plasma expanders, consulted with Ortho, General Surgery and Radiology.

And all the time Luca was chanting, *Come on, Stan, come on Stan, come on Stan. Don't die. Don't die. Don't die.* If it took everything he had, Luca was not going to let this man die.

Not that he'd ever been particularly emotional about life-and-death situations. Being a trauma specialist, he saw the struggle between the two on a regular basis. Like two powerfully competing forces pulling in opposite directions. He worked hard to save every patient but not even he was arrogant enough to assume that hard work was always enough.

Sometimes, no matter what he threw at a patient, they died.

He got that. People died.

Children, teenagers, athletes, mothers, forty-year-olds with everything to live for.

People died.

Hell…they were all dying.

But the truth was, Stan had struck a chord. And probably for the first time ever he actually felt personally invested in a patient. And not because Stan had threatened him with a knife but because Luca knew all about the demons that had driven him.

He knew how it felt to be betrayed by the person you loved. How it felt to have your whole world yanked out from under you. And how life-changing that could be.

He knew how it felt to be a father one moment and then suddenly not.

To feel powerless.

To feel alone.

It may have been a whole bunch of years ago but some things never left you.

He glanced at Mia as she took a phone call from the lab. Mia, who was working just as hard to pull Stan through. The man who had threatened to stab her, who had slashed her arm with a knife.

What was driving her?

The same things that had driven her to cry out in her sleep that night? That had spurred her to seek amnesia in his arms?

What were the things that haunted her? That made her tough and feisty and not the *cuddling* type?

Had Stan stirred them up for her as he had stirred things up from *his* past? *Daddy, come back.* That's what she'd cried out that night. Did Stan remind her of her father as he had reminded him of his sixteen-year-old self?

'Haemoglobin's eight,' Mia announced. She ordered another bag of blood to be hung and administered stat. 'Let's get him to Theatre for that laparotomy,' she said. 'He's bleeding from somewhere.'

As if by magic, an anaesthetist, a nurse and two orderlies arrived and Luca dragged himself out of his reverie to help with the handover.

Within ten minutes Stan had been whisked away and the two of them stood in an empty trauma bay. The floor was littered with packaging and discarded dressing material that had fallen short of the bin. And where there'd been frantic activity and the beeps and alarms of monitors seconds ago, there was now absolute quiet.

Luca glanced at Mia watching Stan disappear down

the corridor with a look on her face he couldn't quite work out.

He put his arm around her shoulder. 'He'll be okay,' he said, even though he had no earthly idea why he'd said it and absolutely no way of knowing how true it was.

Mia nodded. Physically, sure…maybe. After an extended recovery period and if they could control the bleeding and get him through about a hundred complications that could arise.

But mentally?

Would Stan ever be the same again? Was her father?

For a few insane seconds she leaned into the hug, soaking up the comfort, surprised to find that she needed it as a block of unexpected emotion lodged in her chest, invading her throat, threatening to choke her.

And she hated it.

She pulled away, stripped off her plastic gown and peeled off her gloves, disposing of them in an overflowing bin.

'I'll follow up with John,' she said.

And left Luca behind in the bay.

Later that evening, Mia accompanied Evie to the party. She'd finally caved to her friend's relentless insistence that she go. Stan's case had been playing on her mind all afternoon and she knew she wouldn't be able to settle to a book. She needed a distraction and there was no doubt Luca distracted the hell out of her.

That brief comforting hug had been playing on her mind too but she pushed it aside. The distraction she needed from Luca did not involve anything as nurturing as comfort. She needed hard and ready. Hot and sweaty. Down and dirty.

And since she knew he gave it better than anyone else—could obliterate everything else from her brain—only he would do.

The party was in full swing when they finally stepped inside two hours late. Familiar faces milled in groups all around Luca's apartment and greeted them enthusiastically, despite their tardiness. Shift workers accepted that shift times varied and punctuality was fluid.

Mia felt Luca's eyes on her instantly and looked directly at him. Neither of them smiled as music pulsed around them and their gazes ate each other up.

Luca, surprised to see her, devoured the sight of her as she shrugged out of her leather jacket and made her way over to Luke Williams, one of The Harbour's plastic surgeons specialising in burns, and his partner, Lily, a nurse at SHH.

Mia was wearing a tight denim skirt that didn't quite reach her knees, a pair of long rainbow-striped socks that ended in little bows just below her knees and a singlet-style shirt that did up snugly across her front with corset-style lacing.

Thank goodness his apartment was centrally heated.

Her hair hung loose around her shoulders and an image of him removing that lacing with his teeth surrounded by the curtain of her golden hair wreaked havoc in his groin.

His gaze drifted to the reddish-pink scar on her upper arm visible from all the way across the room. It reminded him of that night and what had happened.

It reminded him of today. Of anguish so familiar he

had recognised it immediately. Of those brief few seconds with Mia after Stan had left for Theatre when he'd felt a strange moment of solidarity, of connection.

He pushed the thought aside. Stan had made it out of surgery and was stable in Intensive Care. And Mia had stepped away from him.

Work was work.

This was a party.

He took a swig out of his long-necked beer, his eyes never leaving her. She laughed at something Luke said and shook her head, her hair swinging enticingly around the cleavage barely contained by the faux corset top.

She glanced at him and their gazes locked, the message in her eyes heating his loins. He took another pull from his beer, keeping up the eye contact, matching her frank, unwavering stare. If she wanted to play chicken, he was up for it. He smiled to himself as Lily said something to her and Mia was forced to break contact first.

Why had she come when she'd been so adamant she wouldn't?

Just for the sex she was patently up for? Or was there something more to it? Had Stan rattled her again? Or maybe that moment they'd shared had? Had she come to prove it hadn't? Or to explore if it had?

The thought alarmed him and Luca served himself up a mental slap. What the hell business was it of his? Her motivations? He knew what he wanted and it didn't involve second-guessing a gorgeous woman who had come here to have sex with him. Whatever she was offering, he was going to take it.

And have a damn fine time doing so.

* * *

Mia wandered around the different groups of people, stopping to chat, talk shop, laugh with her friends and colleagues. And all the time she was conscious of Luca tracking her around the room. He hadn't even said hello to her but she could sense his intense interest, feel the weight of his gaze, the heat of his laser-like focus trained squarely on her back.

Sure, he was playing the perfect host—attentive and charming as he moved around the apartment—but underneath that bronzed Latin skin she could sense the leashed desire he was just barely keeping a lid on. His glances may be smouldering with lust but she could also feel his impatience as they slowly circled each other.

She walked past a large bay window and stopped to admire the view. She knew he'd have one. A man with heated bathroom tiles would certainly have a view!

The iron arch of the illuminated Sydney Harbour Bridge and the floodlit white sails of the Opera House glowed like beacons in the night. Of course, these could also be seen from the upper floors of SHH but it was still a pretty amazing sight, no matter how many times she'd been privy to it.

The hairs on the back of her neck prickled and she was instantly aware he was zeroing in.

Luca sauntered up to her. 'I didn't think you were coming,' he murmured.

Mia didn't turn to look at him. She could see his reflection. Tall, broad shouldered, looking very fine in snug blue jeans and a close-fitting black T-shirt.

All he needed was *Security* emblazoned across the front. Or maybe *Italian Stallion*.

'Nice view.'

Luca, who hadn't taken his eyes of her said, 'Indeed.'

He took a sip of his beer. 'The view from my bedroom is even better.'

Mia smiled. 'Don't you have guests to entertain?'

Luca chuckled, turning so his back was to the window. Their arms brushed and he felt a kick in his groin. 'They seem to be amusing themselves just fine.'

Mia turned too just in time to see Finn entering with a stunning-looking redhead she'd not seen before.

'I didn't think Finn would come,' she mused. Evie had been sure of it but she herself hadn't been convinced.

'Why not?' Luca frowned.

'He's not really the social type.'

He shrugged. 'He is tonight.'

Apparently. Very social, if the redhead's relaxed intimacy was anything to go by. Mia flicked a glance towards Evie and watched her friend's face fall a little. She gave an inward sigh, wishing she understood Evie's attraction to the maverick surgeon.

Sure, his legendary status was alluring and he was sexy in a rumpled kind of way. And single. But that just-rolled-out-of-bed look didn't do it for her.

She preferred clean-shaven men.

Like the one standing beside her.

'So...' Luca dropped his head so his mouth was near her ear. 'About that view?'

Mia felt goose-bumps break out on her arms as her belly constricted. But Evie was looking around with an overly bright smile on her face and Mia knew that her friend needed her.

'Patience is a virtue,' she murmured.

She heard Luca chuckling as she slunk away.

* * *

Half an hour later Evie was standing in a circle, ostensibly talking to Mia, Luke Williams and a couple of nurses from the emergency department. But her gaze kept wandering to Finn, who was sitting on the wide windowsill of the bay window, talking to Rupert. He had dismissed the redhead when Rupert had approached and now they seemed to be having quite an intense discussion.

Finn was nursing his usual Scotch and it didn't look like he appreciated what Rupert had to say. After another minute Rupert shrugged and walked away.

'Excuse me, guys. I'll go and grab another drink.'

She felt Mia's concerned gaze on her as she slipped away but no one else paid any attention. Evie grabbed a beer out of the ice-filled sink then wended her way through to Finn.

Finn watched Evie approach through the prism of his glass. She lifted a beer bottle to her lips and tipped her head back as she drew close. When she was done her lips were moist and he found himself wondering what she tasted like.

He tensed at the errant thought, which cranked up the throb in his already aching arm. That, on top of Rupert's little chat, made him even crankier.

'Well, well, well. I thought the Lockheart heiress would be into champagne.'

Evie let the insult slide off her back. She'd learned to chug beer and drink shots at uni just to annoy her parents.

'Beer is better.'

She stood in front of him, one hand shoved into the front pocket of her skinny jeans, the other one wrapped around the bottle. She was wearing a floaty top that fell off her shoulder, which he studiously ignored.

He raised his glass to the light. 'Scotch is the only drink.' It smoothed out the edges and helped with the pain. Physical and mental.

Evie inspected him. Sprawled on the windowsill, his shaggy look was sexy as hell. Unlike other guys she knew, the stubble was real, hinting at disregard rather than fashion. It also lent authenticity to the boast she'd once overheard—apparently he only ever got three or four hours' sleep a night.

She shook her head. *Why?* Was it deliberate? Did his brilliant mind never shut off or was it involuntary? Was the mysterious injury responsible for Finn's chronic insomnia? Or had his time in the army left him with nightmares? It was rumoured he'd been to Afghanistan and Iraq.

Or was it just the redhead or any of the other women he was seen with, keeping him up all night?

She didn't understand why she felt so compelled to try and figure him out. But she did. 'What did Rupert want?'

Finn, the glass halfway to his mouth, paused slightly before lifting it to his lips and draining the entire glass.

'I need another drink,' he said.

'I heard you and Rupert talking a couple of weeks ago. It was in the evening…in the outpatients department.'

Finn felt his hackles rise. 'Spying for Daddy?' He knew how chummy the hospital's biggest benefactor was with pernickety Eric Frobisher.

Evie heard the low menace in his voice and watched as his piercing blue eyes practically bored into her.

'He mentioned surgery.' Evie paused and perused his hard, shuttered face for any signs of softening. 'Is there something wrong, Finn?'

Finn heard the quiet strength in her voice. As if it never occurred to her that he wouldn't confess. The kind of strength that came from growing up in a nurturing environment where a person's opinion, even a child's, mattered.

'I think you should stick with diagnosing complex heart conditions.'

She ploughed on despite his rigid jaw and frigid stare. 'There are rumours about you being wounded in the army. Do you have some residual effects from that?'

Finn's heart pounded in his chest. Only little Miss Rich Girl would dare to push him like this. He stood, instantly towering over her, and was gratified to see her take a step back, to see she wasn't so sure of herself after all. 'I need a drink.'

He brushed past her without looking back.
Conversation over.

At two am only Mia and Evie remained as Luca shut his door on the last of his guests. He caught Mia's eye. She'd been a walking, talking temptation all night and now it was time to pay the piper.

Mia grinned at him. 'I'm going to stay and help Luca clean up,' she said to Evie, carrying some glasses into the kitchen and setting them on the substantial granite bench top beside the sink.

Evie nodded, tired after her long day shift and distracted by thoughts of Finn, who had hastily downed a drink after their *chat* then left with the redhead clinging to his arm. 'I'll help.'

Luca, picking up some more glasses behind where Evie was located, shook his head and mouthed, 'No.'

Mia grinned some more. 'No, Evie. You're done in. Go to bed. I won't be far behind you.' She was so revved up she'd probably come in under a minute.

'Oh, but—'

'No buts,' Luca insisted. 'Go. We'll be fine.'

Evie *was* exhausted. 'Well…if you're sure…?'

Luca nodded, vigorously aware that Mia had turned on the tap and was leaning over the sink. 'Absolutely.'

He ushered Evie out the door and shut it with quiet determination then leant against it, hard. He watched Mia fill the sink with glassware through a haze of high-octane lust.

'Leave that,' he said as he slowly prowled towards her.

Mia looked at him and grinned. It faded in a flash at the naked intent in his gaze. 'It's just a few dishes,' she said lamely as her insides melted to the consistency of chocolate sauce.

Just like his lust-drunk eyes.

Luca reached her side, flicked off the tap, swept the remaining dirty dishes into the sink with a huge clatter, grabbed her around the waist and boosted her up onto the bench.

Mia opened her mouth to protest against the tinkling glass and chipping crockery but mostly the cold granite on the backs of her legs. But Luca didn't give her a chance. He stepped between her thighs, forcing them apart, and claimed her mouth in a kiss that silenced all her inane worries.

A kiss that lit a fuse that ignited a powder keg. After

two weeks of abstinence and an evening of sexual chess they devoured each other like a raging bushfire.

Luca slipped his hands under the hem of her skirt, pushing it up her thighs, exposing her flesh and her heat. He dragged her core hard against him, the bench top just the right height, moaning when Mia locked her ankles around his waist, wedging them together as intimately as they could be fully clothed. She gasped as he kissed down her neck—hard, biting kisses that stiffened her nipples to unbearable points.

Yes. This was what she needed.

This.

Something to forget the day.

She grabbed for the snap on his jeans as he squeezed a breast with his hand. She undid his zip, pushed his underwear aside and grasped his warm velvet girth.

His mouth slammed against hers on a full, throaty groan as he fumbled with the lacing of her shirt, half undoing, half tearing at the fabric until it succumbed to his will. He dragged his mouth from hers, down, down, down to her breasts, ripping aside the cups of her transparent bra and gorging on the ripeness of her nipples.

Mia's back arched, one hand automatically holding his head to her, the other squeezing his rampant erection, rubbing herself against it, whimpering as it caused the most wicked friction.

'Back pocket,' Luca whispered as he lifted his head to pay equal homage to her other breast.

Mia fumbled. His lips were creating havoc and she felt like she'd been to the dentist and been given a full body shot.

Limp with lust. Prostrate with pleasure.

Her fingers found the hard edges of foil and whipped

it out triumphantly as his hand pushed aside her undies and stroked against her so intimately she thought she was going to die.

Too much more of that and she'd be done.

It was bloody-mindedness alone that accomplished sheathing him as he sought and found where she was hottest. Where she was the most ready.

'Ah,' she cried as the friction hit just the right spot. 'Now,' she cried, tilting her pelvis in supplication. 'Now.'

Luca didn't need a translation. He ran his palms up her back, anchored both hands over her shoulders, leaned forward to suck hard on a ripe, plump, moist nipple and rammed into her in one quick decisive thrust of his hips.

Their combined groan no doubt caused a blip at some seismic centre somewhere.

And then they were moving and pounding together in unison, rocking and rocking, higher and higher, gasping and sighing and reaching for breath until it all coalesced in one magical moment and the stars shattered around them.

CHAPTER SIX

A WEEK later Mia was examining a severe case of cellulitis around a ten-day-old calf laceration when Luca entered the cubicle. He smiled at her and her breath hitched.

'Can I help you, Dr di Angelo?'

'You don't happen to have an otoscope by any chance? They all seem to have gone walking.'

Mia didn't register his words. Just the way his eyes crinkled at the edges as he looked at her with a gaze that paid way too much attention to the dip of her cleavage. And the way his lips moved, all soft and full, exactly the same as when they stroked down her neck.

Luca quirked an eyebrow as Mia's normally clear blue gaze became a little heated. 'Mia?'

She blinked and her cheeks warmed as she realised she had no idea what he'd asked for. 'Sorry?'

Luca grinned. It wasn't often he saw her blush and he liked it. It seemed completely at odds with her feisty, my-way-or-the-highway demeanour, softening her. Cranking up the strong sense of attraction another notch. 'Otoscope?'

'Oh. Yes.' she shook her head to clear it as she removed the equipment from the pocket she'd jammed it in earlier. 'Here.'

Their fingers brushed as he took it and Luca smiled again as he felt the pulse of awareness in his fingertips and knew she'd felt it too. 'Thank you.'

It took Mia a few seconds to realise he'd disappeared as her body recovered from just the faintest contact with his.

'He's a bit of a hottie, dear.'

Mia looked down absently at Mable Richardson, her eighty-six-year-old patient. She had snowy white hair and a wicked gleam in her eyes.

'He could park his slippers under my bed any day.' Mable sighed. 'If I was only forty years younger…'

Mia stared at her patient open-mouthed, shocked by such ribald frankness from an octogenarian.

Mable cackled. 'I'm old, deary, not dead.'

Mia laughed. From the twinkle in her eyes, Mable was obviously one of those lovely old ladies who loved to shock.

'Laugh all you want.' Mable patted Mia's hand. 'You blink one day and suddenly you're eighty-six. Mark my words, young lady—take your opportunities when you get them.' And then she winked.

'Mable, you're incorrigible.'

Mable cackled again, seemingly delighted by Mia's description. 'I hope so, deary.'

Mia returned her attention to Mable's gardening wound, which had developed an infection in the subcutaneous tissues. Had Mable seen something pass between her and Luca—something intangible—that had prompted such an observation, or was she just someone who appreciated good eye candy when she saw it?

Not for the first time she wondered what the hell she and Luca were doing. Okay, there'd been no more liaisons since the party and they'd only been together a few times anyway. But it was a few times more than she'd ever allowed any other man. And, if his rep was accurate, the same applied to him.

Why did this man, Luca di Angelo of all men, have this...pull, this sway over her?

No.

Mia smiled absently at Mable as she pulled the gurney rail up decisively and excused herself to arrange for Mable's admission for several days of intravenous antibiotics.

She wasn't going to analyse what had gone on.

She wasn't going to give it any importance by pontificating over it.

They were attracted to each other. They'd had a good time. And that was that.

Period.

A couple of hours later the red emergency phone rang and Luca picked it up. He scribbled notes as he listened to the ambulance comms officer on the other end.

Mia and Evie looked at him as he hung up and Mia quirked an eyebrow. 'Multiple casualties, first five minutes out, from the Douglas army base. Some sort of an explosion. Two critical. One with penetrating chest trauma, the other with a partially severed leg.'

Caroline, on triage, appeared at his elbow and said, 'On it.'

Luca thanked her. 'I'll page Finn,' he said.

Then everyone scattered to do their jobs, ensuring the trauma bays were fully stocked for the incoming wounded and other departments alerted, including Pathology, Radiology and the operating theatres. Luckily it was Sunday when demand for these services was reduced.

Finn, in his standard surgical uniform of blue scrubs, arrived just as the first ambulance was pulling in.

'You take the chest trauma,' Luca said to his colleague, donning a yellow paper gown. 'I'll take the leg.'

Finn nodded, accepting a gown from Evie and quickly securing it before snapping disposable gloves into place.

'Evie, you go with Finn. Mia, you're with me.'

Finn opened his mouth to protest but Mia and Luca had already split off and ultimately it didn't matter who worked with him as long as they were competent. And, as reluctant as he had been to believe it, Princess Evie knew her stuff.

'You ready for this?' he demanded as the paramedic opened the back door.

Evie nodded, determined not to show him how much his enquiry rankled. 'Of course.' She gave him a serene smile to hide her gritted teeth.

A cry of pain, like that of a wounded animal, penetrated Finn's cynicism and tore his attention away to the soldier on the gurney, his dusty boots and army fatigues eerily familiar.

It took him back a lot of years.

He knew all about cries like that. Had heard them too often to forget. Had held Isaac, rocked him, as the yelling had quietened and finally abated, leaving only silence as the life had drained from his brother's trusting eyes.

'Twenty-eighty-year-old sergeant, bomb disposal

officer at Douglas, took the full impact of an explosive device. Safety gear rendered some protection.'

Finn shook his head and blinked as the rapid-fire handover spat out at him like the rat-a-tat of a machine gun. He couldn't think about Isaac. About a distant battlefield.

This soldier needed him.

But *this* soldier was about Isaac's age and cried out in pain just like Isaac had.

Finn pushed it away, knocked it back as the gurney moved rapidly into the emergency department.

'Matthew! Matthew!' the soldier called, pulling the oxygen mask aside with bloodied hands.

The paramedic continued his handover above the soldier's increasingly frantic cries. Evie listened intently while Finn stared at the young man's bloody face.

'Matty!'

'Matthew is his brother,' the paramedic informed Finn and Evie quietly as he helped transfer the soldier to the hospital gurney. 'He's the second soldier. With the…leg.'

Finn gave a grim nod as he looked at the blood-soaked combat shirt that had been cut away from the bleeding chest wound. Isaac had cried out for him, too. He could still hear the panic in his brother's voice. *Finn! Finn!*

'Matthew. Are you okay, Matthew?'

Finn moved in close to the soldier's head while all around him nurses jumped into action. Tears had cut grimy streaks through his grisly war paint of dirt and blood.

'Oxygen saturations eighty-nine, tachy at one fifty-nine,' a nurse relayed.

Finn's heart thundered in his chest as he fought back a tide of memories he'd thought he'd long ago buried deep. 'What's your name, Sergeant?'

Finn's enquiry was quiet but held a note of authority not forgotten from his own time in the army. It seemed to settle the soldier's agitation. He looked at Finn, his eyes filled with pain and emotional anguish.

'Phillips, sir, Sergeant Damien Phillips.' Damien grabbed Finn's gown, yanking him close, jarring his already throbbing upper arm and neck. 'Don't let me die. I don't want to die.'

Finn suddenly felt the weight of the promise he'd made to his brother all those years ago. It burned as fiercely on his conscience at this moment as it had that day sprawled in the dirt of a land far away. A promise he'd known, crippled by his own injuries and with help too many precious minutes away, he couldn't keep.

A promise that had haunted him.

But he could make good on a promise to Damien. In this top-notch facility and with his top-notch skills.

And he'd be damned if he'd lose another soldier on his watch.

'I won't, Damien. I won't.'

Evie looked at him sharply as a nurse passed her a chest tube. The soldier and Finn were practically nose to nose but, still, the husky promise surprised her. And not just because of the raw emotion she could hear in it.

Had Finn gone mad? Why on earth would he make such a promise? Damien's injuries were extensive—no one could promise that. Not even someone with Finn's legendary skill!

'Blood pressure ninety systolic.'

Finn glanced at her and she sucked in a breath at the brief flash of anguish, like the sweep of a light-house beacon, she saw there. His piercing gaze clouded temporarily with something she couldn't put her finger on—pain, compassion, loss?—then cleared as he stood abruptly.

'Let's get him prepped for Theatre,' Finn ordered.

Two hours later, in the thick of the operating theatre after Finn had demanded she scrub in, Evie's shoulders ached and her neck was stiff as they battled to plug the holes in Damien's heart. They'd replaced his entire cir-culation with donated blood products twice over. And he was still bleeding.

No one was surprised when a life-threatening ar-rhythmia caused a sudden dangerous dip in his blood pressure.

But Finn didn't give up.

He had the young soldier's heart in his two blood-ied hands and was squeezing it as if he could make the heart start beating again through sheer force of will.

He'd promised.

Too much death. Too many young men like Damien. Like Isaac.

Damn it! He'd promised.

But as the downtime extended, even he could see the futility of it. Finn found it hard to breathe as he gently removed his hands from around the soldier's heart and stepped back. He peeled off his gloves and glanced at the clock.

'Time of death fifteen thirty-one.'

No one spoke as they watched Finn walk out of the theatre. But a little bit of Evie went with him.

An hour later after attending to all the legalities, Evie felt drained, totally strung out from the after-effects of adrenaline and their exhaustive yet futile efforts to save Sergeant Damien Phillips's life.

Except it wasn't over because she had to find Finn, who wasn't answering his page. He had to sign some paperwork.

And she was worried about him...

Her fingers trembled as she pushed the change-room doors open. She needed to get out of these scrubs. They reminded her too much of the tragedy she'd just witnessed.

Of Finn's hands squeezing Damien's dying heart.

Her heart leapt in her chest as Finn came into view. He was sitting on the floor, staring at the wall, the lockers supporting his back. His knees were bent up and his hands were hanging between them, his surgical cap dangling from his fingers.

She swallowed. 'I've been paging you.'

Finn heard her voice as if from far away. He didn't want her there. He didn't want her to look at him with those calm hazel eyes of hers, eyes that saw too much, and mouth some horrible cliché.

He wanted to go home, pour himself a Scotch. And then another one. Drink until he could be sure he wouldn't dream about Isaac.

He kept his gaze firmly fixed on the wall. 'I've been ignoring you.'

Evie stared at him, dismayed at the return of his churlish tone. She should have expected it but for some reason, after their frantic efforts with Damien and the shared horror of losing him, she'd thought it'd be different.

He'd be different.

Irritated, she sauntered over to the patch of wall he was fixated on and deliberately parked her butt on it. Now he had no choice but to look at her. She folded her arms.

'There's some paperwork for the coroner you need to sign out in the office.'

Finn flicked his gaze up to her determined face. 'Fine.'

They stared at each other for a moment, the blue of Finn's eyes even more pronounced against the blue of his scrubs. Evie battled the urge to debrief, as she would normally with a colleague who had shared such an emotionally intense situation. Even a churlish one. But everything about Finn said, *Back off.*

But, then, when hadn't it?

'Damien's been taken to the morgue and—'

Finn pushed himself to his feet, interrupting her words. He bit down on a wince as a hot needle jabbed viciously into the nerves that ran down his right arm.

'We're not talking about Damien,' he said, turning to his locker, his back deliberately to her.

Evie took in the expanse of his back in his scrubs as she reeled from the vehemence in his words.

But I want to talk about him. I had my hand in his chest too, felt his heart pulsating. I need to talk about him.

She pushed off the wall and took a tentative step towards him and even though she knew she was overstepping the line, she didn't seem to be able to stop.

'Finn.'

His back stayed stubbornly turned away. Evie stared at it and let out the breath she'd been holding. She waited for a moment and stepped closer. 'Maybe it'd help…to talk about it?' she murmured.

His silence was absolute and out of pure frustration she tentatively placed her hand on his left shoulder. Despite the flinch she felt right down to her soul, Mia kept it there. His muscles were knotted with tension, practically vibrating beneath her hand, and she moved closer again until her body was almost touching his.

Finn shut his eyes as her scent and her warmth enveloped him. He could sense her right there behind him. Could hear the soft huff of her breath and the empathy oozing from every pore. A part of him wanted to unburden so badly it was shocking in its intensity.

Would it hurt to lean back a little, to have just a moment today that made sense?

Even if it didn't?

Evie held her breath as his body swayed a little and then seemed to slowly relax back against hers. His scrubs felt warm on her skin and she could sense the vitality of him as they stood in silence, cradled against each other, her cheek brushing his shoulder blade.

It was a magical moment and she shut her eyes to absorb every second. Everything suddenly seemed… right. Evie felt safe. She felt understood.

'You were brilliant today,' he whispered.

Evie eyes fluttered open at the barely discernible words. Had he said it or had she only imagined it? She opened her mouth to return the compliment but a beeping pager shattered the intimacy.

Finn's eyes opened instantly. His surroundings came

into sharp focus, the feel of Evie pressed against him suddenly too, too close for comfort.

What the hell was he doing?

He shrugged her away. 'I have to go,' he said gruffly.

Evie stepped back from him, reeling from the quick severing of the fragile emotional connection they'd just made.

He didn't even look back as he departed.

Mia headed straight for Pete's Bar after work later that evening. It had been a harrowing day for all of them, with Evie seeming particularly stressed when she'd finally returned to the department. They'd arranged to meet for a drink and a bit of a debrief session. Her friend was obviously taking the soldier's death hard.

Evie, however, was nowhere to be seen amidst the surprising Sunday night crowd as Mia made her way to the bar.

Luca, on the other hand, was easily spotted by her specially tuned senses and even if she'd been able to resist his devilish smile, she couldn't resist his I've-been-waiting-for-you stare.

Luca slid over as Mia approached, a sense of inevitability taking hold. What was it about this woman that made him want more? Her complete lack of sexual inhibitions or was she just a novelty, something familiar for a change instead of just another pick-up?

Or maybe it was her emotional unavailability? Knowing that she wanted the same thing he did—no commitments, nothing but a good time.

He watched the tame swish of her ponytail as she came closer, knowing what that hair looked like loose and wild and knowing from the heat in her gaze that tonight was going to get very wild indeed.

Mia refused to look at Luca as she slid in beside him. She didn't want to alert the two other occupants to what was going on between them. She and Luca were sex—just sex—and she didn't want the others to get the wrong impression.

She greeted Charlie Maxwell, the orthopaedic surgeon who had operated on the partially severed leg earlier, and Carl Todd, the anaesthetist. They were chatting about the bomb blast at Douglas and the two operations that had followed.

'He's not out of the woods yet,' Charlie said, taking a mouthful of his cola. He was on call and could well be called back to amputate the leg. 'We managed to save it but I'm not entirely convinced it'll be viable in the long term. There was extensive blood loss and a lengthy ischaemic time.'

Mia was always surprised whenever Charlie was serious. The lovable, laid-back, ex-pro surfer with his shaved head and wicked sense of humour gave new meaning to the Aussie word 'larrikin'. It was hard to tell at first glance that beneath it all he was a dedicated and committed professional.

'The trip from the army barracks isn't exactly short,' Mia mused. They were the nearest tertiary hospital to the barracks but in a situation where every second was vital, it was just a little too far away.

'Absolutely,' Charlie agreed. 'You guys did a great job getting him to me as quickly as you could.'

They chatted about the procedure for a while and Mia was pleased to hear that the patient was still stable in ICU with good pulses when Charlie rang to get an update.

Working on saving the leg today with Luca had been an exhilarating experience, and it was good to know that their efforts had contributed to the thus far positive operative outcome.

She glanced at Luca and felt her breath hitch as he chose that moment to glance at her. Heat surged up the side seam of her jeans where their legs touched. Under the table, his hand slid onto her thigh.

She felt her breath seize in her lungs. But, as his fingers started to smooth the fabric of her jeans in light patterns, she didn't remove it.

'Well, at least you had better luck than Finn,' Carl commented, dragging Mia's attention back to the conversation. He inclined his head to indicate the man in question, who was sitting at the bar by himself, staring into his Scotch.

'He worked like a demon, trying to save the other soldier. It was like he was possessed or something.'

Even knowing how much Carl liked to embellish things, Mia was startled by the anaesthetist's description of the frantic efforts in Finn's theatre that afternoon—no wonder Evie needed to debrief.

'Evie's pretty wrecked,' Mia commented when Carl finished.

'She's in the wrong specialty. She'd make a great surgeon,' Carl mused. 'Kept her head no matter how testy Finn got.'

Mia glanced at Finn again just as Suzy plonked herself down in the chair next to him. The theatre nurse was a regular at Pete's and Mia had seen her flirting with Finn here before, but a blind fool could see that Finn was not in the mood for company.

He gave her one of those polite frozen smiles she'd seen Finn give once too often to hapless medical students or to Eric Frobisher in particular, but Suzy seemed as oblivious or impervious to Finn's signals as Eric did.

Luca's signals, however, as his fingers continued to brush against her thigh, were loud and clear. Mia fought the urge to turn her body towards him, raise her mouth to his.

Carl looked over his shoulder again. 'Well, well, well. Looks like Finn's found a little distraction for the night.'

Mia just stopped the eye-roll. Carl was a top-class anaesthetist and still fancied himself as a bit of a ladies' man but he obviously wasn't a student of body language—he was way off the mark.

Luca winked at her. 'Oh, you think so?' he asked, watching an obviously distant Finn.

Carl took a swallow of his beer. 'Oh, yes.' He tapped his nose three times with his index finger. 'I've been around long enough to tell when there's hanky-panky going on between the staff.'

Luca felt Mia's thigh tense beneath his palm and he grinned. 'Really?' he murmured as he resisted Mia's sudden attempt to remove his hand from her thigh.

He easily won the necessarily subdued struggle.

Carl nodded. 'Of course. I picked Luke and Lily long before anyone else did. And this bloke…' he jerked his thumb towards Charlie. '…is virtually an open book.'

Charlie looked affronted. 'Me? What about him?' Charlie pointed to Luca. 'His reputation *preceded* him.'

'Ah, well.' Carl laughed. 'That's true.'

Luca laughed good-naturedly. 'And what about Mia?'

he enquired innocently, daring to stroke his fingers closer to the apex of her thighs. He didn't even wince when his ankle suffered a short, sharp jab from a hard pointy toe. 'Any gossip on her?'

Carl shook his head with a faux crestfallen look. 'Oh, no. Mia informed me a long time ago that fooling around with someone from work was a recipe for disaster. I think they were the words, right, Mia?'

Mia nodded her head graciously. She'd told Carl that most emphatically one day just after he'd tried to come on to her. And she meant it as much now as she had then.

So why the hell was she sitting at a booth with an Italian devil who was practically bringing her to orgasm in front of two oblivious colleagues?

Surely Carl could see the pheromones wafting off her body?

'What?' Luca feigned shock, looking down into Mia's face, gratified to see heat shimmering in her eyes like a mirage as his finger found her inner seam. He noticed her knuckles whiten as her grip on the edge of the table tightened. 'There's been no work flirtations?'

'Oh, no,' Carl answered for her. 'As far as I can tell, there's been no one. And I have a pretty good radar,' he added, tapping his nose again and smiling at Mia.

Luca flicked a finger across the seam that ran down from the bottom of her zip where it joined the two inner thigh seams. He felt her resistance melt to nothing as her legs eased apart a little and he thought, *Carl, you are a fool!*

Mia knew she shouldn't. They were in a public place, for crying out loud. A place that was crawling with staff from The Harbour. But his fingers were creating such delicious havoc…and no one could see…

She spread her legs a little further and smiled at Charlie as she changed the subject.

Evie was late to Pete's but that was the nature of the job. A last-minute patient had kept her involved for a while, which had been fine by her. Becoming absorbed in her work had helped keep her mind off Finn and what had happened between them today.

Because, whether he liked it or not—whether *she* liked it or not—something *had* happened. She'd had a glimpse of his humanity and no matter how many patients she'd seen since, she just couldn't banish that from her head.

And that brief moment when he'd leaned into her… It had felt like some kind of…surrender.

She'd never seen Finn emotionally vulnerable but today had been different. Today he'd leaned on her. Actually let himself go for once and trusted her enough to drop the cantankerous-but-brilliant-surgeon facade and just be a doctor who'd lost a patient. Be human. Be a man.

She could still feel the imprint of him against her. The flat of his shoulder blade against her cheek, the warm, solid roundness of his shoulder beneath her palm, the press of his broad back against her chest, their hearts beating almost as one.

She wasn't stupid enough to read anything into it. But she was intrigued. She wanted to know more. She wanted to know what had happened in his past to make Damien's case so personal to Finn. So personal that he'd let his guard down to her, of all people. Let her touch him. Let himself touch her back.

You were brilliant today, Evie.

Those words had meant more to her than any compliment she'd ever received-professional or personal. She hugged them to herself as she crossed the road to Pete's.

If Finn was at Pete's, she was going to repay the compliment. She was going to buy him a drink, tell him he was brilliant and badger him until he talked.

Staff at The Harbour always talked about what a maverick he was, what a legend. They held him in awe, hoisted him on high like some kind of trophy, made him untouchable. Like he was a machine, a robot. But they seemed to forget, underneath it all he was also a man.

But she hadn't. She'd seen the man today.

And men needed to be touched too.

Finn probably most of all.

Finn wasn't really listening to Suzy as she prattled on about some movie she'd just seen. He didn't want her there, he didn't want to talk or make light conversation.

He didn't want to hook up. Even if Suzy was extremely attractive and obviously up for it.

He came to Pete's for one reason only. To drink.

Sure, he could drink at home. And he'd do that too. But drinking a little in public tempered the urge to drink a lot when he got back to his apartment.

The Scotch helped with the pain from his injuries and it helped obliterate the events that had caused them.

Suzy couldn't do that. No woman could. Not even Lydia.

And then Evie's lovely face entered his vision and

for one crazy moment panic rose in him as he thought he'd conjured her up. But then she pushed the heavy door open wider and their gazes met.

For a moment there was a shimmer of recognition between them, a whisper of what they'd both endured together, and then she smiled at him, a smile that seemed to see right inside him. A smile that said, *I know you're hurting; let me help you.*

And for one mad instant he wanted that. He wanted to feel again what he'd felt that afternoon in the change room cocooned against her. That strange kind of peace—like nothing he'd ever known.

The panic intensified.

The sheer power of these strange, unwanted feelings Evie evoked overwhelmed him. He dragged his gaze away, his heart beating like that of a wild animal suddenly caged and fighting for his life. She didn't know him. She didn't know anything about him. How could she? Princess Evie couldn't even begin to comprehend where he'd come from, the things he'd seen, the promises he'd broken.

He turned to Suzy and dazzled her with a smile. 'Whaddya say we get out of here?'

Evie, her heart light as she spotted Finn, made a direct line for him. She stopped three paces later when she realised he wasn't alone. The smile he gave the blonde, one she'd seen him with here before, took her breath away and she struggled with the sudden urge to turn on her heel and run.

Or slap someone. *Back off!*

But he wasn't hers to make such an order. The realisation brought with it a sudden crushing sense of despair. Just because they'd shared a moment, that didn't make him hers.

Finn smiled down at Suzy as she leaned forward and whispered in his ear. Her cleavage was exposed to his view and he looked his fill.

It was an impressive cleavage and he was a man, damn it.

A man who appreciated a woman's body but did *not* get emotionally involved with them. And the sooner Evie got that through her head, the better.

He wasn't some wounded hero that needed saving. He was a cantankerous bastard beyond redemption.

'C'mon,' he said, sliding off the stool, putting his hand out to help Suzy off hers but looking directly over her head, meeting Evie's shocked look with practised indifference. 'Let's go back to my place.'

Evie couldn't move for a moment, the cold of Finn's piercing gaze freezing her to the spot. He seemed totally unreachable as his eyes told her things he couldn't say in a crowded bar.

Like*, what happened this afternoon meant nothing. You mean nothing.*

Suzy smiled up at Finn, disconcerted to find he wasn't looking at her. 'I thought you'd never ask.'

Finn dragged his gaze away from the emotions in Evie's hazel eyes. There was hurt and disgust and even a touch of scorn.

And he deserved every one of them.

He threw another dazzler Suzy's way before tucking her hand in his, straightening his back and making a beeline for the door.

Evie watched him go, a veritable storm of emotions raging inside. Anger, repulsion, despair.

Where was the Finn from earlier? The one who had leaned into her and told her she was brilliant?

She looked back to find Pete watching her. He was holding up a cold beer and a shot glass and his gaze radiated warmth and sympathy.

Thank God for Pete.

CHAPTER SEVEN

TWENTY minutes later Charlie drained his glass and stood. 'I'm going to go and check on my patient.'

'That's very dedicated of you,' Mia teased, wishing both he and Carl would leave so she could drag Luca into the nearest dark corner and have him finish what he started, instead of taunting her in secret with those very clever fingers.

But she'd soon learned that two could play at his game and Luca was looking decidedly uncomfortable himself.

'Of course the delectable Nurse Barry has nothing to do with it,' Carl added.

Charlie grinned. 'I'm affronted, Carl.' And grinned again.

Carl tossed back his beer. 'Hang on, then, I'll walk you out.'

They said their goodbyes and Luca and Mia were finally left alone. Luca dropped his mouth to her ear. 'You're going to pay for that. Let's go. Now.'

Mia smiled as his voice, thick with lust, emphasised his accent. A surge of anticipation tightened her pelvic floor. 'If you can't take it,' she murmured, sliding slowly out of the booth, 'you shouldn't be dishing it out.'

'Here you are, Mia. Sorry I'm late,' Evie said, plonking herself down on the opposite seat, pushing a tray of orange juice, beer and shot glasses onto the table. 'I'm warning you now, I plan on getting very, very drunk.'

Mia shut her eyes briefly. *Damn. Evie.*

Luca's caress had managed to erase all trace of the reason she'd come to Pete's tonight in the first place. She glanced at Luca, saw lust rippling through the dark chocolate pools of his eyes and felt everything clench. She forced herself to look away.

'I can see that,' Mia murmured, as Evie raised the shot glass to her lips.

'Oh, hello, Luca,' Evie said as she slammed down the first shot and lined up her second. 'So glad you're here. Maybe you can explain to me how the male mind works?'

Luca looked from Mia to Evie and back to Mia again. He'd had a vision of how the evening was going to pan out and this had not been part of it. He watched as Evie threw back her second shot and knew enough about women to know that he had one too many y chromosomes to be a part of this conversation.

He glanced at Mia, who shrugged an apology at him, a small smile playing on her lips. He stroked up the centre seam of her jeans and was gratified to see the smile disappear.

He patted her leg twice. 'I think I'll go and leave you lovely ladies to it.'

Mia scooted out and Luca followed her, her rear end at an enticing level before he stood and towered over her.

He nodded at Evie. 'Goodnight.'

Evie grunted something as she contemplated her

third shot and he turned to Mia. 'I'll see you...' he quirked an eyebrow at her '...soon?'

Mia watched as Evie downed another tequila. 'Later.' She grimaced.

Luca dropped his gaze to her mouth then sighed. 'Later.'

It was low and raw and whispered along her nerve endings and Mia felt decidedly wobbly as she slid back into the booth, her insides melting.

'Are you okay?' she asked Evie, refusing to turn and watch Luca walk out of the bar. Pete had already given her a speculative look as she'd sat—she didn't want anyone else in the bar wising up.

Evie shook her head. 'Nope. But I will be.' She slammed another shot back. 'Real soon.'

Mia sipped her orange juice. 'You won't be in the morning.'

'Well, I have two days until I'm back on shift to recover.'

Mia pushed the beer towards her friend and dragged the tray with three more shots on it out of reach. 'You may well need them.'

Evie didn't protest, just sipped at her beer.

'Carl was telling me you had a pretty harrowing time in Theatre with Finn. Tell me about it.'

Evie raised her eyes to her best friend. 'Oh, Mia, it was the most incredible thing I've ever witnessed. Finn was...he was...magnificent.' She sipped her beer again. 'And then he went and acted like a total jerk.'

Mia nodded. 'Okay, start at the beginning.'

Three hours later Evie had unburdened and Mia had managed to stagger home with her and put her to bed.

She left a jug of water, a glass and two tablets by Evie's bed for when she woke up feeling like someone was drilling for oil in her brain, her mouth as dry and putrid as the newspaper that lined a budgie cage.

She watched her friend sleep for a moment. Evie really had it bad. She didn't know it yet, of course, but a man who drove a girl that crazy was more than some nutty crush.

Which was why her way was much better. Give them your body but keep your heart and mind out of contention. Use them for sex then walk away.

Like her and Luca.

Except she hadn't walked away, had she?

She looked at Evie's face, troubled even in an alcohol-induced slumber. If this was what pining after a man got you then she wanted no part of it.

She had to end it with Luca.

After tonight.

Mia glanced at Evie's bedside clock—it was nearly one in the morning. Would Luca be awake?

She remembered how hard he'd been beneath his jeans as she'd fondled him under the table.

He'd be awake.

Her own body was still humming like an electrical substation generating enough heat to power the entire eastern seaboard.

She smiled to herself as she hurried to her bedroom, stripping off her clothes, pulling her hair out of its ponytail, opening her wardrobe, yanking her long winter coat off its hanger and stepping into its folds, the lining cool against her bare, heated flesh. She overlapped the edges and tied the cord securely around her

waist—there were buttons but they were going to take
too long to undo for her purposes.

Mia inspected herself in the mirror. She looked very
modest in the calf-length coat and heels. Should she, on
the slim off chance at after one in the morning, happen
to bump into someone in the lift, they couldn't possibly
be aware she didn't have a stitch on under the coat.

Neither would Luca.

Mia smiled at her reflection. All she needed was a
little eye make-up and some lippy and she'd be perfect
for an early-morning booty call.

Hell, if this was going to be their last time, she might
as well blow his mind.

Luca was brooding in front of his magnificent bay window when he heard the knock. He allowed himself a
smile for the first time since arriving home alone with
a raging hard-on over three hours ago.

Anticipation tightened his groin as he stalked to the
door and yanked it open to find a rugged up Mia leaning casually against the jamb.

'Oh, good.' She smiled. 'You're awake.'

Luca sucked in a breath. Her hair was loose and her
eyes were heavily kohled in shades of grey and black,
emphasising their blueness. Her mouth was painted fire-
engine red. He moved in close until their bodies were
almost touching. 'It's hard to sleep in my condition,' he
murmured.

Mia pouted. 'Poor darling. Can I come in? I could
help you with that.'

Luca's gaze drifted to her mouth. 'Are you sure? I
wouldn't want you entering into a recipe for disaster.'

Mia laughed as devilish memories from Pete's surfaced. Luca touching her under the table, stroking between her legs. She lifted a finger and traced his bottom lip, almost moaning out loud when he sucked it into his mouth. 'Carl's a sore loser,' she whispered.

Luca, his body taut with longing, swirled his tongue around her finger and gently released it. 'Come in, take your clothes off. You are way overdressed.'

He stepped back and Mia strode into the room. The heat enveloped her and she turned to find Luca watching her from the shut door. She untied the coat and shrugged out of it. It fell to the floor and she was standing before him in nothing but a pair of heels.

'Will this do?' she asked.

Luca's brain temporarily powered down as his hungry gaze ate up her body. Her long legs, the jut of her breasts, the flare of her hips, the shadow of her sex.

Mia's nipples hardened at the intensity of his scrutiny. It felt more intimate than if he'd touched her and she suddenly felt like he could see right inside her. She fought the urge to cover herself.

Luca swallowed. 'Spin around.'

His husky command spread tentacles of heat through her belly and she performed a slow teasing rotation, looking over her shoulder at him as she circled her hips like she'd seen once in a documentary on pole dancing.

Luca's belly clenched tight. He pushed away from the door and was in front of her, reaching for her in seconds, his hands sliding around her waist, his mouth descending.

And then he was kissing her and she was kissing him back. Long, deep, wet kisses that had her gasping and sighing and begging for more as she pulled at his clothes, desperate for some skin on skin.

Her nipples rubbed against his naked chest and Luca groaned deep in his throat. Then he swept her up into his arms and strode through the apartment, their mouths locked, their hearts beating to a rhythm that pulsed like a rock concert through the air around them.

Luca reached his bed and threw her on it. Mia was startled as she free-fell, landing softly but breathing hard. Somewhere along the way she'd lost her heels so she was one hundred per cent naked now.

She looked up at a half-undressed Luca. His lips were moist from their kissing, his shirt was half off, his zipper undone.

'You look good,' she murmured.

Luca grinned. 'You look better.'

Then he was stripping off his clothes, reaching for a condom, sheathing himself, then joining her, tangling his limbs with hers, kissing her mouth and her neck and her breasts, ignoring her entreaties to finish it as he licked lower. And lower.

It wasn't until she lay spent beneath him that he succumbed to his own body's dictates, entering her slowly, revelling in her exultant cry, rocking and pulsing, building her again until he was pounding and pounding, pushing them both to impossible heights and then pushing them both over into oblivion.

It was several minutes before either of them was physically able to speak. Luca, who was now lying on his back, recovered first.

'Do you realise this is the first time we've actually done it in a bed?'

Mia, her brain cells still reorganising themselves after a mass meltdown, just nodded. It took her another couple of minutes to process and for a spike of worry to register.

Somehow landing in Luca's bed made this whole thing seem more intimate. The other places had personified their relationship—the on-call room, the shower, the kitchen bench. Quick and impersonal.

Places to get off then move on.

They had spelled temporary, fleeting, momentary.

But to be in his bed, in his bedroom? What the hell did that spell?

Mia didn't think it was prudent to stick around and find out. Just as soon as she could move without her legs collapsing, she was out of here. The perfect opportunity arose when Luca went to the bathroom to relieve himself of the condom but her legs refused to co-operate so she was still lying stark naked on his bed when he returned.

'You look good there,' Luca murmured as he approached the bed.

Mia watched him draw nearer, unashamedly naked, his beautiful smooth face and body a sight to behold. Desire stirred in her belly.

Right, that was it! *Get up now, McKenzie!*

Except the phone beside Luca's bed chose that moment to ring, scaring the living daylights out of her. She glanced at the clock. 'Who on earth is ringing at this ungodly hour?'

Luca felt his heart rate accelerate. *People who lived in places where it wasn't an ungodly hour.*

He reached the phone in three purposeful strides and snatched it up. *'Ciao.'*

Mia saw another chance to escape but Luca talking in his native tongue was such a treat, even if she didn't understand a word, she just lay and listened to him. He sat on the side of the bed his back to her, and she resisted the urge to run her palm up and down the broad expanse of his ribs. To contrast the white of her skin with the tantalising copper of his.

The first sign that the phone call wasn't social was Luca raising his voice. He raked his hand through his hair and seemed to be demanding something of the caller. She heard the word '*nonna*' a lot. Wasn't that Italian for grandmother? Had something happened to his grandmother?

There was some more rapid-fire conversation before Luca hung up, tossing the hands-free receiver onto the bedside table with a clatter.

Mia pushed herself up on to her elbows, staring at the solid wall of his back. 'Is everything okay?' she asked tentatively.

Luca dragged himself back from the brink of the abyss the phone call had taken him to. For a moment he'd forgotten Mia was even there. He was inordinately pleased she was.

Which didn't sit well at all.

He rubbed the back of his neck. 'No. That was a cousin of mine. My grandmother is dead.'

Mia heard the husky rawness behind the blunt delivery and in that instant she forgot that she was naked, forgot that she was supposed to have already gone, forgot that she didn't get involved. The driving need to offer him comfort, as she would do anyone—a friend, a patient a colleague—overrode everything.

She sat and scooted over to him shunting in behind him, spreading her legs to accommodate him, his bottom fitting snugly into the cradle of her pelvis, her thighs bracketing his.

She leaned her torso into him, her breasts squashed against his back. Her hands found his arms, her palms running up and down the warm solid weight of his biceps.

'I'm sorry,' she murmured, her cheek resting against his shoulder blade. 'Were you close?'

Luca nodded. Regret, never far away, twisted the ever-present knife deep into his heart. He had been the apple of his nonna's eye. Even after that horrible day that had changed his family life for ever.

She'd been the only one who'd believed there was more to Luca than the irresponsible teenager who had let everyone down.

Turning his back on her had been a particular wrench.

'We spoke once a week.' It was how he knew his family still hadn't forgiven him.

Mia absently brushed her mouth against Luca's back once, twice, three times. His muscles seemed to be quivering beneath her lips and she knew she couldn't leave him like this.

'It's okay, Luca,' she murmured. 'C'mon, lie down for a while.'

She scooted back, until she was sitting propped up a little against the bedhead, and placed a hand on his shoulder. For a moment she thought he was going to resist but then he let her pull him down so the back of his head was cradled against her shoulder, her arm braced across his chest.

Luca lay still as Mia settled the sheet in around them. He turned his face and nuzzled her arm, inhaling her fragrance, letting the beat of her heart close to his ear soothe the ache in his chest.

'Do you want to talk about her?' she asked, trailing the fingers of her free hand up and down his arm.

Luca shook his head. He didn't want to talk, he didn't want to think. He just wanted to lie here next to her and forget the world.

'Okay. We'll just lie here for a bit, then.'

So they did.

She had absolutely no intention of staying. Absolutely no intention of falling asleep. No intention whatsoever other than to offer a little bit of comfort and companionship in Luca's time of need.

She really, really didn't mean to fall asleep.

Or stay the night…

Mia woke to the most delicious feeling of warmth. Of being wrapped in a cocoon of contentment. She stretched languorously against all that solid heat behind her then snuggled back into it again. A heaviness at her hip spanned her waist and curled around her breast. A delicious sensation buzzed her neck. A hardness nudged at the cleft of her bottom.

Hmm. Luca.

She sighed as sleep wrapped her in a sticky embrace. For five seconds.

Then panic set in.

Luca!

Damn! What time was it?

She cracked open one eye, then the other, squinting at the digital clock on the bedside table. Eight-fifteen.

In the morning.

Damn, damn, triple damn!

She lay very still for a long moment, listening to him breathe, not daring to do so herself. It was deep and even. Was he asleep? His lips had brushed her neck only seconds ago but had that been involuntary?

His hand at her breast, tantalising and erotic, seemed lax. Not that her nipple seemed to know the difference as it scrunched and scraped erotically against the flat of his palm.

Neither, for that matter, did his erection. She could feel it nestled against her, big and heavy.

Ready for action.

How the hell could he sleep with that thing? Surely his brain was being deprived of oxygen?

Mia waited a bit longer for signs of life. Other than his erection.

No. He was definitely asleep.

She took that as her cue to get the hell out. What had she been thinking? She didn't do this. She didn't stay the night. She didn't...spoon.

Hell, she didn't even cuddle.

And he knew that!

Okay, no one she'd ever been to bed with had received a phone call that their grandmother had died either—but that was beside the point. She was supposed to have left hours ago. She couldn't let one man's personal life alter years of self-discipline.

She'd very nearly failed medical school, thrown away her future, by letting men and booze rule her life for those couple of crazy years after she'd found out about her father, about her mother's deception. She'd made a promise to herself back then that it would never happen again.

And Luca was no exception.

Yes, he'd transcended her staunch one-night-stand policy. But he was still just a convenient body—hot, sexy, best she'd-ever-known body—and that was all.

Dead grandmother or not.

Her decision from last night—before she'd totally messed up and stayed—to end things with Luca suddenly just got a whole lot more urgent.

Mia didn't breathe again until she'd slunk very carefully out of his bed and tiptoed out of his room. Thankfully the central heating was still on because it looked like a frosty old day through those big bay windows as a stiff breeze blew across the harbour, rippling the surface like goose-bumps on flesh.

She strode to the centre of the room and scooped up her jacket, shrugging into it, again ignoring the buttons as she tied it at the waist.

Now, where the hell were her shoes?

She quickly scanned the shoeless route from the lounge to Luca's bedroom. Her gaze stopped at his doorway.

Please, don't make me go back there.

She didn't need the temptation of a sleeping Luca. She hadn't looked back as she'd fled the room and she didn't want to know now either. She needed to get out.

She'd leave her bloody shoes if she had to. Even if her feet would be half-frozen by the time she reached her apartment.

Yes, she needed to tell him this wouldn't be happening again. Especially now. Especially after last night.

But she could leave that for tomorrow. For now she needed to get out. And quickly.

Her panicked gaze backtracked, sweeping a broader area than before. It snagged on a partially obscured heel somehow under the bar stools that lined the central kitchen bench.

Wow. She must have kicked them off wildly—or had Luca pulled them off then tossed them across the room?

Her mind had been mush at the time.

Mia quickly retrieved it, trying not to think about just what she and Luca had done on that kitchen bench. How he'd swept aside the dirty dishes and taken her right there on the cold granite bench top.

Stop it! Don't go there!

Mia shook herself. One shoe down, one to go. She refined her search—if one had ended up near the kitchen, the other one could be anywhere. She dropped to her knees in front of the lounge suite and looked under the chairs.

Bingo!

She reached under for it but the lounge didn't have a lot of clearance and she had to get down lower to even get her fingers to it. She extended her arm further and finally dragged it out, giving a triumphant murmur as she sat back on her haunches.

'What are you doing?'

Mia lurched abruptly to her feet. Luca was leaning against the doorframe, in nothing but underpants, his arms crossed, a small frown making a harsh line out of his beautiful mouth. There was a shadow in his eyes that was a perfect foil for the one darkening his jaw and seemed to match his serious countenance.

'Luca.' Mia, excruciatingly aware of her nakedness beneath the coat, absently kicked first one foot up behind her and then the other as she slid the shoes in place, 'Sorry…couldn't find my shoes.'

Luca watched as she shimmied into her stilettos.

Usually he liked the way women did that. It was sexy. But this morning the death of his grandmother and the burden of guilt he felt over his absence in her life weighed heavily.

As did Mia being witness to it all.

This morning he was immune to sexy.

When he'd woken alone he'd been relieved. His vulnerability last night had shaken him. He wasn't used to being that emotionally exposed to anyone, least of all a woman. Marissa had burned him for life in that regard and he had no desire to repeat the experience.

The last thing he needed this morning was to see pity in Mia's eyes.

He needed to be alone.

'I need coffee,' he said abruptly, pushing away from the doorframe.

Mia watched him stride to the kitchen, a very different man from the post-coital Luca she'd come to know. No sexy smile, no lazy laugh, no knowing gaze. And certainly very different from the man she'd held last night, who'd fallen asleep in her arms.

He seemed to have erected a wall and was putting her firmly on the outside.

Which was great. *Exactly what she wanted.* Exactly what she'd been hoping for. No need for the big talk after all. Just slip out of his apartment and consider it over.

Perfect.

If only her body wasn't rebelling. The site of his strong, naked back, the way the muscles played beneath the fine moulding of copper flesh, the sexy indentation of the small of his back was causing a riot amongst her hormones. She ground her feet into the carpet to stop herself taking a step towards him.

When had her body started to crave his like this? It was so…base.

'I'm going to go,' she announced to his back. 'Check that Evie hasn't slipped into an alcoholic coma. And you have a lot to organise today.'

Luca frowned as he filled the percolator with water. 'Organise?'

'Flights, time off work, packing.'

'Flights?'

It was Mia's turn to frown. 'For the funeral? I'm sorry, I assumed your grandmother lived in Italy? Is she here in Sydney?'

He hadn't told her that. But, then, why would he? They didn't…chat. They'd had sex a few times. That's what they did. That's all they did.

Until last night.

And it was why they were over now. Now that their relationship had evolved to a level of emotional intimacy neither of them wanted.

Luca flipped the switch on the coffee machine and turned to face her, his hands gripping the bench behind him, his knuckles white. 'I'm not going to the funeral.'

Mia blinked. 'What?'

'I'm not going,' he repeated.

'But…I thought you said you were close to your grandmother?'

Her yearning for a grandmother of her own, someone who could have softened the harsh realities of her childhood, been a buffer even, returned as Mia struggled to understand what Luca was saying.

Luca nodded. 'I am.' He raked a hand through his

hair as he realised what he'd said. 'I was… I haven't been back to Italy since the day I left and, trust me, no one in my family wants me to return.'

The edge of bitterness in his voice surprised Mia and instead of turning and walking to the door, which would have been the wisest course of action, she wandered closer to the kitchen.

'No one?'

He nodded grimly. 'Sicilians have long memories.'

Mia slid onto one of the stools, the urge to comfort him as strong as it had been last night despite his *keep-out* expression. 'Look, I don't know what happened with you and your family—'

She held up a hand as he opened his mouth to interrupt. He looked like he was going to tell her to mind her own damn business, which was fine by her. Apart from knowing he'd left Marsala at the age of sixteen, he hadn't told her about his past or the fact that he'd never been back.

And she didn't want to know. That wasn't what they were about—it was nothing to do with her.

Except she understood. She understood how things could be so bad that you'd never go back. How many times had she visited her mother in the last five years? Half a dozen? And how long ago had she given up on trying to keep in contact with a father who had moved on to a new family after the woman he'd loved had totally destroyed his old one?

'I don't want to know, Luca, but it was a long time ago, yeah? Maybe things are better now?'

Out of habit or manners, Luca poured two coffees and pushed one towards her. Even though he didn't want her to stay. He could see empathy in her gaze and wanted no part of it. They were just about sex—nothing else. Sex was all he did. He'd lost his head for a little while, but not any more.

'They're not.'

Mia stared down into the thick dark coffee—the colour of Luca's eyes. 'I'm sorry,' she murmured.

He shrugged. 'It's the way it is.'

Mia looked up sharply. She could see regret in his espresso gaze and hear a slight rawness to his accent. And suddenly she was mad. *Damn it!* Why was it that way? Why was he still being made to suffer twenty odd years later—this was his family. What had he done that had been so bad? Why did she feel guilty about not keeping her family together, about not keeping in contact when neither of her parents bothered? Why should she give a damn when they didn't?

'You should go,' she said.

Luca saw something glittering in her stained-glass-window eyes. They shone with an intense brightness that for a second looked almost like tears. But then it crystallised into determination.

He shook his head. 'Some things are better left alone, Mia.'

Mia shook her head emphatically. 'No, damn it! She was your grandmother and you loved her. And you need to go to her funeral and to hell with what everyone else thinks. You need this for you, Luca. You deserve this. Don't let them take this from you because of some stupid ancient history.'

Luca wasn't entirely sure that this passion was all about him and his predicament but he appreciated the sentiment. It was surprisingly good to have someone on his side in this whole family mess, even though she had no clue of the facts.

Another spurt of guilt made him uneasy. Would she be this passionate about it if she knew the background? Was she only being this vehement because she thought she knew him well enough to surmise that he'd been wronged by his family?

'Don't think I'm the injured party here, *cara*. They had every right to ostracise me. To be angry with me.'

His voice sounded far away in another time and Mia paused. She hadn't expected any explanation but she had expected him to defend himself when offering one. They'd ostracised him and he just accepted it?

'Still?' she demanded, regrouping. 'After all these years? Doesn't that make you angry?'

Luca shook his head. He'd given up being angry about it a long time ago. Regret was a constant companion—if he could go back and change things he would—but he'd worked through his anger.

'No. Not any more,' he said.

Mia couldn't believe how calm he was. She could feel a burning in her chest at his ostracism and hers. Her father leaving physically and her mother leaving emotionally had completely excluded her from the possibility of a normal life.

How could people who supposedly loved you act so callously? Even in grief? Her heart pounded, there was a ringing in her ears, her hands shook as she clasped them around the coffee cup.

It would be so easy to lose it. Just lose it. She hadn't been this stirred up in years. Maybe not since the day she'd discovered her stillborn baby sister hadn't been her father's child and that's why he'd left. That her mother had been lying to her for years.

She had a sudden insane urge to cry, which both scared and horrified her in equal measure. What the hell was wrong with her?

Mia McKenzie did not cry. Not in front of friends or colleagues and most certainly not lovers.

Not ever!

Luca was a man she'd had sex with a few times and slept with once. She shouldn't care about any of this.

She pulled herself back from the edge. Just. 'Well, I think you're wrong, but...' she shrugged with as much nonchalance as she could muster when her brain was melting down '...it's none of my business.'

She stood. She had to get out of there. The intensity of her feelings was scaring the hell out of her. He plainly didn't want her hanging around and she'd been trying to leave since the moment she'd woken with his hand on her breast.

Luca nodded, gripping the bench harder as the foolish urge to reach for her took hold. To put a hand on her shoulder, tug her into his arms. She looked a little wan and frankly he'd rather spend the day putting some colour back into her cheeks than thinking about his grandmother and the mess he'd left behind in Sicily.

But she'd turned away and was walking rapidly towards the door. Do not pass Go. Do not collect two hundred dollars.

'*Ciao*, Mia,' he called out.

Mia heard the finality in his voice and knew it was goodbye.

CHAPTER EIGHT

EVIE woke at ten-thirty feeling as if the New Year's Eve fireworks, for which Sydney was famous, had been let off in her head. All at once. She groaned out loud and stuffed the pillow over her head to quell the racket.

Not that it helped, given that the noise was coming from inside her skull, not from the outside.

The previous momentous day with Finn and then the bitter disappointment of the night came back in a rush and she groaned again. *Damn the man to hell*. It was his fault she felt this way.

She could only hope he'd been blessed with a hangover of equal proportion. But, of course, he wouldn't have. Because the man could drink whisky like water. And because little Miss Suzy Happy Ending had been draped all over him when he'd left.

She didn't even want to think about why that bugged her so much. The man could sleep with whomever he liked. And quite often did. In the years they'd co-existed at The Harbour, he'd slept with a string of women.

It was no skin off her nose.

Just because Stuart's devastating betrayal had made her more selective with men, it didn't mean the entire world had to follow suit. If Finn wanted to sleep with every floozy Suzy that came along, more power to him.

Evie pulled the pillow off her head—damn it, now he'd made her think of Stuart. She'd been such a fool for that man, believing that he'd loved her when he'd been using her all along for her family connections.

She'd been humiliated and heartbroken and had endured the rather cruel twist of fate that had seen the hospital rumour mill peg her as the bitch of the piece. Apparently Dr Evie Lockheart had considered herself too good for the lowly Stuart.

It had taken her a long time to win back people's respect after that.

She was damned if she was going to lose that hard-won respect by making a fool of herself over another doctor. Especially one as arrogant and infuriating as Finn Kennedy.

The apartment was quiet when she entered the open-plan living area, pulling on a thick woolly dressing gown over the clothes she'd worn all day yesterday and apparently to bed too. She had a vague memory of Mia getting her home and helping her into bed but she must have drawn the line at undressing her.

She flicked on the jug and waited impatiently for it whistle. The aroma of coffee infused her senses as the boiling water hit the granules and Evie's stomach grumbled. She opened the fridge to grab the milk, only to find there was none.

Her stomach revolted. The fireworks in her head popped louder.

Oh, hell—she couldn't do black coffee. She just couldn't.

Without giving any thought to her appearance, she

shrugged out of her gown, grabbed a mug, pushed her feet into some discarded shoes by the door and was standing outside the lift in under thirty seconds.

Susie and John were bound to have milk.

Finally the lift arrived on her floor and for a second Evie almost wept. It was a short-lived emotion as the doors opened to reveal Suzy, also in the same clothes as last night, looking like she hadn't slept a wink. And not in that horrible bed-hair, bleary-eyed way that Evie was sporting. Oh, no. In that loose, relaxed, I've-had-all-my-kinks-ironed-out way.

Suzy smiled a bright, peppy smile. 'Hi, Dr Lockheart,' she chirped.

Evie cracked a small smile and gave what she hoped was a gracious nod because the alternative—launching herself at young, peppy, cute Suzy—was just not physically possible with a headache the size of Sydney Harbour.

Finn stared at the ceiling, absently massaging his right thumb to relieve the painful tingling, and wished he felt better after a very pleasant night with a gorgeous athletic young woman. But he didn't. And it had nothing to do with his physical injuries.

He kept seeing the look in Evie's eyes at Pete's last night. Those twin hazel pools had been like a damn open book as she'd telescoped her disapproval. The disgust and scorn he'd seen there he could live with. He saw them in the mirror every morning and he was pretty immune to them by now.

The hurt had been a lot harder to get past.

It reminded him a lot of Lydia and those horrible few years. Trying to make things better for her—easier—but only making them worse. His brother's widow had turned to him in a dark moment of grief and it had begun a long-drawn-out, complicated affair that he'd needed yet resented all at the same time.

Lydia had needed something that he hadn't been able to give—comfort. After a childhood in institutions and the horror of losing his brother, Finn just hadn't been capable of it. He hadn't known how to comfort himself let alone a grief-stricken widow.

It had been a relief when she'd finally moved on enough to end it. And yet, strangely, he'd also felt bereft. His one link to his little brother, the little brother he'd defended and protected from one care home to the next, the only constant in his childhood, had no longer been there.

The fact that he hadn't loved Lydia, or she him, hadn't mattered so much after she'd walked away.

So he knew exactly how a woman looked when she was hurt. And there'd been no doubt about it—Dr Evie Lockheart had been hurt last night. And he'd been responsible.

But, damn it all, could he help it if she'd read too much into a fleeting moment?

A temporary weakness?

Princess Evie could keep her goo-goo eyes to herself. He was fine. *Just fine.*

Mia was shocked to see Luca standing on her doorstep later that night. Between her morning-after regrets and Evie's monster hangover the day had dragged more slowly and become more depressing than a wet week.

She had been in her pyjamas and ready for bed when the knock had sounded. The cold air from the hallway rushed around her and she pulled her hot-pink polar fleece dressing gown closer.

'Luca?'

'Who is it?' Evie called from the couch, where she'd been watching old sitcom reruns all day.

'It's just Luca,' Mia threw over her shoulder as casually as she could. Because it could never be *just* Luca. The man was dressed in a suit and looked like a matinee idol, even with his face set grimly.

She really, really shouldn't want to drag him to her bedroom. But, heaven help her, she did.

Evie, her face fixed on the screen, laughed. 'Does he want to borrow a cup of milk?' And she laughed again.

Luca frowned. 'Huh?'

Mia shook her head. 'Long story.' She noticed a suitcase standing nearby in the hall. She raised an eyebrow. 'Going somewhere?'

He nodded. 'I decided to follow your advice.'

'You're going back to Italy?'

'Yes.' He gave her a ghost of a smile. 'To hell with them, right?'

Mia searched his face for a moment, pleased that he was doing the right thing but puzzled as to why he'd bothered to stop by and tell her.

The man was about to fly halfway around the world to go to his beloved grandmother's funeral against the wishes of a family he wasn't on good terms with and hadn't seen in over two decades—he probably didn't need her questions.

'Right,' she said awkwardly.

'I'll be back in five days,' he said.

'Five days? Hell, Luca, you're going to be next to useless when you return.' She saw something flit through his eyes and quickly added, 'Professionally,' in case he thought she'd meant it any other way.

She had no doubt that his *other* functions would be in *fine* working order.

Not that she cared or would be thinking about his other functions at all.

'I've arranged cover at work for seven days and business class helps.'

Mia nodded. 'I'll bet.'

'John said his housekeeper, Gladys someone...'

'Henderson,' Mia supplied. The spritely sixty-year-old cleaned their apartment too.

'Yes, that's her. She's going to keep an eye on the apartment for me.'

'Okay.' Mia waited for him to say more. Or to pick up his bags and leave. He didn't. She frowned. 'Why are you here, Luca?' she asked wearily.

Luca put his hand in his pocket. 'To thank you.' He looked at her intently, her fluffy pink dressing gown somehow just as sexy as the winter coat from last night. 'You were right. I needed to do this.'

Mia shrugged. 'No worries.'

He chose his next words carefully. Normally he didn't have to give 'the speech' but Mia was different. Somehow she'd got past the barriers that he'd erected since Marissa and she deserved him to be straight with her.

He wanted her to know that it wasn't her—it was him.

He just didn't do emotional connections and he especially didn't need that baggage now, heading off to face some pretty big demons.

He was surprised, though, at how hard the words were to say. At his reticence.

'I know I wasn't good company this morning and—'

'It's okay, Luca,' Mia interrupted, knowing from his eyes what he was going to say and suddenly not wanting to hear the words come from his mouth. 'I get it. You and I were always just a one-time thing that went on for longer than it should have. Neither of us do this sort of thing. I think we can just walk away and chalk it up to experience.'

Luca pursed his lips. It was an easy out for him but, still, her even easier acceptance rankled. It shouldn't have. It should have been a relief.

But it wasn't.

'I think it's best,' he murmured.

It was. It had to be.

'Of course,' she assured him. So why didn't it feel like it? Why did she feel worse than she had all day?

They stood in the doorway, looking at each other for a moment, not speaking. *It was for the best. It was.*

'I'm sorry.' Luca grimaced, checking his watch. 'I have to go, I have a taxi waiting.'

Mia nodded, her heart hammering in her chest. 'Sure. I'll see you when you get back,' she said. 'At work.'

'Yes,' he agreed, fighting the urge to seize her in his arms and kiss her and the even more bizarre urge to ask her to go with him.

To complicate it much more than it already was.

'At work,' he repeated. Then he turned away, picked up his bag and strode down the corridor to the lift, not daring to look back.

Mia stared after him, watching until he disappeared.

It—whatever *it* was—was over. She should be over the moon.

She wasn't.

'That seemed pretty intense. What was it about?' Evie asked.

Mia swivelled her head to find her friend walking towards her. At least she finally looked interested in something else other than overdosing on salt and vinegar chips and Boston pub life.

'Nothing,' Mia said, recovering sufficiently to withdraw into the warm apartment and shut the door.

'Didn't look like nothing to me,' Evie mused.

'It is now,' Mia assured her.

For five days and nights, despite her every effort not to, Mia thought of Luca constantly. Her feelings fluctuated wildly from complete understanding and agreement with their decision to walk away from each other, to worry about how it was all panning out in Marsala, to an uncharacteristic yearning for something she couldn't even put her finger on.

Add to that a healthy dose of sexual frustration from vivid dreams and Mia was a wreck.

The dreams were the worst.

Happily-ever-after fantasies—erotic one moment, white-wedding poignant the next. They woke her often, rendering her perpetually tired. And cranky. The staff avoided her. Her patients asked the nurses their questions. Even Evie stayed out of her way.

In fact, by day five her best friend was suggesting she burn off some of the bitch with a good old-fashioned bar pick-up somewhere.

Then, on the sixth night, Luca came striding into the

department at almost midnight. His luscious wavy hair, speckled with raindrops from the stormy weather outside, looked like it had hadn't seen a comb in a while and it was the first time she'd seen him unshaven.

He looked like hell.

And her body responded with a primal lurch.

If anything, with the heavy growth of blue-black stubble and the wicked way he filled out a pair of jeans, he looked more like the devil she'd first pegged him as than ever before.

But she knew him much better now.

Well…better than she had, anyway.

'Luca?' Her heart pounded in her chest. Damn it, this wasn't how she'd planned on greeting him on his return. Where was her polite smile and cool nod? 'You're not due back until tomorrow!'

Luca ran a hand through his already unruly hair. She was a sight for sore eyes. It had been a harrowing time in Sicily and even though they weren't together—had never really been together—he wanted to drag her to the on-call room and get lost in her for a little while.

Just one more time.

'I couldn't sleep and I heard the ambulances.' He shrugged. 'Thought I'd drop by and see if you guys needed a hand.'

Mia saw the flash of desire in his deep dark eyes, like a candle in a well, and felt it slug her right in the belly. She was grateful for the bustle of the department around them. If he'd come to her door, she'd have been lost in a look like that. Their parting conversation from six days ago smothered by a fierce surge of lust and a strong urge for privacy.

She blinked, taking a mental step backwards. 'You look tired. Are you up to it?'

'I'm fine.'

Mia raised an eyebrow. 'You don't look it.'

Luca waved a dismissive hand. 'I'm exhausted and my body clock's screwed up but I'm not sleepy. In fact, I'm buzzing. I'm good to work.'

Mia scrutinised him for a moment but that was just plain dangerous. Besides, she understood how jet-lag could mess with your body but have the opposite effect on your brain. And they were pretty slammed at the moment.

'Okay, sure. There was an industrial fire with several burn victims, we're down a couple of nurses and Evie's attending an arrest on one of the wards. It's bedlam.'

He nodded. 'Okay.'

She waited for him to move on, brush past her, leap into action, but he didn't. He just stood looking at her, weary and subdued. 'How…how was it?'

Not that she cared. Not that she wanted to know.

Luca rubbed at his stubble. 'Bad.' A nurse bustled past them.

Mia heard the low accented rumble right down to her toes. 'Do you want to talk about it?'

What the hell?

She didn't want him to talk about it. She didn't want to listen. She didn't want to know. The only thing she was interested in was the magic he could wreak on her body.

And even that was now off limits.

His life was none of her damn business and she liked it that way!

Luca shook his head. He didn't. He really, really

didn't. Three days of dealing with family history had been enough to bear, without rehashing it. What he wanted was to forget it. Lay her down and let their magic take him somewhere else.

A place where he wasn't a hormone-driven, starry-eyed sixteen-year-old. Where he hadn't got his brother's girlfriend—now wife—pregnant. A place where there were no toxic family relationships, where he hadn't let anyone down, where no one disapproved.

And Mia was the perfect woman for that. Gorgeous, sexually uninhibited and emotionally unavailable.

That's what he needed. Talking—not so much.

'I just need to work.'

Mia nodded. 'Cubicle two.' And held her breath as Luca brushed past her.

Two hours later the department had quietened down. The minor burn victims had been triaged, assessed and transferred to the burns unit. Of the two more serious burns, one had gone to Theatre, the other to ICU.

Mia was able to breathe again. To think of something other than ABCs and burns percentages and fluid requirements. She glanced at Luca, who was writing in a chart. He glanced up at the same time and the heat flaring between them could have lit the Sydney Harbour Bridge for all eternity.

Okay. *Enough.* They'd been lovers—briefly. That was all and now it was over. They'd agreed. This... sexual ESP stuff couldn't go on.

It just couldn't.

She stood. 'Can I speak with you please, Dr di Angelo?' she asked quietly, looking around her at the completely disinterested staff going about their own business.

Luca looked up at her, the quiet steel in her voice at odds with the heat in her eyes. 'On-call room?'

Mia felt the kick in her pulse. *The things they'd done in that on-call room...* But the fact was that their privacy was absolute there—the perfect place to tell him this couldn't go on.

'Sure.'

Mia turned and led the way on very shaky legs, hyper-aware of his gaze glued to her back. When she finally reached her destination she headed straight for the kitchenette and grabbed two mugs, absently going about the business of fixing them coffee. She heard the door shut behind her. Then lock. She was conscious of Luca leaning against it, watching her.

Mia turned to face him, her butt resting against the sink. He looked dark and wild and every fibre of her being wanted to melt into his arms. 'We agreed not to do this any more.'

Luca hung onto the doorknob. She was right. They had. But he'd thought of nothing else for the last few hours. Since returning home. Hell, since leaving. And he'd happily walk away. But he needed tonight.

He didn't know why. He just knew he did.

'I know.'

Mia shook her head emphatically. 'I don't do this, Luca. We,' she wagged her finger back and forth between the two of them. 'We don't do this.'

Luca pushed away from the door and prowled over, halting in front of her. Close enough to see the frantic flicker of the pulse at the base of her throat, the flare of her nostrils, the dilation of her pupils.

'I know.'

Mia felt the rumble of his voice curl her toes. Lust, full and throaty and undisguised, thickened his accent. He crowded her against the sink and her fingers automatically curled into the sleeves of his shirt. Their bodies touched from hip to shoulder and it felt so good she almost whimpered.

Mia swallowed and clawed desperately for some self-control. 'We're alike, you and I, Luca. We have scars… trust issues. We guard our hearts. We don't get involved. It's why we're emergency doctors—patch 'em up and ship 'em out, right? No time to get involved. It's who we are.'

Luca looked deep into her eyes. 'Who are you trying to convince Mia—me or yourself?'

Mia glared at him. Damn it, she was trying to walk this thing back. *Why wasn't he meeting her halfway? Why was he trying to change the boundaries he'd set before he'd left? Damn it all, the boundaries he lived by.*

They both lived by.

'Am I wrong?' she challenged.

Luca shook his head. 'No.' In fact, she was one hundred per cent accurate. But that didn't stop the primal beat of a jungle drum thrumming through his blood. His gaze brushed her mouth. 'But I need this. I wish I didn't. But I do.'

He placed a hand on the cold stainless-steel of the sink either side of her and dropped his head, claiming her mouth on a muffled groan. She opened for him instantly, her tongue seeking his, and his barely leashed desire blazed to life with all the heat and intensity of a solar flare.

His hands skimmed up her body and buried themselves in her hair, pulling at the band tying it back, releasing it in a tumble of blonde, his fingers seeking the spot where nape met scalp. Her corresponding moan went straight to his groin.

Yes, yes, yes. This was what he needed. A place to feel good, to feel like a successful, virile man again instead of a home-wrecking boy. A place to forget.

He pulled away from the softness of her mouth to explore the delights of her neck. 'I missed you,' he murmured against the pulse fluttering in her throat.

Because he had. Thoughts of her had been his constant companion while he'd been away. Had often been his only relief from what had been a tense and stilted time.

His hands left her hair, travelled to her hips, gripping them hard as he lifted her onto the narrow edge of the sink, stepped between her legs, forcing them apart, grinding his monster erection against the place where he knew it fitted perfectly.

Mia gasped as her hips responded to the blatant invitation. She wanted him inside her so badly she could practically feel his hardness stretching her.

Here on the sink. In the on-call room. With the bustle of an entire emergency department just outside the door.

This was madness!

'Luca, stop, no, please, stop.'

She pushed at his shoulders as his tongue laved a wet track from her ear to her collarbone. Her heart pounded in her ears and for an insane moment she thought it was someone pounding against the door. 'We really need to stop this.'

Luca pulled away, his chest heaving. 'If you want me to stop, I'll stop.' His breath sawed in and out of his chest as he stared into blue eyes that were hazy with lust. He pulled her in tight to his hips. 'But I don't think you really want me to.'

Mia's head was spinning, her chest was bursting, her belly was clenched in a tight knot. Common sense warred with primal craving. He rotated his hips against hers and she bit down a moan.

To hell with it. She wanted it, needed it—needed him—too much to deny it.

'This is it, Luca. After this, there is no more.'

The words were barely out before Luca was whispering, 'Done,' and reclaiming her mouth.

Mia welcomed the sweep of his tongue and the triumphant noise at the back of his throat when she opened to his long, deep, hot kiss. She especially welcomed his harsh intake of breath as her hands found his zipper and tugged it down.

'Wrap your legs around me,' he murmured, scooping her hips off the edge and grasping her buttocks firmly in his hands as he hauled her off the sink and headed for one of the rooms. Her ankles locked around his waist and he almost stumbled as her hands continued their quest to get behind his zip while her tongue flicked at the pulse thudding at the base of his throat.

He kicked the door shut behind them and tumbled them onto the couch her legs wide, her knees bent, his hips perfectly aligned with hers. His shirt was off in five seconds. Hers followed closely after.

And then a pager beeped.

Mia froze. Luca cursed in his mother tongue.

They both lay there for a few seconds, not moving,

their frantic breath and the trilling of a pager the only sound in the room.

Mia pushed against Luca's shoulders. 'Let me up,' she requested, hating how husky her voice sounded.

Luca pushed off her, sitting back on the couch, his chest naked, his fly gaping open. He raked a hand through his hair while Mia ripped the pager off her waistband and read the liquid crystal display. 'Chopper retrieval,' she relayed. 'MVA near the Blue Mountains.'

She swung herself into a sitting position, her scrambled thoughts sluggish as she tried to switch into medical mode. Luca handed over her shirt and she looked at it absently for a moment before realising she was sitting there in her bra and a pair of jeans.

Too close to Luca for comfort, she stood and fixed her clothing. She straightened her shoulders, pulled her hair back, cleared her throat. She headed for the door and paused with her hand on the knob. 'I'd better go.'

Luca watched her from the sofa. 'This isn't over, Mia.'

Mia knew they couldn't keep doing this. Whatever the two of them were doing had overstepped both their boundaries and all this sexual gratification was doing was prolonging the inevitable. If they'd been meant to be together one last time, they wouldn't have been interrupted.

The pager was a sign from the universe.

'Yes, it is,' she said without looking back, and then swept from the room.

Luca watched her disappear and knew in his bones that there would be no changing her mind. It shouldn't have mattered. He'd done this dozens of times with dozens of women. Had had a good time for a while then walked away without looking back.

No harm, no foul.

Except it did matter. Somehow these past weeks with Mia had come to mean more than a sexual pressure valve.

Mia mattered.

CHAPTER NINE

TWENTY minutes later Mia and Luca were sitting opposite each other strapped into the rescue helicopter, watching the rooftop helipad lights bend and twist as they refracted through the raindrops clinging to the chopper's windows. Luca had volunteered to go with her due to the shortage of nurses in the department and the ICU retrieval team also being out on a call.

'Okay, folks, welcome to Brian Air. Please ensure your tray tables are in an upright position and your seat belts are fastened low and tight. It's going to be an interesting ride.'

Mia grinned at the amplified patter in her earphones despite the tension she felt at sitting opposite a man she'd been mere minutes away from feeling deep inside her. Brian was one of the pilots who had been flying rescue choppers for ever and his skill and experience were much appreciated on a stormy night.

Even his sense of humour.

'Please don't tell me we're heading into a storm, Brian.'

'Would I do that to you, Mia, my lovely?'

Luca gritted his teeth at the easy banter. He had a sudden urge to break something of Brian's. Something non-essential, of course. He still had to be able to fly the damn chopper.

'There is some storm activity but I'll be skirting around it. Safe as houses. Cross my heart. Would I lie to you?'

Mia laughed. 'You? Never.'

Brian laughed back. 'Got yourself a man yet?'

Mia's smile died, her gaze locking with Luca's. 'I'm too busy for a man.'

Brian tsked into his headset. 'Now, if only I was twenty years younger. What's wrong with men these days, Luca? Are they blind?'

Mia tried to look away from him but Luca's brooding gaze held her captive.

'Not all of us,' Luca murmured.

Mia pursed her lips. 'You know me, Brian—don't like to be tied down.'

Luca had no doubt the words were for his benefit and he switched off to the patter as he shifted his gaze from Mia to the now far-away lights of Sydney. The steady beat of the rotors above him echoed the thud of his heart beat as he tried to catalogue the swirl of alien feelings churning in his gut.

In less than two months Dr Mia McKenzie had taken over his life. And he wasn't sure exactly when it had happened. All he knew *for sure* was that the thought of never being with her again was not one he relished.

She'd been the one he'd thought of while he'd been away. Not the air hostess in business class who'd slipped him her card. Not the many beautiful Sicilian women who had smiled at him with frank interest on the streets of Marsala. Not even Marissa, his brother's wife, the woman he'd foolishly thought himself in love with all those years ago.

Mia. It had been Mia who he'd thought of. Mia he'd picked up the phone to ring after his brother had paid him a visit at his hotel and told him to go home. *And then put down again.* Mia who he'd credited as he'd talked to his grandmother standing by her fresh grave after the other mourners had left. Mia who had got him through a killer flight as he'd fantasised about their re-union.

He stole a glance at her as she flicked through the retrieval paperwork balanced on a clipboard on her lap. She was gorgeous even in a big yellow helmet that made her look as if she was trapped inside a giant insect eye and flight overalls that seemed two sizes too big for her.

He looked away again as the insanity of it all hit him. He'd always been able to walk away. Always. None of this made sense.

And none of it made him happy.

It was official—he was having a truly hellish week.

'So the ambulance crew on scene have the patient stabilised and ready for transport,' Mia said, conscious of his eyes on her and desperate to get back to a professional footing after their *coitus interruptus.*

Their patient had suspected spinal injuries requiring rapid air evacuation for maximum treatment success and that's what she needed to focus on.

Luca nodded. 'Should just be able to scoop and run.'

Mia hoped so. The rain had picked up and the chopper seemed to be being buffeted by some decent wind. She could see lightning in the distance and guessed that was the storm they were skirting around. At the best of times Mia wasn't the greatest flyer in the world and she knew that Brian wouldn't be flying if he didn't think it was safe but the sooner they were back at The Harbour in one piece, the better. And then there was Luca, sitting opposite her, watching her with brooding eyes and causing another kind of storm. Inside her. She'd never met a man she couldn't handle and she hated it that she couldn't shake him. From her thoughts. Her dreams.

Her daydreams!

'Think I might get a bit of shut-eye,' she said into her mike. It was, after all, nearly three in the morning and she'd long ago learned the value of power-napping.

She didn't wait for anyone's permission, just closed her eyes. And dreamed of Luca.

A loud bang woke her with a start fifteen minutes later. The chopper spun wildly and her head was filled with Brian swearing and putting out a mayday call. Her eyes flew to the man opposite her. 'Luca?'

Luca saw alarm and fear in her eyes and felt his own pulse leap as the helicopter seemed to be losing altitude as it spun. 'Brian?' He spoke into his headphones. 'What's happening?'

'Lightning took out the tail rotor,' Brian said calmly, while desperately trying to regain control of the spiralling chopper.

'I thought you said you were skirting around the storm?' Mia said above the noise of her pistoning heart and the whine of the labouring engine. She braced one hand against the stretcher beside her and the other against the aircraft shell to steady herself in the midst of the crazy spinning.

'I am. Mother nature can be a bitch like that sometimes.'

*How was it possible that Brian could even sound
upbeat during a mid-air emergency?*

'Are we going to crash?' she asked.

'Hell, yeah,' Brian said matter-of-factly. 'Brace your-
selves, guys, we're over national park and there're a lot
of trees down there.'

Mia tamped down on the rather alien urge to become
hysterical. It wasn't what she usually did in a crisis but,
hell, they were going to crash. She was twenty-nine and
she was going to die. She hadn't witnessed the northern
lights. She hadn't bought herself that cute little retro
convertible. She hadn't been to the ballet.

She hadn't been in love.

Except she had, of course.

And the man she loved was going to die with her.

Her gaze locked with Luca's. What a really, really
horrible time for such a profound revelation. No time
to hug it to herself like a delicious little secret.

'Oh, God,' Mia whispered, her throat suddenly as
dry as ash, her eyes trying to take in every detail of
Luca's face.

'It's going to be okay, Mia,' Luca said.

He reached out his hand, hoping his grandmother
was out there somewhere watching over them. He was
damned if he was going to die before telling Mia how
he felt about her.

Whatever the hell that was.

If he'd learned anything this past week it was that
life was short and you couldn't live in the past.

Mia slipped her hand into his and gripped tight. It
was cold and she was trembling and he'd have given
anything to erase the glimpse of mortality he could see
in her eyes.

'Just because we crash it doesn't mean we're going to die. Does it, Brian?' Luca queried.

He was calm, so bloody calm. How could Luca be this calm as the helicopter spiralled out of control in a death plunge? Her brain was spinning just as wildly. Desperately trying to remember helicopter crash statistics while grappling with regret that she wasn't closer to her parents and sorrow that her fledgling love for Luca was going to be snuffed out before she'd even had the chance to explore it.

'Not on my watch,' Brian chirped. 'Okay, guys, hold tight. Prepare for impact.'

Mia squeezed Luca's hand hard. 'I've never seen *Swan Lake.*'

Luca smiled at her. 'When this is over, we'll go and see it together.'

There was no time for her to smile back. The crippled chopper hit trees with a violent jolt, halting the rapid downward spiral most effectively. Mia squeezed her eyes shut as the impact raced through her body like a giant shock wave. She vaguely heard cracking glass, a loud expletive followed by a guttural cry from Brian and then nothing other than the screech and grind of the rotors could be heard as they sliced through the canopy. Mia, eyes still shut, hit her head several times against the shell of the cabin and she was grateful for her helmet as the chopper lurched and listed, dropping a little then stopping then dropping again as the branches beneath buckled beneath its weight before it finally came to a shuddering halt.

After a good twenty seconds of no movement, Mia cracked open an eye. She could hear Brian talking to Air Control, she could smell rain and fuel and eucalyptus, she could feel the wind buffeting the chopper and hear it whistling inside the cabin. Her eyes adjusted to the sudden darkness and she could see Luca sitting opposite, wonderfully intact.

She was alive. *They were all alive!*

'You okay?' Luca asked.

Mia thought about it for a moment. Everything felt fine. She nodded. 'Yes…I think. You?'

Luca nodded back. 'Yes.' And then he grinned. '*Swan Lake,* here we come.'

Mia grinned back. Her first instinct, to throw herself at him, was pulled up short by a moan coming from the front.

'Brian? Are you okay?' Luca asked.

'Leg's busted,' the pilot panted as he killed the engine.

Luca glanced at Mia. The pain in Brian's voice was obvious. 'Is that a guess or can you see it?'

Brian swore again. 'Tree branch breached the cab, drove into my leg. I can see the bones.'

They exchanged glances again. Luca felt a moment of guilt at his earlier wish that Brian would break something. 'Any other injuries?'

'Nope. Don't think so.'

Luca wasn't totally reassured. Often people could have wounds they weren't even aware of if there was one overriding painful injury.

'Okay, so we need to get you out of there onto the stretcher so we can splint your leg and give you something for the pain. Lucky for you, you crashlanded a mini emergency ward, they have all the best drugs.'

Brian gave a half laugh, half snort at Luca's attempt

to keep things light. 'Ah. You cottoned onto my dastardly plan.'

Luca unbuckled. Mia followed.

'Wait,' Brian called out. 'We need to assess how this bird's being supported. I don't know how precarious it is and moving around could dislodge it. I'd hate to survive the first crash only to be killed on impact with the ground.'

Luca paused. He could tell that Brian was trying to make light of the situation but he also knew that Brian was still thinking like a pilot. Which, given his horrific injury, was amazing.

'Okay,' Luca said. 'How do we do that?'

'If you can open your door safely, grab the torch and have a look out, see if you can see what's supporting us. But move carefully until we know. The crash would have activated our emergency locator transmitter so Air Control will know where we are but they'll want a sit rep—once we know what we're up against, I'll let them know.'

Luca glanced at Mia. The chopper had come to a stop in a reasonably level position with a slight tilt to the left so he was pretty certain that movement wouldn't be an issue but that all depended on what was beneath them.

'Buckle up,' he said as he reached for the torch strapped to the cabin above his head and gently removed it.

Mia felt a trickle of dread drip down her spine. 'Be careful.'

Luca nodded, aware that they might well be precariously balanced and not keen to be the one that upset the apple cart. It was good to know that their ELT had been activated and that help would no doubt soon be on its way. But Brian, while he was being very stoic, needed urgent medical attention, so they couldn't just sit around and wait.

He swivelled in his seat and shone the torch out the window. Through the now driving rain he could see that the door appeared to be free of any vegetation so he gingerly reached for the handle and gently eased it open. The freezing rain assaulted him almost immediately as he carefully lowered himself to the floor of the cabin, hung his head out and shone the torch under the chopper.

They appeared to be wedged between three massive looking tree trunks huddled together. The bottom of the cabin was supported by sturdy interwoven branches which appeared knotted. The tail also seemed wedged between two trunks further back.

Luca shone the torch down towards the forest floor. Whether it was the rain or the dark or the sheer distance, he couldn't make it out. It was nothing but a swirling abyss of cloud and night.

He crawled back in and gently shut the door. His overalls were soaked around the shoulders and the part of his face not protected by the helmet was as wet as if he'd just stepped out of the shower.

He scrambled to his feet and gave a very slight experimental bounce. When the chopper stayed firm he gave another bigger one. 'I think it's fine.'

He relayed the info to Brian who spoke with Air Control. Luca experimented some more, shifting slowly and carefully around the cramped confines of the chopper, which was hardly made for ease of movement anyway.

It seemed stable and he let out a little sigh of relief.

'Bad news.' Brian's voice interrupted Luca. 'The weather has worsened. High winds and driving rain are going to make rescue impossible for a while. It's too dangerous to send another chopper and a winch crew. Meteorology think the system's going to hang around for quite a few more hours so we're stuck up this tree until daylight. Like the bloody Swiss Family Robinson.'

Mia heard Brian laugh at his own joke then suck in a breath on a deep guttural groan.

'We've got to see to him,' she said.

Luca nodded. 'I think the chopper's stable enough to drag him out of his seat and onto the stretcher. It's going to hurt, though.'

Mia nodded grimly. Hell, yeah. 'We could get him to splint his leg first—we carry vacuum splints—it might help a bit.'

Luca nodded. 'Okay. Let's do it. Unbuckle, but slowly. And leave your helmet on. Let's make sure this bird can take both of us moving around before we get too carried away.'

Mia unbuckled and stood slowly. Luca held out his hand and she glanced at him as she took it.

'You're freezing,' he murmured, enclosing her hand within his.

Mia was surprised to realise she was—she'd been in survival mode and hadn't realised it. 'The wind's getting in somewhere,' she said absently, caught up in the warmth of his hand.

Despite how soaked his shoulders and arms were, his hands were like a toasty pair of gloves. In fact, his mere presence was like a beacon of light in this cold, dark, scary scenario they'd landed in.

Luca was here and he was warm and solid and one hundred per cent in control.

'Near Brian, I think,' Luca murmured, steadying her. 'Grab the splint,' he said. 'Slow and easy. I don't know how much weight distribution is aiding stability.'

Mia nodded and reluctantly let go of Luca's hand. She'd felt safe under the influence of his touch. Which made no sense. They were still stuck up a tree. In a helicopter. In the middle of a storm.

Which just went to prove what she'd always thought— love was crazy!

She took a tentative step and then another towards the storage cupboard. Like boats, helicopters made excellent use of space and Mia knew what was in every nook and cranny. The floor felt solid beneath her as she inched her way closer.

She grabbed the splint and the pump and turned to face Luca. 'What now?'

He held out his hand and she passed him the gear. He gestured her close. 'I'm going to drag him out from behind. You stand by at the stretcher for when he's out. Let's get an IV going and give him some morph.'

Mia looked at the cramped confines of the single pilot's seat. The end of the stretcher protruded into the front cab area where in most commercial choppers there would have been a second seat.

'Are you going to be able to manoeuvre him out from behind?'

Luca grimaced. 'I hope so. I'm not sure how stable the chopper will be if I have to climb up onto the stretcher and pull him from there. The tail's wedged fairly solidly so I doubt it'll tip backwards. I'm not so sure it won't tip forward.'

Mia swallowed. So this was the meaning of being stuck between a rock and a hard place. But Luca seemed so confident—like GI Joe, Action Man and Inspector Gadget all rolled into one.

'It's going to be fine, Mia.' He smiled. She returned his smile with one that was suddenly wobbly and thanked any and all deities out there that if she'd had to be in a helicopter crash, at least Luca had been with her.

'Okay. Let's do it.'

Twenty minutes later, after a lot of effort and pain, Brian was on the stretcher, an IV had been inserted, fluids were running, nasal prongs with a trickle of oxygen had been applied and, because they could, he was being monitored. His badly fractured leg had been left in the splint and he'd drifted off to sleep on a morphine cloud.

Finally they both settled back into their seats. The wind howled around the chopper and whistled through the shattered glass at the front. She could feel the slight shuddering of the aircraft as the wind buffeted it from what seemed like all directions. The steady beep, beep, beep of the monitor seemed alien amidst the wild brutality of Mother Nature.

'How long do you think the oxygen will last?' Mia asked into the growing silence.

She knew that Brian didn't really need it but she was aware it was a finite commodity and that they had no idea how long they'd be there. They'd completed a thorough primary and secondary survey of Brian's injuries but what if they'd missed something? What if his condition worsened?

'Quite a few hours, I expect. It's only running at one litre.'

Mia nodded. Would that be enough? How long would it be before they were rescued? The way the wind howled and the rain beat incessantly against the window, it didn't look like any time soon.

She tried really hard not to think about the precariousness of the situation. Their position might feel stable enough but that didn't alter the fact that they were still in a great deal of danger.

'So, now what?' Mia asked.

'We should get some sleep too,' Luca said into the silence.

Mia shook her head, reaching across to feel once again for the pulses in Brian's foot. They were there but feeble and Mia guessed the injury was compromising the blood flow lower. 'I'm worried about the circulation,' Mia murmured. 'It'd be awful to survive a crash like this then go on to lose your leg.'

Luca, who was worried too, gave her a reassuring smile. 'Hopefully we'll be out of here before it comes to that.'

Mia nodded. Suddenly aware she was still wearing her helmet, she pulled it off.

Luca placed a stilling hand on her forearm. 'You should leave it on,' he said.

Mia shook her hair free and finger-combed it. 'I'll feel ridiculous sitting here for the next who knows how long in this stupid helmet.'

Luca sought her gaze. 'If whatever's supporting us gives way, that helmet could be your lifeline.'

Mia glanced away from the stark reality she saw in his deep, dark eyes. 'Well, I doubt very much it'll prevent my neck from being broken, which is the most likely outcome if this thing plummets to the ground.'

Luca knew she was right. Spinal compression injury would be the true killer. That and the many other possibilities in between flitted through his mind as he watched Mia with a growing sense of helplessness.

He hated being powerless to affect change in this situation. That all three of them were dependent on things outside his control—the weather, branch structure, the expertise of others.

He'd been taking care of himself for a long time now. So, he suspected, had she. This kind of impotence was reminiscent of his past. And he'd had a little too much of that already this last week.

He took off his own helmet and ruffled his hair.

'We're going to be fine,' he murmured. If he had to hold this helicopter in place through sheer force of will, he would. *He wouldn't let Mia down*. He tapped the top of her helmet. 'Keep it close.'

Mia nodded. 'I don't suppose Air Control said what was happening with the patient we're supposed to be evac'ing?' Luca had talked with Air Control while she'd been inserting the IV.

'They're coming in by road. No choice now.'

Mia knew that would be an hour or so's drive in these treacherous weather conditions, even with lights and sirens. The mountain roads were dangerous when wet and low cloud would further inhibit speed.

'Hopefully the patient's spinal condition is minor,' Mia commented, rubbing absently at her arms. Although she doubted very much they would have been sent out on such a night for a chipped vertebra.

'You cold?' Luca asked.

'A little,' she admitted. The breached cabin was a perfect conduit for the freezing wind and the temperature inside the crippled aircraft had dropped considerably.

They'd covered Brian in a space blanket but now her adrenaline had settled and their activity had ceased she was starting to feel cold gnawing at her arms. 'You must be too,' Mia said. 'Your overalls are wet around your shoulders and chest.'

Luca wasn't really. His body was still on high alert, his metabolic rate steaming along like a whistling kettle. But they were probably going to be there for a while…

He leaned across and dragged a pack out from under the stretcher, locating the stash of space blankets folded neatly into playing-card-sized packaging.

'Here,' he said, passing her one. Then he opened another and unfolded it. The thin, metallic, foil material crinkled noisily, like a chocolate wrapper, as he proceeded to scrunch it up.

'What are you doing?' Mia asked as she unfolded hers and stood so she could wrap it around her entire body.

'I'm going to plug the hole with it,' Luca murmured.

'Ah…good thinking,' she said as she moved aside to give him more room to manoeuvre.

Luca carefully leaned over Brian's seat and gingerly stuffed the whistling hole with the scrunched-up foil blanket. 'That should do it,' he said, standing back to admire his handiwork.

'Sounds like it,' Mia agreed as the whistling magically stopped.

He smiled down at her and in the confines of the helicopter a hunched Luca seemed to take up all the space.

She hadn't had time to think about her startling revelation from earlier, but now it was all she could think about.

She was in love with Luca di Angelo.

For better or worse. And surely this *had* to be the worst?

'It's going to be okay,' Luca murmured, lifting his hand to cup her cheek. 'You're going to be okay.'

Mia wasn't sure if she'd ever be okay again. She'd gone and done something she'd sworn she never would—fallen in love. How could life ever be okay? How could it ever be the same?

The air seemed to thicken as they stood hunched over in the middle of the helicopter, staring at each other. The howl of the wind and the steady beeping of the heart-rate monitor twirled around them like a symphony.

Brian chose that moment to stir, crinkling the space blanket and setting off the monitor alarm. Luca's hand dropped as he started guiltily and immediately switched his attention to the stretcher.

Luca placed his hand on the pilot's shoulder. 'Hurting, Brian?'

Brian's eyes drifted open and he gave them a goofy smile. 'Nope. Everything ish wonderfullll,' he slurred. 'That morphine is gooood stuff.' And his eyes drifted shut again.

Mia, who was once again checking Brian's foot pulses, smiled. Obviously the pain relief was working.

'How are they?' Luca asked.

'The same, I think. The foot seems a little cooler, though.'

They resumed their seats, Luca wrapping himself in a space blanket as well. He checked his watch. 'Nearly four-thirty,' he said as he peered out the rain-spattered window.

They sat in silence for some minutes, both looking out at the watery blackness. 'This wasn't quite how I imagined my first visit to the Blue Mountains would pan out,' Luca murmured.

Mia's gaze slid from the window to his profile. 'I recommend driving next time.'

There was a pause as their eyes met and then they both laughed. Mia's stomach rumbled. 'Are you hungry?' She grabbed her backpack from its hidey-hole. The foil of the space blanket crinkled with her every movement. 'There's usually some exceedingly fattening, sugar-loaded snacks in here.'

She gave a triumphant whoop when she located two chocolate bars and handed him one. She tore off her wrapper and sighed as she savoured that first sinful bite. 'To think, this could be the last chocolate I ever eat.'

Luca glanced at her sharply. 'Don't talk like that.'

Mia shrugged as the other lasts competed for equal placing. Last time smelling eucalyptus. Last time seeing rain.

Last time being with Luca.

She wondered if she confessed to these crazy new feelings whether Luca would pretend that he reciprocated. He could renege when they were safely back in Sydney, she wouldn't hold him to it, but if she was about to meet her fate then…why not utter the words?

Because she didn't want her last moments filled with an awkward silence and an even more awkward Luca trying to figure out how to let her down gently before they crashed to a fiery death.

Or worse—watch him lie to her.

Yes, he wanted her. But that was different from love. And, faced with her own mortality, nothing less would do.

She sighed again. 'Just being realistic.'

Luca shook his head. 'We're in a stable position. Air Control has our ELT signal. We just need to wait out the weather and then they'll get us out of here as soon as they can.'

Mia nodded. Listening to the sure, steady note in his voice, she believed him. 'I know.'

They finished their chocolate serenaded by the moaning wind and the rhythmic beeping of the monitor. Luca shut his eyes briefly and let his head flop back against the headrest. The fine crinkle of the space blanket sounded like crickets chirping as he shifted to get comfortable, stretching his long legs out into the confined space.

His legs brushed hers and he lifted his head. 'Sorry.' He grimaced as he shifted them slightly to one side.

'It's fine,' she murmured.

Their gazes locked and for the longest moment they just sat and watched each other. Luca was the first to break the connection.

'So...you've never seen *Swan Lake*?'

Mia didn't say anything for a minute. Then she just shook her head. 'Have you?'

He nodded. 'My grandmother adored things like that. Opera was her first love but she enjoyed ballet too. And she insisted we all be well versed.' He smiled at the memory. 'She took me and my sisters to Rome when I was twelve because it was playing at the Teatro dell'Opera.'

Mia remembered he'd mentioned having sisters before. She heard the affection in his voice and felt a corresponding ache of longing deep inside. Her life had been far from family outings to the opera and ballet.

'You have three sisters, right?'

'Yes.' He toyed with leaving it at that but was surprised by the urge to confess all. 'And a brother.'

His accent thickened and Mia heard the regret in every syllable. He'd mentioned he'd been ostracised and she could hear the pain in every husky nuance. How terrible to have lost an entire extended family. Two people had been hard enough.

'What happened, Luca?'

She'd told him she hadn't wanted to know. And she hadn't. But that was before feeling the power of a love so deep that, even now, despite its newness, it was nestling in to her bones, bedding in for the long haul.

Now she wanted to know everything about him.

She wanted to know it all.

Luca hesitated at her soft enquiry, knowing the answer involved a trip down memory lane. And he'd just flown halfway round the world to come back from there. But somehow, with his recent trip back to the scene of the crime and the potentially dire situation they were in, it didn't seem so confronting.

In fact, it seemed kind of cathartic.

And in this strange metal cocoon, perched in the treetops of an ancient forest, it seemed as if they were the only two people in the entire world. Despite the beeping of Brian's monitor, the occasional staccato chatter from the radio and the ever-present potential for disaster, the atmosphere was intimate.

Maybe it was the rain—the whole dark, stormy night

thing—but somehow the mood was conducive to confidences and deep dark secrets.

And it was Mia. The one woman he instinctively knew would understand. But where did he start?

CHAPTER TEN

MIA watched and waited. She could see Luca was grappling with some demons and she held her breath, hoping like crazy he'd open up to her.

'I fell in love for the first time…' Luca paused. 'The only time…when I was sixteen.'

Mia steeled herself against the jab to her chest. He seemed so definite. So absolute.

He snorted. 'At least, I thought I had. I think lust or infatuation is probably more appropriate when I think about it now.'

Mia tried to ignore how the spike of jealousy hurt. *It was an ancient love affair, for crying out loud!*

'She must have been a hell of a girl,' she said, forcing lightness to her tone, and turned to look out the window because she couldn't bear to see what love looked like in his eyes. Not when it was for another woman.

He nodded. 'Oh, yes. Her family was an old, important family in Sicily and our two families had had a deep and abiding friendship for generations. She was promised to my brother.'

Mia's gaze snapped back to his. 'Promised? Like an arranged marriage?'

Luca smiled at her shock. 'Yes, Mia. An arranged marriage. This is Sicily where the old ways still rule.'

Mia blinked at the strange concept. 'But…you fell in love with her instead?'

Luca shook his head. 'As well.'

Oh. Mia felt goose-bumps on her arms as if the wind had found its way in again and blown right up beneath the blanket. There was nothing as heart-wrenching as brother against brother. She hunched into the space blanket a little more with a corresponding ruffle. 'Ah.'

Luca gave a grim nod. 'Yes. Ah.'

She quirked an eyebrow. 'Were there pistols at dawn?' she joked.

Luca gave a half-smile. 'No. That might have been quicker.'

Mia sobered. 'It was bad.' She wasn't sure if it was a question or a statement.

Luca nodded. 'Marissa and Carlos had a tempestuous relationship. He was twenty-three and she was eighteen when the engagement became official. He worked in Rome and was away frequently so Marissa and I hung out a lot. And when they were together they argued frequently then made up again. I think they both loved the drama of it all. And I…'

Luca paused as he remembered how love-struck he'd been. 'I watched like a desperate puppy from the sidelines. And when she came to me and said that they were done and that it was me she'd wanted all along… I didn't question her motives. It didn't occur to me that she would be disingenuous. That I was some pawn to make Carlos jealous.'

Luca shook his head. What a fool he'd been for

Marissa. What a stupid, naive fool. He glanced at Mia and marvelled at how little it suddenly seemed to matter.

'And then Marissa got pregnant and she told Carlos, who she apparently was still seeing, that the baby was mine. She told me it was his and the families came to loggerheads…' Luca shrugged. 'It was like the Capulets and the Montagues times one thousand.'

Mia couldn't really laugh at the joke. She could sense Luca was just skimming the surface and could only begin to imagine the repercussions.

'So who was the father?'

Luca shrugged. 'She miscarried and it became a moot point.'

'I'm sorry,' Mia murmured. 'That must have been hard for you. Losing a baby at any stage is difficult.' She'd been ten when her brand-new baby sister had been stillborn and that had been truly awful. 'And you were so young.'

Luca was momentarily taken aback. His family had been too angry at the time to acknowledge the emotional impact on him, let alone support him through it. Until today his grandmother had been the only person who had understood how much grief the incident had caused him.

He nodded then paused for a moment to pick up the thread of his story. 'A massive rift developed between the two families and it was only Marissa and Carlos's engagement that kept them together. I became the scapegoat.'

Mia felt his pain right down to her toes. And finally she understood his compassion with Stan that first night, a man who'd loved a woman that hadn't been faithful.

'But…surely your parents, your sisters…? They're your family…they're supposed to love you. No matter what.'

Even as she said it she felt a fraud—her parents had certainly forgotten all about what they were supposed to do, bogged down in the quagmire of their grief and anger.

Luca shook his head. 'Sicilians don't forgive very easily and I learned right then and there that love is no guarantee of anything. That any relationship, no matter how strong, can go toxic. I was sent to live with my grandmother in Palermo and as soon as I was out of school I left and didn't go back.'

'Until this week.'

Luca nodded. 'Until this week.'

'Was it hard…seeing them again? Your brother. And Marissa?' Luca shook his head. It had been a relief. Seeing Carlos and Marissa together no longer hurt. 'No.' Mia wished he'd elaborate. *Was he still in love with her?* But she shied from asking it, too frightened of the answer.

'Was there any mellowing?'

He shook his head. 'I was pretty much persona non grata.'

An almighty gust of wind seemed to shake the helicopter and her anger swirled inside the cabin with as much potency. 'That's not fair.'

Luca shrugged, looking out the window. 'Life's not fair. But I'm very pleased, very grateful to you, that I went. That I got to say my goodbye. Nonna anchored me during a very turbulent period in my life. To my shame, I don't think I appreciated that till many years later. I was angry for such a long time.'

Mia watched his brooding profile as he seemed trans-
fixed by rain spatter patterns. 'I'm sure she knew.'

Luca nodded. 'I hope so.' He sat staring out at the
inclement abyss for a moment before turning to her and
saying, 'I've never told anybody this. I'm not really sure
why I'm telling it to you.'

All he knew was how right it felt.

Mia gave a small smile. No matter what, she did not
want to read too much into such an admission. People
were never the same on holiday or just before plunging
to their deaths in a helicopter.

It was practically an unwritten law. 'It's okay. Near-
death experiences tend to encourage confidences.'

Luca chuckled. 'Maybe you're right.' He sobered before pinning her with a speculative stare. 'Your turn.
What makes Dr Mia McKenzie tick?'

He knew there were things, deep-seated things, that
made her the wonderful, non-cuddly woman he'd come
to think of as naturally as he inhaled and exhaled.

It was Mia's turn to look out the window as his question made her squirm. She wasn't so sure she wanted a
man who thought every relationship had potential for
toxicity to know her deepest, darkest stuff.

'Same things as everyone else, I guess,' she hedged.

Luca watched her avoid his gaze. Right…so this
wasn't going to come easy. But he was suddenly desperate to know what made her the woman she was. Why
she didn't stay the night. Why she didn't cuddle.

Why she was looking anywhere but at him.

'Okay. Let's start with an easier question. Why did
you become a doctor?'

Mia barely suppressed a snort. How could he know
the answer to that question was about as entwined with

her baggage as was possible? She glared at him. 'Why did you become a doctor?'

'A child nearly drowned in a lake near where my grandmother lived when I was a teenager. I helped revive her. I knew then and there I wanted to be a doctor.'

Of course. Trust Luca to have an answer. She only wished hers was as cut and dried.

Luca leaned forward in his chair, placing his elbows on his knees, and the foil crinkled. 'Come on, Mia. I told you mine.'

The beeps of the monitor seemed to mock her every thought. Oh, what the hell...

She glanced out the window again. 'My mother had a baby. A stillborn baby, when I was ten.'

Mia didn't want to be sucked back to that time but here, in the darkness, surrounded by the fury of mother nature, it seemed impossible not to be. 'One minute I was going to have a baby sister to dote on. The next minute she was gone. The doctors were so good. Kind and compassionate. Not just to Mum but to me too. I guess I made up my mind then.'

Luca watched her as she stared intently out the window as if the meaning of life was lurking in the treetops. 'That must have been a hard time in your life. Your parents must have been devastated.'

Mia snorted. 'You could say things were never quite the same again.'

Luca frowned. 'They didn't make it?'

Mia shook her head. 'My father walked out a few weeks later and found himself another family. My mother took to our couch and zoned out for the rest of my life. Last time I checked, she was still there.'

Things suddenly became much clearer for Luca. The

most important man in her life had deserted her at an age and during a time when she'd needed him most. And her mother had been too grief-stricken to fill the gap.

'I'm sorry,' he murmured. 'You were just a child. You didn't deserve to be abandoned like that.'

Mia could almost feel the intensity of her ten-year-old pain as she stared out the window. She rolled her head to look at him. 'I hated him for so long.'

Luca shrugged. 'But of course. You needed him and he wasn't there for you. Or your mother.'

Mia gave a harsh little laugh. 'My mother.' She shook her head. 'My mother let me believe that he was the bad guy. That he'd found a better family. But she lied to me for years.'

'Oh?' Luca frowned.

'I found my mother's file when I was a med student working at The Harbour. The baby wasn't my father's.'

Mia rolled her head back to face the window. The find had been cataclysmic and still sucked her breath away.

'I confronted her about it. She admitted that Dad walked out because he'd found out about the baby's paternity. She didn't defend herself or apologise for letting me think the worst of him. She just said that I didn't understand what it was like to be married to a man who worked twenty-four seven.'

Luca watched as a range of emotions flitted across her face. Her emotional fragility after the Stan incident suddenly tightened into crystalline focus. It must have stirred up all those old childhood hurts.

'Did you…did you contact your father…try and reconcile?'

Mia bit down on her lip—she would not cry. No matter how hard that particular part in the saga had been. No matter how polite and distant her father had been. He'd been hurt too deeply both by her mother and by her own refusal to have anything to do with him over the years.

'I did. But it was too late...the damage had been done. And he had three little children who adored him. Frankly, I was a painful memory that he'd put away in a box somewhere.'

The rawness in her voice caught him somewhere right in the middle. His solar plexus. *His heart?* His family's abandonment of him seemed to pale in comparison. At least he'd been older, more emotionally equipped to deal with it. 'I'm sorry. That can't have been a good time in your life. Especially when you were in the middle of your studies.'

Mia gave a little laugh. 'You could say I went off the rails for a while there. A lot of booze and partying. A lot of hooking up with men who I always thought wanted more but were only out for casual sex. Which led to more drinking.'

Ah, so that's what she'd been referring to when she'd told him she'd once liked alcohol a little too much. And maybe it also explained her reluctance to get involved in anything more than a one-nighter. Mia had taken firm control of her life.

'You did well to stop the spiral,' he commented. Mia nodded. Luca had chosen a good word. She *had* been spiralling. Into self-doubt and self-loathing. Each new man, each drink, had made her feel more and more sullied.

'I failed a major exam. Had to resit it. It scared me

silly. I suddenly realised that there was no point throwing away my future over a past I couldn't change.'

Luca nodded. 'Yes.' It was a lesson he'd had to learn too. 'It seems you and I have a lot in common.'

'Oh?' Mia quirked an eyebrow as she looked at him again. 'You got all boozy and floozy too?'

Luca chuckled. 'No. Well, no more than any other angry young man, I suppose. It took a while to realise that I couldn't change what had happened. To accept that my family were never going to take me back. But once I did, it sort of freed me a little.'

Mia studied his face. 'So that's it, you're totally Zen with the whole thing?'

Luca smiled. 'No, not totally. Let's just say I'm a work in progress.'

Mia's heart filled her chest as she smiled back. 'Guess that makes two of us.'

They smiled at each other for a moment then Brian groaned. Mia checked his pulses as Luca administered another small dose of morphine. And when they sat back down again they settled into a companionable silence, each caught in their own thoughts.

Mia yawned. 'We should get some sleep,' Luca suggested.

She nodded. She wasn't sure if it was the confession or the hour but she was suddenly bone-deep tired. And it seemed like the most natural thing in the world to shut her eyes as the man she loved shut his.

Mia wasn't sure what time it was when she woke. Or even what had woken her. But watery daylight lit the inside of the chopper and there was a strange buzzing, crackling noise that she didn't think was coming from the rustling of the space blanket.

She came fully awake as Luca leapt up, muttering, 'The radio.'

And then it was all stations go. No time to feel embarrassed about spilling all their private, closely held secrets in the dark or to analyse what opening up to each other meant. To work out where they stood. Or even to retract them.

No time at all.

The weather had settled and the rescue chopper was fifteen minutes out.

Forty-five minutes later, Mia was harnessed to a rescue officer, dangling over the drizzly treetops, looking down at a wrecked helicopter and a calm, solid Luca. Her eyes filled with tears as her heart swelled so large and full it felt like it was going to burst from her chest.

He was everything she'd ever realised she needed. But he'd only ever loved one woman. And maybe he still did. He certainly thought that all relationships had the potential to go toxic.

Just her luck that when she finally fell in love it would be with someone as damaged as herself.

Luca awoke with a start, vaulting upright. It was dark and he was momentarily disorientated. He'd been dreaming about Mia dangling over a dark, swirling, freezing mist. About her screaming his name as her hand slid from his and she fell.

His heart pounded like a freight train as he realised he was in his room. He glanced at the clock—six-thirty.

But was it morning or evening?

And what bloody day was it?

He flopped back against the mattress, taking deep breaths, forcing himself to calm down. It was just a dream.

A really bad dream.

Mia was safe. Brian was safe. They were all safe.

Mia...he'd lost track of her in the whirlwind that had descended on them the minute they'd set foot on the helipad at The Harbour. Whisked away for tests and debriefing and questions from all kinds of different official people and dozens of people dropping by to wish them well. When he'd finally been told he could go, there'd been no sign of Mia and Evie had told him that she'd taken Mia home and tucked her into bed.

His first instinct had been to go to her. But he'd checked it. She needed to sleep. Just because she'd opened up to him, didn't negate that they'd both been through a trauma and been up most of the night.

So he'd headed for his bed too. And despite his conviction that his speeding mind wouldn't allow him respite, the combination of the jet-lag and adrenaline had him out for the count within minutes of his head hitting the pillow.

But now he was awake. Wide awake. And he knew why. He knew why with every thud of fear still echoing in each heartbeat. He knew why he was dreaming about Mia. Why the overwhelming panic and despair at losing her—in the crash, in his dream—had woken him from deep and utter exhaustion.

He was in love with her.

He'd foolishly thought that they were just a casual thing. That they were having a bit of fun. Some great sex, a distracting flirtation.

But obviously his brain hadn't been listening.

Because while his body had been enjoying itself he hadn't realised his emotions had become involved. That their entire relationship had been based on a series of emotional connections—interlocking, weaving them together.

Stan and the emotional tumult of his case—for both of them—had been the first connection. Being held at knifepoint had been the catalyst for their initial sexual liaison. Sure, he'd dismissed it as a very nice, very surprising turn of events. But it hadn't been the uncomplicated one-off he'd been fooling himself it was.

It had occurred after a highly charged emotional incident.

And then later, when they'd worked together to save Stan's life, they'd forged an even deeper bond.

His grandmother's death had ramped it up a little more. Forced them to an even deeper level of emotional intimacy without him even knowing it. She'd been there to comfort him. To hold him. To tell him to get his butt on a plane and go to her funeral.

That had been more than just sex, no matter what she'd said.

For heaven's sake, she'd stayed the night. She never stayed the night. *She didn't even cuddle.*

And then there was last night. Sharing that near-death experience and then opening up to her, like he'd never done before. Unburdening all the ugly things about his past he never spoke about. Listening to her as she'd unburdened hers.

He'd been pretending it was casual. Having a great time with hard and fast sex, indulging in the physical to override anything deeper. But somewhere along the way it had become more than that.

AMY ANDREWS   179

For him anyway.

He loved her. And it didn't frighten him. He didn't want to run from it like he had in the past. Maybe returning to Sicily had laid some ghosts to rest. Maybe it was almost dying in that helicopter crash. Maybe it was *Mia* almost dying in that helicopter crash.

But he wanted to live. He wanted that grand love poets had written about. And he wanted it with Mia. His scarred, scared Mia.

He didn't want to live another day without it.

Mia woke to a terrible racket. She'd been so tired when Evie had finally dragged her home and pushed her into the shower, not even thoughts of Luca had been enough to keep her awake as she'd collapsed naked into bed.

It took her a moment to realise the racket was coming from the front door. 'Go away,' she groaned as she dragged the pillow over her head and shut her eyes again.

'Mia? Mia! Open up!'

Mia sat up as the voice registered. *Luca?*

'Mia!'

Luca's urgent tone penetrated the fog of fatigue. She was throwing back the covers and pulling on a robe before her sluggish brain even registered her purpose.

'Mia!'

'Coming!' she called as she hurried out of her bedroom, tying the robe firmly at her waist, half tripping over a discarded shoe on the way.

Why on earth was he pounding her door down? Her heart rat-a-tat-tatted in time to the knocks as it romanticised his presence. But she doubted he was knocking like a madman to tell her he loved her. More likely the building was on fire.

Which made her unaccountably grouchy.

She reached the door and snatched it open. Her breath caught in her throat. He stood before her in track pants and a hoodie, his feet stuffed into thongs, his hair rumpled, that stubble still peppering his jaw, a blanket mark reddening one cheekbone.

The man had never looked sexier.

'Where's the fire?' she snapped, because it was that or do something really silly like invite him into her bed.

She'd meant it when she'd told him they couldn't keep sleeping with each other. She couldn't love him and only have some of him. Know that he was waiting for the whole thing to go toxic.

Luca took in her tousled blonde hair and the outline of her breasts beneath her gown and smiled. 'You look good,' he murmured appreciatively.

Mia gripped the door at the lust she saw glittering in the deep brown depths of his eyes. 'I sure hope you didn't wake me for that.'

Luca smiled. 'Can I come in?'

'Luca,' she sighed. She was not going to be sucked in by that sexy smile.

'Please.' He spread his hands. 'Just for a moment.'

Mia almost shut the door on him. She was tired and at a really low ebb. Didn't he know she wanted nothing more than to curl up in bed with him and sleep for a hundred years?

Why didn't he just leave her alone?

Hoping she wouldn't regret it, she stood back and inhaled as he passed. She hadn't meant to but he smelled so good she let his aroma wrap around her like a warm cloak. She stood by the closed door, arms folded, as he strolled to the centre of her lounge room.

Luca turned to face her. She seemed remote. Both physically and emotionally.

That didn't bode well.

He took a step towards her. 'I figured out why I told you all that stuff last night.'

Mia regarded him warily. She hoped he hadn't figured out why she'd told him her stuff. The only way she could keep her dignity here was to hide her feelings. 'Really?'

He took another step. 'I've known somewhere deep inside for a while that you understood me, truly understood me, and I thought that it was just our family issues, our unhappy pasts uniting us in a way that few people could relate to.'

Mia nodded. She'd recognised him as a kindred spirit almost from the beginning.

'But it's more than that, Mia. You got under my skin, sneaked up on me when I wasn't looking. I was fooling myself that we were just keeping it casual but I was wrong.' He raked a hand through his already rumpled hair. 'I've been walking blindly down this track towards you all along and it's only now that I see what's really happening.'

Mia's heart started to thump erratically in her chest. What was he saying? That his toxicity sensors were twitching madly? That he was getting too close and it was time to get as far away as possible? 'Oh? And what's that?'

'I'm in love with you.'

Mia didn't say anything for a moment. She didn't

move. She didn't breathe. In fact, she was pretty certain her heart even stopped for a few beats.

'Mia?'

'What about Marissa?' she blurted out, because that was way simpler than the crash of other thoughts and emotions that were churning inside her.

'Marissa?'

'You said she was the only woman you ever loved.'

Luca frowned. 'I was sixteen. And infatuated. That wasn't love. I knew that the moment I saw her in the church in Palermo last week. I was a boy with a crush. What I feel for you…in here…' Luca patted his chest. 'It's a thousand times deeper, wider, stronger. You're the one I want to talk to, make love to, wake up to.'

Luca watched her face as she grappled with the news. She looked like she was fighting it. Trying to come up with ways to block it out. Block him out. He covered the distance between them until he was standing within touching distance.

'I know that you think you can't do this—have a relationship with someone. That it's not you. That you're not the *sleeping-over* type…'

'Me?' Mia scoffed, arms still firmly crossed. 'What about you? Aren't you afraid this will go toxic too? Because I'm not going to get involved with someone who's waiting for me to slip up or who's out the door at the first sign of trouble wearing a gas mask.'

Luca, buoyed by the concession that she might actually be thinking of getting involved with him, placed his hands on her shoulders and rubbed his thumbs against the polar fleece of the thick robe.

'I'm not saying that this doesn't scare me, that it's not new territory, but as you said last night I can't let an unhappy past, one that I can't change, ruin a chance at a happy future. Neither of us can, Mia.'

Mia felt tears well in her eyes. This couldn't possibly be true, could it? *Could he actually love her back?*

'Oh, Mia,' he murmured, drawing her against him. 'Don't cry, Mia. I love you.'

Mia shut her eyes tight as his accent washed over her like syrup and she allowed herself a moment to inhale the essence of him. Less than two months ago she hadn't even known this man. Just last night she'd realised the utter depth of her feelings for him. And realised he couldn't love her back.

Could she have been wrong?

'This is just the near-death experience talking.'

She tried to break out of his grasp but Luca held her tighter. Her voice was muffled against his shirt but he heard every word.

'No, Mia, no.' He eased her gently back. 'It may have been the jolt that removed the blinkers from my eyes, but this isn't sudden. I've known deep inside, deep in my heart since that night in the on-call room, that you were special. That you were more than just another woman.'

The sincerity in his eyes and in his husky accented voice called to her on a primal level. She laid her head back on his chest as she allowed the possibilities to bloom. 'I thought we were going to die last night and that I'd never get the chance to love you.'

Luca hugged her close as her words sang like an opera in his heart. 'You love me,' he said.

He'd hoped, he'd wondered, he'd wished. But to hear her say the words meant more than his next breath.

'I didn't want to,' Mia murmured.

Luca chuckled as he stroked her hair. 'Well, it's just as well we don't always get what we want.'

'Oh, Luca.' She pulled back and looked into his eyes, oozing love and joy. 'I love you so much, I couldn't bear anything to happen to us.'

Luca placed a finger across her mouth, shushing her, knowing what she was thinking. 'I'm not your father, Mia. And you are not Marissa. We're us and we won't make the same mistakes.'

And then he lowered his head and drifted the sweetest, softest kiss across her mouth she'd ever experienced. Her eyes fluttered closed and she sighed.

'Promise?' she murmured against his lips.

Luca chuckled. 'Promise.'

EPILOGUE

Two weeks later a limousine carrying Luca in a tuxedo and a glamorously dressed but blindfolded Mia glided to a halt outside the Sydney Opera House.

'We're here,' Luca announced.

Mia laughed. 'Luca, for the last time, where are we going?'

'Patience,' he teased, kissing her nose. 'Patience. Although we could just drive around in the back all night...' he dropped a kiss behind her ear '...and christen the seats...' His lips nuzzled her neck.

Mia laughed and pushed him away playfully. 'Oh, no. No way.'

The door opened and Luca grinned at the chauffeur. 'Okay, then, let's go.' He helped Mia out and once she was standing steadily he removed her blindfold.

Mia blinked as the illuminated sails of the Opera House filled her vision. She smiled at him. 'We're going to see a show?'

Luca smiled down at the woman he loved. 'The ballet, actually.'

Mia looked at the tickets he thrust into her hands. She read the fancy printing several times before it registered. She looked up at him, the man she loved, so tall and handsome and so, so hers.

'*Swan Lake*,' she whispered, hugging the tickets close. 'Oh, Luca…thank you.'

Mia beamed up at her Italian angel. She wasn't sure when she'd stopped seeing the devil but tonight all she could see was a pair of luminescent wings and a bright golden halo.

And he was all hers.

* * * * *

THE FIREBRAND
WHO UNLOCKED
HIS HEART

BY
ANNE FRASER

MILLS
BOON

First published in Great Britain 2012
by Mills & Boon, an imprint of Harlequin (UK) Limited.
Harlequin (UK) Limited, Eton House, 18-24 Paradise Road,
Richmond, Surrey TW9 1SR

© Anne Fraser 2012

ISBN: 978 0 263 89786 9

Harlequin (UK) policy is to use papers that are natural, renewable and recyclable products and made from wood grown in sustainable forests. The logging and manufacturing process conform to the legal environmental regulations of the country of origin.

Printed and bound in Spain
by Blackprint CPI, Barcelona

Maybe it was the way he was looking at her—maybe it was because she was tired—or maybe it was because she didn't want to be friends with this man.

She wanted only to think of him as Harry's father—her employer—she didn't want him to try and be her friend. It felt...dangerous. He made her thoughts fly in directions she didn't want them to go.

'I'm tired,' she said. 'If you don't mind I think I'll turn in for the night.'

Suddenly his hand was in her hair and he leant down and kissed her lightly on the lips. For a moment the world spun. 'Goodnight, then, Colleen. I'll see you in the morning.'

Dear Reader

I almost always write my Medical™ Romances from my personal experience as a nurse, and this one is no different.

When Harry is badly injured in a car accident his father, barrister Daniel Frobisher, is determined to do everything in his power to save the son he didn't know he had and barely knows. His research for the right person to help his son leads him to sparky nurse Colleen McCulloch.

Following an accident that left her brother brain-injured, Colleen has made it her mission to make sure every patient under her care is given the best possible chance to improve. So when she meets Harry, who has lost almost everyone he loves, how can she resist taking up Daniel's offer of a job? Particularly when it gives her time away from her disastrous love-life...

Soon sparks fly, and as Colleen begins to see the tortured and grieving man behind Daniel's cool façade, professional distance goes out of the window and she becomes involved with this small, hurt family. And if Daniel makes her feel something that no man has ever made her feel, doesn't she just have to find a way to deal with that too?

I hope you enjoy Colleen and Daniel's story.

Anne Fraser

CHAPTER ONE

'I'M SORRY, but the answer is still no,' Colleen said.

Daniel Frobisher leaned back in his chair and wiped an imaginary fleck of dust from his dark-grey suit. He narrowed his eyes at her as if he couldn't believe what he was hearing.

He looks like a tiger studying his prey just before it attacks, Colleen thought. He was in his late thirties, she guessed, with light brown hair and intense green eyes. He had the kind of face that you wanted to stare at as if it were a painting. Long, straight nose, full mouth and cheekbones most models would give their designer gowns for. He was almost too good-looking. Men who looked like him were too *unreal* somehow.

'I'll pay you well. Very well,' he said in his Oxbridge accent and then went on to name a weekly sum that made Colleen's head reel. What he was proposing was more than she earned in a month. More than she earned in two months, come to think of it, but money wasn't the issue here.

'I don't need the money; besides I'm perfectly happy with my life the way it is,' Colleen said firmly. The last part wasn't exactly true, but there was no need for the man in front of her to know that.

This wasn't the first time she had said no. She had told Daniel Frobisher's assistant—what was his name again? Haversham or something—the same thing over the phone only a few days ago.

'If Mr Frobisher can't spare the time to come and see me for himself, I'm afraid that tells me that he is not committed to making his son better,' Colleen had told Haversham. 'In order to make the greatest improvement, his son is going to need round-the-clock, intensive treatment. That means his father helping. A lot. And if he can't spare the time to meet me…' Colleen paused '…it's a non-starter.'

'Mr Frobisher is a very busy man,' Haversham replied. 'He would have come personally if he could have. He asked me to represent him in this matter.'

This matter? It was Frobisher's *son* they were talking about.

'Look, please tell him I'm sorry about his son, really I am. But if Mr Frobisher is as wealthy as you say he is, there are other arrangements he could make that would work better for him.'

She had said a polite goodbye, and forgotten all about it until this morning, when Daniel Frobisher himself had appeared, demanding to see her.

'There is a gorgeous-looking man asking to see you,' Lillian, the receptionist, had said, having come to find Colleen in the staff room where Colleen was giving her report to the on-coming staff before leaving for the day. 'I told him you were busy, but he says he needs to speak to you—right now.' Lillian's eyes had been round. 'You've been keeping him a secret from us, you naughty thing, although I can quite understand why. If I was two-timing my boyfriend—especially with someone who looks like that—I don't think I'd be telling anyone either.'

'I'm not two-timing Ciaran with anyone,' Colleen had protested. 'How can you even suggest such a thing? Tell whoever it is that he'll have to wait—or to come back on Monday.'

'Honey, whatever you've been up to with that man, he's not going anywhere.'

Mystified, Colleen had peeked around the corner. Lillian was right. Whoever he was, he was a hunk. Just because she was engaged to Ciaran didn't mean she couldn't recognise yumminess when she saw it. But the man pacing the floor, irritably checking his watch every couple of seconds, wasn't anyone she had met before. She would have remembered.

'I've never seen him before in my life. Did he give you a name?' Colleen had whispered to Lillian.

'Says he's called Mr Frobisher.'

So the too-busy man had come in person this time. Well, she'd be telling him exactly the same as she'd told Haversham. But he'd have to wait until she'd finished the handover to the night staff and changed out of her uniform.

After finishing the report, Colleen had gone to say goodbye to her patients, most of whom were getting ready for the day, either on their own or with help from the nursing staff. She had to use some fancy footwork to avoid being mowed down by Jake in his motorised wheelchair. 'Hey, Jake, you're not at Silverstone now,' she had chided affectionately. Jake was one of their longest residents on the rehab ward. When he'd come to them he'd been immobile and angry following a motorbike accident that had robbed him of the use of his legs.

But since he'd been given the motorised chair, he'd become determined to be as independent as possible. He would be going home in a couple of weeks and she'd miss his cheeky grin.

Her last stop had been the room immediately opposite the nurse's station. Kiera Flannigan was an eighteen year old who had been involved in a serious road-traffic accident six months earlier that had left her paralysed from the neck down. Like Jake, she had initially refused to have anything to do with the rehab programme that had been devised for her. Colleen had spent hours by her bed, cajoling her, talking to her, refusing to let the teenager give up. And her efforts had paid off. Kiera was still paralysed—there was no hope of an improvement—but she was able to use a special computer that allowed her to use her breath to type on to a screen as well as guide her wheelchair around the ward.

'Hey, Colleen,' Kiera had typed. 'Are we going dancing tonight?'

'Too tired, Kiera. Need my beauty sleep,' Colleen had replied. 'What have you got planned for the day?'

'School work. Ugh,' Kiera had typed. 'Exams soon. Would rather go dancing.'

Colleen ached for the pretty girl. She'd been with them for four months and, like Jake, she'd be going home soon. The staff on the unit had done a charity bungee jump to raise money so that Kiera would be able to take her computer home with her. The rehabilitation unit—the only one of its kind in the south of Ireland—was funded entirely by charitable donations and, although people were generous, there was always a need for more money to buy specialised equipment such as Jake's motorised wheelchair and Kiera's computer. At the moment the coffers for equipment was running very low.

'And the blog? How's that doing?' Colleen had asked.

'A hundred hits a day,' Kiera had typed. When Kiera had mastered the computer she'd complained of being bored. There was only so much she could do to keep herself occupied. Colleen had suggested she start a blog for other spinal-injury patients. Kiera had eagerly taken to the idea and it had been an immediate success.

Thirty minutes later, having changed in to her civvies, Colleen was ready to leave. In reception, Frobisher was still pacing up and down and looking at his watch with barely concealed impatience. She'd forgotten that he was waiting to see her.

'I'm Colleen McCulloch,' Colleen said. 'You wished to see me?'

Frobisher stopped his pacing and glanced at his watch pointedly.

'Sorry for keeping you waiting,' she said, slipping on her jacket.

He held out his hand. His grasp was firm. 'Daniel Frobisher. Look, is there somewhere we can talk?'

He was so tall she had to tip her head back just to meet his eyes.

'I'm afraid you've wasted your time coming here. The answer is still no. I already told your Mr Haversham I can't take on the care of your son. I'm sorry, but as you can see, I already have a job. I did give him a couple of other names to try.'

'I've taken time I could ill afford to come here, so I think you could at least hear me out.' There was no mistaking the impatience in his voice and Colleen felt herself prickle.

Before she knew what was happening, Frobisher grabbed her by the elbow and was steering her out of the ward. 'I can't stay in this place,' he said tersely. 'I've had enough of hospitals to last me a lifetime. Is there somewhere else we could go to talk?'

'As I said, there's nothing to talk about.' Colleen tried to pull her arm out of his grasp, but his grip was too strong. Was he planning to abduct her? From the grim look on his face she wouldn't put it past him.

She told herself not to be ridiculous. He was hardly going to bundle her into a car in full view of half of Dublin.

But that was exactly what he did. His car, all sleek black and chrome with darkened windows, was waiting right outside the front door of the hospital, where nobody, absolutely nobody, not even Mr Sylvester, the head of the unit, was allowed to park. She was in the back of the car alongside Frobisher so fast she hadn't even had a second to call for help.

He was really beginning to annoy her, sick son or no sick son. She tried the handle of the door as the chauffeur-driven car moved off.

'Would you please stop this car and let me out. This minute!' Colleen tried to keep her voice steady. 'Driver! Stop the car. Immediately.' She scrabbled in her bag looking for a weapon, but all she could find in the jumble of used tissues and coins was a notebook, a pen, her purse and a bottle of perfume. She pulled it out and brandished the bottle at him. 'If you don't, I'll spray you.'

Instead of letting her out, Frobisher pressed a button and a glass screen swished up between them and the driver. 'You're going to disarm me with perfume?

Then what? Do the same to my driver?' Amusement flickered in his green eyes and softened the severity of his angular face. 'All I need is thirty minutes of your time.' His eyes grew solemn. 'I promise I'll bring you back as soon as we've talked. All I want is for you to hear me out before you make up your mind.'

Something in the way he said the words, the unexpected timbre of sadness in the tone, made her pause and look more closely at him.

Despite his astonishing good looks there were lines around his eyes and a tightness to his mouth as if he were unused to smiling. Instinctively she knew that this man was in pain. A whole lot of pain. Not that it excused his high-handed behaviour, but she could at least spare him a few minutes.

'Very well,' Colleen conceded reluctantly. 'I'll listen to what you have to say—not that I think it will make much difference, mind. But I'm not going to do it here. I'm starving. I missed my tea break and if I don't have something to eat soon I'll probably pass out on the floor of this car. There's a café I go to all the time just around the corner. Tell your driver to stop there.'

'You promise you won't try to run away?'

Colleen smiled at the image of her running down the streets of Dublin with this man hot on her heels. If there was a more unlikely scenario, she couldn't think of one. 'I promise. I'll give you as long as it takes for me to eat. But that's it.' She held out her hand. 'Do we have a deal?'

Cool fingers pressed hers. Yikes! Did the man have a buzzer in his hand? Something had to have caused the electric shock that ran up her arm. Quickly she pulled her hand away.

When he saw the café a look of astonishment crossed his face. Admittedly, the café wasn't much from the outside, but inside it was warm and cosy and sold the best Irish breakfasts this side of Dublin. Colleen often stopped there on her way to or from home or work—not least because her best friend, Trish, owned the place.

'Are you sure you want to eat here?' Daniel said doubtfully. 'I could suggest somewhere else.'

There was no way she was going to drive any further with this man.

'It's either here or nowhere,' Colleen said firmly. 'It's only a five-minute walk home for me from here. And I need my bed.'

As soon as the words were out of her mouth she regretted them. She didn't want to give him any clues to where she lived. She had the uneasy feeling that he would have no compunction about staking out her flat once she had made him realise that she was serious about not taking the job.

'Okay, you're the boss.' Then he smiled. It was only the briefest smile, vanishing almost before Colleen was sure she had seen it, but in that millisecond his face was transformed, making him look younger and, if possible, even more devastatingly good looking.

The windows of the café were steamed up from the combined breaths of customers filling up on Trish's renowned breakfasts before setting off for work or college. Trish scurried over to them as soon as they were seated in Colleen's favourite place by the window. Behind Frobisher's back, Trish wriggled her eyebrows and pretended to fan herself with her hand.

'I'll have my usual, please, Trish,' Colleen said, pretending not to notice.

'And you, sir?' Trish was practically drooling.

'Coffee. Black. No sugar.'

With a wink at Colleen, Trish sashayed away. Frobisher didn't even look at Colleen's friend. He had to be really worried about his son not to. Trish was gorgeous and most men fell instantly in love with her as soon as they set eyes on her. She was always fending off wannabe suitors.

'Okay. You asked me to listen to you so I'm all ears— though to be honest, I can't think there's anything you can say to me to convince me.' She softened her tone. 'As I told Mr Haversham—and you—I already have a job here. A job I just happen to love and have no intention of leaving. Besides he told me your home is in London. I'm afraid that in itself makes it impossible. Even if I weren't working already, I couldn't leave Ireland. So you see, you've wasted your time coming out here, Mr Frobisher.'

'Call me Daniel.'

'Daniel, then. Have you tried an agency? From what Mr Haversham told me, your son needs round-the-clock care. There are one or two excellent units in London that I could recommend.'

Trish came back with two coffees and a plate of egg, sausages, bacon and toast. Daniel's expression changed to one of mild incredulity. Had the man never seen a woman eat before? As Colleen added enough ketchup to her satisfaction and speared a slice of sausage on her fork, Daniel fished a photograph out of his top pocket and handed it to Colleen. She set aside her knife and fork and studied the picture. It was of a beautiful woman with blonde hair and shining eyes. It had been taken on a beach with the sun setting in the background. The woman had her arm around a boy who was smiling self-consciously into the camera. Judging by the brilliant green eyes, which were exact replicas of the ones staring intently at her, there was no doubt whose child he was.

'That was taken just over two years ago,' Daniel said softly, 'when my son, Harry, was ten.'

Haversham had told her Harry Frobisher was twelve. Didn't Daniel have a more recent photograph of his son, or was this simply his favourite one?

'That's your wife with Harry?'

'My ex-wife. We were divorced. Eleanor was killed outright in the accident that injured my son.'

'I'm so sorry.' Colleen had to stop herself from reaching out and laying a comforting hand on his. Instinctively she knew the gesture would not be welcome.

Daniel's expression was unreadable. 'She had just collected Harry from his boarding school when it happened. They were on their way to the airport...' He hesitated as if his thoughts were turning inwards, reliving the horror.

'And your son was badly hurt?' she prompted gently.

Pain flashed across Daniel's face. 'Harry's injuries were severe. He was in a coma for almost a week. For a time I thought he wasn't going to make it.' Daniel's voice had become clipped, almost as if he were talking about something that had happened to someone else.

'Harry regained consciousness a month ago. He can't talk and his movement is limited.' Daniel's mouth twisted. 'For God's sake, he can't even feed himself. My child is a prisoner in his own body.'

'It's early days yet,' Colleen said softly. 'He could

improve a great deal in the next six months—with the right kind of care.'

Daniel took the photograph from her hands and placed it carefully back in his pocket.

'So they tell me. But I'm not convinced he wouldn't do better at home, getting individual attention from someone with your reputation. I don't just want good care for my son; I want him to have the best. From everything I've learned about you, I believe you are the person he needs. I understand you were a physiotherapist before you became a nurse. I also understand that you specialise in looking after young patients and have had personal experience of this kind of injury.'

Colleen paused, the forkful of egg and toast halfway to her mouth. 'How do you know that?'

'Let's just say that I did my research.' He studied her calmly. 'I would never offer anyone a job without checking them out. You trained at Guy's. I asked Professor Ludwig and without any hesitation he recommended you. I believe if anyone can fix my son, it's you. And I'm prepared to do anything, pay anything, to make that happen.'

'*Fix* your son?' His choice of words chilled her. What—as if he was a broken car or something? Nevertheless, she spoke as gently as possible, knowing from experience that parents sometimes took years to accept their child's prognosis. 'I'm afraid it's not as easy as that. Even if he gets six months of intensive care and rehabilitation, it doesn't mean he'll ever make a full recovery. He may never be the child he once was. In fact—and you should be prepared for this—it's *unlikely* he'll be the child he once was. A brain injury that kept Harry in a coma for a week must have been pretty severe.'

Daniel leaned across the table and fixed his startlingly coloured eyes on Colleen. 'At least say you'll think about it.'

God, she hated it when people put pressure on her. Despite her unease about the way this man chose to go about finding someone to look after his son, she couldn't help but feel sorry for him. No one should have to go through what Daniel was going through. She knew that better than most. Ten years ago, her youngest brother, Cahil had been in the same situation as Harry. That's why she did what she did. But however much compassion she felt for Harry, what Daniel was asking was impossible.

'I'm sorry—the answer is still no.' Colleen pushed the last piece of sausage around her plate and dunked it in tomato sauce. 'Look, I'm sorry about your son, really I am. But I've got a job and I can't just up and leave. And I've got a life here in Dublin—a fiancé, my family...'

'Three brothers—' Daniel's green eyes bored into hers '—two of whom still live at home. Your youngest brother, Cahil, suffered a head injury ten years ago. I believe he's now his school's football-team star striker.'

For the first time in as long as she could remember, Colleen was speechless.

'You're engaged to your childhood sweetheart, Ciaran, but don't live together,' Daniel continued. 'You've started to build your own house and when you have enough money to finish it then you'll get married. Some may think that's old fashioned...' he paused '...unusual, even.'

Anger knotted in her stomach. To think she'd felt sorry for him! Research into her suitability as a nurse for his son was one thing—even if she hadn't applied for the job—but digging into her personal life? That was too much.

'How dare you snoop into my life…?'

'I prefer to call it research and I dare because I want to do what is best for my son.'

'No doubt you do—but it still doesn't give you the right to—'

'You could get a six-month sabbatical from your job. What I'm willing to pay you will be more than enough for you to finish building your house, with plenty left over for a wedding. In addition, I'm also prepared to make a substantial contribution to your rehab unit. I looked into their accounts and my donation would enable them to buy some much-needed equipment. I've spoken to your boss and he's agreed to release you for up to six months—by the way, he has nothing but praise for your nursing skills. As far as being separated from your fiancé and your family is concerned, you'll have as much time off as you need once Harry is on the mend and I'll even arrange a private plane to fly you back to Dublin whenever you want.'

Colleen let out a whoosh of air and sat back in her seat. 'You've thought of everything haven't you?'

'I've had to. For Harry's sake, I will do whatever it takes to make him better.' Daniel swallowed and for a second the mask slipped again and she saw such naked pain in his eyes that she sucked in a breath.

'My son needs me,' Daniel continued. 'And I need you. Help me get my son back. Don't think of doing it

for me, if that makes it easier. Think of doing it for him.'
For a few seconds silence hung between them. 'Please.'

Colleen studied him for a moment. She had the impression that this man wasn't used to pleading. His insistent green eyes and his obvious distress about his son drew her in, making her want to help him, but still she hesitated. He was asking a great deal and she didn't know enough about Harry to know whether she was the right person for the job.

Daniel pulled another photograph from his pocket. 'This was taken three weeks ago.'

Colleen took the second photograph from him. Harry was lying in a hospital bed. Despite the tube running from his nostril he still looked beautiful with his silver-blond hair and smooth pale skin. Her stomach twisted at the blankness in his green eyes.

Her mind spiralled back to those early days when Cahil had been injured. He, too, had lain in a hospital bed, looking up at them with unseeing eyes. The doctors hadn't held out much hope. But Mammy had refused to give up on her child. She had insisted on taking Cahil home and as a family they had worked around the clock to coax him back to health. It had taken months to get him to feed himself and even longer before he was walking and talking again, but now, as Daniel pointed out, he was recovered enough to play for the school football team.

Daniel must have seen her hesitation. 'At least say you'll meet him,' he pressed. 'Come to London with me. If, after you've met him, you still feel you can't take up my offer, I promise you, there will be no hard feelings. Your unit will get its donation irrespective of what you decide.'

Before she had a chance to answer, Daniel's mobile rang. He looked at it and frowned. 'I'm sorry, but I really have to take this.' He stood up and headed for the door. 'I'll just be a few minutes.'

As soon as he'd stepped outside, Trish scurried over to the table and sat down opposite Colleen.

'Who the hell is that gorgeous hunk of flesh? Why haven't you told me about him? God, Col, I didn't know you had it in you!'

Colleen's head was still full of images of Cahil and Harry. She shook her head to clear it and looked outside to where Daniel was talking on his phone.

'What? Oh, that's Daniel Frobisher. He wants me to go to London to be his son's private nurse.'

Trish looked disappointed. 'I thought he was your new lover.'

Colleen knew she shouldn't really be shocked. Trish always said the first thing that came into her head. She glared at her best friend.

'Have you forgotten I'm engaged?' she said, indignant.

Trish let out a whoosh of air. 'And have you forgotten about the doubts you've been having? That in itself is a good reason to go to London. It will give you space to make up your mind about how you really feel about Ciaran.'

Perhaps Trish was right. Ever since she and Ciaran had become engaged, Colleen had been feeling unsure. She should be on top of the world, instead of feeling as if she was being dragged towards a deep hole.

'It's only pre-wedding jitters,' Colleen said, more emphatically than she felt. 'I do love Ciaran, of course I do. I feel comfortable with him. Isn't that what marriage is about? Mutual respect, shared interests…?' She glanced towards where Daniel was standing, still talking into the phone. She couldn't imagine anyone feeling comfortable with him. He was too intense, too restless, too… Just too much of everything!

'Heavens to glory, girl!' Trish said. 'Feeling comfortable with someone is not a basis for marriage. If you want comfort, why don't you buy yourself a pair of slippers? Oops, I forgot. You do have slippers. Those crazy things that look like you're wearing two dead lambs on your feet. Where's the excitement with you and Ciaran? The glamour? The passion? The can't-keep-your-hands-off-each-other kind? Where's the drinking champagne at lunch time?'

'I don't like champagne,' Colleen said with another nervous glance outside. If Daniel came back inside, he'd hear everything Trish had to say. Her friend was in full flow and Colleen knew she wouldn't stop until she'd had her say. 'I prefer tea, as you well know.'

'See! That's exactly what I mean. You don't *have* to like champagne to drink it. Most people drink it because they like the bubbles and because it makes them act all silly.'

'I don't like acting silly.'

Trish's expression grew serious. 'No, you don't. You used to, though. Now you never let your hair down. Life is supposed to be fun, Col. Look, I'm not saying Ciaran isn't a nice guy, but nice is the operative word. You need someone to pull you back out of that safe, cosy, insular world you choose to live in these days. How old are you, Col? Twenty-six? And have you travelled, made wild, passionate love on a beach, bought a pair of shoes you couldn't afford because they made you feel a million dollars? No, you wear bunny slippers and dress like a farmer's daughter most of the time and your idea of a big night out is a trip to the local pub to play pool with Ciaran and your brothers. Not exactly the romance of the century, is it?'

Colleen squirmed in her chair. God, Trish made her and Ciaran sound so boring. It was too much, even from Trish!

'But I am a farmer's daughter. Anyway Ciaran likes me the way I am.'

'You're a beautiful woman, Col; anyone would give their eye teeth to look like you—which is stunning, God help the rest of us—whatever you chose to wear. But when was the last time Ciaran looked at you? I mean, *really* looked at you?'

Instead of Ciaran's face, an image of dark green eyes, drilling into hers, flashed into her head. She glanced outside. It was clear Daniel was coming to the end of his call. She had to shut Trish up before he came back inside.

'I wouldn't dream of making love on the beach,' she hissed. 'Sand would get everywhere and someone might see. But of course, if I wanted to, I could do that with Ciaran. We might yet.'

The door swished open and Daniel was walking towards them. Trish stood up and bent over Colleen.

'The question is, *do* you want to?' she whispered.

Colleen was feeling decidedly unsettled when Daniel sat down in the chair Trish had just vacated. Unwelcome though Trish's word were, they only echoed what Colleen had been thinking these last few months. Perhaps Trish was right and Daniel's offer was just what she needed? Time, on her own, to think.

'I'm sorry about that,' he said. 'I didn't expect the call to take so long.' He smiled at her and unaccountably her heart thumped against her ribs. 'Have you had time to come to a decision?'

Damn! Why did the way he looked at her make her feel as if they were the only two people in the room?

Daniel's green eyes brought back the image of Harry lying on the hospital bed. Colleen's heart twisted. She knew she couldn't walk away, not without meeting Harry at the very least. Ciaran always said she was a soft touch.

'I'll come to London and meet your son,' she said, finally. 'I'll make my decision then. However, if, for any reason, I don't think I'm the best person to care for your son, either because he doesn't react well to me, or because I think he'll be better off in a rehab unit, then I won't take the job. Is that understood?'

There was no mistaking the relief on Daniel's face. 'In that case,' he said, signalling for the bill, 'shall we get going?'

CHAPTER TWO

'GET going? What now? Right this minute?'

'No time like the present. I need to know whether you're going to take the job. You're off duty for the weekend, aren't you?'

Was there anything he didn't know about her life?

Daniel was flicking through his wallet, otherwise he would have noticed that Colleen's jaw had dropped. She closed it quickly.

'I can't go *right now*.'

'Why not?'

'Because I need to pack, make a couple of calls, have a sleep.' She couldn't just go to London at the drop of a hat. Trips needed careful planning. 'Besides don't you need to make plane reservations?'

Daniel dropped a twenty-pound note on the table and, without waiting for his change, took Colleen's elbow and steered her towards the door. This elbow-steering thing he had was beginning to get out of hand. She cast a desperate glance at Trish who grinned and held two thumbs up. So no help there then.

'I have a plane. It's waiting for us at the airport. I'll take you home and you can pick up anything you might need. You can sleep on the plane.'

'But..' Her voice come out as a squeak.

Daniel held the door open and ushered her out. He stopped and stared down at her with his mesmerising eyes. 'Look, you agreed to meet Harry. The hospital wants to discharge him on Monday, Tuesday at the latest. If I don't take him home, they'll transfer him to the nearest rehab unit and I'm not having that.' He smiled tightly. 'I promise you, I'll have you back home tomorrow at the latest.'

He opened the car door and once again she was bundled inside. But there was no reason she could think of, apart from the ones she had raised and he'd swept aside, not to go with him. Ciaran was going to Wales with her brothers for the weekend to watch some rugby match. It hadn't even occurred to him to ask her whether she wanted to go, too. Not that she did, but it would have been nice to be asked. Come to think of it, when had she and Ciaran last done something on their own? Something on the spur of the moment, something romantic? Once more, she felt a sinking sensation in the pit of her stomach.

'Okay, I'll come, but I have to go home and collect some stuff first.' At least Trish couldn't accuse her of not being spontaneous this time. Truth was, it felt good. Exciting. She would text Ciaran and let him know she was going to London. Maybe that would rock him out of his complacency.

'Good girl,' Daniel said. 'Where to?'

Good girl! What was she—a puppy?

Colleen gave him the address and, as the car moved away, she sent Ciaran and her mother a quick text telling them she was going to London and would call them later. Colleen usually went home for her days off, even when Ciaran wasn't there, but wasn't Mammy always telling her that she should stay in Dublin and enjoy herself with her friends sometimes? Why was everyone so determined to tell her to enjoy herself? It wasn't as if she went around with a face like a camel's behind all the time. Sheesh!

When the car pulled up outside her flat, Colleen jumped out and ran up the step, telling Daniel she'd be half an hour. To her consternation, when she stopped to open the communal door with her key, she realised that Daniel was standing behind her. The faint scent of expensive aftershave drifted up her nose and she could almost feel the energy vibrating from his body.

For some reason her hand was shaking and she struggled to get the key to work. Daniel leaned over her shoulder. 'Let me,' he said. The touch of his hand on hers sent that electric shock up her arm and she dropped her hand, letting him take charge of the key. Now she was enclosed by the circle of his arms and she had to concentrate hard to stop her breath coming out in gasps. Anyone would think she'd never been close to a man in her life.

'I thought we agreed you would stay in the car,' she said. Annoyingly, despite her efforts, she still sounded breathless.

'Did we?' he said, mildly. 'I don't remember that.'

Daniel followed her up the three flights of stairs to her flat. This time she managed to open the door first time. She turned to him. She didn't want him inside her home. She needed some time to compose herself. 'Thank you. I can cope fine from here.' She thought she managed the note of sarcasm perfectly.

To her dismay he ignored her and followed her inside her studio apartment. Couldn't the man take a hint? But she could hardly order him out of her flat without appearing rude, and she was never rude.

Spying a pair of tights lying discarded on the arm of a chair, she hurried across and scooped them up. Then, through the open door of the bathroom, she noticed her panties and a towel on the floor so she hurried over to scoop them up, too, before shoving the whole lot into the washing machine. Her coffee cup from last night and her supper dishes were still in the sink, but she'd been in a rush to get to work after being held up by a fascinating programme on the television on anteaters.

'Nice place,' he said drily. He picked up a magazine from the floor. *The Bride*. His lips twitched. 'Interesting dress she's wearing.'

Colleen snatched it from his hands and shoved it on top of the pile she'd still to read. It tottered there for a moment before the whole lot slid to the ground, fanning out on a heap on the floor. Knowing her face was probably beetroot, she took a deep breath. She never, ever got flustered. What the heck had got into her?

Daniel grinned at her and for a second she thought her heart had stopped beating.

'I'll be back in a sec,' she said and sought the refuge of her bedroom. She closed the door and leaned against it. *Look*, she told herself, firmly, *he's only a man in a fancy suit, even if he does have a heartbreaking smile*. God, God, God. Where had the last thought come from?

She set about packing her weekend bag, forcing herself to concentrate on remembering everything. Slippers? Check. Clothes, including clean underwear? Check. Toiletries? She'd pick them up from the bathroom on her way out. What else? Did a person need a passport to travel on a private plane?

She poked her head out of the door. Daniel had made himself comfortable on one of her chairs and was flicking through *The Bride* magazine, an incredulous look on his face.

'Do I need my passport?' she asked.

'Yes. Er…Dublin isn't part of the UK, if you remember?'

Colleen slammed the door shut. Now he'd think her an idiot too! By the time they got to London, he'd probably have decided to employ someone else. But why should she think that? He was interested in her for her professional skills—not interviewing her as a potential wife!

Once her bag was packed, she looked in the mirror to check her hair. She was pale with dark smudges under her eyes, but there was nothing she could do about that. Sleep was what she needed. In her feverish haste to pack her bags so that she could get Daniel out of her flat her hair had come loose from its braid and wisps were falling into her eyes. She grabbed her hair brush and redid the plait, making sure every last one of her unruly locks was contained. Then she added a slick of lipstick and she was ready. Or as ready as she'd ever be. For once she wished she had listened to Trish on one of their many futile shopping expeditions—at least as far as Trish was concerned—and had bought a dress she could have worn. Something that would give her confidence.

Daniel got to his feet when she came back out of her bedroom with the slow indolence of a lion waking up from a sleep.

'I just have to get my wash bag and I'm ready,' she said.

He took her overnight bag from her hand. 'Let's go, then.'

Daniel slid a look at Colleen as they were driven towards the airport. She wasn't anything like he'd expected.

When she'd turned Haversham down he'd been shocked. No one had ever refused to do something for Daniel before. And the salary—one most people would have found it hard to refuse—hadn't made the slightest difference. Her refusal had made him more determined to secure her services than he'd been before. And he'd been keen then. Especially after the ringing endorsement her old consultant at Guy's had given her. 'She's a tiger,' he'd said, 'and she never gives up. Don't let that innocent face fool you. What Colleen wants, she gets. Nothing and no one stands in the way of Colleen McCulloch when it comes to what is best for her patients. She's not always conventional, but she's always right. That's what makes her special.'

Somehow he'd imagined the redoubtable Nurse McCulloch, whom everyone he'd spoken to had praised to the sky, to look older, to be more severe. Instead she looked like a teenager with her curls escaping from its elastic band and falling in wisps over her face that she constantly and ineffectually tried to tuck back in. He liked the way her mouth turned up at the corners as if in a permanent smile, even the way her eyes flashed when she was annoyed about something. He'd even liked the way her flat looked. Okay, some might say that it looked as if the occupant had been fighting with a pack of wild

animals that had found their way into her home, but
there was a good feeling about her small flat with its
bunches of wild flowers arranged haphazardly in jam
jars. It reminded him somehow of his mother's holiday
home in Dorset. The memory made his stomach clench.
That cottage had been Eleanor and Harry's home until
the accident. Now his son was lying in a hospital bed,
unaware that *his* mother had died and that all he had
left was a father whom he barely knew.

Daniel stole another look at Colleen. He was more
determined than ever to have her as Harry's nurse. He
hoped to hell she lived up to her reputation.

CHAPTER THREE

So this was how the other half lived? Colleen thought, looking around the interior of the plane. If she were honest, a tiny little bit of her was impressed. Only a minuscule bit, mind. The other part of her felt slightly ridiculous having the attentions of a stewardess all to themselves on the tiny, if luxurious, twin-propped plane. And ridiculously under-dressed in her boy jeans and T-shirt, carrying nothing but an imitation designer handbag over her shoulder.

Almost as soon as they'd taken off, Daniel had taken out some papers and a laptop. Once she'd had a good look around and got over the excitement of being on a private plane—and she couldn't pretend for the life of her that she wasn't—even if it might make her look like a country bumpkin in Daniel's eyes—she'd fallen asleep.

She'd only woken when Daniel had bent over her and whispered that they were landing and she needed to fasten her seat belt. For a moment when she'd opened her eyes, she couldn't remember where she was. She'd been having a lovely dream. A dream where she was behind someone on a horse and they were galloping off somewhere. As she stared groggily into Daniel's eyes, she realised with a guilty start that the person on the horse hadn't been Ciaran. It had been someone with green eyes—the man looking down at her, in fact.

She had hidden her embarrassment by escaping to the small onboard toilet and splashing her face with cold water.

When they were escorted through Heathrow airport and towards a sleek, black, stretch limousine. Colleen noticed people nudging each other, puzzlement etched on their faces as they tried to place them. Daniel with his snazzy suit and air of confidence had to be someone famous and as for Colleen, she must be some pop or film star—someone of importance—surely under-dressing to fool the media?

The thought made her smile. She might as well enjoy her moment in the limelight—it was probably the only one she would have until her wedding day.

They sat in silence as they were driven to the hospital. Daniel had his laptop out again and was deeply immersed in whatever he was reading. She'd never met anyone quite so focused on the task in hand before. One minute his attention was completely concentrated on making her do what he wanted, the next minute he was totally engrossed in whatever was on that laptop of his. She simply couldn't make him out. But it was his son that concerned her. How badly had his brain been injured? What was his prognosis? She wouldn't take this job unless she was sure she could help him.

Whizzing along the motorway seeing London city silhouetted in the distance, Colleen felt a thrill of excitement. She'd always planned to come back to London, but somehow the opportunity had never arisen. Ciaran wasn't the adventurous type. He always said that he didn't see the point in travelling to foreign places when you had everything you needed on your own doorstep.

Although she'd never admit it to Trish, sometimes Colleen longed for a bit more excitement. Was she just being foolish for secretly wanting Ciaran to whisk her away to Paris for a weekend? As he'd said, it'd be a waste of money when they needed every penny to get their house finished before the wedding. But a girl could dream, couldn't she?

The car swung sharply to the right, pulling up outside the familiar buildings of Guy's, the hospital where Colleen had trained. She knew from what he'd told her that Harry had been in ITU before being transferred to the high-dependency unit and then to the paediatric ward.

In the ward, posters covered the walls in an attempt to make the unit as cheerful as possible. Every room was a single and a large bright day room filled with toys lead off to the left.

Daniel paused at the very last room and held a finger to his lips. 'We have to go in quietly. Harry gets startled by any loud noise and it unsettles him.'

'Why don't you go in to see Harry, first, while I chat to the nurses?' Colleen suggested. 'Then I'll come in and say hello.'

Daniel nodded briefly and Colleen went to find the nurse in charge of the ward. When she explained who she was and why she was there, she was directed to an office. A woman with short dark hair looked up from her paperwork and held out a hand. 'I'm Sister Lipton.'

Sister Lipton waited until Colleen was sitting down

before she continued. 'So you're the person who's to be Harry's private nurse?' she said. 'Mr Frobisher has told us of his plans.'

Colleen didn't bother to correct her. She had yet to decide whether she was going to take Harry on.

'I have to tell you that I think taking Harry home at this point is a mistake,' Sister Lipton continued.

'Can I ask why?'

The nurse frowned. 'Apart from the fact that there are excellent rehab facilities in London, there is the small matter of the fact that Mr Frobisher doesn't seem to know how to interact with his son.'

'Oh?'

'Harry was in ITU for a week with a GCS score of three. During that time Mr Frobisher, perfectly understandably, refused to leave his son's bedside. But instead of talking to Harry, as we suggested, Mr Frobisher mostly spent his time working on his laptop. Furthermore, I gather he caused the nurses some problems with his demands.' She sighed. 'He insisted on bringing in specialists of his own to assess his son. In fact, he had all sorts of demands. Some of them reasonable. Some less so.'

Colleen hid a smile. She had no doubt that Daniel hadn't been the easiest relative to have around. But what Sister Lipton said about Daniel not interacting with Harry was more of a worry. Nursing staff could only do so much; the rest was up to the patient and their loved ones.

'Mr Frobisher tried the same sort of thing when we moved Harry here once the lad was stable,' Sister Lipton continued. 'I'm afraid he and I clashed more than once. In many ways I won't be sorry to see the back of him.'

'But you don't think he should have Harry at home? I can assure you that I've worked with patients like Harry for many years and Mr Frobisher is fully committed to ensuring that Harry receives as good quality care at home as he does here.'

'That may be,' Sister Lipton said. 'But it's Harry's attitude to his father that worries me. When Harry first regained consciousness he was very agitated. As you know, we see that a great deal with patients like Harry, but it didn't take long for us to notice that it was his father's presence that seemed to distress the boy. We asked Mr Frobisher not to spend so much time on the ward. He wasn't happy, as you can imagine, but even he could see he wasn't helping matters. And as we expected, Harry was—and is—much calmer when his father isn't around.'

Colleen decided to let that pass for the moment. She would make up her own mind. As it stood, Daniel was all the family Harry had left. No one should be keeping the pair apart. Besides, she was getting irritated with Sister Lipton's assumption that she knew best. It had been the same when Cahil had been in hospital. No one had wanted Mammy to take him home, but nothing could stop her mother when her mind was made up. It was one of the ways they were exactly alike. And taking Cahil home, surrounding him with the people who loved him most, had been the right thing to do.

'What can you tell me about Harry's treatment and progress to date?' she asked.

Sister Lipton took her through a detailed summary of Harry's medical treatment. 'As far as we can tell, there is no reason why Harry shouldn't make a good recovery over time. There appears to be no lasting damage to his brain. In fact, we're a little surprised that he hasn't progressed quicker. He seems to understand simple instructions, but we'd really be expecting him to be saying more than the odd word by now. He also has some movement, but not as much as we would expect at this stage.'

'We both know that patients even with apparently identical injuries can progress at different rates. No brain injury is exactly the same,' Colleen said. 'I've seen many cases, as I'm sure you have, where recovery is sudden and dramatic. Perhaps this will be the pattern for Harry?'

No doubt Sister Lipton was an excellent nurse but the way she had spoken about Daniel had made Colleen's blood boil. Just like patients, relatives were different when it came to how they dealt with their loved ones' injuries. Perhaps Lipton was the kind of nurse who expected the relatives to treat her with deference. Frankly Colleen preferred the relatives who made it their business to be involved with their child's care. And despite Daniel's high-handedness, she was sure he only wanted the best for his child.

When Colleen had finished speaking to Sister Lipton, she went along to see Harry.

With the blinds drawn, she could barely make out the frail figure lying on the bed in a tangle of sheets. An older woman in a nurse's uniform was checking Harry's blood pressure while Daniel stood looking out of the window.

Careful not to make any sudden noise, Colleen approached the young boy and her heart constricted. Even in sleep, Harry's forehead was creased in a frown. His legs and arms twitched, as if he was being chased by the hounds of hell. Poor mite.

As if sensing her presence, Harry's eyes slowly opened and stared right at her. His eyes were the same startling green as his father's, but where Daniel's were sharp and focused, Harry's were clouded with confusion.

'Hi, Harry,' Colleen said softly, 'My name is Colleen. I'm a nurse and I look after people who have hurt their heads.'

Harry's eyes shifted from Colleen to Daniel and back again.

Keeping her voice as soothing as possible, Colleen continued. 'May I sit down on your bed, Harry? That's great. There's no need to be scared, I'm here because your dad asked me to come and meet you. He loves you very much.'

Mutely, Harry continued to stare at her.

'Harry, I want to hold your hands—is that okay?' She slipped her fingers round his. They felt stiff and cold. 'That's excellent, Harry. Now squeeze as tight as you can, sweetheart. Squeeze as if I've just pinched your MP3 player and all your favourite tunes.'

The minutes passed and still Harry continued to stare at her. Colleen willed him with every fibre of her being to respond. *Please, Harry, come on, you can do it, darling. Squeeze, squeeze.*

She hadn't realised she'd been holding her breath until she felt the slightest of pressure from Harry's fingers. His eyes locked on hers, only for a moment, but long enough for her to see the fear in his eyes. She held the boy's hand until he relaxed and the fear gradually receded. She already knew there was no way she could walk away from this child.

'That's excellent, Harry. Well done. We're going to be great pals, I just know it. In a few days we're going to take you home with us.'

Harry's eyes shifted until he was looking over Colleen's shoulders. She was aware that Daniel had come to stand behind her.

'Go!' Harry said clearly.

'What is it, Harry? Do you want me to go?' Colleen asked.

With an enormous effort Harry raised his hand until he was pointing at Daniel. It was obvious that he wanted his father to leave the room.

Colleen turned around. Daniel looked shaken. 'Why don't you wait for us outside?' she said.

Daniel hesitated. 'Go on,' Colleen said. 'I'll only be a moment.'

When Daniel left she turned to face Harry again.

'What is it, Harry? Don't you want to go home and be with your father? I'll be there, too.'

Harry looked at her. A tear slipped from his eye and Colleen brushed it away.

'Mum,' he said. 'Want Mum.'

'Oh, Harry, I'm so sorry your mum isn't here. But your dad wants you at home with him. Together we're going to do everything we can to make you better. You can speak a little now, so there's no reason your speech won't come on. And you can move your arm, so with a bit of work we should be able to get much more movement back. It'll mean hard work, but your dad and I will be there to help you every step of the way. C'mon, what do you say? Shall we give it a go?'

Green eyes studied her for a moment. ''kay,' Harry said finally, before turning away and closing his eyes.

Outside Daniel was pacing up and down, looking as if he wanted to find something to kick.

'Maybe he should stay here,' he said. 'He clearly doesn't feel comfortable with me.' It was the first time Colleen had seen Daniel look anything less than certain and her heart went out to him.

'The brain injury could be causing confusion, or it could be that he simply doesn't recognise you. Patients with head injuries often suffer from memory loss on and off for quite some time. When we get him home and he has his familiar belongings around him, I'm sure he'll settle down.'

A look of relief crossed Daniel's face. 'You said "we". Does that mean you'll take the job?'

'It does. I think I can help.'

Daniel pulled a hand through his hair and studied her. It was a few minutes before he spoke. 'At least I got one thing right. I found you. Thank you for agreeing to stay. Harry needs you.'

And something tells me you do, too, boyo.

'Okay,' she said, 'let's make plans to get your son home.'

CHAPTER FOUR

COLLEEN had flown home later that day on Daniel's plane. Moving to London for what could be months necessitated more than the few belongings she'd packed. And if Harry was to be discharged on Tuesday she needed to be back in London tomorrow evening at the latest. Daniel had offered to send someone to her flat to pack her things for her, but she'd refused. No one was going to trawl through her cupboards except her. After she'd packed and cleared out her fridge, she had phoned Ciaran to let him know what she'd decided. He'd been disappointingly blasé about the fact he wouldn't see her for a few weeks.

She was being daft, of course she was. Ciaran loved her. Just because he didn't create fireworks because he might not see her very often over the next few months was no reason to feel a little…disappointed? Deflated? Unappreciated?

Relieved?

If anything, the last twenty-four hours had deepened the feeling of unease she felt whenever she thought about her impending marriage.

As before, she flew back to London on Daniel's private plane. Her third flight in less than two days. She could get used to this way of travelling. No endless queueing for her bags to be checked, or to go through security or to have her passport examined. Everything happened as if by magic. As soon as she stepped into the arrivals' hall, Daniel's driver was waiting to take her suitcase, his car right outside, so she barely had to walk.

Colleen reached for the car door before the chauffeur had a chance to open it for her. She looked up at him and smiled. 'I'll lose the use of my own arms if I don't use them.'

'Yes, madam.'

'Oh, no. None of that madam stuff. Please call me Colleen.'

'Yes, madam.'

Oh dear.

Suddenly the driver grinned and held out his hand. 'I'm Mike.'

She shook it, feeling relieved. Much more of that madamising malarkey and she would have gone crazy.

They had driven through London before coming to a halt in front of large wrought-iron gates that swung open as if sensing their arrival.

Once again, Colleen got to the door before Mike could do it for her.

'I don't suppose I can carry my own bags?' she said to him.

'No need. They'll be taken up to your room and unpacked for you,' Mike replied, taking her embarrassingly bedraggled-looking bags from the boot.

Colleen looked up at the most enormous mansion she'd ever seen. It was like something out of *Country House Rescue*, except she had no doubt that there would be no crumbling plasterwork or peeling paint in Daniel Frobisher's palace. Hooking her handbag over her shoulder, she skipped up the sweep of steps. As if by magic, the huge front door swung open, revealing a man in his early fifties, wearing the same black suit, white shirt and tie as the uniform of the chauffeur.

'Welcome to Carrington Hall, Miss McCulloch.'

Colleen held her hand out. 'Mr Haversham, I presume?'

The man couldn't have looked more shocked had she attacked him with a deadly weapon. Colleen let her hand drop.

'Mr Haversham is Mr Frobisher's personal assistant. I'm Burton, Mr Frobisher's butler.'

Did people really still have butlers? This felt more and more like she was in a period costume drama.

'Please call me, Colleen. Don't you have a first name, Mr Burton?'

'Just Burton, miss. Please follow me,' the butler said, taking her bags from Mike. 'Mr Frobisher sends his apologies. I am to tell you that he is unable to welcome you personally, but unfortunately he has pressing business to attend to. He says he'll see you at dinner.'

Colleen hid her dismay. Daniel had made all that effort to get her here in the first place, but couldn't spare the time to greet her! If he truly cared about Harry, shouldn't his son and not a business deal be his first priority? The sympathy she'd been feeling towards him faded. If he thought he could hand Harry over to her and leave it at that, he'd made a mistake. She was here to help him care for his son and Daniel's involvement was absolutely critical. She had to make that clear and the sooner the better.

'He had pressing business, did he? Well, I would like you to get Mr Frobisher on the telephone and let him know that his presence is needed here.'

Burton raised an eyebrow. 'I'm afraid that won't be possible. Mr Frobisher does not care to be interrupted when he's working.' Was she mistaken or did Burton shudder slightly, as if remembering a time when he had made the mistake of interrupting his boss? Well, she wouldn't be so easily intimidated.

'If you could let me have his telephone number, then I'll call him myself.' Colleen scrambled around in her bag for her phone, eventually finding it caught up in some sweet papers. One day she would have to find the time to give her bag a good clear-out. She waved her mobile at Burton. 'Number, please?'

This time, the penguin-suited man did shudder. And folded his arms. And looked at her with unmistakable resolve. 'As I said, Mr Frobisher will see you at dinner. In the meantime, maybe you'd like to see your room?' He looked at her and his lip curled. 'And freshen up. Perhaps change?'

The cheek. There was nothing wrong with her freshly washed jeans and T-shirt. She was here to work—not look like something from a catwalk.

'I'd rather go straight to Harry's room to make sure everything's in order,' Colleen said stiffly. She'd only been here ten minutes and already she was wondering what she'd let herself in for. 'That's why I'm here. I understand from what Mr Frobisher said that his son will be coming home the day after tomorrow. I'm sure there is a fair bit to organise before then.'

Burton jumped back, startled, as she swept past him. The marbled hall with its high-vaulted ceilings and imposing staircase took Colleen's breath away. This was more like the entrance to a private hotel than a house. But despite the grandeur, it wasn't a place she would call home. It was too dark and gloomy with its wooden panelled walls and deep-green wallpaper.

'But, miss, Mr Frobisher insisted…'

'Mmm…well, see, here's the thing.' Colleen waved a finger in the air. 'I'm here for Harry. Everyone—and I mean everyone—is second in importance to that. So, which way to Harry's room?'

'If you wait here, miss, I'll just get Mr Frobisher for you. He's working from home today,' Burton replied, regaining his composure.

So Daniel wasn't even at work? He was here all the time, yet couldn't be bothered to make the time to greet her. If possible, she felt even more uneasy. None of this matched the little she knew of Daniel. In Dublin and at the hospital, she hadn't doubted for a second that he cared about his son.

She heard Daniel's footsteps on the marbled floor before she saw him. Somehow she'd expected him to be suited and booted again, not wearing faded denim jeans and an open-necked pearl-grey shirt. His dark hair was kind of mussy, as if he'd been pulling his hands through it, and he had the beginnings of a five-o'clock shadow. It made him look more approachable and really quite sexy in an uptight British way.

'Colleen, welcome. Did you have a good flight?' he asked, with only the briefest of smiles.

'Everything about my trip was great, thanks,' Colleen replied, coolly.

'I gather you wish to speak to me. What is so important that it can't wait?'

'I'd like to see Harry's room, but Mr Burton appears reluctant to show it to me. He seems to want to pack me off to my room so I can change. I tried to tell him that I don't need to rest or change or freshen up, or whatever it is that he seems to think I need to do, but he's not having it. I'm not in the least bit tired, I'm almost as clean as I was when I showered this morning and I want to see Harry's room. Is that a problem?'

A smile, more genuine this time, crossed Daniel's face.

'Of course not. Burton was just following instructions. Guests normally like to settle in to their rooms when they arrive.'

'But I'm not a guest, sure I'm not.'

Something glinted in Daniel's eyes. If she didn't know better, she would have sworn it was laughter. He regarded her calmly without saying anything. She already that knew that he wasn't exactly a chatterbox. But if he thought his silence would make her back down meekly, he had another think coming.

'Here's the thing,' she continued doggedly, trying to ignore the way her heart was racing, 'I'm here to do the best job I can for Harry, but in order to do that—what I say goes. Do we understand each other?' Colleen held her breath as she waited for Daniel to reply. Despite the instant connection she'd felt with Harry, she couldn't work here unless she had free rein to do what she thought was best for him. She needed to make that absolutely clear from the start. Daniel studied her through narrowed eyes.

'Perfectly. But let me make something clear, too. If,

at any time, I feel you are not up to the job, I will find someone else.'

He was pinning her with that look again. Her heart was galloping like one of the horses in the field back home. Jeepers, life in this household wasn't going to be easy.

'Have you forgotten that you were the one who hounded me to take the job and not the other way round? But that's fine by me, just as long as whatever happens, you don't renege on your donation to the rehab unit.'

'I never go back on my promises, Colleen.' The words were quietly spoken, but held a thread of steel. 'And something tells me you don't either.'

Colleen just couldn't make Daniel out. For two pins she'd insist on being taken back to Ireland. If it weren't for the fact that Daniel was right—she never backed out of a promise. She'd told Harry she'd be here when he came home and she'd keep that promise.

'Despite the way you went about securing my services, I've agreed to care for your son and I would never, ever let my—er—relationship...' *damn, that was the wrong word, but it was too late now to find a better one* '...with a parent affect the way I treat a patient.' And that was true. Even if she'd never felt like kicking someone before.

His smile was catlike. 'At least we understand each other.'

Colleen let her breath out slowly, willing her heart rate to return to normal. 'Okay, now that that's out of the way, shall we get on?'

Daniel looked at his watch. 'It's okay, Burton, I can manage from here.' He turned his gaze back to Colleen. She'd forgotten just how green those penetrating eyes of his were—even when he was frowning. 'I can give you ten minutes. Follow me. Harry's bedroom is on the second floor.'

Colleen remained silent for the rest of the way up the curving stairs and along the carpeted hallway lined with old-fashioned portraits of stuffy men in uniforms and aristocratic women in evening dresses. Daniel threw open the very last room at the end of the long corridor.

'This is Harry's room,' he said over his shoulder. 'I've installed a hospital bed as you can see. You're in the suite next door.'

Colleen glanced round, taking in the bare walls and almost-empty shelves. An electric wheelchair stood in front of the unlit fireplace. She walked over to the bookshelf and tilted her head to the side, reading the titles along the spines: *Great Expectations*, *The Decline and Fall of the Roman Empire*, a couple of other tomes and a raft of other titles she didn't recognise. Either Harry had unusual tastes for a twelve year old or these books didn't belong to him.

She could sense Daniel's impatience as he waited until she'd finished.

'Would you like to see your room now?' he asked.

'There's plenty of time for that later,' Colleen replied.

He shrugged. 'All right. You'll find some uniforms laid out for you.' He gave her an appraising look. 'I'm pretty sure they'll fit perfectly.'

'I'm pretty sure they will, too, but I won't be wearing a uniform.' She pulled the heavy curtains back from the window and gazed down below. It was hard to believe they were in the centre of London—with the greenery in the garden below the concrete buildings of the city seemed miles away. She turned back to face him. 'It's important that Harry feels at home. Me wearing a uniform is not going to give him that impression. He's already spent almost two months in hospital and I doubt he wants to be reminded of his experience there.'

Daniel tipped his head. 'I see your point. It didn't occur to me.' He pulled his hand through his hair—she'd been right in her guess about where the mussy hair came from . 'Clearly, I'm making a pig's ear of this.'

His words, along with his baffled expression, disarmed her. He was after all, a father who wanted the best for his child. But she didn't want to feel sorry for him—she already sensed that there was going to be more than one battle of wills between them. In many ways it was easier to deal with the arrogant, self-assured Daniel of earlier.

'Don't be too hard on yourself,' she said gently, 'you've never been in this situation before.' She took a last look round the room. 'Okay, that's fine—I've seen enough. Could I see the rest of the house, please?'

She followed Daniel back down the stairs and across the vast hallway. He swung open the first door on the right, leading Colleen into a large lounge. Heavily polished rosewood tables complimented several worn chocolate-brown leather couches, which framed an enormous, slightly threadbare Oriental carpet in front of a head-height marble fireplace. Surely with all his wealth Daniel could get a new carpet and some modern furniture? The rug on the floor had clearly seen better days. She pointed to the fireplace. 'Grief, Santa wouldn't have any problem coming down your chimney, would he?'

Daniel didn't answer, but she thought she saw that

glint in his eyes again. There was a definite twitch of his lips.

Bay windows streamed in light with a broad view of the lush green garden bursting with flowers and shrubbery that she'd noticed from upstairs.

'As I said in the contract I faxed over to you, there is a heated swimming pool in the basement as well as a gym that you are welcome to use. You may have your meals in your room, or with Harry, or in the dining room. I'll leave that up to you. I've engaged night nurses to look after Harry from eight in the evening to eight in the morning, and you will be free to do whatever you wish between those hours. You may take every second weekend off and my plane will be at your disposal should you wish to go back to Ireland for the weekend. A car will always be available to you—'

'I am able to read, Daniel,' Colleen said with a smile. 'The contract was very detailed.' She paused. 'How easy is it to get down to the pool?'

'It's down a flight of steps and along a corridor.'

'Any chance of getting a lift installed?' she asked. 'Then we could take Harry down to the pool for his physio. A lot of patients find the water makes it easier for them to move their arms and legs.'

'I'll get Haversham on to it straight away. Anything else?'

'What's through the double doors there?' Colleen pointed to the middle of the room.

'The dining room. Look, if you want a tour of the house I'll ask Burton to show you around. I should get back to work. I'm expecting a conference call in…' he glanced at his watch '…five minutes. We can talk later. Over dinner, if you care to join me.'

'Can I see the dining room?'

With a barely concealed sigh of irritation, Daniel waved his hand. 'Help yourself.'

Colleen pushed open the doors and grinned. This room was perfect. 'Daniel, would you come in here, please?'

'What is it?'

'I think this should be Harry's new room.'

'I've just shown you his bedroom—it's what he's familiar with.'

Colleen shook her head. 'It's too far away from the rest of the household. And it will be difficult getting him up and down the stairs.' She pushed open the French doors leading out on to a patio. 'This room will make a perfect bedroom for him.' She swung round. 'If you could arrange to have the furniture cleared out of here straight away so we can get Harry settled in.'

'No.'

'No? What do you mean "no"?'

'Harry is sensitive to noise. There is no way he'd get the peace and quiet he needs down here.'

The silence stretched between them. Clearly when he said he'd give her free rein in the care of Harry, he meant it still had to be on his terms. It was time to change tack. 'I'd kill for some tea—any chance of a cuppa?'

'Sure. I'll get Burton to bring a tray to your room.'

'Can't we have it down here? It's obvious to me that we need to discuss Harry's care in more detail.'

Daniel frowned and looked at his watch—again. 'I really have to take that call. We can discuss whatever it is you wish to this evening.'

'I'm sorry, but that won't work. Harry is coming

home the day after tomorrow and we've got to get everything ready for him.' She forced herself to keep her tone as neutral as possible, although frustration and annoyance was beginning to bubble again.

Daniel's expression hardened. 'Everything *is* ready for my son.' His tone was clipped. 'I've made sure of that. All you've got to do is do your job. That's what I'm paying you for.'

This wasn't going to be as easy as she thought. He needed to be reminded that she was a professional and was not prepared to be bossed around.

'Haven't we just had this conversation, Daniel? You have to trust that I know what I'm doing.' She kept her voice even. 'I wouldn't suggest changes if I didn't think they were important.'

'Forgive me,' Daniel replied with a disarming smile. 'It's just that I'm not used to relinquishing control. And, if I'm honest, I'm just so damned nervous about Harry coming home.'

Colleen found herself smiling back. Of course he was bound to be anxious. No wonder he was being prickly. Anyone would in his situation.

Colleen pulled out one of the high-backed dining chairs and sat down at the mahogany table. Taking her notebook out her bag, she thumbed through it. 'Have you told him what's happening on Tuesday? That that's the day he's coming home?'

Daniel leaned his arms on the back of a chair. 'I did. I don't know how much of it he took in. Sometimes he won't talk at all, so we've worked out a system. One blink means no, two means yes. When I told him I was taking him away from the hospital and you were coming to look after him, he blinked once.' Daniel ran his hand through his hair. 'I have no idea whether that means he doesn't understand or whether that means he doesn't want to come home.'

'It's important not to push him too much right now, but I think if he didn't want to come home, he'd have made that clear.'

Pain flashed in Daniel's eyes. She knew he was remembering yesterday, when Harry had demanded he leave.

Colleen leaned forwards in her chair. 'With regards to Harry's room, please hear me out before you dismiss my suggestions.' She held up her hand as Daniel looked as if he were about to speak. 'I know you say Harry is frightened of noise, but it's more important that he doesn't feel separated from the rest of the household. If we move his room into the dining room, he'll soon get used to the hubbub; in fact, he will probably find it reassuring. When the weather's good we can open the double doors or take him out to the garden. It will be much easier than installing a lift to take him from the first floor to the basement.'

She waited for him to challenge her again, but to her surprise, he nodded. 'Okay, I can see it's worth a try. If the noise does upset him, we'll move him back to his old room.'

Daniel's unexpected capitulation surprised, but pleased her. She really didn't want to spar with him over every aspect of Harry's care.

'Point two…' she counted on her fingers. 'No hospital bed. Bring Harry's old bed in here or buy him a new one. Three—where are his belongings? You know, such as his computer, MP3 player—the normal things lads his age have. I didn't notice any in his room upstairs.'

Daniel shook his head as if he didn't understand the question. 'Apart from his iPod, which I have, the rest of his stuff is probably still at the house he shared with his mother in Dorset. But Harry isn't able to move, never mind use his computer.'

'Not now, no. But he needs to be surrounded by familiar things, his own things.'

'Fine. I'll arrange that.' He stood up. 'I take it that's all. I've really got to go back into work.'

'Afraid not. Not by a long chalk, so forget about work for a while.' Colleen tapped her pen down her notes. 'What sport does Harry like?'

'Oh, for God's sake!' Daniel swung towards her, hands bent down on the table. 'What kind of question is that? My son…' His voiced cracked. He raked a hand through his hair and turned away from her. Colleen heard his intake of breath as he struggled to regain his composure. 'We don't know if he'll ever walk again, never mind play sport—and I don't want him reminded of that fact.'

'You don't know yet what Harry will be capable of,' Colleen replied softly. 'But you've got to have hope—and you've got to give him hope. Give him goals to aspire to.'

Daniel thrust his hands in his pockets and walked towards the French windows. She waited patiently for him to reply.

Finally he cleared his throat. 'Cricket. Cricket and rugby.'

'Does he follow any special team? Any heroes he admires?'

Still with his back to her, he shook his head. 'I don't know. My wife Eleanor would know—would have known. I took Harry to a cricket match at Lord's once but, well…let's just say it wasn't a great success.'

Colleen stared at Daniel, puzzled. He didn't seem to know very much about his son.

'Does Harry know his mum is dead?' Colleen asked quietly.

This time Daniel did turn round, his startlingly handsome face expressionless. 'He hasn't asked where she is. I don't even know if he's aware of who he is or what's happened to him. I talked it over with the staff and I decided I couldn't tell him. Not yet. Not until he's stronger.'

'That's okay. However, we should be prepared for him to ask at any time. With brain injuries, the loss of memory and confusion can last for weeks, maybe months. But it can also come back quite suddenly.' Colleen kept her tone matter of fact. 'If you could arrange to get as many of Harry's personal belongings back here, that would be a start. You said that he was attending boarding school, and it's the school holidays, so maybe you could encourage his friends to visit.'

Daniel puffed out his cheeks, looking relieved that he had something practical to arrange. She had no doubt that he'd be clinically efficient in getting all her recommendations carried out to the letter—now that he'd agreed with them. The next part would be trickier.

Colleen remained seated, signalling that she wasn't quite finished yet. She tilted her chin up and kept her gaze steady as she looked at him. 'I understand you've secured the services of a speech therapist as I requested.'

'Yes. She's ready to come whenever you say the word.'

'And a night nurse to keep an eye on Harry during the night. I am happy to be woken if she needs me, of course.'

Daniel nodded. 'A couple of the nurses from the ward Harry's been on have agreed to do a rotation of shifts on their days off. They'll also cover the weekends when you're back in Dublin.'

'Good. The fewer new faces, the better.' She sat up straighter. 'There's one more member of Harry's team whose role we haven't mentioned yet. In fact, the most important one.'

Daniel frowned. 'I haven't authorised any one else on the payroll, but of course if you can think of anyone we should get to help, that's not a problem.'

'I meant you.'

'Me?' He looked startled 'I don't know the first thing about looking after a child with head injuries—that's why I employed you. I've also got my work. There's no way I can…' He stopped and looked down at her. 'What would you want me to do?'

Colleen sighed. 'Daniel, it's going to be tough, I promise you that. Harry has a long road ahead of him and he'll need you every step of the way. I don't care about your work—that's up to you. But I can tell you that unless you're with Harry, reading to him, playing his favourite music, reminding him of the good times you shared, we may never break through to him.' Colleen held his gaze. 'Harry needs someone to fight for him. He needs *you* to fight for him. Make him believe that he is the centre of your universe—that he matters to you.' She looked at him. 'You asked me to save your son and I'll do everything in my power to help him.

But, Daniel, make no mistake—it's you he really needs right now.'

Daniel walked over to the window and stood there without saying anything.

As the silence stretched between them, anxiety coiled in the pit of Colleen's stomach. Did Daniel even understand what she was getting at?

'Needs me?' When he finally spoke, his voice was harsh. 'I wish it were that easy.'

'You love him.' She spoke softly. 'But you need to show him. Trust me, everything else will follow from that.'

He turned around. With the sun at his back, she couldn't read the expression in his eyes.

'Trust you?' he repeated with a short laugh. 'Well, Colleen McCulloch, it seems I have no option but to do just that.'

And before she could think of a response, he walked out of the room.

CHAPTER FIVE

BEFORE Daniel left to make his conference call, he passed Colleen back over to Burton to show her to her room on the first floor. Its size—four times that of her room at home—made her gasp. In the centre was a canopied four-poster, a working fire to her left and a sofa with two chairs. Through a door on her right was an *en suite* bathroom with claw-footed bath that was big enough for two. It felt as if she had stepped back in time to the 1920s.

'Please make yourself at home, miss,' Burton said. 'There is a bell pull by the side of the bed; if you need anything, please ring. Do you have any preferences for dinner?'

'I eat just about anything.' Colleen said. She patted her hips. 'As you can probably tell.' Now why did she say that? It was just that Burton and the whole set up in this house made her nervous.

'Very well, Miss. Afternoon tea is at four in the small sitting room. Dinner is at seven.'

'Thank you, Mr...er...Burton, but I think I'll skip afternoon teas. The hips, you see.' But as the door clicked closed behind Burton, she realised she was speaking to an empty room.

She walked over to the large sash windows and gazed out at the formal gardens below. In the centre was a statue of a Greek figure holding something in his hand. Could it possibly be Cupid? The thought made her smile. It was unlikely. A statue like that spoke of a whimsy this house didn't have.

She left her bag on the floor and made her way back downstairs. It was deserted. She went in search of Burton, opening door after door to find room after room, beautifully decorated but, like the rest of the house, totally devoid of life. Grand it might be, if slightly out of date, but this house wasn't loved. It was a mausoleum—not a home. So it was up to her to make it welcoming for Harry.

Colleen arched her back and stretched out her aching muscles. The past few hours had been busy. Burton had helped as had Mike, who, finally, had given up with the madam stuff and was now calling her Colleen. Although Burton had tried to persuade her to leave organising the room to him and Mike, Colleen had insisted on staying to make sure every single instruction was carried out to the letter. Even if it meant helping to heave round the furniture so that it was placed to her exact satisfaction.

She stood back and surveyed the once-elegant dining room with a critical eye, finally nodding with approval. Harry's bed had been retrieved from wherever it had been removed to and had been positioned against the back wall in the centre of the room facing the French doors. The heavy brocade curtains had been replaced by neutral curtains that let in more light, making the room less oppressive. Colleen had left the childish posters and books upstairs exactly where they belonged. She'd been out to the garden and brought back masses of fragrant roses to arrange in vases later. Now all she needed was Harry's things—his current favourite books, posters and games, for a start. They would be at the house in Dorset, no doubt. In that case, Daniel would need to fetch them. She would raise the subject over dinner. Mike had told her that Daniel had gone to visit Harry at hospital. She could have gone, too, of course, but Daniel hadn't even let her know he was going. Any softening she had felt towards him had disappeared again.

After thanking Burton and Mike for their help, Colleen ran up to her room. Someone—it had to be Burton—had somehow found the time to unpack her bags for her, and now her meagre possessions were hanging in the wardrobe, looking a bit lost and forlorn.

The thought of the austere and formidable-looking Burton putting away her underwear made her cringe.

Although it was July and the days were warm, her room had been chilly earlier and someone had thoughtfully lit a fire. She walked over and warmed her hands by the flickering flames.

As the firelight bounced off the small diamond in her engagement ring, she wondered if she should give Ciaran a call, but then, almost instantly, decided against it. He'd be totally caught up with the rugby match; besides she didn't really feel like talking to him.

The realisation sent a shiver down her spine. At one time she would have been straight on the phone to him. They would have laughed over Burton's stuffiness and she would have shared the details of her trip and this incredible house. But the truth was, until now, she'd hardly thought about Ciaran. She wrapped her arms around herself, trying to force warmth into her bones. Perhaps it was because events of the last couple of days—her tussles with Daniel and her anxiety to ensure that everything was perfect for when Harry came home—were preoccupying her? But the feeling of unease wouldn't go away. Was Trish right? Was it possible that by marrying Ciaran she was about to make the biggest mistake of her life?

No. She loved Ciaran. Of course she did. It was just pre-wedding jitters. That was all.

At seven she headed back downstairs to be met by Burton.

'Good evening, miss,' Burton said. 'As the main dining room is now out of commission, I have arranged for dinner to be served in one of the other rooms. Mr Frobisher is waiting for you in the library. If you would follow me?'

As if she couldn't find the way herself! However, after being led up one flight of stairs and down another past several rooms before coming to the library, Colleen had to admit that she would have never found the room herself. In fact, a map of the house wouldn't be a bad idea.

Daniel was sitting in a leather chair that faced out over the garden. The room, furnished simply with a couple of leather chairs, a writing desk and floor-to-ceiling shelves of books, was freezing. Daniel clearly didn't feel the cold.

He jumped to his feet when Burton announced her as if she were a guest at a posh wedding.

'Good evening, Colleen. Have you settled in? Please

let me know if there is anything we can do to make your room more comfortable.' Now *he* sounded like Burton.

'I've stayed in hotels that are significantly less comfortable than my room,' Colleen said with a smile. Then she decided to get straight to the point. 'What I would like to know is why you didn't tell me you were going to the hospital to visit Harry? Didn't it cross your mind that it might be appropriate for me to come, too?'

'I didn't tell you I was going because I wanted to remind him that you were here first—in case he'd forgotten.'

'It would have been better for him to see me again. The more familiar he is with me before he comes home, the better.'

Daniel's lips formed a narrow line. 'I think you should let me decide what is best for my son at this point.'

'Although you have employed me as the expert?' Colleen didn't even attempt to keep the exasperation from her voice. 'Didn't we just agree that this morning?' She bit her lip, annoyed with herself. She had to keep reminding herself that underneath the cool exterior and piles of money and trappings was a man who was trying to do the best for his son and was scared to death of doing the wrong thing. She had to tread as gently with the father as she would with Harry if she was to have any hope of doing a good job.

However, there was something she needed Daniel to do before Harry came home.

'We've moved Harry's room into the dining room as we discussed,' she said.

'So Burton tells me.'

'But the room is bare. Would it be possible to go to

the home he shared with his mother and bring back his stuff from there? We might be able to recreate a room for him here that feels familiar. What was his room in Dorset like?'

'I'm afraid I have no idea. I've only been there once in the last couple of years.'

Colleen tried to hide her astonishment, but if Daniel noticed he didn't so much as betray it by a flicker of his eyelids. 'However,' he continued, 'there is nothing to stop me having Mike fetch Harry's belongings. He could do it tomorrow.'

'I would like to go myself,' Colleen said. 'It will give me a feel of what Harry was like before his accident. In fact, I think we should both go.'

'I can't. I'm afraid I have meetings tomorrow.' This time there was a flicker of something in his eyes, although what it was, Colleen couldn't say. Irritation? Embarrassment? Guilt? For sure, he should be embarrassed. So far, from what she could gather, Daniel knew very little about his son and, despite everything he'd said, didn't seem particularly keen to get involved with him. But to be fair, there could be all sorts of reasons for him not visiting the home where his son lived. Perhaps relations between him and his ex-wife had been strained. He wouldn't be the first parent who had to collect his child for visitation rights from neutral territory. On the other hand, perhaps he had still been in love with his wife. Maybe the thought of seeing her had been too difficult. Nonetheless, whatever the reason for his reluctance, it was important that Daniel come with her.

'I really think we should both go,' she insisted.

Daniel stood up and took a couple of steps towards

her. He looked as if he'd just stood on some chewing gum and it had stuck to his foot and he was looking for the perpetrator and, boy, when he found him, he was going to sort him out.

'Good God, Colleen. Are you going to challenge me at every turn? I am Harry's father,' Daniel said. 'In the end the ultimate responsibility for his well-being rests with me.'

Colleen had to dig her nails into her palms to stop herself from retorting that so far he didn't seem to have a clue what was best for his son. And she was damned if she was going to let him intimidate her. She jumped to her feet, too, but immediately regretted it when Daniel took a step towards her. She had forgotten how tall he was, how unnerving his eyes were. Despite every instinct telling her to back down, she held her ground. 'And I thought I made it clear that as long as I am to be Harry's nurse, I will decide what is in your child's best interests as far as his rehab is concerned.'

For a long moment the air between them seemed to shiver. Colleen held her breath.

Suddenly and quite unexpectedly Daniel grinned and Colleen's heart did something very peculiar inside her chest. He really was the most astonishingly good-looking man. If only he would smile more often, perhaps people would be more likely to do as he asked.

'I'm sorry. That was unforgivably rude of me. You are absolutely right. I employed you because I believe that you do know what you're doing. I guess I'm not very good at deferring to someone else when it comes to making decisions. But give me time.'

Once again he seemed completely different to the person who'd been glowering at her a few moments earlier. What was it with this man that made her feel constantly wrong-footed? One minute she was ready to hate him, the next, he made her feel all mushy inside. It must be because she felt sorry for him. Well, not sorry exactly. Daniel wasn't the kind of man a person felt sorry for. Empathetic? No. Sympathetic! That was the right word. Any soft feelings she had were because she *sympathised* with him. Now she'd sorted that inside her head, she felt better.

He reached out and before she knew it his hand was at the back of her head. She felt a sharp tug, then her hair was released from its ponytail and falling around her shoulders. 'That's better. Now you don't look quite as fierce.'

He was laughing at her. Colleen felt her cheeks redden, but whether it was from anger or something else, she didn't want to think about. All she knew was that this man made her feel off balance—and she wasn't used to feeling that way. She reached out and grabbed her scrunchie, tied her hair back into its ponytail and regarded him steadily.

'If it's all the same to you, I think I'll have dinner in my room tonight.' She was pleased to hear that her voice sounded normal. 'I'm tired and we have a long day in front of us tomorrow. I'll be ready to set off for Dorset no later than eight tomorrow. Shall I meet you in the hall?'

He was still grinning, but there was something disturbing in his smile… Something that sent a shiver down her spine, because her reaction to his smile wasn't something a woman who was engaged should be feeling. What on earth was the matter with her? She had to be overtired and that was making her over-emotional.

Relief made her feel light headed. Really, it was obvious when she thought about it.

'Eight o'clock tomorrow it is,' Daniel said and opened the door for her. He bent his head to hers. 'Are you sure you won't change your mind about dinner?' His breath fanned her neck and little goose bumps popped out all over her body.

'No, thanks,' she said formally, and, resisting the impulse to bolt from the room, she bade him goodnight with what she hoped was a nonchalant smile and walked away.

CHAPTER SIX

UNTIL she saw Daniel pacing the hall at exactly eight the next morning, Colleen hadn't been sure whether he'd keep his word. She had fully expected to find Burton meeting her to tell her that Daniel had been called into work and that Mike would be taking her instead. But as Daniel was wearing jeans and a casual short-sleeved shirt, it seemed he had decided to take the day off work after all.

A team of contractors were busy working in the hall. Daniel hadn't wasted any time getting the lift organised. He was deep in conversation with a man who appeared to be the foreman.

As she waited for him to finish, she hid a yawn behind her hand. Last night, she had tossed and turned, unable to sleep for wondering what she had let herself in for. She kept replaying that moment when he'd let down her hair and her disturbing reaction to him.

When he saw her in the hall, he came towards her. His eyes were shadowed as if he too had spent most of the night awake.

'As I'm going to be unavailable for most of the day, I spent most of the night on conference calls with America. Thank God, they're awake when most of the

UK is asleep,' he said as if he'd read her mind. She hoped to hell he couldn't. There were all sorts of wayward thoughts rattling around in there.

'Wouldn't want you to miss out on a business deal now, would we?' Colleen muttered under her breath, but Daniel had already turned away and was issuing a stream of instructions to Burton who was standing by the door waiting patiently with both their coats in his hand.

'Shall I expect you both for dinner, sir?' Burton asked in his mournful voice that by now Colleen was realising was the way he always spoke. God, she'd love to see him crack a smile. Did no one in this house have anything to be happy about? Then she felt ashamed. Of course they didn't. Not too far from here was Daniel's son, who was severely injured, and as Burton had obviously come with the bricks, he had probably known the late Mrs Frobisher well.

'It's a two-hour journey to Dorset and another two hours back,' Daniel said. 'I don't know how long we'll need to spend at the house, but I hope to be back in time for evening visiting at the hospital. Ask Mike to meet us down at the house with one of the cars. Tell him to bring the Bentley. We'll need the boot space.'

So Daniel had a Bentley? It wasn't the kind of car she associated with him. Surely Daniel was more of a Porsche man?

And it seemed she was almost right. The car waiting outside wasn't a Porsche—it was some other equally sleek sports car, but it was definitely more in keeping with what she knew of Daniel. *Which was exactly what?* she thought. *A big fat zero, more or less. How many cars did he have, anyway?* She decided to ask him as

Burton helped her into the passenger seat of the car as if she were completely unable to move her own legs.

'No idea,' Daniel answered her question as they sped away with a spurt of gravel. 'Six? Seven? I don't know and I don't particularly care. I inherited them from my father. He collected cars. They're mostly kept garaged at the house in Cambridgeshire.'

'How can you not know how many cars you have?' Colleen said. 'And Mike told me you have, what is it, four houses? I would have thought that two max was enough for most people.'

'I imagine you have an opinion on most things,' Daniel said, sounding amused.

Colleen smiled. 'My brothers are always saying that I should give people a chance to speak before I rush in and tell them how I see it.'

Daniel smiled back and the tension in the car eased as he weaved his way through the London traffic, pointing out various landmarks as they went along.

When they reached the motorway, he turned on the radio and fiddled with the buttons until he found a station playing classical music.

'This okay for you?' he asked.

'Actually I prefer country and western myself,' Colleen said. She slid him a glance and smiled again. 'I did admit to having an opinion on most things.'

Daniel caught her look and his lips twitched.

'But I also like rock—you know, the golden oldies—as well as more contemporary artists,' Colleen continued hastily. She preferred it when he didn't look at her like that, as if she were an intriguing creature from another planet.

Daniel found a station to satisfy them both and for the next hour and half they sat in silence, each wrapped in their own thoughts.

'So you're getting married?' Daniel said suddenly. 'Have you decided on a date?'

'No, not yet. But with the salary I'll be earning, I'm hoping for an autumn wedding.'

'You don't sound very excited.'

Didn't she?

'But I am excited!' Colleen protested, the words not sounding convincing even to her own ears. 'We've been waiting for this day to come around for so long. We've even started building a house.'

'What does he do? Your fiancé.'

Colleen slid a look in his direction. 'I thought you knew everything about me. You had me *investigated*, after all.'

His green eyes glittered back at her and she felt that strange sensation in her stomach again. Maybe she should stop looking into his eyes?

'My research didn't include your fiancé.'

'Ciaran works on the family farm with my brothers.' Colleen decided it was time to change the subject. The discussion was bringing back that sinking feeling in the pit of her stomach. And she wasn't here to talk about herself. She was here to do a job and that meant finding out everything she could about Harry and his life before the accident.

'Were Harry and his mother close?' she asked.

'Of course. Aren't all mothers and sons?'

Colleen bit back the retort that rose to her lips. Not all mothers and sons. Certainly not all fathers and sons.

Wasn't this man sitting next to her living proof of that? He seemed completely oblivious to the irony in his last statement.

'I mean, Harry was at boarding school before his accident, right? How did he like it?'

Daniel looked puzzled. 'I'm pretty sure he liked it well enough. I wanted him to have the best education money could buy. It's the same school I went to and my father before me. It never did me any harm. In fact, it toughened me up. Made me self-reliant and confident.'

Colleen choked back the words that came to mind. In her opinion it explained a lot.

'And Eleanor was happy about this?'

'It was her idea. She'd been to boarding school herself and the best local schools were over-subscribed. Of course she missed him, but we both agreed it was for the best.'

Best for whom? Colleen wondered. She couldn't see how it was best for a young child to be sent to live with a bunch of strangers. It wasn't as if Harry even had a brother there to help him through the inevitable homesickness. She remembered the time her youngest brother had gone away with the scouts on a two-day camp. He'd phoned home on the first night and insisted their parents come and fetch him home.

'Eleanor thought he'd have company there,' Daniel continued. 'Harry was shy, or so she said. She thought it would give him confidence to be with others his own age.'

Even worse. Sending a shy, lonely boy away from home—how could anyone think that was the right thing to do? However, she wasn't going to voice her opinion. Not now at any rate. Daniel was hurting enough as it was.

'He came home every weekend. Mostly to his mother and the cottage in Devon. A couple of times to Carrington Hall.' He pulled his hand through his hair in that characteristic way Colleen was beginning to learn meant he was baffled. 'After the second time, he refused to come again. Probably because there was no one of his own age to play with, I guess.'

Colleen's heart went out to Harry. She could see the little boy wandering around that big house looking for company and not finding it. No wonder he stopped wanting to come. Hadn't the same thought crossed his father's mind?

'He was only at boarding school for the last two years. He was at day school until he came back to the UK,' Daniel said.

'Came back to the UK?'

Daniel's fingers tightened on the steering wheel. 'Harry was born in Buenos Aires. He lived there with his mother and stepfather. They only returned to the UK when Harry was ten.'

Colleen waited for him to continue, but it was a few minutes before he did.

'Harry's mother and I divorced before Harry was born. She took him to Buenos Aires with her and the man she married when our divorce came through. Eleanor and David separated when Harry was nine. That was when she decided to bring him back.'

That made it worse. Couldn't Daniel see? Not only was Harry in an unfamiliar place, but he'd also been separated from the man who he'd known as his father for most of his life. Although it explained why Daniel didn't seem to know his son very well, there was something that didn't quite add up.

'But you visited Harry in Buenos Aires?'

Daniel's jaw clenched. 'No.'

'Why not?'

Daniel expelled a breath. 'I guess there is no reason why I shouldn't tell you. In fact, it may help.' He paused. 'Eleanor and I married when we were both very young—too young. She was eighteen and I was nineteen. Our parents tried to stop us, but we were in love, or so we thought, and the more they tried to stop us the more determined we were. At first we were happy. We had a flat in London and used the house in Dorset that we're going to now at weekends. My father's disapproval didn't extend to cutting me off from the family money. Not that it would have made a difference if he had. To cut a long story short, I was ambitious. Soon I was working every hour I could and only coming home late at night. I even worked weekends. Eleanor started spending more and more time in Dorset. She met someone there and asked me for a divorce. She told me she was pregnant by him, so I didn't stand in her way.'

'But Harry, he looks like you.'

A shadow crossed Daniel's face. 'That would be because he is my son. I didn't find that out until Eleanor and her new partner split. Up until then she'd led me to believe that Harry was David's child. But if I had had any doubts she was telling me the truth, the moment she showed me a picture of Harry I knew he was mine.'

That explained a hell of a lot. No wonder Daniel knew so little about his son. 'Why didn't you tell me this before?'

'I dislike talking about my personal life.'

'But this is relevant!'

'And how is my personal life relevant?'

'Because anything that affects my patient is important. I need to understand the family dynamics. It can
make a huge difference to a patient's outcome.' She
tried to keep the exasperation from her voice. She took
a deep breath. 'Why did Eleanor wait so long to tell you
Harry was yours?'

'Because she would have known I would have fought
tooth and nail to stop her leaving the country, if I'd
known she was pregnant with my child. I suspect she
only told me when she did, because she didn't want
Harry to miss out on his inheritance.'

'So Harry didn't know you were his father until a
couple of years ago?'

'No.'

'That must have been difficult—for both of you.'

'When I found out I was furious with Eleanor for
keeping him away from me.' His expression darkened.
'All those years. Wasted.'

'How did Harry feel when he found out you were his
father and not the man he called Dad?'

'Angry. Resentful. Mixed up, I guess. I tried to get
to know him, but—' He broke off and shook his head.

'He did come to Carrington Hall to stay, though. He
must have wanted to get to know you, too.'

'He came twice. Then he made excuses not to come.'

'Why did he stop?'

'I don't know. He just did. Maybe he was bored.
Maybe he preferred to be in Dorset with his mother—
he wouldn't say. I didn't think it was fair to make him
come when he didn't want to.' His voice was casual

but there was an undercurrent of something Colleen couldn't quite place. Regret? Hurt? Bewilderment?

'Didn't you miss him when he stopped coming? I mean, you could have gone to see him—or taken him out for the day.'

Daniel's hands tightened on the steering wheel and the temperature in the car dropped a couple of degrees. 'I think you're overstepping the mark, don't you?' he said finally. 'I've told you everything you need to know.'

Colleen felt her hackles rise. Why did this man make it so difficult for her to feel sympathy for him? He had been put in a difficult situation that was none of his making. But had he really tried to get to know his son?

It was another half an hour before he spoke again. 'Harry's best friend at boarding school is a boy called Nathan. You might find it helpful to talk to him about Harry. Haversham should be able to find out how to get hold of him.'

At least Daniel knew one thing about his son.

'Sounds like a good idea. Perhaps you could get Haversham on to it this morning?'

The look Daniel sent her was an indecipherable mixture of exasperation and something else she couldn't quite read. He was so different to Ciaran. With Ciaran everything was an open book and what you saw was what you got. But she knew she had got as much out of Daniel as she was going to—for the time being.

The home Harry had shared with his mother was a surprise. Given the imposing grandeur of Carrington Hall, she supposed she'd expected something similar, or, at the very least, just as grand. However, the cottage was similar to the ones they'd passed when they'd come off the motorway—a neat, compact house with a thatched roof and thick, whitewashed walls covered with roses and jasmine. Although it wasn't what Colleen had expected, the house drew her immediately.

'Does your ex-wife's husband live here now?' Colleen asked as they stepped out of the car.

'David? As far as I'm aware he's still in Buenos Aires. Mrs Hardcastle—Dora—should be here, though. The other help left after the accident, but Dora insisted on staying. She was housekeeper to my mother when I was a child and worked for Eleanor and I when we were married. She went with Eleanor and Harry to Buenos Aires and came back with them. This is the only home she knows.'

He tried the door, but it was locked.

'She's probably gone down to the village,' he said, fishing a set of keys out of his pocket. He smiled wryly. 'I can't remember when I last used these.'

Inside the house was a revelation. Unlike Carrington Hall, it was furnished in bright, welcoming colours and sunlight streamed through the windows. The door led through a small entrance hall and into a sitting room-cum-dining room. The sitting room was furnished with deep, squashy sofas in pale linen and piles of brightly covered cushions. The coffee tables were a mismatch of oak and pine and the scrubbed and dark-varnished wooden floors were covered with deep red rugs. An inglenook fireplace took up most of one side of the sitting-room wall. Just off to the right was a small but adequate kitchen and a door that Colleen guessed led up to the upstairs bedrooms.

'It's beautiful,' Colleen said. 'My idea of a dream cottage.'

Daniel was looking around, his expression bleak.

'My mother loved this house. When I was a child she used to bring me here for the summer. It was the only place that felt like home.' The last words were said so softly and with such regret that Colleen wasn't sure she had heard right. Was she seeing another chink in Daniel's armour? Maybe he wasn't so detached as he liked people to believe?

'Eleanor asked if she and Harry could live here when they came back to the UK, so I gave it to her.' Daniel continued. 'I knew Harry would be happy here.'

Colleen touched him on the arm, wanting him to know that she understood how painful it was for him to come to the place where he had once known happiness. He looked down at her hand and his muscles tensed. She removed her hand and stepped back, feeling as if she'd been stung.

'Shall we have a look at Harry's room?' she suggested. 'See what we should take back with us?'

Harry's bedroom was the first room on the right at the top of the narrow stairs. It was small, with only just enough room for a bed, a side table and a built-in cupboard. On the table was a portable TV with a computer console attached.

'I bought him a new, bigger TV for his last birthday,' Daniel said. 'I don't see it.'

Colleen thought that a large flat-screen television would be totally out of place in this bedroom, but again decided to keep her counsel. The walls in Harry's room were decorated with posters, some from movies and others of cricketers and rugby players.

'Ah. Good lad. I see he supports Wasps. Next to the London Irish they're the best,' she said.

Daniel wandered across to the bookshelves and was looking through the books. He seemed bemused. 'I didn't know he read this! I thought he was still into Harry Potter. Isn't every kid under fifteen into Harry Potter?'

'Children move on in their tastes quite quickly,' Colleen said, keeping her voice neutral although she was dismayed. Daniel had a lot to learn about his son.

Next to Harry's bed was a bedside table. On it was a photograph of him and his mother, similar to the one Daniel had shown her. The pair had their arms wrapped around each other and were smiling into the camera. There were other photos pinned to a notice board on the wall. Photos of Harry with friends, a team photo of him with the school cricket team as well as one of him in swimming trunks holding up a cup. There was also, touchingly, an old photograph of Daniel when he must have been five or six. He'd clearly had not long finished devouring an ice cream as there were traces of the treat still clinging to his mouth and a couple of tell-tale drips on his T-shirt. An austere-looking man was holding him in his arms rigidly, as if unused to holding a child, but the little boy was looking up at the man with such devotion it made Colleen's heart ache for him.

Daniel came to stand next to her and unpinned the photo from the board. 'I remember this,' he said, his voice ragged. 'It was taken one summer when my father came to stay. He and I had spent the day looking for fossils down on Chesil Beach. It was the only day I can remember the two of us on our own just having fun. My father worked day and night at his business.

He was a bit of a workaholic.' He smiled wryly. 'I guess
we had that in common.'

If Daniel's father was as distant as he looked and
sounded, no wonder Daniel struggled with his own
child. Slowly the pieces were beginning to fall into
place.

Daniel placed the photo back on the table. 'I had no
idea Harry had this. There should be one of Harry and
me.'

'You'll have other, good days together,' Colleen said.
'Just give it time.'

Daniel smiled tightly 'You may have gathered by
now that patience isn't one of my strengths.'

There was little Colleen could say to that.

'Okay, let's pack up everything in this room.
Photographs, posters, books, his game console, even
his duvet and cover.'

She started removing the posters from the wall. She
had to stand on a chair to reach one that was higher
up. As she stretched, the chair wobbled, but before she
could fall strong arms grabbed her around the waist and
lifted her off the chair. Daniel set her down on her feet
and she stumbled against him. She felt the muscles of
his chest against her back and his arms tightened around
her. Her skin sizzled and she found herself leaning into
the warmth of his body. She closed her eyes. It felt
so good, so right. Unlike anything she'd ever felt with
Ciaran. Horrified at the direction her thoughts were
going, she stepped away.

'Oops,' she said.

She turned around to find Daniel looking at her with
the strangest expression on his face. The air was suddenly filled with an almost unbearable tension. Her

heart was pounding so hard she could almost hear it. Quickly she stepped away and pretended to survey the room.

'Now, what next?' she said to cover her confusion.

Harry's bed was covered in a duvet with figures from a recent movie. Colleen decided to take that, too. As she lifted the pillow to remove the matching pillow slip she found a torn-out scrap of paper from a newspaper. It was ragged around the edges, as if it had been handled many times.

She picked it up and studied the picture. It was of a man in a black gown and a wig—the kind the lawyers wore in court. Peering closer, she was startled to find that he looked very familiar.

'Who's the geezer in the wig?' she asked, handing it to Daniel.

As he took the piece of paper from her, their hands brushed and a tingling sensation ran up her arm. Colleen snatched her hand away.

'I didn't know Harry had this,' Daniel said softly. 'Don't you recognise me?'

'Good God, that's you?'

'I'm a Q C. A Queen's Counsel. Some people call it Silk. Didn't you know?'

No she didn't know. She hadn't thought to ask Daniel what he did and just assumed he was some sort of business tycoon.

'Are you a prosecutor or a defender?'

He looked at her strangely. 'Does it matter?'

He was right. It shouldn't matter. But it did.

'I work for the prosecution,' he said after a moment.

She couldn't help but be relieved at his answer. She wanted him to be on the side of the innocent.

'But every person has the right to the best defence. In this country, people are still innocent until proven guilty.'

Damn. He was doing that reading-the-mind thing again. She felt her cheeks colour.

Daniel ran his hand through his hair. 'I handle criminal cases most of the time, but occasionally I deal with matrimonial law. Divorces, custody, that sort of thing.'

Colleen whistled under her breath. 'What kind of people have a QC represent them when they're getting divorced?'

'Very rich people,' he said, drily. He lifted an eyebrow. 'Shall we get on?'

It took them only an hour to pack up the rest of Harry's belongings. They left it at the front door for Mike to collect. Daniel was in the process of leaving a note for Mrs Hardcastle when a grey-haired woman with frizzy dark hair appeared at the door. Her lips thinned when she saw Daniel.

'Still here, then?' she said.

'This is Colleen, Dora,' Daniel said. 'She's the nurse who's going to be caring for Harry when he comes out of hospital tomorrow. Colleen, this is Dora Hardcastle. When Eleanor went abroad Dora went with her. Harry's known her all his life.'

'That child should be here with people he loves and who love him,' Dora said, pushing past Colleen and Daniel. 'Especially now he's lost his poor mother.'

'He will be with people who love him,' Daniel said. Despite his even tone, his voice had an undercurrent of steel.

'Aye, well, you say that, but he knows me best of all.

He loves me. And where am I? Stuck here looking after an empty house with nothing but the memories of him and his mother to keep me company.' She pulled out one of the largest handkerchiefs Colleen had ever seen and dabbed surreptitiously at her eyes. 'If it wasn't for the fact I loved his mother like a daughter, I'd be away from here myself.'

'You know you could come and stay with us in London,' Daniel said. 'I've asked you often enough. God knows there is enough space.'

Making sure Dora wasn't looking, Colleen dug an elbow into his side. He looked at her in surprise. *Plead with her to come,* she mouthed at him.

He gentled his tone. 'We…I…would really like you to come. Please say you'll think about it.'

'And what would I be doing up there?' Dora said gruffly, but Colleen could tell from the spark in her eye that the idea appealed to her.

'You could help me look after Harry,' Colleen said. 'We could take turns sitting with him. I agree it's better for him to have as many familiar faces around him as possible. Of course it's a lot to ask of you.'

'I know Harry looks on you as an honorary gran, Dora,' Daniel added. 'He'd like you to be around, I'm sure.'

Dora looked mollified. It seemed as if Daniel had hurt her feelings when he hadn't pleaded with her to return to Carrington Hall after the accident. Men could be so slow sometimes.

Dora tutted and looked askance at Colleen. 'You might be a nurse, but you don't know how Harry likes his eggs, or how to disguise the vegetables in his food so he'll get enough vitamins. I've been looking after that lad since he was born. I've changed his nappies, seen him take his first steps, fed him as a baby. I love him as if he were my own. I hate to think of him up in London without me.'

And she blew her nose, almost disappearing behind her voluminous handkerchief.

'You are absolutely right, Mrs Hardcastle, I don't know Harry's likes and dislikes. Please, please consider coming to Carrington Hall to help,' Colleen said.

'I know it's not fair to ask you,' Daniel added, 'but I'd really appreciate it if you would come and help look after Harry. And I know Harry would be delighted to have you there.'

Mrs Hardcastle's lips trembled and for a moment Colleen thought she was going to cry. However she sniffed and compressed her lips together. 'When is he leaving the hospital?' she asked.

'Tomorrow.'

'In that case I'll come next week. I have some things to organise before then. You tell the lad I'll see him soon. Now if you'll excuse me, I have dusting to do.'

Left alone with Daniel, Colleen sneaked a glance at him. He was smiling. *He should smile more often. On the other hand, maybe he shouldn't.* His smile made her feel quite dizzy.

Daniel's smile grew broader. 'Can you see Burton and Dora sharing a kitchen?' he asked.

'No. Not really.' Colleen smothered a giggle. 'I don't know how comfortable it's going to be having Dora around, but I think you did the right thing. She obviously loves Harry.'

'Anything that is good for Harry is all right with me,' Daniel said. 'Even if it means having Dora in London.'

He grimaced but his eyes were sparkling. 'She and Burton don't exactly hit it off.'

'Dora doesn't entirely approve of you either, does she?'

Daniel's eyes glinted. 'That makes two of you, then, doesn't it?'

'I wouldn't say I disapprove of you,' Colleen protested.

Daniel raised a disbelieving eyebrow and her heart thumped. This man confused her. One minute she was sure she disliked him, the next he was making her heart do complicated manoeuvres. All she knew was that he was having the most peculiar effect on her.

CHAPTER SEVEN

LATER that day, back in London, Colleen surveyed the dining room, now Harry's room, with satisfaction. The heavily embossed walls were covered with posters of Harry's favourite current sport stars and a bookcase was jammed with the books they had taken from Harry's room in Dorset as well as a new selection of paperbacks from Harry's favourite science-fiction writer.

Or so his best friend, Nathan, had said. When Daniel had tracked him down, at home on holiday with his parents in Chelsea, the teenager had said he'd be glad to help Colleen get Harry's room ready. Daniel had sent Mike to pick him up as soon as he'd returned from Dorset.

Colleen was beginning to get a very clear picture of Harry in her head. At least of the child he'd been before his accident. All she was missing was an understanding of what had gone wrong between Harry and Daniel. Daniel clearly cared about his son, but the two of them seemed more like strangers than father and son. Surely two years was long enough for them to get to know each other better than they had?

'So what do you think, Nat? Will Harry like it?' Colleen had asked the serious-looking young lad.

Harry's friend had squinted a bespectacled eye. 'I think so.' He tilted his head as if he was giving the matter some serious thought. 'No, in fact I know he'll think it's cool.'

'Are you sure?' Colleen smiled. 'You don't think he'd prefer posters of the great Irish rugby players instead?'

'Nah. Definitely not. Oh, by the way, I've set up a new game on Harry's computer.' Nathan ambled over to the laptop beside the bed. 'I'll show you how it works. It's the business.'

She watched in admiration as his fingers danced across the computer keys. 'Good work, Nat. You're a star.'

Nathan smiled back, but then he wriggled about in the chair, looking as if he wanted to say something, but didn't know how to begin.

'Harry's accident must have been a terrible shock,' Colleen said, suspecting that the teen might need an opening.

'I went to see him at the hospital. A lot of us went at first. But…' Nathan bit his lip. 'Harry didn't look like himself. None of us knew what to say.'

'Try not to worry about that, Nat. A lot of people find it very difficult to spend time with someone who doesn't seem to know that they're there. But often, even if they seem to be deeply unconscious, they can hear what's being said. If Harry was at all aware, he would have been glad to hear your voice.'

Nathan brightened. 'Maybe I can come and see him when he comes home. Do you think that would be all right?'

'I think it's a great idea, Nathan. You can talk to him about all the stuff you used to talk about at school before the accident.'

Colleen went through her check list again, ticking off the items one by one. The room was ready for Harry. No doubt he would want changes, but they could be made as and when. The swimming pool was an added bonus. Colleen had already decided to get him into the water as soon as possible, but for that, she would need Daniel's help. There was no way she could do it on her own. Besides, the more involved with Harry's care Daniel was, the better—for both father and son. Now what else did she need to do?

As she set her list aside, Daniel walked into the room. Their eyes met and immediately she could tell something was bothering him by the way he ran his hand through his hair. She wondered if he knew that it was a definite tell.

'What time is the ambulance arranged for?' she asked.

'Three o'clock,' he replied. 'The doctor is coming here about five to check Harry over.'

Colleen checked her watch. 'We should leave soon.' She placed a hand on his shoulder. 'It's going to be fine, you'll see.'

Harry's transfer from the hospital had gone smoothly and a short while after being transported home by ambulance, he was safely tucked up in bed in his new room. Sometimes, when he opened his eyes, they were expressionless. At other times he would look frightened as if he had no idea where he was or what was happening to him. Daniel's presence still seemed to agitate him, so Colleen had gently suggested Daniel leave her to get Harry settled.

'It's okay, Harry. You're in your father's house. I'm here with you and I'm going to stay until you're better.' Colleen kept repeating the words and eventually the fear would leave Harry's eyes and he would close them again. She'd seen this before. Patients would have lucid episodes where they'd seem to understand everything that was going on around them, only to have them followed by periods of confusion and apparent memory loss. Hopefully the lucid periods would increase as the days went on.

When she was sure he was sleeping, she went in search of Daniel. She found him in the library, staring down at the glass of whisky he held in his hand. He looked up and in that moment she saw such anguish in his eyes it made her wince. Then the shutters came down again, making her think of the steel doors in a bank vault slamming shut.

'How is he?' Daniel asked.

'He's sleeping. I don't want to leave him too long. I don't want him to wake up and find himself alone.'

Daniel pulled a hand through his thick hair again and frowned. 'For the first time in my life I don't know if I've made the right decision. Perhaps Harry would have been better off in a specialist unit.'

'For what it's worth, I still think you're doing exactly the right thing. You and Harry are going to have to get to know each other all over again. It will take time, but Harry will get used to you and learn that you care about him. In the meantime, he has his familiar things around him, he will have Dora, he has me and, in time, he will realise that he has you too. Nathan has promised to visit as much as he can and that will help as well. As I explained before, these next few weeks are critical.'

'I've handed over as much of my business as I could for the board and Haversham to run as I can. Unfortunately there's other stuff, upcoming court cases, that I can't pass on right now.' Daniel sketched a bow. 'Otherwise, I am completely at your and Harry's beck and call.'

Colleen found it impossible to imagine Daniel at anyone's beck and call.

'What happened to Harry's MP3 player?' Colleen asked. 'I'm assuming he had one.'

'I have it. The police recovered it from the scene of the accident and gave it to me.'

'I'd like to keep it in Harry's room so I can play it. Knowing what music he likes will be another thing it will be helpful to know about your son. If you wouldn't mind fetching it for me?'

Daniel crossed the room and pressed a button. Moments later, Burton appeared at the door.

'Ah, Burton. Could you bring me Harry's MP3 player, please? I think it's on my bedside table.'

When Burton had left the room, Daniel turned back to Colleen.

'Actually, I know what music he likes. I'm not saying I recognise it, but when Harry was in a coma I listened to it. It made me feel closer to him.' A shadow crossed his face. 'When the doctors told me that he might not survive and that I might have to think about organ do-nation…'

It was all Colleen could do to stop herself from going

to him and wrapping her arms around him. That's what she would have done for any other relative who was in as much pain. But something held her back. For some reason, she found it difficult to behave normally towards Daniel.

Daniel shook his head as if to clear it. 'Okay, what else?'

'We're going to have to take turns being with him. I want one of us to be there all the time when he's awake. We should read to him or talk to him or listen to his music with him. He needs as much stimulation as possible and I'll need help turning him regularly. I'll be moving his limbs as much as possible to keep the muscles toned so we can get him back on his feet as soon as possible. I'm warning you, the next few weeks are going to be tough—on all of us.' She got to her feet. 'Let's continue this conversation in Harry's room. I want him to get used to the sound of our voices.'

Back in Harry's room, Colleen sat on the chair next to Harry's bed. Daniel crossed to the window and looked outside.

'No wonder Harry didn't like coming here,' Daniel said softly. 'I hated this place when I was a child.'

Harry stirred in his sleep. Colleen held her breath, wanting to know more.

'My father was a disciplinarian—almost Victorian in his view that children should neither be seen nor be heard.'

'Go on,' Colleen prompted. 'Tell me more. This is the kind of stuff you should be telling Harry when he's awake.'

'I wish Harry could've spent time in Dorset when he

was younger.' He smiled ruefully. 'I wouldn't want you
to think my childhood didn't have its happy moments.
As I said, I used to go with my mother to the cottage
at the weekends. She'd take me down to the beach and
we'd do all the things families do when they're at the
seaside: make sandcastles, get buried in the sand, eat ice
creams. I would have done that with Harry.' He stopped
speaking for a while. 'Eleanor always loved that cottage. She was a great fan of Thomas Hardy. She said it
gave her a thrill to live where Tess of the d'Urbervilles
was set. She always intended to write a book one day.'
Daniel's shoulders were stiff. 'We were happy there.'

Something suspiciously like envy sliced through
Colleen. Daniel had clearly loved Harry's mother once.
Perhaps he still did. Maybe he was grieving for a missed
opportunity to get back with her. She knew so little
about him. *And it's none of your business. Your business is with the child and not the father.* Why, then, did
she feel envious? Was it because it emphasised what she
and Ciaran didn't have?

There was a long silence.

'But you didn't visit Harry in Dorset after they returned?' Colleen asked.

'Eleanor made it clear that I wasn't welcome. But,
God forgive me, I could have tried harder to see Harry,
but something always seemed to come up…' He turned
back to Colleen and the remorse on his face made her
heart twist.

'Maybe we could take Harry there when he's a little
better? Stay for a while if he likes.'

In a moment the mask was back in place. 'I don't
think we should take Harry back to a place that is bound
to remind him that he's lost his mother.'

Colleen said nothing. Maybe he was right. It was too early yet to know what would be best for Harry. Hopefully when he was better he'd be able to tell them what he wanted.

Harry opened his eyes and blinked rapidly.

'Hello, Harry,' Colleen said quietly. 'Remember me? I'm Colleen. You're back in your father's house in London. He's here, too. We've being talking about the house in Dorset.'

Colleen waited for a reaction from Harry, but there was none. 'Now...' Colleen beckoned to Daniel '...we're just going to sit you up. Then I'll read to you. Or would you like me to put your music on?'

They helped Harry sit up in bed, Daniel holding his son against his chest while Colleen sorted the pillows.

'Okay, Harry,' Colleen said, her heart aching for Daniel. 'Blink once if you would like me to read to you.'

There was no response.

'Blink once if you would like me to put your music on.'

Again there was no response.

'Or, I can do both. I could read to you while you listen to music?'

Harry blinked twice.

'Okay, not music, not reading. What about a DVD of *Iron Man*? Your friend Nat tells me it's one of your favourite films.'

Harry blinked once.

Colleen and Daniel exchanged a look over the top of Harry's head. For the first time, Colleen saw hope in Daniel's eyes.

'Look, I need to get to the office,' Daniel said, 'but I'll be back as soon as I can.' He leaned over and kissed the top of his son's head. Harry flinched and turned his head away.

The look in Daniel's eyes changed to one of despair, but without saying anything, he straightened and left the room.

'Okay, Harry, it seems to me you can understand a fair bit of what's going on. That's good. But just in case you forget, I'm going to keep reminding you of where you are and who I am. It might get on your nerves, but until I know for sure what you remember, I'm afraid you are going to have to put up with it.'

Colleen slipped the DVD into the slot and pressed play. 'While you're watching this, I'm going to move your arms and legs for you. It might be a bit uncomfortable, but it needs to be done if we're going to get you back on your feet. Do you understand?'

Another double blink.

'Harry, you were in a car accident. Your head got a bit of a bump. Do you remember that?'

A look of bewilderment crossed Harry's face, followed by a look of panic.

'But you're all right,' Colleen hurried to reassure him. 'Things are going to seem a little fuggy for a while, but don't try to fight it. I'm here with your dad to make sure you get better. All you have to do at the moment is let us look after you.'

The fear left the child's face and, as the DVD started, Harry fixed his eyes on the screen.

Half an hour later, he was asleep again. According to the staff at the hospital, the periods that he spent sleeping were getting shorter. If he continued to improve, sooner or later he would remember about the car accident. And then he would want to know where his mother was. It wasn't a moment she was looking forward to.

CHAPTER EIGHT

THE next few days slipped past quickly. Colleen had established a routine, knowing it was important for Harry. She got up at six and, after showering and dressing, had breakfast in her room. Then she went to Harry's room and received the report from the night nurse. Together they would wash the child and dress him before Colleen fed him his breakfast. After that she would spend the day reading to him or simply chatting to him as she put his limbs through passive movements.

After the night nurse had arrived, and Harry was settled for the night, Colleen would have a tray in her room. Some evenings she'd walk the streets of London, following her nose, delighted when she'd come across a familiar building or landmark. To her surprise, she never felt lonely. Her doubts about Ciaran were still there. Although she spoke to him every now and again, shouldn't they be talking much more often? Making plans for their wedding? Neither of them had raised the subject recently, perhaps because they were apart. Or maybe he was having his doubts, too?

Her musing was interrupted by a knock on her door.

'Mr Frobisher is asking if you would join him for dinner tonight, madam,' Burton said.

'Sure. Tell him I'll be down in a minute,' Colleen said. To her dismay and disappointment, Daniel had been out all day for the last couple of days, only returning late at night. Often Colleen would hear his footsteps echoing in the hall and the sound of his voice murmuring to Harry. She hadn't spoken to him alone since the day Harry had come home from hospital. No doubt he wanted an update on his child's progress.

She found him in the drawing room, a glass of whisky in his hand.

'Ah, Colleen. Thank you for joining me.' He looked tired, Colleen thought. One minute she was furious with him, the next she had to restrain the impulse to touch him—to smooth his ruffled hair with her hand. She'd never met anyone who made her feel so mixed up before.

'I thought we could eat in the kitchen,' Daniel continued. He gave her a wry smile. 'If that's okay?'

'Suits me,' Colleen said. 'I was never one for formal dining.' At that moment she thought of her family—the lot of them piled around the kitchen table, all speaking at once. Up until now she had been too busy to miss them.

'Can I get you a drink?' Daniel asked.

Colleen shook her head. 'If I have any alcohol at all, I'll fall asleep.'

Daniel looked concerned. 'I'm sorry. We've been working you too hard.' He waited for her to sit, before sinking into a chair by the fire. 'I've organised the plane to take you home tomorrow for the weekend.'

Colleen covered a yawn with her hand. 'I'm not going.'

Daniel raised his eyebrows in a silent question.

'Harry is spending longer and longer periods awake. He's improving more quickly than I'd hoped,' she said.

'But that's good, isn't it?'

'Yes. But it means that he might remember the accident any day now.'

Daniel placed his glass carefully on the table and closed his eyes. 'And when he remembers the accident, he's going to ask where his mother is. God, what am I going to tell him?'

'The only thing you can tell him is the truth. He'll be upset—distraught. He might even regress a little.'

'But you'll be here?'

'He needs me,' Colleen said simply. *And you do, too,* she thought. *For all your wealth and position, there is nothing you can do to stop your child having to face the awful news that his mother is dead.*

'Thank you,' Daniel said. 'I'll make it up to you.'

'It's my job.' But that wasn't the whole of it. The truth was, despite everything she'd been taught about keeping a professional distance, she had become involved with this small, hurt family.

The clock ticked into the silence.

'I like to get Harry up every day,' Colleen said, 'even if it's just to sit. But I think he's well enough for us to try to take him out when the weather's okay. Maybe take him to a cricket match. We could all go.'

'I tried to get to his school cricket matches as much as I could. He was in the team, you know. Unfortunately I didn't get to them as often as I would have liked.'

'Work?' Colleen guessed.

If he heard the disapproval in her voice, he chose to ignore it.

'I took him to Lord's for his tenth birthday. It didn't

go quite as I planned.' Daniel's smile was bleak. He took a sip of his drink. 'I wanted to spend his birthday with him. The first birthday we would spend together. He seemed so excited when I picked him up. He barely looked at the present I'd bought him. I thought it would be a new start for us. A common interest. Something we could share.'

'Go on,' Colleen said quietly.

'I'd arranged the best seats and a picnic with all his favourite things. Eleanor had told me exactly what he liked. At first everything seemed to be going so well. He was chatting away, telling me about his matches, pointing out his favourite cricketer. And then, I don't know, something went wrong. He clammed up.'

Colleen was puzzled. 'Was it something you said?'

'I don't think so. I had guests. You know, business acquaintances I needed to speak to. It was when they arrived that Harry went all quiet. Maybe they made him shy.'

Colleen couldn't control herself any longer. 'Oh, you great big lummox of a man. Can't you see what went wrong? Here was a little boy, being taken out for a birthday treat by a father he barely knew, thinking he was going to have you all to himself—for once. Then these strangers appear and take all his father's attention. What kind of birthday treat was that for the lad?'

Daniel looked stunned by her outburst. 'I would have been happy if *my* father had taken me to a cricket match.'

Agitated, she jumped to her feet. Hadn't he listened to anything she'd said? Daniel *had* to start being more involved with his child.

'And,' she continued, 'you have to spend more time

with Harry. You've hardly spent any time with him so far. I know you have your cases, but isn't it time you put Harry first?'

Under any other circumstances she might have found the look of incredulity on Daniel's face amusing. She doubted anyone had ever spoken to him like that.

'I've changed my mind,' she said. 'I think I'll have a tray in my room if it's all the same to you. We can talk again tomorrow.'

But as she spun on her heel, Daniel's voice came from behind her.

'Colleen, wait.'

She stopped in her tracks.

When she turned around, Daniel was looking as if the demons of hell were fighting a war behind his eyes.

'When I found out that Harry was mine, I was bowled over,' he said slowly, almost as if the words were being pulled from somewhere deep inside him. 'I never thought that having a child would make me feel the way it did. Eleanor had talked about having children, of course, but only as a distant future possibility. I couldn't actually imagine ever being a father. While we were married it didn't seem there could be room for a child. When I found out Harry was mine, I was shocked—and furious with Eleanor that she'd kept him from me, but mostly I was amazed and delighted— even if I was scared to death that I wouldn't live up to Harry's expectations. I wanted to get to know my son, but what I didn't anticipate was that he wouldn't feel the same way. I didn't know it was going to be so damn difficult to talk to him.

'Taking him to a cricket match was the only way I could think of being with him. I thought that if I took it slowly—gave him time to get to know me—he'd eventually feel relaxed in my company.' He smiled ruefully. 'I can see now I made a mistake by inviting colleagues to the match.'

He pulled his hand through his hair. 'This father business doesn't exactly come easily to me.'

Colleen held her breath. She could see how hard it was for Daniel to tell her this. She sat down on the chair opposite him, mortified and ashamed by the way she'd spoken to him.

'I'm sorry,' she said. 'I shouldn't have said what I did.' And why had she? Why did she react to him instead of being able to treat him like she would normally treat any other patient's father—in a cool, caring, but professional manner?

'I like to have control in and of my life,' Daniel continued. 'But I haven't been able to control anything that's happened to Harry. Not knowing he was my son, trying to get to know him, his accident—I couldn't control any of it.' He clenched his jaw.

Colleen wanted to reach out and touch him, as if her touch could absorb some of his pain. But she instinctively knew her sympathy wouldn't be welcome.

'When Harry was desperately ill, when they thought he might die, I would have swapped my life for his in a minute. But I couldn't. I would've given everything I own in the world if that would have made him better, or brought his mother back, but for once in my life I was powerless.'

He stood up. 'Helping to get him better—that's something I can do. But I can't do it alone.'

The admission seemed to cost him the last bit of his self-control. He turned away from her.

'If you'll excuse me, Colleen, I think I'm going to do some work now.'

Colleen looked at him. He'd allowed her to see his pain. And now, more than ever, she knew she would never give up on this man and his child. She stepped across to the door and reached for the handle. She had only one more thing left to say.

'Thank you for telling me what you did, Daniel. As long as you remember that there is only one thing Harry needs from you.'

Daniel narrowed his eyes then raised a questioning brow. 'And that is…?'

'You, Daniel. Plain and simple, all he really needs is you.'

Finding it impossible to concentrate, Daniel slammed down the lid of his laptop and leaned tiredly against the back of his chair. He found his thoughts once again returning to dwell on the exchange between himself and Colleen. He stared at the closed door of the sitting room. God, what kind of harridan had he invited into his home? No one ever spoke to him like that. It was yes, Mr Frobisher and of course, Mr Frobisher. Damn it. It wasn't unreasonable to expect respect from employees, surely?

But then Colleen was a strange sort of employee. For a start, he needed her more than she needed him. But there were bound to be other nurses out there. More biddable ones for a start. Ones who wouldn't feel the need to challenge him constantly. But the truth was, he didn't want anyone else—no matter how fiery Colleen was. Harry already knew and trusted her.

And of course she had a point. Asking business acquaintances to Harry's birthday treat had been a mistake. He could see that now.

But, hell, he hadn't expected her to react the way she had. God, she certainly didn't pull her punches.

He took a gulp of his drink. He'd just told her stuff that he'd never told anyone before. Stuff that he didn't want to share. She seemed to drag it out of him. Perhaps because for some reason he wanted her to think that he was a better man than the person she believed him to be.

Which made him feel uncomfortable. Why should he care what she thought of him as long as it didn't interfere with her care of his son? He had managed all right up until now, without giving a damn for other people's opinions.

He would just have to be careful how he handled Colleen in future. One thing was for sure, he hadn't got to where he was without knowing how to get the best from the people who worked for him.

Why, then, did he have the uncomfortable feeling that in Colleen, he'd met his match?

CHAPTER NINE

A FEW days later, finding herself in the unusual position of having nothing to do as Dora was sitting with Harry, Colleen made her way down to the kitchen in search of a cup of tea. The smell of baking drifting from the kitchen made her mouth water. Although it was only a couple of hours since she'd had breakfast she was suddenly starving. Maybe she should head back upstaris while there was still time? She'd always intended to lose weight before the wedding, but somehow she only had to look at a cake and the pounds crept on. Thinking about her wedding brought back that uncomfortable feeling in the pit of her stomach.

Perhaps a slice of cake or some home-made bread would help get rid of the butterflies that seemed to have set up home in her stomach? Food always made her feel better.

Before she knew it her legs had carried her into the kitchen; to her delight, she found a freshly baked chocolate cake with lashings of fresh cream just sitting on the table begging to be eaten.

She cut three thick slices and placed them, along with a glass of milk, on a tray to take it up to Harry's room. She was still mulling things over as she made her way up the kitchen stairs, concentrating on balancing the tray of milk and cake. It was no surprise, then, that she walked headlong into Daniel who was at the top of the stairs with his mobile in his hand. Needless to say the contents of the tray went everywhere. Chocolate cake and milk in a sodden mess on the floor, but, worst of all, all over Daniel's dark-grey, once-immaculate suit.

'Oh, my God,' Colleen cried. 'I'm so sorry.' She dabbed at his jacket with a paper serviette she'd retrieved from the floor, but that only made matters worse. Daniel looked as if he'd been in a bun fight. 'I'm such a clumsy idiot. Now you'll be late!'

Daniel was looking down in horror at his suit. Colleen waited for the explosion that was bound to come, but to her surprise he laughed.

'Hell, Colleen, do you think so little of me that you expect me to lose my cool over an accident? I'm just happy to know that Little Miss Perfect isn't so perfect after all.' His hand reached out and removed something from her cheek. 'I have to admit a little chocolate cake makes you seem more human.'

Colleen felt the colour rise in her cheeks, but then she saw the funny side of it, too. 'And I have to say, you look pretty good in chocolate cake, yourself.' There was a roar in her ears as she realised what she'd said. 'I mean—you look less severe...' Oh dear that wasn't what she meant to say either. 'I mean more...relaxed.' Maybe she should just stop talking. The problem was, or so her brothers were forever telling her, she never knew when to hold her tongue. 'It's just that sometimes you look...so scary, you frighten me, never mind Harry.'

The smile left his face. 'I frighten you? I frighten my

ANNE FRASER 105

son?' he growled. He actually growled. If he could hear himself, he would know why she found him scary.

'What I mean is, I wouldn't like to be on the opposing side to you in court. I bet you freeze witnesses with one look from those shockingly green eyes.'

He looked perplexed, but at least the gathering storm clouds on his face seemed to have gone. 'You think my eyes are shockingly green?'

Shut up, Colleen! she tried to tell the one part of herself that was still working—her brain. *Just stop talking and get the hell away from him as fast as your legs will carry you.* 'I don't mean shocking in a bad way. They're such an unusual shade of green I—one can't help looking at them.'

A small smile was playing around Daniel's mouth and those interesting green eyes crinkled at the corners. Colleen's heart was thumping against her ribs. Forget the bit about her brain working. It had packed up and gone on a permanent holiday. Was she doomed to say the wrong thing to this man?

'I take that back about you being a lawyer,' Daniel said, stepping closer to her. 'A lawyer needs to be precise. Now what exactly do you mean about my eyes?' He was so close she could make out the faint smell of toothpaste on his breath, his aftershave, his own distinct male scent. She thought if anyone was watching they would see her ribs moving from the impact of her heart beating against them. Now, she couldn't think of anything to say. The truth was, she didn't know whether she had any breath left to speak with.

At that moment Burton appeared by the door. 'Your car is waiting, sir,' he said in his sonorous voice.

Daniel smiled. 'We'll finish this conversation later,'

he said to Colleen. 'I'll be back in a minute, Burton. I just have to change my suit.' And then he turned and ran upstairs, leaving Colleen wondering what had just happened.

The next morning, Colleen was with Harry in his room. She had finished putting him through the first set of passive movements of the day and was tidying up, keeping up a flow of chat to Harry, when there was a knock on the door. Daniel came in and greeted his son with a smile.

He held out a DVD. 'Look, Harry, I managed to get a copy of the 2003 rugby world cup in Australia—you know the one England won? I thought we could watch it together.'

Colleen hid a delighted smile. She wasn't sure that Daniel wasn't the one who really wanted to watch the match, but at least he'd taken her words last night to heart.

And then something happened that made her heart crash against her ribs. Harry was making a sound. It was indistinct, but he was clearly trying to speak. He hadn't spoken since the day they'd collected him from hospital. There it was again. 'Mu...'

'What is it, Harry?' she asked.

She sat down on one side of the bed while Daniel took the other.

'Mum?' This time the word was recognisable, as was the rising inflection. Clearly Harry wanted to know where his mother was. Colleen glanced at Daniel. His expression was frozen.

Daniel took his son's hand in his. 'Harry...' he started, before glancing helplessly at Colleen. She nodded at him. This was the moment they had all been dreading. But it was Daniel's place to tell Harry about his mother. She took Harry's other hand in hers and squeezed. 'Harry, your father has something to tell you. You're going to have to be very brave.'

'Mum,' Harry said again. There was no mistaking the panic in his voice.

'Harry,' Daniel started again, his voice firmer this time, 'you were in a car accident. On the way home from boarding school. Do you remember?'

There was a slight movement of Harry's head. 'No.' His voice was hoarse from lack of use. Colleen knew for certain though that he understood the question.

'Mum,' he said again. He was becoming increasingly agitated.

'Your mother was badly hurt in the same accident, Harry,' Daniel said. 'The ambulance took her to hospital. I'm afraid her injuries were too bad. She never woke up.'

Harry's eyes filled with understanding and fear. Daniel moved so that he was lying on the bed next to his son. He put his arms around his child and pulled him close. 'I'm sorry, Harry. Your mother is dead.'

Colleen ached for the misery she saw in Harry's eyes.

'No...no...no,' he said over and over. 'Mum. Want Mum.'

As Daniel's arms tightened around him, the boy struggled weakly in his arms. Harry's eyes clung to Colleen's in desperation. 'Dad go,' he said. 'Not Dad. Mum. Colleen, make him go away.'

'I think you should leave,' Colleen said to Daniel. The pain she saw in his face made her flinch. 'I'll stay with Harry.'

Daniel stumbled to his feet. Tears were rolling down Harry's cheeks. He was turning his head from side to side, still intoning the word 'no' as if he could change what he'd been told.

Daniel stood in the centre of the room as if rooted to the spot. She could see he was torn between wanting to comfort his son and doing as Harry demanded. She stood quickly and gave Daniel a gentle shove towards the door. 'Go now,' she said. 'I'll look after Harry. I'll come and find you as soon as he settles.'

With a last despairing look at his grieving son, Daniel left them alone.

When Harry was settled and sleeping, Colleen went in search of Daniel. She looked everywhere to no avail. Finally she made her way to the kitchen. Burton might know where he was.

But to her surprise, Daniel was in the kitchen, nursing a cup of black coffee. Dora was also there, having arrived from Dorset yesterday.

'How is he?' Dora asked.

'He's sleeping now,' Colleen said. 'He was very upset. It will take time for him to get used to the idea his mother has gone. We should be prepared for some difficult days ahead.' She looked at Daniel and her heart melted. He looked so stricken, so much at a loss. His son's rejection must have cost him a great deal.

Dora got to her feet. 'I'll go and sit with him, shall I?'

'That would be good, thank you, Dora. Please call me immediately if he wakes up.'

She waited until Dora had left the room.

'Daniel…' she started, 'don't take Harry's reaction too much to heart. I—'

But before she could complete the words Daniel had jumped to his feet.

'Don't take what too much to heart, exactly? You mean I shouldn't be upset that my son can't bear the sight of me. That he probably blames me for his mother's death.' His green eyes were cold. 'And he'd be right. Is that what you want to hear? Eleanor asked me to pick him up to bring him to Dorset, but I said no. I had an important meeting.' He laughed and the mirthless sound sent a chill down Colleen's spine. 'What kind of man would put his work before his only child? If I had collected Harry as Eleanor had asked, the accident would never have happened. At the very least Harry would still have his mother.'

'Daniel.' Colleen couldn't help herself. She stepped forwards and placed a hand on his arm, but he shook her off, looking at her as if she repelled him.

'I don't want or need your sympathy,' he said roughly.

'Then for God's sake, stop blaming yourself!' Colleen retorted. 'That boy, your son, is going to need you more than ever in the coming days and weeks. He's lost his mother and he needs time to come to terms with it.' She took a breath and softened her voice. 'He's angry with the world and he's directing it at you—and can you blame him? All he has right now is a father he hardly knows. The last thing he needs is for you to withdraw.' Colleen felt her voice crack. The scene upstairs had taken its toll on her, too. Every time she thought she was beginning to understand Daniel, he did or said something that threw her. Last night Daniel had made it clear how much he cared about Harry and she didn't doubt him for a second, but he had to realise it would take Harry time to know how much Daniel loved him. She opened her mouth to apologise, but Daniel had turned on his heel.

'I'm going out,' he said and, without a glance at her, he stormed out of the room.

Later that night, after Harry was sleeping in the care of the night nurse, Colleen paced her room. She felt restless and ill at ease. She wasn't handling the situation with Daniel at all well. She was letting him rattle her time and time again. It seemed she could barely be in the room with Daniel for ten minutes and they were sparking against each other.

She opened her window and the sounds of late-night traffic and the laughter of couples returning from a night on the town drifted on the still night air. Suddenly she was almost overcome by a yearning to be back in the clear air and peace of County Wicklow.

But not with Ciaran.

The realisation chilled her. She loved Ciaran, but she wasn't *in love* with him and she couldn't marry him. Trish had been right all along. The way she felt about Ciaran was the same way she would feel if he was her brother. She felt more alive after seconds in Daniel's company than she'd ever felt in Ciaran's. Not that she was falling for Daniel. No way. No one in their right mind would fall for that pig-headed, opinionated, arrogant, interesting, exciting… *Whoa there*, she told herself, sternly. *Just because you've decided not to marry Ciaran doesn't mean you fancy another man.* Any feelings she had for Daniel were purely because she'd allowed herself to become so wrapped up in Harry—*so wrapped up in Harry and Daniel*, the voice whispered back—and their pain that she just wasn't thinking straight. But she'd never reacted to any of the other fathers like this, even when she'd been totally involved with their child.

Now she'd made up her mind she couldn't marry Ciaran, she had to let him know as soon as possible. She would have to go back to Ireland this weekend. Her heart ached for the pain she was about to cause him, but if she married him without truly loving him, that would be so much worse.

A tear trickled down her cheek and she closed the window with a decisive click. She was over-tired and over-emotional, that was all. She needed to get some sleep. Tomorrow was bound to be another difficult day. Perhaps some warm milk would help.

She pulled her dressing gown over her pyjamas, shoved her feet into her slippers and let herself out of her room. Apart from the light from Harry's night light that seeped from under his door, the house was in darkness. She popped her head around his door. He was sleeping soundly, with Sheena, the night nurse, in a chair beside his bed.

'Would you like anything from the kitchen, Sheena?' Colleen asked.

'No, thank you, love. Dora brought me some tea a little while ago.'

But instead of finding the kitchen empty, Colleen was dismayed to find Daniel sitting at the kitchen table, his long legs stretched out in front of him. He was so still that at first Colleen thought he was asleep. The kitchen was lit by a single table lamp at the far end of the room, casting Daniel's face in shadows. She was about to slip away when his voice came out of the semi-darkness.

'Couldn't sleep either?'

'I thought I'd make myself some warm milk,' Colleen said, 'but I'll leave you in peace.'

'Warm milk?' His voice was amused. 'Who still drinks warm milk?' He gestured towards her with a tumbler of amber liquid. 'Wouldn't you rather have some whisky? I find it works better.'

She wondered if he was a little drunk. At least he no longer seemed angry with her.

'No, thank you,' she said. 'Can't abide the stuff.'

'I'm sure there's some wine around here, if you'd prefer.' He waved his glass in the general direction of the room. 'Or I can ring for Burton to bring us some.'

'Don't be daft,' Colleen said. 'It's after one in the morning. Let the man have his sleep.'

Daniel's teeth flashed. 'Okay, warm milk it is.' He got to his feet and looked around the room. 'I'm sure there's a pan around here somewhere.'

'I should go,' Colleen said.

'For God's sake, woman. Stay. I'm not going to bite you. Anyway, it's me who should be more nervous than you. God knows what you're going to accuse me of next.'

'I'm sorry about earlier and the other night,' Colleen said. 'I shouldn't have snapped at you. You've enough on your plate.'

'Well, Nurse Colleen, to be honest I've had enough of people agreeing with me. It makes a pleasant change to have someone tell me what's really on their mind.'

She couldn't tell from the tone of his voice or his expression whether he was teasing her or meant what he said. She decided to take his words at face value. Otherwise there was the danger they would get into another undignified slanging match.

Daniel was opening cupboards at random, muttering under his breath when each one failed to reveal what he was looking for.

'Grief, Daniel. Don't tell me you've never cooked yourself anything in this kitchen before.' But weren't her brothers just the same? The minute they entered their mother's kitchen it was as if they lost the use of their arms and legs. Colleen took a mug from the top of the dresser where they were displayed for anyone to see.

'This and the microwave will do fine,' she said.

'Microwave? Do you think Dora would allow such a thing in her kitchen?' Daniel widened his eyes in mock dismay. Then suddenly the tension was broken.

'Sit down,' Colleen told Daniel. 'I'll do it. Would you like some, too?'

He peered at his whisky glass as if surprised to find it empty. He reached across the table and grasped the neck of the bottle sitting there. 'I think I'll stick with this if it's all the same to you.'

Colleen watched anxiously as he poured himself a hefty measure and slugged it back in one go. A sober Daniel was difficult enough to deal with, but an inebriated one? As he reached for the whisky bottle again she whisked it away. 'I think you've had enough, don't you?'

He eyed her balefully. 'Did anyone ever tell you that you're a bossy woman?'

'Many times,' Colleen said lightly. 'And I've been called worse things than that, too.'

'Can't imagine why,' Daniel said drily. He sat up in his chair. 'You know, I find myself wanting to know more about Colleen McCulloch. The woman, that is, not the nurse. That's fair, isn't it? After all, you know all my sordid little secrets.'

Colleen emptied some milk into a saucepan and placed it on the stove to heat. 'I wouldn't call your secrets sordid,' she said. 'You're no different to thousands of parents. People get caught up and fail to recognise what's important. I guess it happens to us all at some time or another.'

He leaned back in his chair. 'Letting me off the hook, then? Somehow I can't imagine you failing to recognise what's important. Too perfect for a start.'

Her perfect? She wished! And certainly not recently. A perfect person would never have behaved towards Daniel the way she had earlier. A perfect person would never have got into the mess she had with Ciaran. A perfect person would never have become engaged simply because it seemed the easiest thing to do and their families wanted it. The truth was that was exactly what had happened and now she was going to have to do something about it and hurt someone she loved in the process. Because although she wasn't in love with Ciaran, she did care about him. No. She knew only too well she was far from perfect.

'I don't think my brothers would agree with you,' she said. 'They always claimed that Daddy let me get away with murder.'

She took her drink and sat down opposite Daniel.

'Tell me about your family,' he said. 'I'd really like to know.'

Reluctant to spoil the easy atmosphere, Colleen refrained from reminding him that he'd already looked into her family. But knowing how many siblings she had and what they did, or did not do, for a living was one thing. Knowing what it was like to be part of a noisy, argumentative but loving household, another. She could only imagine how chaotic her family would seem to Daniel if he ever met them. Which, of course, was extremely unlikely to happen.

'Mammy and Dad always owned a farm,' she said. 'At first they farmed livestock—cattle, sheep, that sort of thing—then Daddy decided that horses were the way to go. He sold off all the livestock and invested in a few brood mares. I suspect he thought that horse breeding was more lucrative somehow than cattle. He always hoped to make his fortune, you see. And that was unlikely to happen with a large family and with the prices of livestock falling all the time.'

'Were you poor?' Daniel asked.

Colleen laughed. 'That depends on what you mean by poor. I guess by your standards we were. At least in monetary terms, but in everything else, no, I always felt rich.'

'Explain,' Daniel said.

Colleen quirked an eyebrow at him. 'Is this how you cross-examine a witness?'

To his credit, Daniel looked abashed. 'Sorry. What I should have said was, "Go on, tell me more".'

'I can't remember not feeling happy as a child. At least until Cahil's accident and Daddy became depressed. But before that there was always something to do. Help Daddy on the farm or play with my bothers—when they'd let me, of course. They used to tease me about being a girl, so I was always trying to show them how tough I was. Led to a few cuts and scrapes, I can tell you.'

'Now why don't I find that hard to imagine? I can just see the little girl you were. Hair flying in the wind as you ran barefoot over the hills.'

'Come on,' Colleen retorted. 'We weren't that poor. We had shoes like everyone else.' When she saw him smile she knew she had been suckered.

'No, up until Daddy sold the cattle for the horses we were comfortably off. But somehow he could never get the hang of breeding horses.' Her heart ached as she remembered her father's slip into depression. 'I know he felt a failure, but it wasn't all his fault. One of the brood mares became unwell suddenly and had to be put down, another foaled, but her colt died. And so it went on until he was left with only one of the five he had invested in. Believe me, high-quality brood mares are expensive to buy and even more expensive to keep.

'We tried to help him, at least my older brothers did—I was too young and at school—but things got so bad that eventually my brothers had to stop helping him on the farm and find work in Dublin. My mother hated her sons leaving and my father felt it was his fault. And then Cahil had his accident. Daddy was never the same. It was as if he'd given up on life. Of course I know now that it was depression, but back then I couldn't understand why Daddy had gone from this laughing man to someone who never smiled and just sat in his chair all day long. The family kind of broke apart then. My mother was distraught. She didn't know how to help him.'

Colleen didn't know why she was telling Daniel all this. Perhaps because it was late. Perhaps it was the semi-darkness, or perhaps it was because he had been through his own kind of hell.

'I'm sorry. What happened to your brother? Can you talk about it?'

Colleen drew in a breath. 'Cahil was the youngest. I was eleven when he was born. I think he was as much of a surprise to Mammy and Daddy as he was to me. But they were happy to have another child. By that time they were still well enough off and there was plenty of room on the farm for one more. But when Cahil was eight my other brothers were working off the farm and Daddy needed help to bring one of the horses in from the field. He wasn't keeping so well by this time so Mammy suggested he wait until one of the older boys came back from work. Cahil must have been listening. He always wanted to be like the big boys. He went out to the field without telling my parents. But the horse wasn't used to him. She had a bit of a temper and was about to foal, but whatever happened we can't be sure. Mammy only noticed that Cahil was gone when she called him for his tea. They found him unconscious in the field. It looked as if the horse had reared up and kicked Cahil in the head. To cut a long story short, Cahil was in hospital for months. Mammy wanted him home. Just like you, she had no faith that the doctors and nurses would look after her baby as well as she could. Daddy was beside himself and no use. He could barely bring himself to look at Cahil. So every day after school, I helped Mammy care for Cahil. She was like a woman possessed. The doctors told her that it was un-likely that my little brother would ever be able to walk or talk or even feed himself. But she wasn't having it. She bullied and coaxed my brother and slowly he began to learn to walk and talk all over again. You should see him now. He still has some short-term memory problems and mixes up his words, but as you know he plays for the local football team and helps my mother on the farm. You would never know just by looking at him that once the doctors held out little hope.'

'So that's why you do what you do,' Daniel said. 'I knew there must be a reason why you were so driven. Your patients are just like your brother all over again, aren't they?'

She wriggled under his intense gaze, surprised by his perception.

'I guess so. I know what the power of love can achieve and that's why, no matter how much Harry pushes you away, you have to believe that right now he needs you more than ever.'

'And your father? What happened to him?'

Colleen sucked in a breath as pain lanced through her. 'He died shortly after Cahil's accident. He didn't live long enough to know that his son made an almost complete recovery. He died feeling guilty and a failure. So you see, Daniel, I know all about what guilt can do to a man.'

The clock ticked into the silence. What Colleen had said surprised Daniel. He was certain there was more to her story—his job had given him an instinct for when people weren't telling the whole truth—but if there was more, he would wait until she decided to tell him. If she ever told him. He studied her as she sipped the last of her drink. He would never have guessed that she had her own tragedy in her life. When she wasn't challenging him, hands on hips and grey eyes blazing, her mouth was curved in an almost permanent smile.

With her dark hair tumbling in loose curls over her shoulders instead of clasped back in the usual ponytail, she looked younger, less severe. Her skin was pale, almost translucent, with an alluring sprinkling of freckles across the bridge of her nose that he found unbearably cute. In fact, there was a great deal about Colleen that he found cute. He liked the way her grey eyes sparked when she was in a temper. He liked the way her mouth twitched when she was trying not to laugh. He liked the way she stood up to him, he liked the way she treated his son and he even liked the way she looked, even in those ridiculous bunny slippers she was wearing on her feet and those childish pyjamas. Her dressing gown had fallen open slightly, revealing a spaghetti top, exposing creamy shoulders and just a hint of cleavage. On the bottom half she was wearing boxer shorts depicting cartoon characters. His brain saw all this, registered it logically and coolly, but there was nothing cool about the way his body was reacting. He hadn't seen her legs before—they were usually hidden by the trousers she always wore, but who in their right mind would hide legs like that? They were slim and toned. The sort of legs that just begged a man to run his hands up their silky smoothness. When she'd leaned over him to place his milk on the table in front of him he'd caught a scent of vanilla and strawberries and he'd shifted in his chair to hide his sudden and immediate response to her. Perhaps it was the whisky or perhaps it was because he'd not been with a woman for a long time? But suddenly an image of Colleen lying underneath him, her body all sweet curves and softness, her grey eyes clouded with desire, filled his head. He shook the image away.

Maybe he was seeing her in a different light because she had allowed him to see the vulnerable side of her.

No wonder he was rattled. The last thing he'd expected was that he couldn't get the Irish harridan out of his head. She was nothing like the women he usually dated. All of a sudden he wanted to see her at one of the dinners he attended—the looks on the other women's faces as she outshone them with her simple beauty despite their designer dresses and hundred-pound haircuts. He bit back a groan. Great. That was all he needed right now. A developing case of the hots for his son's nurse—a woman who just happened to be in love with another man.

CHAPTER TEN

COLLEEN stretched languorously as the sun poured in her bedroom window. For some reason this morning, she felt happier than she had since she took up the job here. She smiled to herself. Maybe it was because she had come to a decision about Ciaran and because some of the tension between her and Daniel had disappeared. After all, her job would be so much easier without the constant clashing of wills. Or maybe it was because she had talked to Daniel about her dad? No one in the family could bring themselves to talk about those final days. Not in front of their mother anyway. They were all too scared that a mention of his name would send Mammy into another paroxysm of grieving. Perhaps it was time that they did talk about Daddy? When she was home next she would try.

She jumped out of bed before Dora could arrive with her tea. She couldn't get used to being served her tea in bed by the housekeeper. It seemed so lazy.

By the time she came out of the shower the tea tray had been left on the table. Dora had even added a small vase of flowers. It seemed that Dora was beginning to thaw towards her. But when she bent to pour the tea, she noticed a small envelope addressed to her in unfamiliar handwriting.

Puzzled, she tore it open. It was from Daniel. It was brief and to the point. 'Thanks for the warm milk. And for telling me about your brother. Most of all thank you for caring about my son.'

Something shifted behind her ribs. Daniel wasn't so bad once you got to know him. They had got off on the wrong foot, that was all. And if her heart had done a crazy little pirouette when she'd seen the note was from him, well, that was just a sign of the pleasure she felt that they seemed to have reached an understanding.

As soon as she was dressed she went to Harry's room. After their chat last night, she'd half-expected to find Daniel by his son's bedside and not just the night nurse. Colleen tried to ignore the thud of disappointment— which was, of course, on behalf of Harry, wasn't it?

'Morning, sunshine,' she chirped.

Harry turned his head at the sound of her voice and smiled. Colleen felt her heart melt—what would happen the day that devastating grin finally reached his emerald eyes? Then she'd be a goner, that was for sure. She was getting far too fond of Harry already, but there was something so special about this young man that she couldn't help herself.

The night nurse gave Colleen a quick handover before she left. 'Has Mr Frobisher been in to see Harry this morning?' Colleen asked softly, so that Harry couldn't hear.

The nurse—Sheena—nodded. 'An hour ago. Harry was still asleep. Mr Frobisher didn't stay long, though, said he'd an important meeting to go to and wouldn't be back till later.'

Colleen closed the door behind Sheena. So much for thinking she'd got through to Daniel last night. It was all she could do to stop herself from marching to the nearest telephone and telling Daniel Frobisher exactly what she thought of him! But she had Harry to concentrate on and that was far more important. Instead, she pulled open the curtains and flung the patio doors wide before turning back to her charge.

'Oh, Harry, it's such a beautiful day—too good for staying indoors. Are you up for some fresh air?'

Harry nodded his head slowly and moved his mouth. 'Yes. Outside. Nice.'

Colleen laughed in delight. 'Excellent, Harry— you're doing it! You're almost there—before you know it you'll be chatting twenty to the dozen, giving me a run for my money, eh?'

His grin widened and Colleen put her hands on her hips in mock horror. 'Are you trying to say I talk too much, young man?'

A sound of delight bubbled from Harry. It was the nearest she'd seen him come to laughing properly. Oh, why wasn't Daniel here to see his son take these tiny, but oh-so-significant steps forwards? Despite his protestations of love, words, after all, were easy to say— acts of love were much harder to do. If only he could understand how much he was missing out on.

She tilted her head to the side. 'You know, Harry, I think you're ready to try something new this morning.' Suddenly his eyes widened in fear and his smile faded. Colleen sat on his bed and reached for his hands, stroking them gently. 'No, no, don't worry. Trust me, Harry.

I won't do anything to harm or frighten you, you know that, don't you?'

When Harry didn't reply, she continued, keeping her tone light and soothing. 'Your dad told me how much you used to love swimming, especially when you were little. Well, I think we should try swimming today; it will really help your arms and legs rebuild their muscles. What do you think?'

Still he gazed back at her. 'I know you're not sure about it, Harry, but I promise I'll look after you. You'll be safe with me, you know that, don't you, sweetheart?'

Harry nodded slowly.

Colleen didn't want to let him see how relieved she felt. If he'd refused or become agitated, there was no way she could have forced him. It was vital that Harry trusted her completely so that he would feel safe in the water and hydrotherapy would bring on his mobility in leaps and bounds. Colleen ruffled his har. 'You're my trooper, aren't you? A brave young man, that's what you are! And it'll be fun, you'll see.' With expert practice she dressed him in a pair of boxer shorts and, using the hoist, manoeuvred him into his wheelchair, chatting all the while. Despite her best jokes and quips, Harry didn't smile once. Colleen could sense his apprehension.

She knelt down in front of him. 'I know you're still unsure, Harry, so I'll tell you what. Will it make you feel better if I ask Burton to help?' Colleen grinned. 'Hey, maybe I should ask him to put on a costume and come swimming with us. He might have one of those one-piece bathing suits that goes to his knees.'

She was rewarded with a smile. Now all she had to do was persuade Burton!

'You wait there, now. Give me a minute while I put my costume on and give Burton the good news.'

To give him credit, Burton didn't put up as much resistance as she'd expected. Perhaps he was too used to Daniel's extravagant requests that nothing much fazed him any more—not that she could imagine what those would be. Who knew how the rich and priviliged lived?

Still, she felt a bit guilty laughing at him behind his back. But it had been worth it to have made Harry smile, she thought.

To her surprise, Burton was already there waiting for them and she almost pushed the wheelchair into one of the elaborate marble columns when she saw him. What in all that was holy was he wearing! Far from the old-fashioned costume she'd half-expected, the older man was dressed in the skimpiest briefs she'd ever seen in her entire life. If he'd worn a wig and a false moustache, she couldn't have been more taken aback.

Colleen averted her eyes from his expanse of bare chest and hairy back, although it took a huge amount of will power to keep her gaze from straying away from his. It was as if her eyes had a sudden will of their own. Thank God they had to concentrate on getting the hoist round Harry and lowering him on to the sling at the side of the pool. When he was secure, Colleen slipped into the warm water and between them they lowered Harry in.

Whilst Burton sat on the side, Colleen slipped her arms under Harry's back and eased him free. His eyes cast round desperately and she tilted him towards her, so that he could see her face.

'Well done,' she soothed. 'I've got you and I'm

going to let you go, Harry. Just try to let the water swirl around you.'

It took a fair amount of cajoling and encouragement, but within ten minutes she felt her young patient begin to relax. 'You're doing really well, sweetheart.'

Suddenly she noticed his gaze slip from hers to over her shoulder and he tensed. Colleen turned round in the water so she could see what had caught his attention.

It wasn't what—it was who. Daniel stood uncertainly at the side of the pool. Thankfully he didn't shop in the same store that Buton did and his swimming shorts were far more modest. She couldn't help noticing that they somehow accentuated his tanned, smooth chest and broad shoulders and didn't make his muscular legs look too shabby either.

'Can I join you?' Daniel asked.

'What do you think, Harry? Can your dad swim with us?' Colleen gazed down at the young lad, willing him to relax. She looked up and caught Daniel's eye. Almost imperceptibly, she nodded.

Daniel nodded to Burton. 'That's okay, Burton, I'll take over from here.'

'Very well, sir.' There was no mistaking the look of relief in Burton's eyes. Colleen caught Daniel's eyes and for a moment his lips twitched. Clearly he found the sight of Burton in his swimwear as amusing as she did. Colleen's heart skipped a beat.

With a graceful ease belying his size, Daniel dived in at the deep end and swam towards them. Harry's eyes widened and he flailed his body, pressing himself as close as possible to her. The arm around her neck tightened and his fingers grasped her hair. Ignoring the sharp pain, Colleen kept her tone even. 'Remember when I said you could trust me, darling? Remember when I promised I wouldn't let any harm come to you? Well, it's the same with your daddy. He only wants to help, Harry.'

Harry tore his eyes away from his father and looked at her. His deep-green eyes searched her face, looking for the slightest hint that she wasn't telling the truth, and in that moment she knew that if Daniel let him down now, made one wrong move, the tiny delicate thread holding father and son together would be broken—maybe forever.

'How about letting your dad hold you? That way I could move your arms and legs about a bit in the water?'

'No.' Harry shook his head.

Colleen met Daniel's gaze over Harry's blond curls. His anguish was unmistakable, but yet he didn't move away from them.

She brushed her lips against Harry's cheeks. 'Your dad is a big strong man, darling, and he's going to hold on to you tight.'

Finally Daniel spoke. 'I won't let you go, son. I promise you.'

Gently Colleen untangled Harry's arms from around her neck and eased him towards his father. Between the two of them they held the too thin child, until Colleen felt his under-used muscles finally relax.

Signalling to Daniel with a nod of her head, she again reassured Harry, 'I'm going to let go now, but just so I can move your legs, okay? Your dad's got you safe.'

As Colleen moved away, Daniel eased himself down into the shallow water, cradling his son in his arms. She watched as, ever so slowly, Harry's arms snaked around his father's neck and clasped on to him tightly.

For a split second she could see Daniel's eyes widen in surprise, then he was looking down at his son, beaming from ear to ear. Pulling him closer, until his blond curls were tucked into his neck, Daniel looked at Colleen.

Thank you, he mouthed.

'What would you like to do this afternoon, Harry?' Colleen asked a couple of days later. 'I know Nathan is coming over this morning, but if the weather clears up later, perhaps we could go out for a while?'

As they were talking, Dora came in with Harry's breakfast and set the tray on the table.

'I think you should have a go at feeding yourself,' Colleen said to Harry. 'Now you're bound to make an almighty mess at first, so we'll do it before your wash. How about it? Are you willing to have a go?'

Colleen cut up Harry's toast that had been supplied with his scrambled egg into easily manageable slices. She wouldn't call them soldiers. Harry would hate to be treated as if he were five instead of twelve.

To her delight, Harry managed, although with some difficulty, to pick up one of the pieces of toast in his hand and bring it towards his mouth. She waited with bated breath as he concentrated hard on bringing the morsel to his lips. Finally, after a couple of false starts, he managed to get it in his mouth. The fine motor control required meant that he was improving in leaps and bounds. He was making progress far quicker than she had dared to hope.

Just as they had finished breakfast and Harry was sitting up in his chair by the window, Daniel came into the room. He was wearing dark trousers and an open neck shirt—no tie.

'Hello, everyone,' he said. 'I've taken the morning off work so we can spend it together. What would you like to do, Harry?'

Harry glanced up at his father and smiled briefly.

'Nathan,' he mumbled.

'Nathan's coming this morning,' Colleen said quickly, seeing Daniel's disappointment. 'What about doing something this afternoon instead? I was just saying to Harry that we should try to have a session in the pool, but we could all go somewhere later.'

Daniel ruffled Harry's hair.

'You could have Nathan over another day,' Daniel said. 'I have to be in court this afternoon. It would give us the chance to do something together first. And you can choose.'

The boy pulled his head away and Colleen caught the bleak look in Daniel's eyes before the usual mask came down. *Don't push it*, she wanted to say. *Give him time.*

Harry shook his head again. 'Nathan!'

Daniel's mouth tightened. 'You can have Nathan visit later. I've taken the morning off, despite the fact that I should be going over this afternoon's case, so I think you and I should do something this morning, Harry.'

Harry flung Colleen a look so full of entreaty she couldn't ignore it. Daniel was going about this all wrong. Couldn't he see that?

'I think since Nathan is already coming over, we should leave things the way they are,' Colleen said evenly.

Daniel pulled a hand through his hair and a look

of resignation crossed his face. 'Whatever you prefer, son.' And with one final look at Colleen, he turned on his heel and left the room.

Harry looked angry. As well he might be. 'Dad. Work. Typical,' he said. 'No time for me.'

Although Colleen was thrilled that Harry's speech and understanding was so much improved, it was the relationship between father and son that was concerning her.

'To be fair to him, Harry, he didn't know Nathan was expected. Your dad did want to spend time with you.' She crouched by Harry's side and took his hand. 'You need to be patient with him. He's trying his best.'

But Harry pulled his hand away. 'You on his side.'

'I'm not. If anything I'm on yours. But I know your father loves you. He's just not sure how to show it.'

She reached out and gently turned Harry's face towards her, forcing him to look in her eyes.

'Give him time, darling.'

Suddenly tears were rolling down Harry's cheeks and he buried his head in Colleen's chest. 'Want...my... mum,' he said between sobs.

'Oh, sweetheart, I know you do.' And Colleen's heart cracked as she held the sobbing child.

After Nathan arrived, Colleen left the boys playing a computer game. Nathan was working the controls, but Harry seemed to be engaged with the game, offering 'yes' and 'no's at regular intervals and even an 'idiot' once.

She tapped on the door of Daniel's study and marched in without waiting for an invitation.

Daniel looked up from his papers and frowned. 'Now's not a good time, Colleen,' he said roughly.

'It seems that there's never a good time, Daniel,' she said. 'Have you any idea how upset Harry is?' She was furious. Despite what she'd said to Harry about giving his father time, how much time did he need? After everything they had spoken about, Daniel still didn't have the faintest idea how to go about building a relationship with his son.

'If you think that the occasional visit with him, or the odd DVD, is going to cut it, then you're a bigger fool than I thought.'

'Harry—' Daniel started, but Colleen stopped him with a wave of her hand.

'Your son is making progress—fantastic progress. But do I need to remind you that he has just lost his mother. He loved his mother deeply and that little boy is *grieving*. And not only has he lost his mother, but he's lost the only home he ever really knew. He's lost the ability to play cricket, to play computer games, he can only express himself with great difficulty and he's only just learning how to feed himself.'

'He's managing to feed himself? But that's great.'

'Please don't interrupt me, Daniel. Yes, it's great that he's learning to do that. But it's not so great that he's having to learn to do everything he once took for granted all over again. Your son has shown, *is* showing, great strength of character, God knows he must have got if from his mother—but every day is a struggle for him. What he needs now, most of all, is to know that he is the most important person in your life. That you are with him literally every step of the way. That you will love him, even if he doesn't improve from where he is now. He needs to know that he can count on you. His father. The person who will be there for him through thick and thin and never ever let him go no matter what happens.'

The shell-shocked look on Daniel's face had slowly turned to anger. 'I don't like to be lectured, Colleen. I am making time for him. If I could be with him all the time, don't you think I would? But there is a small matter of my job.'

'Of course. Your job!'

'Yes, my work. When I heard about the accident I was in the middle of the biggest court case of my life. Do you think that mattered to me when my son was seriously ill in hospital and his mother was dead? But believe it or not, no matter what terrible personal tragedies are happening in people's lives, the world continues. People who need you to act for them don't care what's going on in your life, not when they could be sent down for years because they weren't represented properly. I managed to get the case deferred for a while, so I could spend time with Harry in hospital, and then when it was clear that he was going to be there for some time, I tried to hand the case on to a colleague. But the client wouldn't have it. Funnily enough, he trusted me. He believed, rightly or wrongly, that I was the only person who could save his neck, and he was right. I am bloody good at what I do. It's his case that is starting this afternoon—the preliminary hearing—and I should be in chambers as we speak, going over the defence reports one more time, but because my son needs me, I am here. I can't be with him this afternoon, and not very much over the next few weeks, certainly not as much as I would like to be, but I have no choice.'

His breath was coming in short rapid bursts as if the effort of keeping himself under control was costing him dearly. Colleen was stunned by the naked pain in his eyes.

'So why didn't you just tell him that? Explain? The way you have just explained to me? Your son is angry, hurting and not just physically, but he loves you and I suspect from the photograph we found under his pillow—he's proud of you. At the moment he thinks you're not giving him the time or attention he craves, because you're not interested. Tell him the truth. Spend every minute you're not in court, or preparing, with him. Even if it's just sitting with him.' An idea was forming in her head. 'And maybe—I don't even know if this is possible…maybe I could bring him to court some time so he can watch you.'

They were both staring at each other across Daniel's desk. For a moment there was a silence. Something seemed to shimmer in the room. Colleen's heart was pounding so hard she could almost feel it kicking against her ribs. Daniel reached across and tucked a lock of her hair behind her ear.

'Has anyone ever told you, Colleen McCulloch, that you're some woman? Anyone would be lucky to have you on their side and fighting for them. Maybe you should have considered a career in the court?'

Colleen's legs felt as if they were about to give way. She reached behind her for the chair and almost collapsed into it. Why was everything with this man so… fraught?

Daniel leaned back and studied her through half-closed eyes as if she were a problem he couldn't quite get a fix on. 'I'd like Harry to come to court one day.

Perhaps then he'll understand why it was so difficult for me to be around.'

'If you want him there so you can excuse your absence from his life, then I think it's going to take much more than that.'

'Determined not to let me off the hook?'

Colleen used the edge of the desk to ease herself on to still-weak legs.

'I think it's you that has to let yourself off the hook, don't you?' And with as much grace as she could manage on her wobbly legs, she left the room.

CHAPTER ELEVEN

DANIEL was still feeling irritable when he got up the next morning. As soon as he was dressed he crept into Harry's room to say goodbye before leaving for chambers. The night nurse rose from her chair as he entered the room, but he signalled for her to stay seated and crossed over to Harry's bed. His son was still sleeping, his blond hair, so much like his mother's, falling across his brow.

Harry sighed in his sleep and Daniel's chest tightened. Why hadn't he tried harder to get to know his son when he had the chance? He could still have been a lawyer and made a decent living without working almost every waking hour. The money had never really interested him.

Haversham had been handling most of his father's business since Harry's accident and was doing a good job. Realistically, all Daniel needed to do was attend the monthly meetings and study the published accounts. His court cases were another matter, especially the *pro bono* ones. If he didn't take them on, who else would?

He bent down and kissed Harry on the cheek before saying goodbye to the nurse and letting himself out of the room. Who was he kidding? He worked because the truth was he didn't know who Daniel Frobisher was outside work. Doing what he did defined him. But yesterday, spending time away from the never-ending cases piled up on his desk hadn't prevented his cases from being as well prepared as they should be. But if he were honest with himself—and with Colleen around to be his conscience, it was hard to be anything else—he did find spending time with his son difficult. He didn't have a clue how to reach him—how to talk to him, how to simply be with him—not the way Colleen, a comparative stranger, did. But she was wrong about one thing. He would never give up trying to learn how to be the kind of father Harry deserved. Perhaps there was a way to spend time with his son while keeping on top of his cases. Surely all he had to do was work harder?

CHAPTER TWELVE

THE following day Daniel woke up with a smile on his face. He couldn't remember when he'd looked forward to a day off before. In fact, when had he last taken a day off? When had he last gone to the theatre? Or to a concert or even for a drive? Haversham was dealing with the business and Daniel wasn't due in court until tomorrow. From now on things would be different. He would spend proper time with his son, do all the stuff he should have done years ago. The stuff that according to Colleen other fathers did with their children. Starting today. Yesterday in the pool when Harry had clung to him he'd felt as if his heart would break. Up until now he wasn't even sure that he had one to break. It had felt good to hold Harry in his arms. And that was down to Colleen. For the first time he allowed himself to believe that his son would come back to him. Maybe even learn to love him.

The rain had disappeared and the sun was streaming in the window. He would ask Colleen where she thought they should go today. He jumped out of bed and into the shower. Thinking of Colleen made him smile. This house with its large, empty rooms had never felt like home before. Now he found himself listening out for light footsteps on the wooden floors, the sound of her laughter. God, he even liked it when she was confronting him, hands on hips, eyes blazing with indignation. And those hips. He'd noticed them before when she'd come down to the kitchen and he couldn't help notice them again when he saw her in the pool. And it wasn't just her hips. It was her tiny waist and her small but perfect breasts. With her long hair plastered to her face she looked like some sea sprite just risen from the sea. God, she was bringing out the poet in him, too. He was even beginning to think in the same rhythms that she spoke.

As soon as he was dressed, he went to look in on Harry. His son was still sleeping, his light blond hair falling over his forehead and his mouth only beginning to lose its childish softness.

Daniel closed the door gently on his sleeping son and bounded downstairs to the kitchen. He sneaked up on Dora, who was busy stirring a pot on the stove, and wrapped his arms around her waist.

Dora shrieked and spun around.

'Mr Frobisher! I didn't hear you coming in. What's with the boyish pranks? Aren't you getting too old to be frightening an old lady half out of her wits?'

Daniel grabbed a piece of toast from the kitchen table. 'Sorry, didn't mean to frighten you. I just felt like giving you a hug.'

Dora eyed him speculatively. 'What's brought all this on? I haven't seen you look this cheerful for a long time. Far too long a time.'

Daniel sat down on the kitchen chair. 'For the first

time, Dora, I believe that Harry's going to be okay. Really okay. How can I not be happy about that?'

'I heard he's turned a corner. Colleen was down here not a minute or two before you, telling me all about it.' Dora's eyes grew soft. 'I'm so happy for you. That girl seems to know what she's doing.'

'You mean Colleen?' Daniel said casually. 'I always knew she was the right person for Harry.'

'And the right person for you, perhaps?'

Daniel jumped to his feet. That was going too far. 'Sorry, Dora. You know I'm never going to get married again. I was rubbish at it when I was married to Eleanor and I'm never going to put another woman through that again. Apart from that, don't you know Colleen is getting married herself? In a couple of months' time, if I remember.'

'So she told me,' Dora said, drily. 'Anyway, what are you wanting for your breakfast? The usual glass of orange juice to go with your toast. Bacon? Eggs?'

'The full works, Dora,' Daniel replied cheerfully. 'I've a feeling I'm going to need some fortifying for the day ahead. Then I'm going to take Harry's breakfast up to him.'

Once he'd eaten Daniel went back to Harry's room with a tray. His son was sitting up in bed and managed a small smile when he saw his father. It was still nothing in comparison to the smiles he bestowed on Colleen, but it was a start. 'What about breakfast?' he asked. 'Porridge and toast?'

Harry pulled a face.

Daniel laughed. 'Okay, maybe we can hide the porridge from Colleen. But let's give the toast a try.' He turned to the night nurse. 'I can take it from here. You might as well get off.'

'I don't like to. Not until Colleen gets here.'

Daniel looked at his watch. It was still early. 'I doubt she'll be here for another half an hour or so. Don't worry, we can manage, can't we, son?'

To his relief, Harry nodded.

After the night nurse had said her goodbyes and left, Daniel buttered Harry's toast and cut it into small pieces. 'My mother used to do this for me when I was a little boy.'

Tears welled in Harry's eyes. 'Mum used to,' he said.

Daniel's chest tightened. His first instinct was to pretend he hadn't heard. But he could almost hear Colleen's voice telling him that he had to find the words to comfort his son.

'Your mother loved you very much,' Daniel said. 'When my mother died, I was too young to really know that she wasn't coming back. Sometimes I'd want my mum so bad, I thought I would break into pieces. I was angry with her for not coming when I needed her.'

Harry's eyes were fixed on his face. Daniel struggled for the right words. God, he wished Colleen was here. She'd find exactly the right words. He lay down on the bed and put his arm around his son.

'Dora was our housekeeper back then. She told me that my mother would always be part of me. That she was watching over me and that she wouldn't want me to be sad or angry.' His throat was so dry he could barely speak. 'It wasn't always easy to remember that, but I tried to and it helped.' He smoothed Harry's hair with his hand. 'I know that your mother would never have left you if she had the choice and that she is somewhere watching over you—even if it's because of the memories you have of her inside.'

His words sounded so inadequate. He glanced at Harry. Although he looked unconvinced, his eyes had cleared. If only Daniel had tried harder to get to know his son, perhaps he would have found the right words. But there was no point in thinking about what could have been—should have been—he had to deal with the present.

'Hear her in my head,' Harry said. Although the words were slurred, it was the first complete sentence Daniel had heard his son say. The tightness in his chest eased. He was beginning to see a future—not just for his son, but for them together.

When he'd finished helping Harry with his breakfast Daniel slipped a DVD into the player. 'I thought we could watch the match we didn't see the end of the other day. Would you like that?'

'Work?' Harry said.

'Not today, Harry. I plan to spend the whole day with you.' A small smile crossed his son's lips.

They had been watching the match in companionable silence when Colleen came into the room.

'Well, look at the pair of you,' she said, pretending to be cross, 'Watching TV before breakfast.'

'We've already had it.' Daniel nodded his head towards the empty bowl. He'd flushed most of the porridge down the toilet. Not that he would tell Colleen that. 'We're looking forward to when we can have a burger.'

Harry's face lit up. Then he said 'Yes. Burger.' As before, although it was indistinct the meaning was clear.

'I think it's time we asked the speech therapist to come, guys,' Colleen said, looking delighted. 'With her help we'll have you chatting away in no time.'

She picked up the tray. 'I'll leave you two to it,' she said, 'while I have my breakfast. But as the sun's shining, what do you say about going out to get some fresh air this morning?'

'Sounds good to me.' Daniel winked at Harry. 'Take your time with breakfast, Colleen, so we can see the end of the match, eh?'

By the time Colleen returned, however, the sunshine had turned to heavy rain and a trip outside was out of the question. But now that Harry was making progress she wanted to establish a more normal routine. Keeping him in his room all day had never been part of the plan. Dora was sitting in the chair by the window, knitting as she and Daniel chatted.

'Time to get dressed, Harry,' Colleen said.

Harry looked at his father. 'Not Dad. You and Dora.'

Colleen was delighted. Harry's speech was coming on so quickly now that she suspected it was only a matter of time before he was speaking more or less normally.

'Why don't we let Dad go and check his emails while Dora and I get you dressed?' she suggested. Harry was at that age where he'd feel uncomfortable having his father dress him.

Luckily, Daniel seemed to catch on and excused himself. 'I'll be back in twenty minutes. Maybe the rain will have gone by then.'

When Daniel left. Harry scrabbled at his bedclothes. It looked as if he was trying to get out of bed.

'What is it, Harry? What do you want?' Colleen asked.

'Walk.'

Dora and Colleen shared a glance.

'You want to try walking?'

Harry nodded.

'Tell you what, why don't we have you sitting at the side of the bed while we get you dressed? Then we can see how you manage to stand. Your muscles are going to be weak at first, so you might only manage a minute or two at first, but that and the swimming is a good way of getting some strength back in your legs. What do you say?'

They got him dressed in his jeans and a T-shirt, Colleen and Dora taking turns to thread his arms through the sleeves.

'Why don't we stand you up while we pull your jeans up?'

They took Harry's weight between them while Colleen pulled up his jeans and fastened them.

'Okay. Try to take as much of your own weight as you can. Dora and I will be here to catch you if you think you're going to fall.'

Very slowly they decreased their support until Harry was standing. It only lasted a few seconds before he swayed and had to be helped back into his position at the edge of the bed.

'That was fantastic, Harry! Well done. We'll keep trying. But you'll see, soon we'll have you back on your feet and maybe then you can try a few steps. How does that sound?'

Harry grinned up at them. 'Good.' Then he shook his head. 'Don't…Dad.'

'You don't want me to tell your dad, Harry. Is that what you're trying to say?'

Harry nodded.

'But he'll be thrilled. He's been so worried about you.'

Harry's expression settled into one Colleen knew very well. It was the same one she'd seen on his father's face several times before. It seemed the son was as stubborn as the father. But in terms of Harry's progress that was good. Harry would need all his stubbornness and determination in the weeks and months to come.

'Fair enough, sweetie. If you don't want me to tell your father, I won't. From now on it's up to you to keep him up to date with your progress. Unless, of course, something happens and I have to tell him. Deal?'

Harry's smile was back.

'Deal,' he said.

Daniel had quickly dealt with his emails before returning to Harry's room.

'The sun's shining again so I thought the three of us could go out somewhere. Does anyone have any preferences? Of course you're welcome to come too, Dora.'

'Funny, Harry and I were thinking just the same thing. Harry would like to go to Hyde Park, if that would be okay?' Colleen said.

It was uncanny how Colleen seemed able to communicate with Harry even with Harry's speech being so limited. Daniel had seen it happen too often not to know that it was genuine. She would ask a question and, depending on Harry's yes or no, ask another until she had established what Harry wanted. Over the time she'd been here, their unique form of shorthand was developing to a point where she seemed to know what Harry wanted with very little difficulty.

'I'll stay here if that's all the same to you,' Dora said. 'My legs aren't what they used to be.'

As they were about to leave the doorbell rang. Daniel opened it to find a man with longish dark hair and a cheerful smile.

'Hello,' the stranger said in an Irish accent. 'Is Colleen about, by any chance?'

'Ciaran! What on earth are you doing here?' Colleen said, from behind Daniel. 'Not that it isn't good to see you,' she added hastily.

Was it his imagination or did Colleen seem less than enthralled to see her fiancé? The thought cheered Daniel immensely.

He watched Colleen lift her face for Ciaran's kiss. So this was the man she loved? This unremarkable individual with his bad haircut and washed-out jeans was the man Colleen was intending to marry? He simply couldn't see it.

'I thought, if you couldn't come to see me, I would come to see you, Col,' Ciaran said.

Col? What kind of name was that? It didn't suit her.

Ciaran pulled Colleen into his arms and hugged her.

Colleen returned the hug half-heartedly. She glanced at Daniel and flushed, before wriggling out of Ciaran's embrace. She turned to Harry, who had been watching them with interest.

'Harry, this is my fiancé, Ciaran. Remember I told you about him?'

Harry nodded and with a huge effort lifted his hand from his lap and held it out towards Ciaran.

Ciaran took it and shook it. 'Col's told me a lot about

you, Harry. It's grand to meet you at last. She tells me you're a rugby fan. Well, so am I.'

Colleen looked at Daniel, delight written all over her face, and he grinned back. Harry's movements were becoming more and more purposeful.

Then she frowned. 'I'm sorry, Ciaran, but now's not a good time. We're about to go out to the park. Where are you staying? Perhaps we can meet up later?' She looked at Daniel for confirmation.

He nodded reluctantly. After all, Colleen was entitled to time off. He had no right to stop her seeing her fiancé. Even if the thought made him feel…resentful was the word that came to mind.

'I came straight here,' Ciaran said. 'I thought there might be a B&B nearby.'

'You are welcome to stay at Carrington Hall,' Daniel found himself saying. He didn't want Ciaran staying here. In fact, he wanted him a thousand miles away. But he couldn't *not* ask him. There were seven empty bedrooms in the house. The very least he owed Colleen was to make her fiancé welcome. Even if it was the last thing he wanted.

'Oh, Ciaran will be happy with a B & B,' Colleen said, quickly. 'Isn't there one nearby?'

Of course—Colleen and her fiancé would want to have somewhere they could meet in private. Daniel ignored the knot in his stomach

'If that's what you'd prefer, of course,' he said, 'I'll ask Burton to arrange it.' He signalled to Burton, who nodded and picked up the telephone.

'There is a decent establishment a couple of streets away, sir. I'll give them a call now.'

'And of course you should have the day off. Harry and I will manage on our own,' Daniel said.

But as he glanced at his son he saw a stricken look cross his face. Obviously, despite the improvement in their relationship, Harry wasn't ready to be alone with him. The buoyant feeling he'd had when he'd woken up was fast disappearing.

Colleen must have seen Harry's reaction too, as she quickly crouched beside Harry and took his hand. 'What? And miss Harry's first trip out? No way. Ciaran won't mind waiting until we get back, will you?'

'Or I could come with you,' the idiot said, cheerfully. 'It's not as if I've got anything else to do—'

'I'm not sure Harry should be introduced to new people at this stage,' Daniel interrupted. 'It's perfectly all right if you just want it to be the three of us, Harry. I'm sure Ciaran will be happy staying behind. He's probably tired.'

'Oh, I think if Harry's fine with Ciaran coming, then that's okay. Harry would tell me if he didn't want him along. Wouldn't you, sweetie?'

Harry smiled and nodded.

'The Duchess Hotel has a room available, sir,' Burton said. He turned to Ciaran. 'It's just a short walk from here, sir, but I could ask Mike to take you.'

'Why don't I walk with you as far as my hotel?' Ciaran said. 'Col, we could meet there when you've had your walk.'

Could that be relief on Colleen's face? No, that was wishful thinking on his part. No doubt she preferred to see Ciaran alone away from prying eyes.

With the decision made that Ciaran would accompany them as far as his hotel, the four of them set off.

Colleen insisted on pushing Harry. As the pavement was too narrow for the three of them to walk side by side, Daniel found himself alongside Ciaran.

'Did you fly?' he asked.

'Just jumped on a plane at Dublin this morning. Luckily there was space. If there hadn't have been, I would have taken the ferry.'

'You should have said. I would have sent my plane for you.'

'I wanted to surprise Col. She's looking grand, isn't she?'

Daniel followed Ciaran's gaze. Colleen's ponytail was swinging as she walked and her bottom undulated deliciously with every step she took. Daniel bit back the groan that rose to his lips.

What exactly did Ciaran expect him to say? *Yes, she's looking good. She looked even better in her bikini. In fact, I think she's quite beautiful. She has a smile that lights up a room.*

'Yes. She has a great deal of energy.' Good God, couldn't he have thought of something else to say?

Ciaran laughed. 'You can say that again. Col's never happy unless she's bustling around and has plenty to do. The only time I see her sitting still is when she has her nose in a book. She's been like that as long as I can remember.'

'How long have you known her?' Daniel asked, his curiosity piqued.

'Since she was about ten. I was—am—pals with her older brothers. She was always a bit of a tomboy.' Ciaran frowned. 'Is she okay? I mean, she sounded a bit strange the last time I spoke to her on the phone.'

'She seems all right to me,' Daniel replied.

* * *

Daniel was pleased when Ciaran peeled off at his hotel. Thankfully there was no repeat of the earlier hug. Colleen simply gave Ciaran a wave and, as Daniel took over chair-pushing duty, she fell into step beside them.

It felt odd to be out like this, almost as if the three of them were a family. Which was ridiculous. Harry was all the family he wanted or needed.

The park was mobbed with people, riding bikes, picnicking and generally relaxing in the first real sunshine of the month. Daniel caught a badly aimed frisbee as it came his way and returned it, and was pleased to see it went in the general direction he'd planned.

'Is there anything you'd like to do in particular, Harry?' he asked. But to his dismay his son's expression had darkened and he turned his face away from him.

Quickly Colleen crouched by the side of Harry's chair. 'I know it's tough, Harry, seeing all these people doing stuff you used to do. But you've got to believe me when I tell you that I really believe that in time you'll be able to do more—a lot more. There's no reason why you might not be able to throw a frisbee yourself. Do anything you put your mind to, in fact.'

Perhaps this hadn't been such a good idea after all. All it was doing was reminding Harry of what he could no longer do. Harry pointed over Colleen's shoulder. Daniel had been so intent on keeping an eye on the frisbee throwers that he hadn't noticed another group playing cricket. Suddenly he saw something fly towards the air directly towards Harry. Before he was even aware of what he was doing he had thrown himself forwards just in time to catch the missile in his right hand. However, his impetus threw him on to the ground where he landed in an untidy heap.

Feeling an idiot, he was about to jump back up when suddenly Colleen was there, leaning over him, anxiety flooding her grey eyes.

'Are you okay? Speak to me, Daniel.'

He no longer felt the need to move. It was kind of nice to have Colleen bending over him. She bent lower to peer in his eyes and as she did so her ponytail fell forwards, enveloping him in the smell of strawberries and vanilla. He groaned.

'What have you hurt? Can you sit up?'

He considered laying it on a bit thicker, but decided against it. They had Harry to think about. He grinned at her and jumped to his feet. He looked down at his hand. He was still holding the missile, which turned out to be a cricket ball. If that had hit Harry, God only knew what damage it would have done. He turned towards his son. Harry was smiling.

'Good catch, Dad,' he said.

Colleen looked at Ciaran across the table and took a deep breath. 'I have something to tell you, Ciaran,' she said. She hadn't expected Ciaran to jump on a plane and come and see her. But now he was here, she had to tell him.

For once Ciaran looked serious. 'I think I know what it is.'

'You do?'

'Come on, Col, we've known each other for ever. You've never been any good at keeping things hidden from me. You've decided not to marry me. Am I right?'

'I am so sorry, Ciaran.' She reached a hand across the table and Ciaran took it. 'How did you guess?'

Ciaran smiled sadly. 'It's been this way for a while, hasn't it? I've known for months you were having your doubts, but I thought if I said nothing, things would just get better. Anyway, it's not just you whose been having doubts. I love you, Col, you know I do, but I've met someone recently and she looks at me the way someone who's in love with you is supposed to look at you. The way you and Daniel look at each other—as if you have stars in your eyes.'

What on earth did he mean? If only Ciaran knew how often she and Daniel argued.

'That's nonsense, Ciaran. I sometimes think Daniel would like nothing more than to give me a good shake and as for the way I feel about him…'

'You're in love with him. Anyone with a pair of eyes in his head can see that.'

'In love with Daniel?' Had Ciaran completely lost the plot? 'No way.'

'And he's in love with you. I knew it the moment I saw the way he looks at you.'

'You're got it completely wrong, Ciaran. Daniel and I can barely be in the room together for two minutes before sparks start to fly.'

Ciaran leaned back in his chair. 'Exactly,' he said.

Colleen's head was spinning. Was Ciaran right? Could this crazy feeling in the pit of her stomach, this urge to be around Daniel, this feeling as if every nerve ending was tingling whenever he was around, be love? If so, it didn't make her feel good. It made her feel awful.

No, of course she wasn't in love with Daniel. It was

just that she'd never met anyone like him—someone who made her feel more alive than she ever had before. But that wasn't love. That was lust. And as for him being in love with her? Hah! Nothing was less likely.

'You've got it all wrong, Ciaran. But I'm glad you're okay about us not getting married.' She smiled back at him. The relief of breaking off her engagement and knowing Ciaran wasn't upset, made her feel lighter than she had in days.

She twisted the ring from her finger and handed it to him.

'I hope we can still be friends.'

'Hey, we're breaking off our engagement, not falling out. Of course we'll always be friends, Col. And I will always love you—and your crazy family. You know that, don't you?'

She returned his grin. 'So tell me about this woman who looks at you with stars in her eyes, Ciaran. I want to know everything.'

CHAPTER THIRTEEN

DANIEL let Burton take his jacket. It had been another tough day in court, but he was confident they would get the verdict they were seeking. In a day or two the trial would be over and he could take time off to be with Harry. He had cleared his diary, refusing to take any more cases for at least four weeks. Harry would have his undivided attention during that time.

'The doctor is here to see you, sir,' Burton said.

Daniel's heart thudded. Had Harry relapsed? Handing his briefcase to Burton, he hurried into his son's room. The doctor was leaning over Harry, listening to his chest.

'Hello, Dad,' Harry said.

Daniel's chest felt tight. 'Hello, son.'

The doctor straightened. 'Your son is doing well,' he said. 'His speech is pretty much back to normal and, despite a continuing weakness in his right side, it looks like he's making excellent progress.'

'What do you think of our star boy, then?' Colleen said, her grey eyes sparkling.

'I think he's amazing,' Daniel said. He perched on the side of Harry's bed and ruffled his hair.

'Not a baby, Dad,' Harry said.

The doctor packed his stethoscope away in his bag. 'You should have a rest, Harry. You've had a busy day. Although you're improving, don't try and do too much too soon.'

'We've been in the pool again this morning,' Colleen added. 'Nathan and Burton helped.'

Guilt coiled in Daniel's chest. He should be the one helping his child. But over the coming weeks he'd be able to do just that.

'I have a couple of days more in court, son,' Daniel said. 'But after that, I'm on holiday. We can go into the pool every day and maybe you and I could go to a cricket match?'

Harry looked at Colleen, anxiety darkening his green eyes. Daniel felt the look like a blow to his solar plexus.

'Don't worry, Harry. I'm not going anywhere,' Colleen said quickly. 'Not until you're ready.'

'I think I want to sleep now,' Harry said.

Daniel stepped outside with the doctor, leaving Colleen to settle Harry.

'Will he make a full recovery?'

'It's too early to say how much he'll continue to improve, but, yes, if you all carry on doing what you're doing, I see no reason why your son won't be able to return to school after the summer. He may still require a wheelchair, but that in itself shouldn't prevent him. I am warning you, however, that he may experience some lack of concentration and some mood swings for some time yet, so be prepared.'

Mood swings and a loss of concentration were nothing compared to the prospect of having his son permanently disabled. His decision to seek out Colleen had been the right one. Perhaps his son would have improved anyway, but he couldn't help but believe his rapid progress was at least partly down to Colleen.

Daniel had waited outside until Colleen emerged, closing the door gently behind her.

She looked up at him and smiled. He loved her smile. It made it seem as if there were a thousand candles burning behind her eyes.

'He'll sleep for a couple of hours. I told him to press his buzzer when he wakes up.'

'I don't know how to thank you,' Daniel said.

'All in a day's work,' Colleen said breezily.

'Don't be modest, Colleen,' Daniel said. 'It doesn't suit you. I know what Harry and I owe you; if there's anything I can do to thank you, you only have to say the word.'

'I'm being thanked well enough,' she said. 'You already pay me three times the going rate.'

'That's not what I meant.'

Colleen looked at him with her steady grey eyes. A man could happily drown in those eyes. How come he'd never noticed before?

'It's enough,' she said. 'It's great, though, that you've taken time off. We can get Harry into the pool every day. We can take him places—to see you in court—to a cricket match—anywhere he fancies.'

'Perhaps we could go somewhere this weekend?' Daniel suggested.

'You could go anywhere you like, but I'd like to go home this weekend. There are things I need to get sorted.'

A strange feeling coiled in Daniel's chest. He didn't want Colleen to go home—even for a weekend.

'I'd prefer it if you could stay this weekend.'

'I'm sorry. I would like to, but...' She tailed off. 'I really need to go home. I wouldn't ask to go if it wasn't important.'

Of course, she wanted to see her fiancé. The thought gave him no pleasure. He especially didn't want to think of her with Ciaran. But he had no right to try to stop her.

Just then Dora appeared with a tray. 'I have some sandwiches and cake. Where would you like it?'

'No more cake.' Colleen groaned. 'Another couple of weeks of your baking and I won't be able to fit into anything.'

'There's nothing wrong with the way you look,' Daniel protested. 'Nothing at all.'

To his delight, Colleen blushed. She was the only woman he knew that did. And it only made her more appealing to him. He'd choose Colleen McCulloch with her what-you-see-is-what-you-get manner over the superficially glamorous women he usually dated, any time.

'You can always use the gym downstairs,' Dora suggested. 'Seeing as someone has spent a fortune on it.'

'I hate the gym. It's like a medieval form of torture,' Colleen replied with a smile. 'But I may well be forced to give it a go.'

'We'll take tea in the garden,' Daniel said. 'Please join me, Colleen. I could do with not having to think about my case for a couple of hours.'

'I don't suppose one little sandwich will hurt,' Colleen replied. 'And I was planning to take my book into the garden to read. If we sit near Harry's room, we can hear him when he wakes up.'

Daniel took the tray from Dora. He knew he should ask the older woman to join them, but this was too good an opportunity to get Colleen to himself for a while. So they could talk about Harry, of course.

The wrought-iron table and chairs were only a short distance from Harry's room and Daniel set down the tray and sat down.

'It's a beautiful day,' Colleen said, picking up the bone china teapot. 'I hope the weather stays like this for a while. How do you like your tea?'

'Like my coffee. Black,' Daniel replied and watched her through half-closed eyes as she poured the tea. She took a satisfied sip and closed her eyes, turning her face to the sun. 'I wonder what they're doing back in Ireland,' she said. 'No…wait…I know what they'll be doing. Ciaran will be seeing to the horses with my brothers. Mammy will be in the kitchen, making dinner with the dogs at her feet.'

'Do you miss them?' Daniel asked.

'I've never really been away from them for very long. I spend all my days off on the farm.'

'I gather you've known Ciaran a long time.'

'Since for ever, it seems. We were in high school together. He was friends with my oldest brother and used to hang about the farm. I can hardly remember a time when I didn't know him.' His chest tightened when some of the light went out of her grey eyes.

'Do you love him?' The question surprised even him.

'Actually, Daniel, Ciaran and I have broken up. The other day—when he came to London.'

A wave of delight surged through Daniel. But why was she looking so sad?

'Was it Ciaran who broke it off?' If it was Ciaran

and Colleen still loved him, that would account for the look in her eyes. His delight faded.

'I'd really rather not discuss it, Daniel.'

That wasn't good enough. He had to know how she felt.

'Mum! Mum!' The panicked cry came from Harry's room and Colleen and Daniel were on their feet and running. 'Colleen!'

They burst into Harry's room. The boy was struggling to sit up, a look of terror on his face. 'Where's Mum?' he cried. 'I want her. Please, Colleen, I need her.'

Daniel was across the room and gathered his son into his arms, cradling the sobbing child against his chest.

'Shh, Harry. It's okay. I'm here. Dad's here.' He looked at Colleen for support. God, how often would this happen? Colleen didn't move. Daniel continued to hold his son until the sobs quietened to only the occasional hiccups.

'Mum. She's dead, isn't she?' Harry said. 'I keep dreaming she's here next to me.'

'She is next to you. She might be dead, Harry, but she's looking over you from wherever she is. But I'm here.'

'Don't leave me, Daddy,' Harry said.

Daniel hugged Harry tighter. 'I'm never going to leave you, son. Not ever.'

Colleen had left Daniel comforting his son. She could have intervened, but it was Daniel that Harry ultimately needed. The sight of Daniel holding the son who looked so much like him made her heart twist. It would take time before the rift between them was completely healed, but if Daniel would keep his promise it was a start. It wouldn't be long now before she could go home and leave this small family to get on with their lives. The thought made her heart ache even more. Damn it! Hadn't she promised herself that she wouldn't get overly emotionally involved with them? She was here to do a job and if that job was nearly done, she should be happy and not filled with dismay.

She went upstairs to change for dinner. As the evening was warm she would swap her usual jeans and T-shirt for a summer dress. She also decided to let her hair down. Peering at her reflection in the mirror, she was irked to see that there were shadows under her eyes. Maybe she should do as Dora suggested and spend some time in the gym? She'd spent so much time inside with Harry lately; no doubt all she needed was some fresh air and exercise.

She found Daniel and Harry, who was sitting up in bed, watching a DVD. Although Harry wasn't looking at Daniel, neither was he turning his head away.

'Hello, you two,' Colleen said. 'What are you up to?'

'It's the test match between England and Pakistan. It's almost finished. Do you want to watch it with us?'

'Don't understand the first thing about the game. Now if you were watching a rugby match that would be different.'

'Not like cricket? Is she nuts, do you think, Harry?'

A small but unmistakable smile crossed Harry's mouth. It seemed that more than physical progress was being made. Although his eyes were red rimmed, he seemed more settled than she'd seen him for a while.

'Look, I've had an idea,' Colleen said 'I'm going

home this weekend. But why don't you both come too? One of our dogs has just had a litter of puppies and I'm sure you'd like to see them, Harry. You can also meet my brother Cahil. He had a head injury a few years ago and you might find it helpful to meet him. He'll know exactly what you are going through. What do you say?'

The idea had just come to her, but the more she thought about it, the more it seemed like a plan. She could see her family and be able to keep on top of Harry's therapy.

A broad smile crossed Harry's face. 'Puppies! Could we have one, Dad?'

'If Colleen can part with one, I don't see why not.' Daniel frowned and looked thoughtful. 'But Harry and I couldn't put your mother out. Doesn't she have a pretty full house as it is?'

'Oh, Mammy can always fit in another couple of bodies. She loves having people to stay and she'd love to fuss over Harry. Now her children are all almost grown up, she's always asking when any of us are going to have kids so she can have children about the farm again.'

A shadow crossed Daniel's face as if something she had said displeased him. Perhaps the thought of roughing it was a step too far? After all, this man was used to having a whole house to himself. He was more used to five-star hotels than a crowded farmhouse. 'But…' she went on hastily, 'please don't feel you have to come.'

'I want to go,' Harry said. 'Please, Dad. I want to see the horses and the puppies.' He looked anxious. 'I want to stay with Colleen.'

It was only natural that the child didn't want to be separated from her. He had got used to her being around. But as his relationship with his father improved,

he'd need to become less reliant on her. If Daniel was
upset that Harry didn't seem keen to have him on his
own for the weekend, he gave no indication of it.

'If you're sure your mother won't mind a couple of
extra guests, then we'd like to come,' he said. 'We could
take the plane on Friday and come back on Sunday evening.'

'That's settled, then,' Colleen said. 'I'll let Mammy
know. Now, why don't we all have dinner together?'

After dinner when Harry was back in bed and Daniel
reading to him from one of the books they had brought
back from Dorset, Colleen had phoned her mother to
let her know there would be two extra guests at the
weekend. She'd already told her that Ciaran and she
had broken up, but her mother hadn't seemed the least
bit surprised. The phone call finished, Colleen let herself out of the door and into the garden. Although it
was eight, the sun was still up. Harry had managed to
feed himself pretty well after Colleen had cut up his
food for him. It was another step in the right direction.

'Can I join you?' Daniel's deep voice came from behind her. Her heart thumped.

'Sure. I was just about to go exploring. Is Harry
asleep?'

'Yes. Why don't we walk this way?' Daniel took her
elbow and an odd zinging sensation shot up her arm.

'I want to thank you again,' he said. 'You've made
such a difference to Harry and in such a short time.'

'He's a determined boy. Takes after his father, I suspect.'

'Why don't you ever take a compliment when it's
given to you?'

'I'm happy to accept compliments any time,' Colleen said. Annoyingly, she sounded breathless as if she'd been on a gallop on one of the horses.

'In that case, you should know that you look beautiful tonight.' His voice was easy, almost teasing, but there was an unmistakable undercurrent in his words. Was it possible Daniel Frobisher was flirting with her? Had Ciaran been right when he said Daniel was attracted to her? She immediately dismissed the thought. Daniel's words were just the well-oiled ones of a man used to charming people.

Daniel reached across and touched her gently on the cheek. 'Do you know two dimples appear just here when you smile?'

The touch of his fingers made it difficult for her to breathe. Okay, so he was definitely flirting.

'Have you kissed the Blarney stone recently?' she asked, striving to keep her voice light.

He laughed. She liked it when he laughed. It made his face soften and his green eyes glint. Good God, what was she thinking? And her just recently unengaged? It wasn't as if she and Daniel had anything in common—apart from Harry, of course.

'Maybe you *should* be a lawyer. You always have a ready answer. I'm going to miss you when you leave.'

She felt a pang of loss at his words. The faint scent of his aftershave drifted on the still evening air.

'I won't be leaving for a while,' she said. Again she felt that hollow sensation in the pit of her stomach. One day she would be back in Ireland, her time here a distant dream.

'What's wrong, Colleen?' he asked. 'Are you okay?'

She shook her head. 'Now what could be wrong? My

patient is getting better. His father is taking time off to be with him. Soon I won't be needed here.'

'Harry will miss you terribly,' Daniel said. 'And so will I. We've got used to having you around.'

Used to having her around. Like a friend. Her heart sank. Maybe it was because she was tired. She didn't want Daniel to be her friend. It felt unsatisfactory, yet... dangerous.

'I'm tired,' she said. 'If you don't mind, I think I'll turn in for the night.'

Suddenly his hand was in her hair and he leant down and kissed her lightly on the lips. For a moment the world spun. 'Good night then, Colleen. I'll see you in the morning.'

After a night spent more awake than asleep, Colleen gave up trying to sleep and slipped out of bed. She glanced at her watch. It was only six. Too early to wake Harry. She supposed she could go for a walk, but it was raining hard outside.

But she needed to get rid of this restless feeling some-how. Making up her mind, she pulled on a pair of shorts and a T-shirt and headed down to the gym. Exercise would help.

The gym had weights, which she ignored, a tread-mill and another machine Colleen hadn't seen before. She decided that half an hour on the treadmill would do the trick. If only she could remember how to use it. The last time she'd been to the gym was with Trish a couple of years ago. But how difficult could it be?

There was a quick-start button so Colleen pressed that. The treadmill started to roll beneath her at a rapid–but-doable walking speed. This was okay.

But then, to her consternation, the running machine started to speed up. She broke into a jog, but the machine kept increasing speed until she was practically sprinting. She glanced around frantically for a stop button, but before she could reach it, she stumbled and, before she knew it, the machine had thrown her off as if it were a badly behaved horse.

She lay in a crumpled heap on the floor, wondering what had just happened and trying to get her breath back.

'Are you having a nap down there?' an amused voice came from above her.

She looked up to find Daniel looking down at her, grinning. Slowly her eyes travelled down from his face. He was wearing a sleeveless T-shirt that emphasised the muscles in his arms and a pair of low-slung tracksuit bottoms. What little breath she had caught in her throat. She closed her eyes as her cheeks burned.

He crouched next to her. 'Normally people stay on the machine,' he said.

'Very funny,' she gasped. Hopefully he'd put her shortness of breath down to being on the machine. She struggled into a sitting position. 'I don't know what happened. One minute I was going along just fine. The next the damn thing was trying to make me do a seven-minute mile.'

'It's programmed to go to twelve mph after a two-minute warm-up,' Daniel said. 'That's the setting I always use. You needed to set it manually for your speed.'

His jade eyes were alight with mirth.

'You might have told me,' she said huffily.

'I would have, had you asked. Did you hurt yourself?' His hands were on her ankles, gently pressing.

A flash of heat ran up Colleen's legs all the way to her pelvis. 'I'm fine,' she said.

'Hey, relax. Let me just make sure.'

She closed her eyes and tried to ignore the way her body was overheating from the touch of his deft fingers on her skin. What was the matter with her? How could her body be responding this way? It had never behaved like this when Ciaran had touched her.

'Everything seems in one piece.' His voice sounded hoarse.

Colleen forced her eyes open. He was looking at her intensely. Their gazes locked and Colleen's breath stopped in her throat.

He placed his hands under her arms and pulled her to her feet. He held her against him for a long moment. She became aware of the heat of his skin burning her fingertips before he muttered something under his breath and released her so abruptly, she staggered a little. Or was it because her knees were weak?

'I'll set the treadmill for you,' he said, 'at a more appropriate speed.'

All Colleen wanted to do was to escape to her room so she could examine these strange sensations coursing through her body. 'No, you obviously wanted to use it.'

'I was going to lift some weights,' Daniel said. 'I can do that while you're on the machine.' He was punching something into the buttons on the front of the machine. Colleen had no choice but to step back on and, with her knees still feeling as if they were made from plasticine, started running at a more sedate pace.

As the equipment was in front of the running machine, she was forced to watch as Daniel lay down on a bench and started lifting weights.

The way his muscles contracted and bunched every time he raised the weights above his chest did nothing to help the warm feeling in Colleen's abdomen.

After fifteen minutes of her trying to concentrate on keeping her wobbly legs moving, Daniel stood up and pressed a switch. The treadmill slowed to a stop.

'I think that's long enough for your first day.'

'I was managing fine,' Colleen protested. 'I could have gone on for twice as long.'

Daniel smiled at her and, if she hadn't known it was impossible, her heart rate went up another twenty beats.

'It's better to mix your work-out routine,' he said. 'A bit of cardiovascular with a bit of resistance training.'

Resistance training was just what she needed, but not the kind he was referring to.

'Come on. I'll help you lift some weights,' he said.

Unable to find enough breath to refuse, she let him lead her over to the bench he had been lying on.

She lay down on the bench with her legs draped over the end.

Daniel placed a bar with weights on either side in her hands and stood behind her.

'Okay, now lift them straight up,' he said.

She did as he instructed.

'That's good, but don't lock your elbows.' She felt his hands on her elbows. 'Keep a little bend here.'

There was no way she could do this. If he continued to touch her the way he was doing, she would start to whimper. She placed the bar back in its holder, looked at her watch and faked dismay. 'Goodness. Is that the time? I must go. I want to have a shower, then it'll be time for the night nurse to leave and I don't want to keep her waiting.'

She sprang to her feet, only too aware of his amused eyes on her.

'Thanks…er…for your help. I'll see you later?' And before he could say anything, she flicked her fingers at him and, as casually as she could manage on legs that felt like rubber, walked out of the room.

Daniel watched Colleen's retreating back until she'd disappeared. He reset the treadmill to its usual setting and started to run. He would do an extra five miles this morning, he decided. He needed something to distract his head—and his pelvis—from the image of Colleen in her skimpy shorts and T-shirt. He felt a smile tug at his mouth. What was it about her that drew him? It wasn't just that he found her so sexy, it was the way he felt good around her. She captivated him in a way no woman had before. He never quite knew what she was going to do next and he found himself constantly listening out for the sound of her voice, her laughter, her quick steps.

He turned the speed up and ran faster.

Dear God, it wasn't just that he had the hots for her—somewhere along the way, he had fallen in love with her. And no amount of telling himself otherwise was going to make the slightest difference.

CHAPTER FOURTEEN

THE flight to Dublin was short and uneventful. They hadn't had to queue at security. All they had to do was show their passports and then they were ushered on to the plane. Daniel had carried his son up the short flight of steps as if he weighed no more than a bag of sugar. The three of them had played 'Go Fish' during the flight—after explaining the rules to a baffled-looking Daniel. She hadn't seen much of him since that day in the gym, and when she did, he had treated her with his usual courtesy. She'd almost managed to make herself believe that she was mistaken about the charged atmosphere between them.

'I win,' said Harry, waving his empty hand in the air. 'You're useless at this, Dad.'

'Just as well I don't have to make my living as a card player, then,' he laughed. He looked good in his short-sleeved, open-necked shirt and jeans. Almost too good.

And he and Harry were getting on well, although Harry would tell his father off every now and again for babying him.

The journey to the farm had taken an hour and Colleen had felt herself relax as soon as Daniel had steered the

car off the motorway and on to the country roads leading to the farm. Her mother had cleared out one of the
unused farmworker cottages for Daniel and was planning to put Harry into Colleen's old room as it was the
only one on the ground floor.

As soon as they stepped out of the car Colleen's
mother came rushing up to greet them. 'I've put the
dogs away in case they jumped on Harry,' she said. As
soon as Daniel had transferred Harry to his wheelchair,
she bent down and shook Harry's hand. 'I'm Sheila,
Colleen's Mammy. You must be Harry. Welcome to our
home.'

Harry smiled shyly. 'Thank you for asking me.'

Sheila straightened. 'And you must be Harry's dad.
Daniel, isn't it? Well, come in, Danny and Harry. Let's
get you fed. Colleen tells me you're wanting to see the
puppies. We'll do that after you've had a taste of my
special dumplings. Why don't you go and say hello to
your brothers, Colleen, while I settle our guests?' She
waved a hand in the direction of the hills. 'They're out
there somewhere.'

'It's okay, Mammy. I'll catch up with them later.
I want to be around when Harry sees the puppies.
Actually, I can't wait to see them myself.'

The large, scrubbed pine table in the kitchen was laid
for tea. There were plates groaning with sandwiches,
others piled high with home baking, while her mother's
enormous tea pot took centre stage. It was always like
this, Colleen thought, happily. The minute she stepped
inside this room it was as if she'd never been away.

Daniel pushed Harry in his wheelchair up to the
kitchen table and Colleen handed the sandwiches
around. It was an inspired choice by her mother as

Harry would be able to feed himself. If she'd made soup, he would have needed help. Colleen knew instinctively that the lad would have hated that in front of people who were strangers.

'Do you like horses, Harry?' Sheila asked.

'Yes. I can't ride, though.'

'Colleen could take you up on Dobbin if you like. He's as gentle as a lamb and my daughter rides better than most people can run.'

Daniel stopped eating and stared at Colleen in surprise.

'I'm a woman of many talents,' she quipped.

'Why? What else can you do?' Daniel said with a wink at Harry.

Colleen pretended to think. 'Mmm. Let me see... I can do a Sudoku puzzle in under three minutes and I'm an okay pool player. Learnt from my brothers.'

'Don't let her fool you, Daniel. She wipes the floor with most of the men down at our local.'

'We should have a game some time,' Daniel said.

Colleen smiled and shrugged nonchalantly. 'Sure, as long as you don't mind losing.'

The look he gave her left her in no doubt that that wasn't going to happen—not in his lifetime at any rate. Or was she reading too much into his lingering gaze that was oh so difficult to pull away from. Flustered, Colleen pushed her chair back from the table. 'Leave the dishes, Mammy, I'll do them. You sit down and relax for a bit.'

Sheila looked incredulous. 'What do I need to relax for? Besides, wouldn't it be good if you showed our guests to their rooms?'

Colleen knew there was no point arguing with her

mother. 'Let's get Harry settled first, then.' With a tilt of her head, she beckoned Daniel to follow her and Harry down the hall.

'Harry's in my old room,' she said over her shoulder. 'It's got French doors leading out to the back courtyard as you can see.' The three of them squeezed into the small bedroom and Colleen coloured at the poster of a once-popular Irish boy band on the wall.

Harry looked at Colleen and grinned. 'You didn't like them, did you?'

'Hey, they're Irish. Of course I love them.'

'Seems the more we find out about Colleen, the more she surprises us!' Daniel said. The gleam in his eyes made her heart lurch.

'Can we go look at the puppies now?' Harry asked. 'I want to choose the one that's going to be mine.'

'Of course we can.' Anything to get away from Daniel and that breath-stealing look in his eyes. 'Then we'll show your dad his room.'

Daniel looked around the tiny bedroom of the cottage where he'd be staying for the next couple of days. He lay down on the narrow bed. If he stretched his arms out wide he could touch both of the walls simultaneously and if he stretched out to his full height, his feet would touch that wall, too. Come to think of it, it was very like the room he'd had in boarding school. That had been about the same size and was equally sparsely furnished. But this room didn't fill him with dread as that room had. This room was bright and, with the addition of a vase of wild flowers on the bedside table, more welcoming than most rooms in which he had stayed in the past. The whole house had the same sort of feel.

The McCullochs weren't rich, anyone could see that, but what they might be lacking in wall-to-wall TVs was more than made up for by the warm and friendly atmosphere.

And Colleen was at the centre. Just as she was at the centre of his and Harry's life. And he didn't want her just because he needed her—he wanted her because he couldn't imagine a life without her. Now she was no longer engaged, it was time for him to find out whether she could love him.

Leaving his unpacking for later, he went to find her.

Colleen was pushing Harry in his wheelchair towards him.

'Are you coming to see the puppies, Dad?' Harry said excitedly. Already his son seemed happier than Daniel had ever seen him. Although he needed time alone with Colleen, it would have to wait for a few minutes. Soon, he hoped, they'd have all the time in the world.

The puppies, who were in a small enclosure in one of the other, unused outhouses, were, as Colleen had guessed, an instant hit. Harry watched in delight as the chocolate Labradors squirmed and wriggled over their mum in an attempt to feed. He was far more de-lighted with the puppies than any present Daniel had ever given him. Once again, Colleen was right. Harry wanted company and attention, not gifts. How come he hadn't been able to see that before?

But he knew the answer. He hadn't known it before because he had needed Colleen to show him what love meant.

'They're only small yet,' Colleen told Harry, 'so you won't be able to take one home for another couple of weeks. You can choose one today though, if you like. She reached out for the biggest puppy and placed it in Harry's lap. What about this one? He has the cutest white socks.'

Harry petted the puppy for a few moments before pointing to the littlest one who was struggling in vain to shove his brothers and sisters out of the way so he could feed, too. 'I want that one.'

Colleen looked doubtful. The puppy Harry had pointed to was the runt of the litter and so small it was possible it might not make it.

'Won't you prefer one of the others? That little one isn't doing so well.'

But Harry stuck out his lower lip. 'That's why I want him. He's weak, like me. But he's going to get better, get stronger, like me.'

'If that's the one you want, that's the one you're going to have,' Daniel said firmly. If he and Harry were about to lose Colleen, this was the least he could do to make it up to his son.

Not that he was ready to let Colleen walk out of his life. Not by a long way.

A short while later, back in the house, Sheila shooed them outside.

'Why don't you and Daniel go for a walk, Colleen? Harry will be fine with me.'

Before Colleen could object, Daniel had taken her by the elbow and steered her outside.

'We'll be back shortly,' he said.

'Where would you like to go?' Colleen asked when they were outside.

'Why don't you show me around? I've never been on a working brood farm before.'

'Okay. If you like. By the way, have you seen Ciaran?'

'Ciaran?' Daniel asked with a frown.

'Yes, Ciaran. The same Ciaran who came to London.'

Daniel stopped abruptly and looked down at her with the strangest expression on his face. 'I want to ask you something,' he said.

'Sure. Although I don't promise that I can answer it.'

Daniel looked around. 'Is there anywhere more private?' he asked. 'Maybe on the other side of the house? Where no one can overhear us?'

'There's a bench down by the lake, but what is it, Daniel? Is there something wrong?'

'Let's go down there and then we can talk.'

Was he going to tell her that her services were no longer needed? That Harry was making such good progress that they could manage on their own? The thought filled her with dismay. She couldn't bear the thought of leaving them, but the truth was that Daniel only saw her as his son's nurse. Oh, she'd no doubt Daniel needed her and liked having her around, but one day soon he and Harry would no longer need her. Harry was making so much progress and his relationship with his father was improving day by day. Which was brilliant. Everything she'd hoped for. Why, then, did it feel as if her heart was been slowly ripped into tiny pieces?

She led the way down a slope at the back of the house until they came to a bench built of stones. Her father had made it when he and her mother had first moved to the farm. He'd always said it was the place he came to when he needed to work out a problem. They sat down next to each other and Colleen was acutely conscious of Daniel's thigh touching hers. She longed to rest her head against him and let the world carry on without them—keep everything the way it was—even for a short while.

'Okay, shoot. Ask me your question,' Colleen said, pushing the thought away. She still had a job to do.

'How many times have you been in love?'

The question took her so much by surprise that she laughed out loud. 'I can't see that that is any of your business,' she said. 'When I said you could ask me anything, I thought it was about Harry. My private life is—private.'

'But you know everything about my private life. Come on, Colleen, we're friends, aren't we?'

Friends? Is that what they were? 'I guess so,' she said slowly. 'Still doesn't mean you can ask me personal questions.'

'Just humour me, please.'

'How many times have I been in love? I had a crush on a boy in my class when I was eight that lasted about a year, but I don't think that counts. Then with Ciaran, I guess.'

'So how did you know that you were in love?'

Colleen laughed again, but it sounded forced, even to her own ears. 'Let me get this right. I'm here because you're looking for some kind of agony aunt. You've met someone and don't know whether it's the real McCoy, is that it?'

Who? Who had he met? When did he have time to be with a woman? As far as she knew, when he wasn't working he was with Harry—or her.

'No. I would know.'

'And how would you know?'

'Because being with that person makes me happy. I want to be with her all the time, want to see her smile, want to make her laugh, want to comfort her when she's down, want to make love to her all the time.' Something in his tone, as if he found the words difficult to say, made her realise he was deadly serious.

'The way you felt about Eleanor when you first got together?' she asked. Envy ate into her soul. It would be something to be loved by Daniel.

'No, the way I felt about Eleanor was different. I wanted her—I thought she was beautiful. But...there was something missing. I only realised that for sure when...' He cleared his throat. 'I only realised that later.'

Colleen's heart was racing. 'I'm not sure where this is going, Daniel.'

He turned so he was facing her. He pushed her hair off her face and, gently cupping his hands on either side of her neck, drew her towards him.

She was frozen to the spot as he brought her lips down on hers, so lightly at first it was almost as if she were imagining it. Then the pressure grew firmer and before she knew what she was doing, her fists were knotting into the front of his shirt as she tugged him closer to her. He groaned and pulled her to her feet, pressing her body into his. She felt as if she were on fire from the tips of her toes to the skin on her scalp. It was as if her body had a mind of its own. She wrapped her arms around him, wanting his kisses to be deeper, moulding her body to the length of his. The world receded as she was sucked into a vortex of desire. His hands dropped to cup her bottom and as she pressed her into him, she felt the unmistakable proof of his desire.

She moaned as an answering red-hot flame of desire shot through her pelvis.

She'd never felt like this before. She wanted to rip his clothes from his body, so she could feel his naked skin on hers. She wanted her body to melt into his. She had never wanted anything more in the world.

Suddenly he stopped kissing her and stepped back. She felt bereft and chilled with the sudden loss of his warmth. They were both breathing heavily.

'Did Ciaran ever kiss you like that?' Daniel said hoarsely. 'Did he make you want him so much you can hardly bear it? Did he fill your waking thoughts, your dreams?'

No, was the answer. *Not ever.* Thoughts clambered around her head. But why was he talking about Ciaran?

'Did Ciaran ever love you the way you deserve to be loved? Have you ever responded to him the way you responded just now?' Daniel continued.

'What's Ciaran got to do with anything?' she asked, totally bewildered.

'I need to know if you still love him.'

Colleen gave a shaky laugh. 'Of course I don't. I wouldn't have ended our engagement if I had.'

'So you broke it off?' The look of relief on Daniel's face made her smile.

'Yes,' she said, softly. 'I thought you knew.'

'I needed to be sure. I need to know that there is nothing to stop us being together.'

Her heart was beating so hard, she could hardly breathe. Daniel wanted her.

'Don't you see?' Daniel said triumphantly. 'We can be a family. You, me and Harry.'

His words tore her apart.

She understood now. It had happened before, of course, with other family members of patients she had nursed. He was mistaking gratitude for love. And she well knew those feelings would fade; when Harry no longer needed her, Daniel wouldn't either.

Her arms dropped to her side. 'Daniel, I...'

He seemed oblivious to the change in her.

'Don't you see, Colleen? You belong with Harry and me. You love Harry and perhaps you could love me, too?'

So he'd kissed her so he wouldn't lose her as Harry's nurse? The thought made her feel ill. The arrogance of the man! Did he honestly think one kiss from him was all it took? He couldn't even pretend he was in love with her!

'And of course you know so much about love—with your own failed relationships behind you—your son and your wife for starters.' She couldn't stop herself from lashing out. She was hurting so much inside she thought she'd break apart. 'I'm an employee, so that makes me fair game, does it? Well, let me tell you, if it wasn't for Harry I'd tell you where to shove your job.' Then, before she could say something she was bound to regret later, she turned her back on him and ran back up the slope towards the safety of the house.

She'd only got a little way up the hill before she felt a hand on her arm and she was yanked around to face Daniel.

'Good God, woman. You don't believe that I kissed you because of some crack-minded idea of keeping you as an unpaid nurse? Don't you understand? I'm crazy about you.'

She looked up at him. His green eyes were blazing

with such passion she knew he believed what he was saying.

'Oh, Daniel. Maybe you do think you care about me. But it's all really about Harry. People often develop feelings for the people who care for them or their families. But it will pass. I promise you. I'll leave and shortly afterwards you'll forget all about me. That's the way it is.'

He took her by the shoulders and she knew by the way his fingers pressed into her that he was having a hard time not shaking her.

'You're wrong. I will never stop loving you—never.'

She reached up and touched him gently on the cheek. 'You believe that…but in time…' Her throat felt thick and she knew tears weren't far away. She pushed his hands away. 'Let me go, Daniel. Just let me go.'

He had made a mess of that. What had he been thinking? That Colleen would realise as soon as he kissed her that the man she should love was standing right in front of her?

The trouble was he hadn't been thinking. At least not with his head. Weeks of having Colleen around and not being able to touch her, listening to her plans about getting married, had been bad enough when he thought that she was in love with Ciaran and he with her. He shouldn't have rushed her. He should have taken his time, made his feelings clear, but instead he'd waded in and kissed her. He simply couldn't help himself. The truth was he had wanted to kiss her for a long, long time.

And why hadn't he told her that he loved her straight away, instead of clouding the issue with talk of Harry?

Good God, a person would think he'd never made love to a woman before.

And there was the rub. He'd made love to plenty of women in the past, more than he could care to name, but he had never been in love before. Not even with Eleanor. Not like this.

So what was he going to do about it?

Not give up. That was for sure. Colleen and he belonged together. She was the missing part of his soul.

All he had to do now was make her believe that.

Colleen headed away from the house and towards the paddock. She wasn't in a fit state to talk to anyone right now. She had to get herself under control first. She touched her lips where Daniel had kissed her. What had got into him? More importantly, what had got into her? She'd responded to him with unadulterated abandon. And if he hadn't started talking about Harry, it wouldn't have stopped there.

Now she wished she'd thrown common sense to the wind and allowed herself to take—if only for the moment—what he had offered her. At least until he came to the realisation he and Harry no longer needed her. But to even think that way was crazy—nuts. She'd only recently broken off her engagement and wasn't about to charge into another one. Especially with Daniel Frobisher—a man whom she'd known for a few short weeks, but who would only break her heart if she let him.

The realisation that she was too late, that she was already in love with him, stopped her dead in her tracks. How could she have been so blind to all the signs?

The mere sight of Daniel made her feel alive in a

way she had never felt before. The slightest brush of
Daniel's fingertips against her skin set her nerve endings on fire.

But it wasn't just physical attraction she felt for
Daniel. She loved being with him. Even if he wasn't
touching her, her body felt electrified in his presence.
She loved his intensity, his passion, his dedication to
his son—everything about him.

She loved Daniel.

She would always love Daniel.

And he cared about her. But for all the wrong reasons. It could never last. Daniel would realise that in
time. When she was gone.

She walked over to the paddock and let her horse,
Star, nuzzle her hand. Why couldn't life be simple? Why
couldn't you love the person who was right for you?
Why couldn't the person you loved, love you back? Why
couldn't Daniel love her for herself and not because of
Harry?

Why did love have to hurt so much?

Colleen tucked the covers round an exhausted-looking
Harry. Despite his tiredness, there was finally a glow to
his cheeks. Sitting down beside him, she stroked a lock
of his blond hair from his eyes. Apart from his immo-
bility, he looked like any other healthy, young twelve-
year-old and her heart ached for him.

'Did you have a good day, Harry?' she asked softly.

Harry grinned. 'The best.' He squinted up at her,
'Your brothers are brilliant fun. Even if they are a bit…'

'Nutty?' Colleen finished his sentence for him
and laughed. 'Sure, am I not the only sane one in the
family?'

When Harry raised his eyebrow he looked so like his father it made her catch her breath. 'If you say so,' he teased back.

Sheila and Colleen had been helping Harry with his walking practice. He could manage the length of the room by himself now. However, Colleen had warned him not to attempt to try walking without her being there ready to catch him, should he stumble.

Colleen leaned over and kissed Harry's forehead. 'Night, sweetheart. Remember, I'm right next door to you if you need anything during the night, okay?' She stood up.

'Colleen, I want to speak to Dad,' Harry said.

'Then I'll get him for you. Are you ready to tell him about your walking?'

'Yes. But I want to talk to him first. Will you stay with me?'

His green eyes so like his father's were filled with anxiety. No matter how much she wanted to avoid Daniel, she couldn't resist the entreaty in Harry's voice.

'Of course I will, if you want me to.'

'I'll stay with Harry while you fetch Daniel,' Sheila said.

Colleen ran across to the cottage where Daniel was staying. He was sitting outside, looking pensive. Colleen's heart tumbled. How would she get through the next few weeks seeing him every day, yet knowing she had to keep her distance?

'Harry wants to speak to you,' Colleen said.

Daniel got to his feet. 'I was just coming to see him. It's beautiful here,' Daniel said. 'Maybe I'll buy a house in Ireland. I think Harry would like that, don't you?'

'I think he might.'

'He's going to be all right, isn't he? At last I can finally believe it and it's largely down to you, Colleen. I wish I knew how to thank you.'

'I don't need thanks. Harry would have made it on his own.'

'Perhaps. But not so quickly.'

The breeze whipped her hair across her face and Daniel reached across and tucked a stray lock of hair behind her ear. 'You should always wear your hair loose,' he said. The touch of his fingers on her face made her skin sizzle.

'Let's go and see what Harry wants,' Daniel said. 'Then I need you to listen to what I have to tell you.'

His words and the look in his eyes held a promise that made her heart do a complicated routine inside her chest.

Inside Harry's room, Harry was waiting in the chair beside his bed with the sleeping puppy on his lap.

'Hello, Dad,' Harry said.

Daniel ruffled his hair. 'Did you have a good day?'

'Yes. I like it here. Can we stay longer?'

Daniel hesitated and glanced over to Colleen. 'I don't know, son. Colleen's family has their own lives to be getting on with.'

'Of course we can stay for a few more days, if that's what you want, Harry. If your dad doesn't mind. He can always go back to London to finish off whatever he needs to, but you and I can stay here until he comes back. Then you both can stay until his leave is up.'

Harry's eyes lit up. 'Can we, Dad? Then Patch will be old enough for us to take home.'

'If Colleen and her family are up for it, then yes.'

Daniel sat down on the bed. 'Is that what you wanted to talk to me about?'

Harry flicked a glance in Colleen's direction. 'Something else,' he mumbled.

'Fire away. You know you can talk to me about anything.'

Something in Harry's expression made Colleen's breath catch in her throat. But she had promised to stay and stay she would. She took the remaining seat beside Harry. Harry was looking at his father. Unshed tears trembled on his long lashes.

'Why did you wait to tell me you were my dad?'

Immediately Daniel was off his feet and crouching by his son's side.

'I didn't know, son. Your mum only told me you were mine and not David's after he left you both. If I'd known, I'd never have let you go. I think your mum knew that. So that's why she didn't tell me.'

Doubt clouded Harry's eyes.

'I didn't tell you this before because I didn't want you to blame your mother. Once I knew you were mine, I thought the important thing was for us to get to know each other.'

'Mum said you didn't want me. She said you were too busy. And you were.'

'People say things when they're hurt, son.' Daniel continued. 'I hurt your mother. And I'm sorry about that. But she was wrong. I do want you. I love you more than I can say. I'm sorry that I missed you growing up and I'm sorry that I wasn't around for you as much as I should have been. But I'm going to spend the rest of my life making it up to you.'

Harry smiled and Colleen's heart splintered. He

looked so much like his father. But that wasn't the only reason her heart felt as if it would shatter into a thousand pieces. Her work with Harry was almost done. All too soon they'd be out of her life and she out of theirs.

'Does that mean you'll buy me whatever I want?' Harry asked. 'Cool.'

Daniel laughed, too. 'What it means is that I promise from now on to put you before my work. No more working at weekends—and we're going to spend every holiday together. You can even choose where we go. You don't even have to go back to boarding school if you don't want to. We can find another school closer that you can attend as a day boy if you like.'

'Hey, Dad. Not so fast. I like my school. All my friends are there. I don't want to spend the rest of my life hanging around with my father—even if he's kind of cool.'

Daniel's eyebrows shot up. 'You think I'm cool?'

'Sort of. For an old man.'

Daniel laughed again. 'Less of the old man, son.'

Harry looked towards Colleen.

'I think there's something else Harry wants you to know, Daniel,' Colleen said, rising to her feet. 'Why don't you go and stand by the door?' Looking baffled, Daniel did as he was asked. 'Are you ready, Harry?' Colleen said softly.

Harry nodded and she helped him to his feet. He swayed slightly as he found his balance. Then she let him go and Harry took one step and then another. Daniel stared at his son and moved forwards as if to help him. Harry stopped. 'No, Dad. I can do it.'

And then, with Harry taking one unsteady step at a time, he walked towards his father and into his arms.

Colleen watched with a lump in her throat as Daniel held his son in his arms. 'I'll leave you two to it, then,' she said. 'I've got to go and see to the horses we had out today—make sure they've got fresh bedding and feed.'

Daniel helped his son on to the bed and lay down beside him, gathering him close.

Colleen closed the door gently behind her, pausing only to look at Daniel lying alongside his son, his arm round his shoulders and the pair of them looking so comfortable together. She felt as if her heart was breaking. She would miss Harry terribly when it came time for her to leave. And as for Daniel? The thought of a life without him was almost too much to bear.

But did she have to live without him?

Love wasn't slow and gentle. Love wasn't boring. At least not with Daniel. It was exciting and unpredictable. It made your legs feel like jelly and your heart sing from a smile. It made you ache in the night from the need to be close. It made the thought of saying good bye unbearable. Colleen had always played it safe. Maybe now it was time to take a chance? Maybe it was time to be rocked out of her safe world? One thing was for sure—it would be a terrifying ride. But also exhilarating. Maybe Daniel did only love her because he felt indebted to her, but she would never know for sure unless she took the risk of finding out.

Happiness washed over her. Maybe Daniel did love her. In the meantime, she would take whatever he had to offer, no matter how short-lived it was.

Daniel eased his arm out from under Harry's shoulders carefully, lest he wake him. Slowly and as quietly as possible, he removed the game console from Harry's lap and, stretching his arm above his head, shuffled off the end of the bed. A floorboard creaked beneath his feet and he held his breath, but Harry didn't move. He was definitely sound asleep.

Reaching for the lamp switch, Daniel hesitated, looking down at his son. He'd always loved him—but never more so than at this very moment. Very gently he stroked a finger down his cheek and in his sleep, Harry smiled.

Daniel could hear the sounds of a game show on the TV coming from the living room. Obviously the family relaxing at the end of a tiring day. He popped his head around the door. Colleen's brothers were all there as well as Sheila.

'If you're looking for Colleen,' Eugene said, 'she's mucking out down at the stables. But if you're looking for company, you're welcome to join us.'

'It's a beautiful evening,' Daniel replied. 'I think I'll go for a walk.' He had to find Colleen. The sky was streaking orange and gold, casting a shimmering light over the lake that was glass still. Was he becoming a romantic? Daniel grinned wryly. So much was changing, himself included, he wouldn't be surprised.

Crunching down the path, he made his way to the stables, wondering if he'd find her still there. But a quick glance in each of the boxes showed resting horses and no sign of Colleen.

He was about to turn on his heel when he noticed a light shining in the barn.

As if sensing his presence, she turned around, showering hay over her shoulder.

'Come to help?' she asked.

'Sure. What would you like me to do?'

Colleen handed him a shovel and pointed to a pile of horse manure. 'Shovel that up for a start.'

Great. Only his love for her could make him touch the stuff. 'Shouldn't your brothers be helping with this?' He knew he was prevaricating, but he was unaccountably nervous. He had to make Colleen believe that what he felt for her had nothing to do with Harry.

'They offered.' Colleen rubbed a hand across her forehead. 'But I love getting back to the farm and mucking in. It keeps me sane.'

Her fingers brushed his and Daniel felt an overwhelming urge to wrap his hand round hers. With her hair tumbling loose from her scrunchie, jeans low on her hips and the porcelain smoothness of her skin, he'd never felt such desire for a woman. Especially one with smudges of dirt on her cheeks and eyes sparking—not with make-up but with fire and laughter. In which case it was better, if he couldn't convince her that he loved her, that soon she'd be leaving him and Harry. He couldn't spend many more days with her and not touch her.

She smiled at him, the moonlight reflecting on her hair turning it to gold.

Daniel removed a piece of straw from her hair and tossed it to the ground. 'That's better,' he said.

She moved towards him and stood on her tiptoes. Her perfume flooded his nostrils, making his head reel. He felt her hands in his hair. 'You have one, too,' she laughed.

He couldn't stop himself. His hands dropped to her waist and his mouth was on hers. He tasted her lips, ten-

tatively at first and then, as she responded, he tugged at
the belt of her jeans and pulled her against him.

When she moaned he deepened his kiss. Her tongue
flicked against his teeth, driving him crazy with desire.
It took all his will-power to pull away from her.

Her eyes were shining and her breath was coming
in short gasps.

'God, I want you, Colleen,' he murmured. 'I've
wanted you since the first time I saw you. I want to
make love to you—badly. But I want you to be sure.'

Her answer was to pull his head back down so his
mouth covered hers once more. 'You great lummox,
can't you see how sure I am?'

When he released her, she grabbed a horse blanket
from one of the stalls and took him by the hand and led
him up a ladder into the hay loft. 'Give me your shirt,'
she demanded.

He slipped it over his head and passed it to her. She
placed the blanket with his T-shirt on top of it and lay
down, grinning up at him. She held her arms out. 'Don't
you know better than to keep a girl waiting?' she asked.

Later, much later, they lay together. Her head was on
his chest, their naked bodies entwined. Rain thudded
against the tin roof of the stables like a million bul-
lets. One of the horses stamped his feet and snickered.
Colleen called out to the horse and it settled down. She
had never felt so peaceful.

'I love you, Colleen.' His voice came out of the darkness. 'I never thought I could love a woman the way I
love you.' He put his hands around her waist and swung
her around until she was sitting astride him. 'Do you
believe me now?'

She grinned down at him. 'Now you wouldn't just be saying that because you've had your wicked way with me, would you?'

'Don't you think I would have said it before I had my wicked way with you? Isn't that the way it's supposed to work?'

She feigned dismay. 'Oops, I got it wrong. Damn.' She felt as if she was floating somewhere above herself.

'So will you stay with Harry and me?'

Some of the happiness dropped out of her world. 'Because of Harry?'

'No, you idiot. Not because of Harry. Because I love you and want to spend the rest of my life with you.' He raked a hand through his hair. 'I didn't think I'd ever say that again. But, yes, Harry is part of the deal. I meant what I said to him earlier. I've got a lot of making up to do. He needs a father.'

'And a mother?'

'Do you think that's why I'm asking? Harry loves you. I love you. I want you in our lives—permanently. I want you to marry me, Colleen. But if you need time, I want you to be with me any way you choose.'

Colleen's heart was singing. 'And here's me just un-engaged. Now you're wanting me to do it all over again.'

'The difference is that I want you to do it all over again, but this time with me. Only me. Only ever me.' His eyes glinted in the dark. 'I'm warning you, Colleen, now that I've found you, I don't intend to let you go.'

EPILOGUE

COLLEEN walked up the aisle on Eugene's arm to where Daniel was waiting for her with Harry standing by his side. The last three months had flown by. Harry had continued to improve so much that he was able to walk reasonable distances on his own. His speech was clearer and, although his concentration was less than perfect at times, they were all confident that, with a bit of extra support, he'd be able to resume his studies where he had left off when he returned to school.

In the pews her friends and family smiled at her. Trish, who was her bridesmaid, was grinning from ear to ear as if getting Daniel and Colleen together had been all her doing. Jake from the unit and Kiera were also there, as was most of the staff from the unit in Dublin. Dora was using her handkerchief to dab at her eyes and even Burton's eyes looked suspiciously wet. Colleen and Daniel were going to fund another special unit for brain-injured patients in Dorset and Colleen was looking forward to getting stuck in to the planning of the unit. As she approached the altar, two pairs of shockingly green eyes turned in her direction.

Daniel held out his hand.

She stood next to him as the final strains of the wedding march faded away and knew that life was going to be a roller coaster, but one she intended to enjoy for every breathtaking minute it lasted.

* * * * *

Special Offers

Every month we put together collections and longer reads written by your favourite authors.

Here are some of next month's highlights— and don't miss our fabulous discount online!

On sale 16th March

On sale 16th March

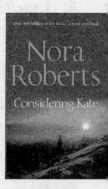

On sale 6th April

Have Your Say

You've just finished your book.
So what did you think?

We'd love to hear your thoughts on our
'Have your say' online panel
www.millsandboon.co.uk/haveyoursay

- Easy to use
- Short questionnaire
- Chance to win Mills & Boon®
  goodies